✠ Praise for Jack McDevitt ✠

"You should definitely read Jack McDevitt!"
—Gregory Benford

"McDevitt tells his complex and suspenseful stories with meticulous attention to detail, deft characterization, and graceful prose."
—*Publishers Weekly*

"Some authors are masters at spinning world-spanning cosmic tales; others are adept at down-to-earth character-driven stories. But only a precious few can combine the two, and no one does it better than Jack McDevitt."
—Robert J. Sawyer

"McDevitt blends straightforward adventure with scientific mystery, peoples his stories with diverse . . . characters, and delivers rewardingly startling solutions."
—*Science Fiction Chronicle*

"Jack McDevitt writes with a keen eye for human nature and the sure hand of human experience. An engrossing storyteller."
—Jeffrey A. Carver

Books by Jack McDevitt

Ancient Shores
Eternity Road
*Moonfall**

Published by HarperPrism

*coming soon

ATTENTION: ORGANIZATIONS AND CORPORATIONS

Most HarperPrism books are available at special quantity discounts for bulk purchases for sales promotions, premiums, or fund-raising. For information, please call or write:
Special Markets Department, HarperCollins*Publishers*,
10 East 53rd Street, New York, N.Y. 10022.
Telephone: (212) 207-7528. Fax: (212) 207-7222.

✠ ETERNITY ✠ ROAD

Jack McDevitt

HarperPrism
A Division of HarperCollins*Publishers*

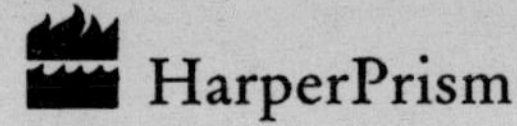

A Division of HarperCollins*Publishers*
10 East 53rd Street, New York, N.Y. 10022-5299

If you purchased this book without a cover, you should be aware that this book is stolen property. It was reported as "unsold and destroyed" to the publisher and neither the author nor the publisher has received any payment for this "stripped book."

This is a work of fiction. The characters, incidents, and dialogues are products of the author's imagination and are not to be construed as real. Any resemblance to actual events or persons, living or dead, is entirely coincidental.

Copyright © 1997 by Cryptic, Inc.
All rights reserved. No part of this book may be used or reproduced in any manner whatsoever without written permission of the publisher, except in the case of brief quotations embodied in critical articles and reviews.
For information address HarperCollins*Publishers*,
10 East 53rd Street, New York, N.Y. 10022-5299.

A hardcover edition of this book was published
in 1997 by HarperCollinsPublishers.

ISBN: 0-06-105427-5

HarperCollins®, ®, and HarperPrism®
are trademarks of HarperCollins*Publishers*, Inc.

Cover illustration © 1997 Joe Danisi

First HarperPrism mass market printing: April 1998

Printed in the United States of America

Visit HarperPrism on the World Wide Web at
http://www.harperprism.com

❖10 9 8 7 6 5 4 3 2 1

For Merry, Scott, and Chris,
my inestimable ambassadors
to the 21st century

Lines from Mark Twain, *A Connecticut Yankee in King Arthur's Court,* The Mark Twain Library, translated/edited by Stein, Bernard, are quoted from the introduction, "A Word of Explanation." Copyright © 1984 by the Mark Twain Foundation. Reprinted by permission.

Lines from Werner Jaeger, *Paideia,* Vol. 1, translated by Gilbert Highet, are quoted from the introduction. Copyright © 1945 by Oxford University Press, Inc. Reprinted by permission of Blackwell Publishers, Oxford.

Line from George Bernard Shaw, *Mrs. Warren's Profession,* is quoted from Act IV. Reprinted by permission of the Society of Authors on behalf of the Bernard Shaw Estate.

ACKNOWLEDGMENTS

The part of me that writes has always included a second person. Thanks, Maureen.

I'd also like to extend my appreciation to Ralph Vicinanza, and to Caitlin Blasdell and John Silbersack at HarperPrism. To Dolores Dwyer for editorial assistance. To Charles Sheffield for his comments on the manuscript. And to Elizabeth Moon, who knows horses, and who would have been a valuable addition to the second expedition.

I asked him how far we were from Hartford.
He said he had never heard of the place.

—Mark Twain,
A Connecticut Yankee in King Arthur's Court

✠ PROLOGUE ✠

They came during the October of the World,
Riding the twilight,
To ensure that men would not forget.

—The Travels of Abraham Polk

The boy was waiting in the garden when Silas got home. "He's back," he whispered, and held out an envelope.

The boy was one of two who had been employed to take care of Karik's villa during his absence. Silas was surprised: He had expected Karik Endine to return with horns playing and drums beating. Or not at all.

The envelope was sealed with wax.

"How is he?"

"Not well, I think."

Silas tried to remember the boy's name. Kam. Kim. Something like that. He shrugged, opened the envelope, and removed a single sheet of folded paper.

SILAS,

I NEED TO SEE YOU. TELL NO ONE.
PLEASE COME AT ONCE.

KARIK

The expedition had been gone almost nine months. He stared at the note, produced a coin and held it out. "Tell him I'm on my way."

The sun was moving toward the horizon, and the last few nights had been cold. He hurried inside, washed up, put on a fresh shirt, and took a light jacket from the closet. Then he burst from the house, moving as quickly as dignity and his fifty years would permit. He walked swiftly to the Imperium, took Oxfoot from the stables, and rode out through the city gates along River Road. The sky was clear and red, fading toward dusk. A pair of herons floated lazily over the water. The Mississippi boiled past the collapsed Roadmaker bridge, swirled between mounds of shapeless concrete, flowed smoothly over submerged plazas, broke against piles of bricks. No one really knew how old the bridge was. Its supports made wakes, and its towers were gray and forlorn in the twilight.

A cobblestone trail led off to the right, passed through a stand of elm trees, and emerged on a bluff. A long gray wall, part of a structure buried within the hill, lined the north side of the road. Silas examined the gray stones as he passed, wondering what the world had been like when that mortar had been new. The wall ended abruptly; he rounded the hill and came in view of Karik's villa. It was a familiar sight, and the recollections of earlier days spent here with wine, conversation, and friends induced a sense of wistfulness. The boy who had brought the message was drawing water from the well. He waved. "He's waiting for you, sir. Just go in."

The villa faced the river. It was an elaborate structure, two stories high, built in the Masandik tradition with split wings on the lower level, balustrades and balconies on the upper, and a lot of glass. Silas gave the horse to the boy, knocked at the front door, and entered.

It hadn't changed. Autumn-colored tapestries covered the walls, and shafts of muted light illuminated the sitting room. The furniture was new, but of the same style he remembered: ornately carved wood padded with leather. The kind you might have seen in the ruling homes during the imperial years.

Karik was seated before a reading table, poring over a book. Silas barely recognized him. His hair and beard had turned almost white. His skin was loose and sallow, and his eyes had retreated into dark hollows. Their old intensity had dwindled into a dim red glow. But he smiled, looked up from the pages of handwritten text, and advanced through a cross-pattern of pink sunlight with his arms extended. "Silas," he said. "It's good to see you." He clasped Silas and held him for a long moment. Out of character, that was. Karik Endine was a man of cool temperament. "You didn't expect me back, did you?"

Silas had had his doubts as the months wore on. "I wasn't sure," he said.

The boy came in with water and began filling the containers in the kitchen.

Karik motioned Silas into a chair, and they made small talk until they were alone. Then Silas leaned toward his old friend and lowered his voice. "What happened?" he asked. "Did you find it?"

The windows were open. A cool breeze rippled through the room. Curtains moved.

"No."

Silas felt an unexpected rush of satisfaction. "I'm sorry."

"I don't think it exists."

"You mean your information was wrong and you don't know where it is."

"I mean I don't think it exists." Karik extracted a

bottle of dark wine and a pair of goblets from a cabinet. He filled the goblets and handed one to Silas.

"To Haven," said Silas. "And old friends."

Karik shook his head. "No. To you, Silas. And to home. To Illyria."

While they drank off the first round, the boy brought Silas a damp cloth. He wiped the dust of the road from his face and draped the cloth around his neck. "Feels good."

Karik's gaze was distracted and remote. "I missed you, Silas," he said.

"What happened out there?" asked Silas. "Did everyone get back okay?"

The older man's expression remained rock hard.

"Who did you lose?"

The Mississippi was visible through the windows. Karik got up, looked out at it, and finished his wine. "Everybody," he said. "I came home alone." His voice shook.

Silas lowered his glass, never taking his eyes off his old friend. "What happened?"

Karik's breathing was loud. "Two drowned in a river. Others dead from exposure. Disease. Bad luck." His eyes slid shut. "All to no purpose. You were right."

A flatboat came into view. It navigated carefully into a wing channel on the west side of the ruined bridge. Its deck was piled high with wooden containers.

Silas swallowed his own disappointment. It was true he had maintained stoutly that Haven was mythical, that the expedition was an exercise in fantasy; but part of him had hoped to be proved wrong. Indeed, he had lain at night dreaming how it would be if Abraham Polk's treasures actually existed. What it would mean to find a history of the Roadmakers, to learn something about the race that had built the great cities and highways, what they had dreamed of. And perhaps even to recover an account of the Plague days.

Eleven dead. Silas had known most of them: the guide, Landon Shay; Kir, Tori, and Mira from the Imperium; Arin Milana, the artist; Shola Kobai, the daredevil ex-princess from Masandik. There was Random Iverton, a former military officer turned adventurer; and the scholar Axel from the academy at Farroad; and Cris Lukasi, the survival expert. And two whom Silas had not known, save to shake their hands as they set out on rain-damped River Road and headed into the wilderness.

Only the leader survived. He looked at Karik and knew his old friend was reading his thoughts.

"It happened," he said. "I was just luckier than the rest." Pain came into his eyes. "Silas, what do I tell their families?"

"Tell them the truth. What else is there?"

He faced the window, watching the barge. "I did everything I could. Things just broke down."

"Do you have a list of next of kin?" asked Silas.

"I was hoping you'd help me put one together."

"All right. We can do that. Tonight, you should invite them here. Before they find out you're home and start wondering where their relatives are."

"Some of them are from other cities."

"Do what you can. Take care of the others later. Send messengers."

"Yes," he said. "I suppose that is best."

"Get to as many people as you can. Bring them here this evening. Talk to them together. Tell them what happened."

Karik's eyes were wet. "They won't understand."

"What's to understand? The people who went with you knew there was a risk. When did you get home?"

Karik hesitated. "Last week."

Silas looked at him a long time. "Okay." He refilled the cups and tried to sound casual. "Who else knows you're back?"

"Flojian."

His son.

"All right. Let's get it over with. Listen: The people who went with you were volunteers. They understood there was danger, and their families knew that. All you have to do is explain what happened. Give your regrets. It's okay. They'll see you're hurting, too."

Karik folded his arms and seemed to sag. "Silas," he said, "I wish I'd died out there."

They fell into another long silence. Silas picked up a tablet and began writing down names. Fathers. Sisters. Axel's daughter, who was a relative of Silas's, having married his cousin.

"I don't want to do this," said Karik.

"I know." Silas poured more wine. "But you will. And I'll stand up there with you."

✠ 1 ✠

It is a fond and universally held notion that only things of the spirit truly endure: love, sunsets, music, drama. Marble and paint are subject to the ravages of time. Yet it might be argued that nothing imperishable can move the spirit with quite the impact of a ruined Athenian temple under a full moon.

There was something equally poignant in the wreckage the Roadmakers had left behind. One does not normally equate concrete with beauty. But there it was, formed into magnificent twin strips that glided across rolling hills and through broad forests, leaped rivers, and splayed into tributary roads in designs of such geometrical perfection as to leave an observer breathless. And here, in glittering towers so tall that few could climb them in a single day. And in structures whose elegance had survived the collapse of foundations and roofs.

The engineering skills that created them are lost. Now the structures exist as an integral part of the landscape, as familar to the children of Illyria as the Mississippi itself. But they no longer serve any function save as a tether to a misty past.

Perhaps most striking, and most enigmatic, among them is the Iron Pyramid. The Pyramid dominates the eastern bank of the river. Despite its name, it is not made from iron, but from a metal that some believe is artificial. Like so many Roadmaker materials, it seems to resist rust and decay. The structure is 325 feet high, and its base measures approximately a quarter-mile on a side. It's hollow, and the interior is given over to vast spaces that might have been used to drill an army, or to conduct religious exercises.

Roadmaker cups and combs, dishware and jewelry, toys and knickknacks have been excavated from the ruins and now fill the homes and decorate the persons of the Illyrians. They too are made of material no one can duplicate; they resist wear, and they are easy to keep clean.

Rinny and Colin rarely thought of the ruins, except as places they'd been warned against. People had fallen through holes, things had fallen on *them*. *Stay away.* There were even tales that the wreckage was not quite dead. Consequently, adolescents being what they were, they favored the ancient concrete pier a mile north of Colin's home when they wanted to drop a line in the water.

On this day, rain was coming.

The boys were fifteen, an age at which Illyrian males had already determined their paths in life. Rinny had established himself as a skilled artisan at his father's gunmaking shop. Colin worked on the family farm. Today both were charged with bringing home some catfish.

Rinny watched the storm build. When it hit, they would take shelter in Martin's Warehouse at the foot of the wharf. Martin's Warehouse dated from Roadmaker times. But it was still intact, a worn brick building with its proud sign announcing the name of the establishment and business hours. Eight to six. (The Preservation Society kept the sign clean for tourists.) Colin shifted his weight and squinted at the sky. "Something better start biting soon. Or we're going to be eating turnips again tonight."

So far, they had one fish between them. "I think they've all gone south," said Rinny. A damp wind chopped in across the river. It was getting colder.

Rinny rubbed his hands and tightened the thongs on the upper part of his jacket. On the far side, a flatboat moved slowly downstream. They were rigging tarps to protect themselves from the approaching storm. "Maybe we better think about clearing out."

"In a minute." Colin stared hard at the water as if willing the fish to bite.

The clouds were moving out over the river from the opposite shore. A line of rain appeared. Rinny sighed, put down the carved branch that served as a fishing pole, and began to secure his gear.

"I've got a bite," said Colin. He grinned. "That's better."

"Right. One each will go a long way."

Colin tried to bring it in, but it resisted. "It's tangled up in something." He pulled hard but the pole bent close to breaking. There was a dark mass in the water. "What *is* that?"

"It's not a fish," said Rinny, disappointed.

A boot surfaced.

A boot with a foot in it.

Colin dropped the rod and the foot sank back into the water.

"I don't understand it." Flojian Endine stood away from the bed so Silas could see the body.

Karik seemed to have shrunk year by year since his abortive expedition. Now, in death, it was hard to remember him as he had been in the old days. "I'm sorry," said Silas, suspecting that he was more grieved than Flojian.

"Thank you." Flojian shook his head slowly. "He wasn't the easiest man in the world to live with, but I'll miss him."

Karik's cheek was white and cold. Silas saw no sign of injury. "How did it happen?"

"I don't know." A sketch of a wandering river running between thick wooded slopes hung on the wall. It was black-and-white, and had a curiously unfinished look. The artist had titled it *River Valley*. In the right-hand corner he'd dated it, and signed his name, and Silas noticed with a mild shock that it was Arin Milana, one of the people lost on the Haven mission. The date was June 23, in the 197th year since the founding of the city. The expedition had left Illyria March 1 of that year, and Karik had returned alone in early November. Nine winters ago.

"He liked to walk along the ridge. See, up there? He must have slipped. Fallen in." Flojian moved close to the window and looked out. "Maybe his heart gave out."

"Had he been having problems?"

"Heart problems? No. Not that I know of." Flojian Endine was a thin, fussy version of his father. Same physical model, but without the passions. Flojian was a solid citizen, prosperous, energetic, bright. But Silas didn't believe there was anything he would be willing to fight for. Not even money. "No. As far as I know, he was healthy. But you know how he was. If he'd been ill, he would have kept it to himself."

Silas, who was a year older than Karik had been, marveled at the indelicacy of the remark. "I'm sorry," he said. "I haven't seen much of him for a long time, but I'll miss him all the same. Won't seem right, knowing he's not here anymore." Silas had grown up with Karik. They'd challenged the river, and stood above the rushing water on Holly's Bridge and sworn that together they would learn the secrets of the Roadmakers. They'd soldiered during the wars with Argon and the river pirates, and they'd taken their schooling together, at the feet of Filio Kon of Farroad. Question everything, Kon had warned them. The world runs on illusion. There is nothing people won't believe if it's presented convincingly, or with authority.

It was a lesson Silas learned. It had served him well when Karik started rounding up volunteers to go searching for his never-never land. Silas had stayed home. There'd been a difficult parting, without rancor on Karik's side, but with a substantial load of guilt on Silas's. "I don't know why I felt a responsibility to go with him," he'd later told whoever would listen. "The expedition was a colossal waste of time and resources and I knew it from the start." Karik had claimed to have a map, but he wouldn't show it to anybody on the grounds that he didn't want to risk the possibility that someone would mount a rival expedition.

There wasn't much chance of that, but Karik had clearly lost his grip on reality. Haven was a myth. It was probable that a historical Abraham Polk had existed. It might be true that he had indeed gathered a group of refugees in a remote fortress to ride out the Plague. But the notion that they had emerged when the storm passed, to recover what they could of civilization and store it away for the future: That was the kind of story people liked to tell. And liked to hear. It was therefore suspect. Silas was not going to risk life and reputation in a misguided effort to find a treasure that almost certainly did not exist. Still, his conscience kept after him, and he came eventually to understand that the issue had not been the practicality of the expedition, but simple loyalty. Silas had backed away from his old friend.

"He looked well this morning," said Flojian, who had never really moved out of his father's house, save for a short period during which he had experimented unsuccessfully with marriage. He'd kept an eye on

Karik's welfare, having refused to abandon him when the town damned the old man for cowardice or incompetence or both. Had the lone survivor been anyone else, no one would have objected. But it was indecent for the leader to come home while the bones of his people littered distant roadways. Silas admired Flojian for that, but suspected he was more interested in securing his inheritance than in protecting his father.

The river was cool and serene. There had been a time when he'd counted Karik Endine his closest friend. But he didn't know the man who'd returned from the expedition. *That* Karik had been withdrawn, uncommunicative, almost sullen. At first Silas thought it had been a reaction against *him* personally. But when he heard reports from others at the Imperium, when it became evident that Karik had retired to the north wing of his villa and was no longer seen abroad, he understood that something far more profound had happened.

Flojian was in the middle of his life, about average size, a trifle stocky. His blond hair had already begun to thin. He was especially proud of his neatly trimmed gold beard, which he ardently believed lent him a dashing appearance. "Silas," he said, "the funeral rite will be tomorrow afternoon. I thought you'd like to say a few words."

"I haven't seen much of him for a long time," Silas replied. "I'm not sure I'd know what to talk about."

"I'd be grateful," said Flojian. "You were very close to him at one time. Besides," he hesitated, "there is no one else. I mean, you know how it's been."

Silas nodded. "Of course," he said. "I'll be honored."

Silas and Karik and their intimates had spent countless pleasant evenings at the villa, by the fireplace, or on the benches out under the elms, watching the light fade from the sky, speculating about artifacts and lost races and what really lay beneath the soil. It had been an exciting time to be alive: The League was forming, inter-city wars were ending, there was talk of actively excavating the colossal Roadmaker ruins at the mouth of the Mississippi. There were even proposals for more money for the Imperium, and a higher emphasis on scholarship and research. It had seemed possible then that they might finally begin to make some progress toward uncovering the secrets of the Roadmakers. At least, perhaps, they might find out how the various engines worked, what fueled their civilization. Of all the artifacts, nothing was more enigmatic than the *hojjies*. Named for Algo Hoj, who spent a lifetime trying to understand how they worked, the hojjies were vehicles. They were scattered everywhere on the highways. Their interiors were scorched, but their pseudo-metal bodies could still be made to shine if one wanted to work at it. (It was Hoj who concluded that the charred interiors had resulted from long summers of brutal heat before the very tough windows had finally blown out.) But what had powered them?

So there had been ground for optimism twenty years ago. The League had formed, and peace had come. But wreckage in the Mississippi had discouraged operations in the delta; funds for the Imperium had never materialized; and the hojjies remained as enigmatic as ever.

They stood at the front door while Silas took in the river and the ruins. "He loved this view," said Silas. "It was his window into the past." The hillside sloped gently down to the water's edge, about a hundred feet away. A pebble walkway circled the house, looped past a series of stone benches, and descended to the narrow strip of beach fronting the river. A tablet lay on one of the benches.

Flojian shook his hand. "Thanks for your help, Silas."

Silas looked at the tablet. A cold wind moved in the trees.

Flojian followed his gaze. "That's odd," he said. He strolled to the bench, almost too casually, regarded the tablet as if it were an animal that might bite, and picked it up. It was drenched from the rain, but the leather cover had protected it. "My father was working on a commentary to *The Travels*."

Silas opened the tablet and looked at Karik's neat, precise handwriting. It was dated that day.

Unfortunately, only a fragment of *The Travels* was then known to exist. There is, in the prologue, a celebrated conversation between Abraham Polk and Simba Markus, the woman who would eventually betray him, over the value of securing the history of a vanished world. *"It's only the dead past,"* Simba says. *"Let it go."*

"The past," Polk replies, *"is never dead. It is who we are."*

"But the risk is too great. We might bring the Plague back with us. Have you thought of that?"

"I've thought of it. But for this kind of prize, any risk is justified."

Apparently in reference to this exchange, Karik had written: *"No, it is not."*

"Odd to leave it outside like that," said Silas. "Maybe he wasn't feeling well." He looked from the bench to the top of the ridge, where Karik customarily walked, to the strip of beach. "He set it on the bench and did *what?* Walked up onto the ridge?"

"I assume that's what happened."

"And he was wearing boots, wasn't he? The first thing the boys saw was a *boot.*"

"Yes."

"There are bootmarks *here.*" They were faint, barely discernible after the rain. But they *were* there. Immediately adjacent to the bench, the marks crossed several feet of beach, and disappeared into the water.

Kon had provided Silas with another gift: an unquenchable desire to know about the Roadmakers, whose highways ran to infinity. Now they were frequently covered with earth, mere passages through the forests, on which trees did not grow. An observer standing on the low hills that rimmed the Mississippi could see the path of the great east-west road, two strips really, twin tracks rising and falling, sometimes in unison, sometimes not, coming like arrows out of the sunrise, dividing when they reached Illyria, circling the city and rejoining at Holly's Bridge to cross the river.

Kon had suggested an intriguing possibility to Silas: The great structures were more than simply roads, they were simultaneously religious artifacts. Several studies had found geometrical implications that tied them to the cosmic harmonies. Silas never understood any of it and exercised the principle of skepticism that Kon himself had encouraged.

If the ruins were simply part of the landscape to Rinny and Colin, no more exceptional than honey locusts and red oaks, they meant a great deal more to Silas. They were a touchstone to another world. It was painful to be in the presence of so great a civilization and to know so little about it.

Silas Glote had found his life's work investigating the Roadmakers. And if it didn't pay well, it supplied endless satisfaction. There was nothing quite like introducing students to the mysteries of the ruins, whose peculiarities they had seen but rarely noticed: the shafts, for example, that existed to no apparent purpose in most of the taller buildings; the ubiquitous metallic boxes and pseudo-glass screens; the massive gray disk mounted near a sign that read MEMPHIS LIGHT, GAS, AND WATER, pointed at the sky; the occasional music that could be heard at night from within a mound on the west side of the old city.

Silas's sense of guilt over staying away from Karik's expedition might have arisen not only from his failure to support his old friend, but also from his mixed feelings regarding the outcome of the mission. In a dark part of his soul, he had taken satisfaction in Karik's failure. He didn't like to admit that fact to himself, but it was nonetheless true.

Karik had not shown him any evidence that he could find Haven, or that Haven even existed. Instead, he had asked him to trust his judgment. *I know where it is,* he'd said. *I have a map. You'll want to be there when we find it.*

Polk's fortress was said to be tended still by scholars, descendants of the original garrison, men and women who had cared for the contents, who restored what they could, who meticulously recopied the texts as paper crumbled.

Haven.

If it did not exist, it should. And therein, to Silas's mind, lay the root of his doubts. If Abraham Polk had not existed, someone would certainly have invented him.

For Chaka Milana, the news of Karik Endine's death conjured up images of her fourteenth birthday. Her brother Arin had taken her to her favorite spot, a quiet glade fronting on one of the Roadmaker buildings, and had painted her portrait.

She had wanted him to do that as far back as she could remember. But she had been too shy to ask, too afraid he would laugh. On that cool, late winter day, however, he'd posed her on a slab of granite in front of a broken wall and an arch whose spandrel was engraved: *MEMPHIS CHAMBER OF COMMERCE—2009.*

The spot was special because Memphis had burned. Much of its ruins were ashes. But here, the little arched building with its fluted columns was whole. And lovely.

"Chaka, please keep still." Arin peered at her, tilted his head while he measured the quality of the light, nodded, and returned his attention to his canvas.

"Are you almost finished?"

"Almost."

They had speculated as to what a chamber of commerce was, and what its functions might be. She liked the stylized characters, with their flares and tails. When she looked at them, a wind from another era blew through her.

When she arrived at the service, Karik's body had been placed on a pyre at the water's edge and covered with a funeral cloth. The corpse was surrounded by wood cases containing his personal belongings, his *anuma*. These were the items which would accompany him on his final journey. The ceremonial torch had been unsealed, and the emblem of the *Tasselay,* the Cup of Life, fluttered on an emerald banner.

Guests filled the house and grounds. Singly and in pairs, they mounted the low platform that had been erected in front of the pyre, paid their respects to Flojian, and gazed thoughtfully at the body.

✠ ✠ ✠

"I think that'll do." Arin flourished his brush, dabbed his signature in the lower right corner, and stood aside. Chaka jumped off the rock and hurried to look.

"Do you like it?"

He had captured it all: the granite, a couple of the Roadmaker letters, the failing late afternoon light. And Chaka herself. He'd added a degree of poise and an inner illumination that she persuaded herself were really there. "Oh, yes, Arin. It's lovely."

He smiled, pleased, his amiable features streaked with paint. It was a family joke that Arin inevitably used himself as the prime canvas.

"Happy birthday, little sister."

She was thinking how it would look on the wall of her bedroom when she saw that a shadow had darkened his green eyes.

A casual visitor could not have been blamed for concluding, from the size and demeanor of the crowd attending the service, that Karik Endine had been blessed with a loving family and a large body of devoted friends. Neither was true. There were no kin other than his son and a couple of neglected cousins. And it would have been difficult to find anyone in Illyria, or for that matter in any of the five League cities and their various suburbs and outposts, who would have thought himself part of Karik's inner circle.

Among those who had known him in better times, he had become an object of curiosity and pity, whose death was seen as a release. But they came out of loyalty, as people will, to the old days. Some felt an obligation to attend because they were connected in some way with Flojian. Others were curious, interested in hearing what might be said about a celebrated man whose achievements had, at the very least, been mixed. These were the people who arrived to celebrate his life, to wish him farewell on his final journey, to exchange anecdotes with one another, and to drink somber toasts to the man they realized, at last, they had never really known. As was the tradition on such occasions, no one gave voice to personal reservations about the character of the deceased. (This happy custom arose not only from courtesy to relatives, but from the Illyrian belief that the dead man lingered among them until the priest officially consigned him to eternity.)

"Thank you."

"You're welcome," he said.

"What's wrong?"

"Nothing." Arin wiped his hands and pretended to study the painting. "Nothing's wrong. But I do have something to tell you." He'd been standing a long time, more than an hour. Now he sat down on the grassy slope and patted the grass, inviting her to join him. "Do you remember Karik Endine?"

"Yes, of course I remember him." He had been an intense little man who seemed always out of breath, who visited the house and locked himself away with her father and her brother. When she was a little girl, he had patted her on the head, but even then she could see he was distracted and anxious to be away.

"He thinks he knows where Haven is. He wants me to go with him to find it."

She knew about Haven, knew that it was a story and not a place. "You're kidding."

"I never kid, Chaka."

"I thought it was made-up."

"Maybe it is. Karik doesn't think so."

"So where is it?"

"In the north somewhere. He doesn't really want to say where. But he says he knows how to get there."

He was so handsome that morning. "How long will you be gone?"

"About six months."

"It seems like a lot of trouble to me. What's the point?"

"It's a piece of history, Chaka. Think what might be there."

"The treasures."

"Yes. Maybe there really was an October Patrol, and maybe they really did save part of the Roadmaker world." He bent toward her. "Abraham Polk probably is made-up, and maybe the whole story's a fabrication. But there might be some truth to it. We won't know unless we go look."

She asked whether she could go, too. He'd smiled that gorgeous smile and ruffled her hair.

"He never really lived in our time." The speaker was round-faced, bearded, ponderous. "One might almost say he really lived with the Roadmakers. In this house, he was only a transient."

Even Chaka knew that Karik had in fact taken to the house and remained unseen in it for nine years. The remark struck her as unfortunate, and she had to work to restrain a smile.

Others expressed similar sentiments, and it became clear to Chaka after a time that no one seemed to have had a recent personal experience to relate. Karik Endine had been a man at a distance, someone glimpsed at the periphery of vision. It seemed that nobody had ever gone to lunch with him. Or shared an intimate hour. Nobody said, *he was my friend*. Nobody said, *I loved him*.

Something else was missing in the tributes. There was no mention of the mission to Haven. It was as if it had never happened.

Flojian tried to look mournful, but after a while he

gave it up and simply walked around wearing a blank expression that probably masked his relief that the old man was gone. He'd shunned an academic life like Karik's for one that seemed more useful, and certainly was more lucrative: He operated a pair of ferries and a service that used horses to drag flatboats back upstream. The villa had been in the family for four generations, but it had fallen into neglect and disrepair during Karik's tenure. It had been Flojian's money that had restored it, and subsequently furnished and maintained it. His father had been a dreamer. Flojian saw nothing wrong with that, but it required men of purpose and action like himself to create a world in which dreamers could live.

Chaka had gone to see Karik shortly after her father's death. She'd never understood precisely what had happened to Arin. So she went to his cottage and knocked on the door, determined to ask him. He'd let her wait a long time, and it had become a war of nerves until Karik gave in and opened up.

"I'm sorry," he said. "I was sleeping."

His tone suggested he was lying. She was still very young but her blood was up by then. "My father told me Arin drowned, Master Endine. But I wonder whether you could explain just what happened?"

He stood in the doorway, ferocious in moonlight. "Come in, Chaka."

"I'm sorry to bother you."

"It's no bother."

"I know my father talked to you." But he had come home and stared into the fire and said simply that Arin had drowned, had got swept away by the current and drowned. And that was all.

Karik offered her a seat. "We were trying to ford a river. We thought we were getting close to the end of the journey, and maybe we got careless. Arin was leading the way, with our guide. Landon Shay. One of the packhorses lost its balance. It panicked and Arin went after it and tried to pull it back." His gaze focused on a distant point. "In the end they both got dragged away. When he saw it was hopeless to try to save the animal, Arin let go and swam for shore. We thought he'd make it, but every time he got close, the current pushed him out again. Finally he got sucked into white water, into rocks." He leaned close. "I think he hit his head. The last we saw of him, he looked unconscious. Then the river took him around a bend. It all happened so fast. We just couldn't reach him, Chaka."

"But you never found his body?"

He reached out for her. "We searched for him downstream. But no. We never found him. I'm sorry. I wish I could have done something."

He had begun to cry. Only a short storm, but fierce all the same because he did not look like a man capable of tears. And when he'd recovered, he'd gone upstairs and come down with an armload of sketches, her brother's work. "These are from the mission," he said, offering them to her and then asking if he might keep one.

"Does anyone else wish to speak?" Flojian looked over the assembly. It was a lovely day, bright and cool and clear. The river was ablaze in the sun. The priest, an elderly woman with white hair and severe features, inserted a couple of sticks into the cookfire and glanced at the torch.

Chaka had wondered about the description of Arin's death. He hadn't been much of a swimmer, and she had a difficult time imagining him daring deep water to bring back a panicked animal. It *could* have happened. But it was out of character. She had concluded that Karik might have added the heroic details to comfort her. It was more likely that Arin had simply been carried away himself and sank like a stone.

She surprised herself by standing up. "I would like to say something." The assembly parted and she walked forward and ascended the platform. She had red, shoulder-length hair, features that had been boyish during adolescence and which retained a rugged, devil-may-care aspect, softened by luminous blue eyes and a warm smile.

"I hardly knew Karik Endine," she said. "My brother made the trip north with him nine years ago. After Master Endine came home, I asked him about my brother." Her listeners stirred uneasily. "I came away with the sense that he was in as much pain as I. I always loved him for that. He was, I think, the most unfortunate man I've known. But he did what he could to ease the suffering of a child he barely knew." The wind was loud in the elms. She stepped down.

Flojian thanked her and asked whether there was anyone else. There was not. "When the ceremony is concluded," he said, "Karik welcomes you to stay." The priest came forward, drew down the Tasselay banner, folded it reverently, handed it to an aide, and took the torch. She held it over the cookfire until it caught, and gave it to Flojian with a whispered admonition to be careful. Flojian now delivered the ritual appreciation to his father, thanking him for the sun and the river and all the hours of his life. When he had finished, the priest intoned a prayer to Ekra the Traveler, who would convey the departing spirit to its next life. They bowed their heads. When the priest had finished, Flojian touched the torch to the pyre.

Within seconds, it was engulfed in flames. Chaka looked away. *Goodbye, Arin,* she said, as if the final link to her brother were being cut.

Afterward, they retreated into the house, exchanged toasts through the afternoon, and talked a lot about how they would miss the deceased. Chaka had a light tolerance for wine, and she was getting ready to call it a day when a short, stout man with a neatly clipped gray beard put a drink in her hand. "You said exactly the right things, young lady," he said.

"Thank you."

She understood immediately from his formal bearing and precise speech that he was an academic. He was about sixty, probably one of Endine's colleagues. "The rest of us babbled like damned fools," he continued.

She smiled at him, pleased.

"We're going to miss him." He tasted his wine. "My name's Silas Glote. I teach at the Imperium."

The name sounded familiar. "Pleased to meet you, Master Glote." She smiled. "I'm Chaka Milana."

"I knew Arin," said Silas.

She recalled where she had heard the name. "He was in one of your seminars."

"A long time ago. He was a fine young man."

"Thank you."

Flojian came up behind them, nodded to Silas, and thanked them both for their comments. "I'm sure," he told Chaka, "he was delighted." This was, of course, a reference to Karik's spirit.

"It was true," she said.

Flojian managed a smile. "Silas was invited to go on the expedition."

"Really?"

"I have no taste for the wilderness," said Silas. "I like my comforts." He turned to Flojian. "How far did they actually get? Did he ever tell you?"

Flojian saw three empty chairs around a table and steered his guests toward them. Toko, his ancient servant, brought more drinks. "No," he said, passing a cushion to Chaka. "He didn't talk about it. Not a word."

"How about the map?"

"I never saw a map. I don't know that there was one." He took a deep breath. "The tradition has always been that it was to the north. On the sea. But what sea?" He rolled his eyes. "Well, it hardly matters." He looked toward Chaka. "Silas blames himself for not going."

"I never said that."

"I know. But I can hear it in your voice. And you do yourself an injustice. Nothing would have been different. Except one more would have died. I suspect you refused him for the same reason I did."

"He asked *you* to go?" Silas blurted the question, and then realized the implied insult and tried to regroup by suggesting that Karik would not have expected Flojian to be interested.

"It's all right, Silas. He was relieved when I passed on the idea." Flojian's voice dropped to a harsh whisper. "But it was abject nonsense from the start and you and I both knew it. We told him so and challenged him to show his evidence. Show the map. But he refused."

Flojian finished his drink and sighed. "He walked out of here with a group of *children*. I apologize for that, Chaka, but it's so. He took advantage of people who believed in him. And he led them to their graves. Nothing changes that, no matter what anyone says here."

Chaka was about to leave when Flojian appeared again and asked whether he could speak with her privately. The request was put so earnestly that she was at a loss to guess his purpose.

He led her to a sitting room in the back of the

house, and drew aside a set of heavy curtains. Sunlight fell on a collection of four books.

The room was comfortably furnished with leather chairs, a desk, a cabinet, a side table, and a reading stand. "This was my father's sanctum," he said, "before he retreated into the north wing." All four volumes were bound and, of course, hand-written. Two were inside the cabinet, a third was on the desk, and a fourth lay open on the reading stand. They were Kessler's *The Poetic Rationale;* Karik's own history of Illyria, *Empire and Sunset;* Molka's *Foundations of the League;* and a fragment copy of *The Travels of Abraham Polk.*

"They're lovely," she said.

"Thank you."

The Molka book, on the stand, was most accessible. The craftsmanship was marvelous: leather binding, vellum of the highest order, exquisite calligraphy, fine inks, golden flourishes in strategic locations, brilliant illustrations.

"They must be quite valuable."

"They are." His brown eyes focused on her. "I'm going to sell them."

"You're not serious."

"Oh, yes. I have no way to protect them. When Father was here, it was one thing. But now, I'd have to hire a guard. No, they don't really mean much to me, Chaka. I'd rather have the money."

"I see." She ran her fingers lightly over the binding.

"A pleasant sensation, isn't it?"

"Yes."

"Well, you must be wondering why I wanted to see you." He opened a cabinet drawer and removed a package. She guessed by its dimensions and weight it contained a fifth book. He set it down on a table and stood aside. "I don't know whether you're aware of it or not, but you made a considerable impression on my father."

"That's hard to believe, Flojian. He never really knew me."

"He remembered. He left instructions that this was to be given to you." The package was wrapped in black leather and held shut by a pair of straps. Chaka released the buckles, and caught her breath.

Gold leaf, red leather binding, fine parchment, although somewhat yellowed with age. "This is for *me*?"

"It's Mark Twain," said Flojian. *"A Connecticut Yankee in King Arthur's Court."*

She lifted the cover and stared at the title page. "Mark Twain's books are lost," she said.

"Well." He laughed. "Not all of them. Not anymore."

There were illustrations of knights on horseback and castle walls and beautiful women in flowing gowns. And a picture of a man fashioning a pistol.

The language was antiquated.

"Where did it come from?"

"That's a question I wish I could answer. It was as much a surprise to me as it is to you." He pursed his lips. "It's somewhat worn, as you can see. But this is the way it was put into my hands."

Chaka was overwhelmed. "I can't take this," she said.

"I think you have to," said Flojian. "It's in his will. Be careful of it, though. I suspect it will command a substantial price."

"I would think so."

"I can make some suggestions with regard to getting full value for it, Chaka."

She closed the book and refastened the case. "Oh, no," she said. "I wouldn't sell it. But thank you anyway."

✠ ✠ ✠

Raney was waiting for her on Sundown Road. He was tall, congenial, with dark eyes and a gentleness that one seldom found in younger men. He was occasionally dull, but that was not necessarily a bad thing in a man. She wore his bracelet on her ankle.

"How did it go?" he asked as she rode up.

The Mark Twain was secured in her saddlebag. Raney didn't seem to have noticed it. "You wouldn't believe it," she said, accepting his kiss and returning an embrace that surprised him and almost knocked him off his horse.

Raney was a garment maker. He was skilled, well paid, and enjoyed the affection and respect of his customers and the owner of the shop in which he worked. The shop was prosperous, the owner feeble, and, as nature took its course, Raney could expect to have few concerns about his future.

He nodded toward the pillar of smoke rising into the sky. "I was surprised that you'd go."

"Why?"

"The man's responsible for Arin's death."

"That's nonsense," she said. "Arin took his chances when he went. There aren't any guarantees upcountry. *You* should know that."

It was a fine sunny day, unseasonably warm. They rode slowly toward River Road, where they would turn north. "He came back," said Raney. "The man in charge of the expedition is the only survivor." He shook his head. "If it were me, I'd have stayed out there."

She shrugged. "Maybe. But what would be the point?"

The river sparkled below them. They talked about trivialities and after a while turned off the road and cantered upslope to Chaka's villa, which stood atop the ridge. Her grandfather had built it, and it had passed to her remaining brother, Sauk, who'd granted it to her in exchange for her agreement to rear her two sisters. Now, Lyra was grown and gone, and Carin expected to marry in the spring.

Raney was staring at her. "You okay?" he asked. "You look kind of funny."

"I'm fine." She smiled as they rode through a hedge onto the grounds. "I have something to show you."

He carried the bag into the house and she opened it. When he saw the book, he frowned. "What is it?"

"Mark Twain. One of the lost books."

"He's a Roadmaker writer."

"Yes."

"Where'd it come from?"

"It's an inheritance, Raney. Karik left it to me."

"Funny thing to do for a stranger. Why?"

She thought she caught a suspicious note in his voice. "I don't know."

"How much do you think it's worth?"

"A lot. But it doesn't matter."

"Why not?"

"I'm not going to sell it."

"You're not?" He gazed at an open page. "What do *you* want with it?"

What was *that* supposed to mean? "Raney, this is *Mark Twain.*"

He shook his head. "It's your book, love. But *I'd* unload it at the first opportunity."

✠ 2 ✠

The Illyrians knew the world was round, though some among the lower classes were skeptical. They knew that infections were caused by tiny creatures they could not see, that the pattern of days and nights resulted from the movement of the world and not of the sun, that the Mississippi rose in a land of gigantic ruins and emptied into a gulf whose waters ran untroubled to the horizon. They were aware that thunderstorms were caused by natural processes and not by supernatural beings, although, since no one could explain how this was so, that view was becoming progressively tenuous with each generation.

They knew that a civilization of major dimensions had occupied the land before them. How extensive those dimensions had been was a matter for speculation: The Illyrians and their fellow dwellers in the Mississippi Valley did not travel far beyond League outposts. They were still few in number; population pressures would not, for many years, drive them into a dangerous and hard wilderness. Furthermore, river navigation was limited: They could not move upstream easily without powered vessels; and travel downstream was hampered in some places and blocked altogether in others by collapsed bridges and other debris.

A metropolis had once existed at the river's mouth, where the Mississippi drained into the Southern Sea. How this had been possible, given the fact that the entire area was swampland, no one knew. Silas and a few others suspected that the swamp was a relatively recent phenomenon and had not existed in Roadmaker times. But the ruin was there nonetheless. And, like Memphis, it had burned.

Six years after Karik's unhappy expedition, the Illyrians had joined the other four river valley cities to form the Mississippi League, one of whose express purposes was to gain direct access to the sea. It was an enterprise still in its planning phases.

The League's acknowledged center of learning was the Imperium, a onetime royal academy located in Illyria. It derived its name from its imperial founders and patrons and from its location in the west wing of the old palace. (The "empire" had consisted of Illyria, a half-dozen outlying settlements, and a lot of optimism.) It was one of the few institutions to survive intact the seven years of civil war and revolution that separated the murder of the last emperor, Benikat V ("Bloody Beni"), from the Declaration of Rights and the founding of the Republic.

The palace had been restored, but it no longer served an official function. The Senate had made a point of their republican roots: Their first order of business under the constitution had been to move out of the imperial grounds and to take up temporary residence in a military barracks until a new capitol could be built. Much of the palace itself was converted into a museum.

Daily visitors could now see the bedroom in which Benikat had been surprised by his guards; the Great Hall of the Moon, where Hethra had invoked the power of heaven to frighten Lorimar VII into submission; and the balcony on which Paxton the Far-Seer had composed his immortal ballads.

In the west wing, men of science, literature, and philosophy served the sons of the wealthy and a specially selected few from the poorer classes. It was a position that carried respect and satisfied the spirit. Silas envied no one. He could imagine no finer calling than spending the winter afternoons speculating on man's place in the cosmos and the reality of divine purpose. (Here, of course, he had to be a little careful: The religious authorities and their pious allies in the Senate did not respond favorably to any opinion that might undermine the faith.)

He had never married.

There were times now that he regretted being alone. The years were beginning to crowd him, and the coldness of the farewell to Karik had depressed his spirits. He arrived home wondering what sort of send-off *he* would be accorded when his time came.

The palace straddled the crest of Calagua Hill, the highest point in Illyria. It was, in fact, a network of connected buildings clustered around a series of courtyards. Springs and hydraulic systems carried water into and waste out of baths and washrooms; interior courtyards and enormous banks of windows provided illumination. There was a web of stairways and corridors, apartments, workshops, sanctuaries, armories, and banquet halls. The royal apartments were still maintained on the south side, where they overlooked the busy commercial center.

Rows of houses, separated by winding unpaved streets, sprawled out from the foot of Calagua Hill. The houses were, for the most part, wooden or brick. They lacked indoor plumbing, as did most residences in Illyria, but they were comfortable and well kept. After the formation of the League, when security ceased to be a major concern, the more prosperous inhabitants had moved outside the city walls. The area had then been given over to a teeming marketplace, full of haggling and bargaining, which sold corn, grains, and meat from local farms; pottery and handicrafts from Argon; wines from downriver; soaps and scents from Masandik; leather goods from Farroad; furniture, firearms, and jewelry from local artisans.

For all its dark associations, the palace embodied the pride of the nation and remained a monument to the magnificence of the imperial imagination. Glittering spires and granite turrets, broad galleries and elevated courtyards, cupolas and vaulted staircases collaborated to infuse in visitors a sense of past greatness and future promise.

From his study, Silas could see the entire southern face of the structure, its arches and mezzanines and guard posts. "Forget the politics," he told his students. "Concentrate on the architecture. If we can create such beauty from stone, what can we not do?"

And yet. . . .

Anyone digging more than a few feet into the soil could expect to collide with ancient walls and foundations. They were everywhere. The Roadmakers had far exceeded his own people in their architectural skills, yet they had gone to dust. It was a grim reminder against hubris. The palace, which had once been alive, was now only a vast mausoleum with a school at one end and a museum at the other. Every year, students wondered whether the Illyrians had already taken the first step downhill. Among the masters there were several, not least of all Silas, who were convinced that the democratic system now in place was little better than mob rule. Ordinary people, they suspected, inevitably vote their own interests. To survive, a nation needs authority and wisdom at the top. The strategy, he believed, should be to find a mechanism to maintain a balance of power among a small number of families. These families would be educated to the throne, and would select the best among them to act for all. As to a practical design for such a mechanism, Silas confessed he had none.

After Karik's body had been consigned to the flames, he had fallen into a contemplative, and indeed almost bleak, mood. If a people could achieve the capability to erect the monumental structures that existed in all the forests of the known world, and yet could not save themselves from extinction, what was one to conclude? It was difficult for Silas to discard his conviction that history should reflect moral and technological progress. It was a battle he'd fought many times with Karik, who argued that history was chaotic and wondered how anybody living among the ruins could think otherwise.

That Silas thought of himself as a history teacher should not suggest that the instructors at the Imperium were specialized. In fact, the body of knowledge was so limited that specialization beyond certain very broad categories would have been absurd. The categories, other than history, were ethics, philosophy, theology, medicine, rhetoric, law, and mathematics.

Several of his students had attended the ceremonies for Karik. Next day, in a seminar, they wondered how so erudite a man could have been so foolish, and they engaged in a long discussion about the ability of even the best minds to delude themselves.

At the end of the class, one of his students lingered. His name was Brandel Tess, and he had been among those who'd attended the funeral rites. He looked troubled. "Master Glote," he said, "one of my friends is Toko's grandson."

"Who?"

"Toko. Master Endine's servant."

"Oh, yes. And—?"

"He says that his grandfather claims there was a copy of *A Connecticut Yankee* in Master Endine's quarters."

"He must be mistaken."

"He says no. Toko swears it was there. He says Karik had it open on a reading table for years, and made him promise not to tell anybody. But now it's missing."

"Did he ask Flojian about it?"

"Flojian told him it was given away."

"To whom?"

"I don't think he thought it proper to ask."

Silas shook his head. "This can't be right," he said, with smooth self-assurance. "There *is* no extant copy of *Connecticut Yankee*." Only six books from the age of the Roadmakers were known to exist: *The Odyssey; Brave New World; The Brothers Karamazov; The Collected Short Stories of Washington Irving;* Eliot Klein's book of puzzles and logic, *Beats Me;* and Goethe's *Faust*. They also had substantial sections of *The Oxford Companion to World Literature* and several plays by Bernard Shaw. There were bits and pieces of other material. Of Mark Twain, two fragments remained, the first half of "The Facts in the Case of the Great Beef Contract," and chapter sixteen from *Life on the Mississippi,* which describes piloting and racing steamboats, although the precise nature of the steamboat tantalizingly eluded Illyria's best scholars.

Brandel shrugged. "Okay," he said. "I just thought you'd be interested."

The tables and benches that had been set out for the funeral rite were still in place. Silas tied his horse to the hitching rail. The ground where the pyre had stood was charred. The ashes of his old friend, in accordance with tradition, had been given to the river by Flojian at sunrise.

He knocked on the front door. Toko answered. He was tall and thin, white-haired, ancient, the soul of dignity. "I expect my master shortly, sir," he said. "If you care to wait." He showed Silas into a side parlor, and placed a glass of wine before him.

Brandel was wrong, of course. There was simply no question about that. Karik would have judged his life spectacularly successful had he been able to find a copy of *Connecticut Yankee*. If he'd owned one, he would have given it to the world. Still, Silas needed to pin down the reason for the misunderstanding.

Dusk had set in. From the window he could watch the first lamps being lit across the river. It was a curiously restful sight and he was enjoying it when he heard the sound of an approaching horse. Flojian rode into the front yard on a dusky mare. Several minutes later Toko opened a door and Flojian strode into the sitting room carrying a glass of wine and a candle.

"Good to see you again, Silas," he said, falling into a chair. "I thought the ceremony went well yesterday. Thank you for your help."

"I thought so, too. We'll miss him." Actually, no one would miss him, and they both knew it. "I wanted to be sure you were all right."

"I'm okay," said Flojian. He tried to smile, but there was an element of pain in the expression. "My father and I weren't really that close. I don't find myself regretting what I've lost so much as what I never had." He used the candle to light the lamps in the room, and then set it in a holder. "But I don't guess there's much help for that now."

"I heard an odd story today," said Silas, rearranging himself in his chair. "One of my students thought your father owned a Mark Twain."

Flojian sipped his wine. "I'm surprised you know about that," he said. "But yes, it's true."

The room chilled. Silas stared at the younger man. It was a moment before he found his voice again. "How long did he have it?"

"I don't know."

"You don't know." Whatever his drawbacks, Flojian was not stupid. "How could you not know?"

"It's easy. He didn't tell me. Refused to talk about it. You know how he was."

"May I ask where he got it?"

"I don't know that either. I asked my father that question and he said it was of no moment, and that's all he would say. Listen, Silas, I only found out about this a couple of days before he died. I didn't know there was anything like that around the house."

"It's *Connecticut Yankee,* I understand."

"That's right."

Silas was essentially a patient man and had never been given to violence. But on that occasion he wanted to seize his host and shake the answers from him. "Where is it now?" he demanded.

Flojian stiffened. "Your tone almost suggests that you have a proprietary interest."

"Damn it, Flojian. *Everybody* has a proprietary interest in something like that. You can't keep it to yourself."

"As a matter of fact, I didn't." The comment hammered down on the still evening air. "Father bequeathed it to Chaka Milana. The young woman you were talking with yesterday."

"Why on earth would he do that?"

"I'm sure I do not know. She was Arin's sister. You remember, Arin was the artist who was lost on the expedition."

"I remember."

Flojian's features clouded. "So he gave her the book. I don't know why. Guilt, probably, or something like that."

"Did he know her well?"

"Oh, I don't think so. In fact, he hardly knew her at all."

"What did she do with it?"

"Took it home, I guess."

"I don't believe this. I hope she knows enough to take care of it." Silas glared at Flojian. "At least, he should have given it to us. Did she know about it in advance?"

"No. In fact, she couldn't have been more surprised."

Silas wanted to flee the room, to begin tracking the book down before the poor woman used it to light her fire. But the story didn't make sense. "Karik had a Mark Twain novel and he didn't tell anybody? Why?"

"I don't know."

"Did he expect that Chaka was just going to take it home and throw it into her hope chest?"

"He really didn't tell me what he thought, Silas."

Morinda lifted the amulet and examined it in the candlelight. Chaka watched the amethyst crescent glitter against its silver setting. It was exquisite. "Yes," she said.

A bow was engraved on the reverse, Lyka's device, the sign of the moon goddess. "It does look very nice on you," said Chaka.

Morinda put the chain around her neck, and unclasped the top of her knit blouse so that the amulet hung between her breasts. "Thank you." She shook her hair out and smiled alluringly. "Yes," she said again.

Hoofbeats outside. "I'm glad you like it."

They were in her workroom, in the rear of the villa. Morinda produced two gold pieces from a black purse. "My husband told me he saw you yesterday at Endine's service."

Chaka nodded. "It was a painful afternoon."

"I'm not surprised. I intend no disrespect to the dead, but a man like that—" She shook her head.

"It was a long time ago." Chaka closed the box that she had fashioned to house the amulet and handed it to Morinda. "There was no one you knew on that expedition, was there?"

"No," Morinda said. "But that's not the point, is it?"

Probably not.

Morinda smiled again, wished the silversmith a pleasant evening, and opened the door to reveal an older man just preparing to knock. "Good evening, ladies," he said.

The man from the funeral service.

"Silas Glote," he said quickly.

Morinda took her farewell while Chaka gestured Silas into the shop. "I didn't forget you, Master Glote," she said. "How good to see you again."

He smiled and gazed at the items on the display shelves. There was an array of bracelets, rings, anklets, urns, goblets, and pins. He seemed particularly drawn to a set of silver clasps designed to secure a man's shirt. "These are quite nice," he observed.

She offered one for his inspection. "They'd look pretty good down at the Imperium," she said.

He held it under a lamp. "Philosophically, we're opposed to such baubles. We seek the inner realities." He smiled. "The inner realities are more within the reach of my pocketbook."

"For you," she said, "I can offer a special price."

She named an amount which really was quite reasonable. The clasps would contrast very nicely with the dark vest he was wearing. "Done," he said, and then laughed when he saw he'd surprised her. "One should not be a slave to any code."

"A wise choice, Master Glote."

He folded his arms and the smile faded. "Chaka, I wanted to talk with you."

"Please," she said. She offered him a chair and sat down beside him. "What can I do for you?"

"I understand you received a legacy from Karik Endine."

"Yes," she said. He was direct, this one. "I was surprised. I'd seen him only once to talk with, and that was years ago. It's really very odd."

"Is it true it's a book?"

"I suspect you know very well what it is, Master Glote."

"Please call me Silas. May I see it?"

She *was* annoyed at Flojian's lack of discretion. Still, she *wanted* to show it to someone who would appreciate it. "Of course." She locked the workshop and led the way through a connecting door into the house.

A fire burned low in the living room. She walked past a fabric sofa and a long table whose top was littered with pieces of jewelry. Twin cabinets framed a window that looked out onto a row of moonlit hills.

Silas's gaze fell on the rifles that were mounted over the fireplace. "Family of hunters," she said.

She took him to the left-hand cabinet and lit a taper. In the flickering light, Silas's features seemed rigid. The cabinet was cunningly made, designed so that the top unfolded, revealing a series of narrow compartments and a drawer. She opened the drawer, and the light from the taper fell on the book.

Mark Twain. Silas's breathing became audible.

"May I?" he asked at last.

"Of course."

He touched the cover cautiously, reverently. The title was written in gold script across soft leather. He pulled the taper closer, but was careful not to get it too near to the volume. He opened it and turned over the title page. The text was in black ink, the letters skillfully executed. He studied the one-page preface. Two paragraphs, followed by the writer's name. Written at Hartford, July 21, 1889.

"How long ago was that?"

"Nobody knows."

"Where was Hartford?"

"We think it's where he was born. But nobody's sure where it was."

He leafed through it cautiously. Was this what it purported to be? That would be the next question, and it might be hard to answer definitively without knowing the source of the book. He turned more pages, lingered over chapter headings, nodded at the precise lines. She watched his lips move, saw a smile appear, saw his eyes glow. "Yes," he said. "It *sounds* right."

Good. "Silas. Are you satisfied this is really Mark Twain?"

He gazed very hard at her. "I know what I *want* it to be. It seems very much like his style, the little I've seen of it." He took a deep breath. "Do you have reason to doubt its authenticity?"

"Why did Endine keep it secret? Why didn't he tell anyone he had this?"

Silas carried the book over to the table, set it down in the light of the lamp, and lowered himself into a chair. The burning oil smelled sweet. "I don't know, Chaka."

"It makes no sense."

"I agree. Still, I think this is exactly what it looks like." He turned more leaves, nodding and smiling until he was barely able to contain himself. "Oh, yes," he said. He began reading lines to her, stopping occasionally to chuckle.

"I've been advised to sell it," she said, breaking the mood.

He looked up, suddenly worried. "I'd recommend you not do that. This is priceless."

"But what else can I do with it? It won't be safe here. I have no servants. I'd have to hire a guard."

Silas grew thoughtful. She understood he would prefer she sell it to the Imperium. In no case did he want it auctioned off, because the scholars could not compete with wealthy collectors, and the book would ultimately go into a rich man's drawing room and become generally inaccessible. "Lend it to the Senatorial Library," he suggested. "It will be locked away, kept secure, but made available to scholars. Meantime, we can set people to making copies."

"What do *I* get out of it?"

"You'll get payment for the sale of copies. It won't be a *lot* of money, but it will be reasonable. Moreover, I'll arrange suitable recognition." He smiled. "We'll have you out regularly for lunch, the finest people in the Republic will feel indebted to you, and you can stop worrying about thieves. If at some future date you wish to sell it, you'll be free to do so."

A long silence settled between them. "Silas," she said at last, "why did he give it to me?"

"I thought you would know the answer to that."

"I barely knew him."

Silas was trying to keep eye contact with her, but his attention kept drifting back to the book. "There must be a reason he settled on you."

One of Arin's sketches, a waterfall, hung on the wall. It was one of the group Karik had given her in that long-ago meeting. "I recognize this," he said.

That couldn't be. Silas had not been in her home before. He saw her confusion. "The *style*." He went over to it. "Not the picture itself. Karik had one very much like this."

"I know. There were twelve altogether. Arin made them during the expedition. That's why he was invited, because Karik wanted a visual record." She shook her head. "I wish he'd been more like me."

"Beg pardon?"

"I can't draw a stick." The old sense of helplessness and anger seeped through her. "When I went to see Karik, after he came back, he gave me the sketches. And then he asked whether he might keep one. It was a river scene. Very quiet, very peaceful. That's the one you saw, I'm sure."

The waterfall was very wide. The sketch was titled *Nyagra*. Arin had included a tiny human to suggest the enormous scale. "May I see the others?"

She brought them from another room. They were separately wrapped in soft cloth. She uncovered them one by one and placed them on the table. They pictured the expedition variously fording rivers, looking down from bridges, moving along ancient highways in the setting sun. All were dated, so it was possible to set them in sequence. Three particularly drew Silas's attention.

One, titled *Dragon*, showed a set of glowing eyes set above a dark forest. Another, dated the following day, depicted a spectral city apparently afloat in a misty sea. It was close to sunset, and enormous dark towers rose in the gathering gloom. This was *The City*.

"Even for the Roadmakers," she said, "It looks incredible."

He nodded and returned to the preceding sketch. "If we can believe this," he said, "It's guarded by a dragon."

She shrugged. "It *does* look like it."

"Wasn't this supposed to be a literal record?"

"I would have thought so."

The shop bell rang. Chaka got to her feet and went off to take care of a customer. When she came back, Silas was once again poring over the book. "I wonder," he said, "if you'd trust me with this for a while?"

"Yes," she said. "If the library would make a copy for me."

"Of course. That will be easy to arrange." She could see he was relieved. "Would you want me to take it now? Tonight?"

"Please," she said.

He smiled, closed and rewrapped the book.

"Not that I don't trust you," she said. "But I wonder if you could give me a receipt?"

"Of course." There were several stacks of paper sheets on the table. She gave him a bottle of ink and took a pen down from a shelf. He wrote:

JANUARY 4, 306

THE IMPERIUM

RECEIVED OF CHAKA MILANA ON THIS DATE THE ONLY EXTANT COPY OF *A CONNECTICUT YANKEE IN KING ARTHUR'S COURT*. TO BE RETURNED ON DEMAND.

(SIGNED)
SILAS GLOTE

"Thank you," she said. "And I've got one other question for you."

Silas picked up the book and cradled it. "Yes?"

"Where do you suppose he got it?"

✠ 3 ✠

Silas should have been delighted with the find. He kept the book in his bedroom that night, leafing through it and reading passages aloud until the first gray streaks appeared in the sky. But he could not shake a sense of foreboding. Karik's footprints had made it clear he'd *walked* into the river. Drowned himself.

Now there was this strange business of the book.

Why had he kept such a secret?

In the morning Silas reluctantly turned the book over to the library. In a society that lacks the printing press, a library is necessarily a facility whose primary concern is security. Users are permitted access to books only under close supervision, and nobody ever takes one home.

The custodians thanked him effusively, gushed and burbled as he must have to Chaka Milana the previous evening. The Director came out and assured Silas that the board would not forget his services, and they were all still poring over the volume when he left.

His morning was free and he was still too excited to sleep, so he paid a second visit to Flojian, finding him at his waterfront shipping dock. He was supervising a half-dozen workmen who were constructing a new ferry. He wore a yellow cotton shirt and gray workpants. "They don't get anything right unless you watch them every minute," he told Silas. "When we started this business, you could trust people to do an honest day's work for a day's pay." He squinted, shook his head, and sighed. "What can I do for you?"

The ferry was going to be a large double-deck barge. When finished, it would use sail, poles, and a bank of oarsmen to cross the river to Westlok. After unloading, it would be hauled upstream by a team of horses to a dock almost two miles north of its east bank point of departure. There it would reload and begin its return voyage cross-river.

Silas expressed his admiration for the vessel, and switched quickly to the subject at hand. "Flojian, I can't imagine why your father never told anyone about the Mark Twain."

"Let's go inside," said Flojian. He led the way into a battered cubicle piled high with ledgers, and pointed Silas to a chair. "When he showed it to me, I pleaded with him to make it public. For one thing, it would have gone a long way to restoring his reputation."

"What did he say?"

"He said *no*. Then he said the only reason he was showing it to me was to make sure I understood the bequest: that the book was to be given to the woman, no questions asked."

"Which means that he wanted it out, but he didn't want to do it himself."

"Didn't want it done during his lifetime, *I'd* say."

"But why?"

Flojian shrugged. "Wish I knew." There was pain in his eyes. "It hurts to have been locked out like that. I was his *son*, Silas. I never did anything to cause him grief. Or to give him reason not to trust me." He looked tired. "Look, I thought I'd find out what was going on in due time. Just be patient and wait for him to tell me. It never occurred to me he was getting ready to take his life."

"I'm sorry."

"Maybe I could have helped if he'd said something."

They were seated in worn but comfortable fabric chairs, looking at each other across a table. Silas pressed his fingers against his temples. "Was there anything unusual in the anuma?" he asked.

"No. Just personal items. Clothes, his pen, his hourglass. Things like that."

"No map?"

"No."

"No journal? Notebooks? Diary? Records of any kind?"

"No. Just mundane stuff."

"You're sure?"

Flojian hesitated. His eyes glanced momentarily away. "I'm sure. I packed it myself."

Silas looked at him.

Flojian squirmed. "Okay. There was a copy of something purporting to be *The Notebooks of Showron Voyager*. But it was a fake."

Silas felt a rush of despair. "And you *burned* it?" Showron was the Baranji scholar who, according to tradition, had been the last known person to visit Haven. He had spoken with its guardians, had examined some of the manuscripts, had even left sketches. "How do you *know* it was a fake?" he demanded.

"Because my father tried to use it to find the place. And he never got there, did he?" He looked at Silas, challenging him to deny the truth of the statement. "Look, don't you think I know what my father's reputation is? People think he was a *coward* because he was the only person to come back. He had to live with that. *I* had to live with it." He got up, walked to the window, and stared out at the dock. "It's no secret I didn't like him very much. He was tyrannical, self-centered, secretive. He had a short temper, and he didn't worry unduly about other people's feelings. You know that."

Silas nodded.

Flojian's gaze turned inward. "When he came back, he withdrew from me as well as from the world. He sat in his wing of the house and almost never came out. That was *his* territory. Okay. I learned to live with it. But I'd be less than honest, Silas, if I didn't admit that his death has lifted a lot of weight from my shoulders." He took a deep breath. "I'm glad he's gone. But I don't care what anybody says: He wouldn't have abandoned anyone."

A long silence drew itself around them. "I agree," said Silas at last. "But that doesn't explain where the *Connecticut Yankee* came from. Have you noticed anything unusual around the house?"

"Unusual in what way?"

Damn the man. Was he, after all, naturally obtuse? Or was he hiding something? "Anything that might tell us where he got it. For all we know, there might even be *other* stuff hidden somewhere."

Flojian's mouth hardened. "There are no other unaccounted-for books."

Silas wanted to point out that the Mark Twain was a major find, that there was a serious enigma here, and that a hundred years from now people would still be trying to understand what happened. We're close to it, so we ought to get some answers. But he knew it would sound ridiculous in Flojian's ears.

"I tell you what," Flojian said. "I'm leaving this afternoon for Masandik. I'll be back in a couple of days. When I return, I'll look through my father's things. If there's anything there, I'll let you know."

Quait Esterhok was a senator's son. Years ago, he had been one of Silas's prime students. He'd been blessed with a good intellect and an enthusiasm for scholarship that suggested great potential as a researcher. Silas had hoped he would stay with the Imperium, and had even persuaded the board to offer a position. But Quait, pressured by his father, had declined and instead accepted a military commission.

That was six years ago. Quait had returned from time to time, had sat in on a few seminars, and had even treated his old master to dinner occasionally. It was consequently no surprise when Silas found a note from him in his mail, and the man himself waiting in a nearby pub favored by the faculty.

The boyish features had hardened somewhat, and Silas saw at once that he'd acquired a new level of self-assurance. Quait rose from a corner stall as he entered, smiled broadly, and embraced him. "Master Silas," he said, "it's good to see you again."

They wandered over to the cookery and collected slices of roast chicken and corn, called for a bottle of wine, and fell to reminiscing. Quait talked about the changes in the military that had come with the foundation of the League. "Everyone does not profit from peace," he laughed. The wine flowed freely, and Silas was feeling quite ebullient when his companion surprised him by putting down the chicken leg he'd been chewing and asking what he knew about the Mark Twain.

"You *know* about that?" asked Silas.

"I think the whole world knows by now. Is it true?"

"Yes," he said. "As far as I can judge."

Quait bent over the table so they could not be overheard, although the loud conversation around them all but precluded that possibility. "Where did he find it? Do you know?"

"No. No one seems to know."

"Isn't that strange? Where could he *possibly* have got it?"

Silas shrugged. "Don't know."

"I had a thought."

"Go ahead."

"It occurred to me that Karik might have *found* what he was looking for."

The possibility had occurred to Silas. But it raised even bigger questions. If Karik Endine had found Haven, he could have deflected much of the disgrace that had settled about his name. "I don't see how it could be," he said.

"You mean, why he didn't say anything? He lost everybody. Maybe his mind went."

"I don't think so."

"Can you conceive of any sequence of events that would lead him to keep such a discovery secret?"

"No," said Silas. "Which is why I think the Mark Twain has nothing to do with Haven." Quait's gray eyes had grown relentless. There was a quality in this man that the boy had not possessed. "Look, Quait, if they found Haven, don't you think he'd have brought back more than one book?"

"But why did he keep it quiet? If *you* found something like that, Silas, would you not mention it to someone?"

"I'd tell the world," Silas said.

"As would I. As would any rational person." He speared a piece of white meat and examined it absent-mindedly. "Are we sure there are no more of these things lying around?"

The wine was good. Silas drank deep, let its taste linger on his tongue. "I've invited Flojian to look for more."

"Who's Flojian?"

"His son."

"Silas—" Quait shook his head. "If I were his son, and I found, say, a Shakespearean collection, I'd burn it."

"Why?"

"Because I was his son. If there's anything there, Karik was hiding it for a reason. I'd honor that reason."

"Flojian didn't like him very much."

"It doesn't matter. He'll protect his father's name. It's too late to come forward with new finds. Look at the way we're reacting to the Mark Twain. It smells too much of conspiracy."

Silas thought it over. "I think you're wrong. If he felt that protective, he wouldn't have turned the Mark Twain over to Chaka."

"Maybe he hadn't put things together," said Quait. "He might have needed you to do that for him. Now he knows his father's reputation, such as it is, is at stake. Has it occurred to you he might have *murdered* the others?"

Silas laughed. "No, it hasn't. That's out of the question."

"You're sure."

"I'm sure. I knew the man."

"Maybe something happened out there. Maybe he thought he could keep everything for himself."

"Quait, you've been chasing too many bandits."

"Maybe. But I'll guarantee you, Flojian's search won't turn up anything."

Silas finished off the last of his roast chicken. "Well," he said, "Flojian's going to be out of town for a couple of days. We could consider burglary."

The culture that had developed in the valley of the Mississippi was male-dominated. Women were treated with courtly respect, but were traditionally relegated to domestic chores. The major professions, save the clergy, were closed to them. They could own, but not transmit, property. The villa granted to Chaka Milana by her younger brother, Sauk, would revert to him in the event of either her marriage or her death.

That Chaka remained unattached in her twenty-fifth year led many of her acquaintances to suspect she was more interested in retaining her home than in establishing a family. Chaka herself wondered about the truth of the charge.

Her father, Tarbul, had been a farmer and (like everyone in the tumultuous times before the League) a soldier. He'd returned from one campaign with a beautiful young captive who was repatriated after the war, and whom he later courted and won. This was Lia of Masandik, a merchant's daughter, and a born revolutionary. "High-spirited," Tarbul had said of her.

Lia had been appalled by the arbitrary chaos of constant warfare, mostly brought on, she thought, by male idiocy. She had consequently invested heavily in the education of *all* her children, determined to give them the best possible chance at independence. This was not a strategy with which her husband had concurred, but he was interested enough in keeping the peace to avoid opposing his determined wife. Ironically, his firstborn, Arin, showed little aptitude for the farm or for the hunting expeditions that were the lifeblood of the father's existence. The boy was given to art and debate and draughts. Not the sort of qualities to make a father proud.

In the end it had been Chaka who'd joined her father in the hunt, and who managed the farm in his absence. On one memorable occasion, during a raid by a Makar force, she had led the defense. "Your mother would have been proud of you," he'd told her. It was the ultimate compliment.

Lia had died after contracting a virulent illness as Chaka approached adolescence. Her father was killed seven years later in a gunfight with poachers. The farm went to Sauk, while she moved eventually to the villa and established a living as a silversmith and jewelry designer.

Chaka wanted a family. She wanted a good spouse, a man who could engage her emotions, whose spirit she would be pleased to pass on to her children. But she simply hadn't found anyone like that yet. And, living in a society in which most girls were married by seventeen, she was beginning to feel a sense of urgency. And of fear. Although she would not admit it to herself, this was why Raney was now prominent in her life. She was, at long last, prepared to settle.

The sundial at the foot of Calagua Hill registered the third afternoon hour. Chaka took time to wander through the bazaar.

She had no competitors among the city jewelry shops, who appealed to those customers who were primarily interested in economy and glitter. Chaka had established her reputation as an artist, from whom one could either buy fine pieces off the shelf, or have them custom made. Nevertheless, she knew the people who ran the other businesses and enjoyed spending time with them. So she whiled away an afternoon that seemed strangely restless. Toward the end of the day she stopped by the library and basked in the admiration and gratitude that *Connecticut Yankee* generated. She was delighted to discover she'd acquired a considerable degree of celebrity.

Silas came in while she was there. He was in a jovial mood and joked about how he and a former student had considered burglarizing Flojian's place. "He's out of town, and the militia could go through the house without waking up Toko," he said. Still, at sundown, she returned to Piper, her mount, feeling out of sorts. This should have been a *good* time for her, a time to celebrate her fortune. Yet she had never felt more alone.

Raney was waiting at the west gate.

He looked good on a horse, far more graceful than one would normally expect from a shopkeeper. He was handsome, and she did not want to let him get away. He was reasonably intelligent, he treated her well, and he would be a good provider. Furthermore, Chaka lived in a society which tended to dismiss romantic notions as so much petty nonsense. Marriage was for procreation and mutual support and economic stability. Her father had summed up this philosophy when he realized she was imbibing some of her mother's ill-advised notions. *Marry a friend, and preferably a friend with means,* he had said. *You cannot do better than that.* He would have approved heartily of Raney.

"I think you're right about the book," she said, as they rode out of the city. "Eventually, I'll sell it. For now, I've turned it over to the Senatorial Library for safekeeping."

"Good." His congenial features showed that he agreed completely with this common-sense decision. "Take your time with it, find out what it'll bring, and get the best price you can. Having the library put it on display's a smart idea. That can't hurt." He grinned. It was a good smile, warm and genuine, the smile of a man at peace with the world. His soft blue eyes were almost feminine. They lingered on her, and expressed more clearly than words ever could his devotion to her. He'd proposed marriage several weeks ago, and she had put him off, told him she was not ready. She'd expected he would sulk or withdraw, but to her surprise he'd laughed and told her she was worth waiting for and he would be patient. "I'll try again," he'd assured her.

His rich brown hair hung to his shoulders. Like most of the young men of the period, he was clean-shaven. He rode silently at her side and there was no tension between them.

Maybe it was time.

She straightened herself in the saddle. "I'd like very much to know where it came from," she said.

"I can't see that it matters, Chaka." He commented idly on the weather, noting how extremely pleasant it was. He looked around, surveying the sunlight and the river, and his glance took in the Iron Pyramid, rising in the south. "He probably found it in a ruin somewhere."

"Maybe." The road wound into thick, lush forest. It began its long climb up the series of ridges that formed the eastern bank. A military patrol cantered past, resplendent in blue uniforms and white plumes. Their officer saluted Chaka.

"What else?" asked Raney, swinging around in his saddle to watch the horsemen ride away.

"I don't know. I think there's more to this than Flojian's telling."

Raney's eyes came to rest on her. "I can't imagine what it could be," he said patiently.

"Nor can I. But I just don't understand what happened."

"Look, the truth is probably very simple. He felt guilty about being the only survivor of the expedition. Anybody would. So he gave you his most valuable possession. It's an offering, an act of penance. He was trying to soothe his conscience. I don't think there's anything very mysterious about it."

"Why did he wait until he died?"

"What do you mean?"

"If he was trying to soothe his conscience, why didn't he soothe it while he was alive?"

"That's easy, Chaka. Because he didn't want to let go of the book. So you become an heir. That way, he wins all the way around. He can be generous with you, and it doesn't cost him anything. We know he didn't like his son, so he makes a statement there, too."

The conversation drifted to other, more mundane, topics. One of the senators had been caught in a tax scandal. Business at Raney's establishment was picking up. One of Chaka's friends had begun studying for the priesthood.

"What I can't understand," she said, as they rode through Baffle's Pass, where the trees intertwine and form a green tunnel almost a hundred yards long, "is that Karik didn't tell anybody about this. Not *anybody.*"

When he saw it was hopeless to try to save the animal, Arin let it go and swam for shore. We thought he'd make it, but every time he got close, the current pushed him out again.

She could not get the image clear in her mind: Arin's clumsy stroke fighting the rushing waters.

Afterward, Chaka was never certain precisely when she made up her mind to break into Flojian's villa. She went to bed that night with a picture of the north wing in her mind, and her stomach churning. Sleep did not come. She progressed from contemplating the ferry operator's secret to considering the consequences of getting caught. She thought about spending the rest of her life wondering why Karik Endine had concealed his discovery. The mechanics of actually doing a break-in did not seem daunting. Presumably the doors and windows on the ground floor would be locked. She remembered seeing a tree whose limbs overhung the house on the north. It should be possible to climb the tree and drop down onto the roof. Once that far, she could get in through the courtyard or from one of the balconies. She'd almost brought the subject up with Raney on the ride home, to give him the opportunity to volunteer. But she knew he would not. He would instead try to dissuade her, and would eventually become annoyed if she persisted, and condescending if she didn't.

Flojian was away. There was only Toko, who would certainly be asleep in the servant's quarters.

Not really intending to do it, she went over the details in her mind, where she would leave Piper, how to approach the property, what might go wrong, how she would gain entrance, whether there were any dogs about. (She couldn't remember any.) As she lay safe and warm in the big bed, she realized gradually there was no real obstacle. And she owed it to her brother to proceed.

She considered how easy it would be, and her heart began to beat faster.

When Silas had joked with Chaka about burglarizing Karik's home, he was, of course, expressing the wish that it would happen but that *he* wouldn't have to do it. This is not to imply that Silas was a coward. His shoulder still ached from a bullet taken during service with the militia. He had stayed behind during the six-month plague to help the priests with the victims. And on one particularly memorable occasion, he had used a stick to face down a cougar.

Nor was he above bending a law or two to get his way. As he often reminded his students, laws are not ethics. But the risk entailed in a break-in daunted him. How would it look if an ethics instructor were caught burglarizing the home of a friend?

He was still smiling at the thought when he

assumed his place in front of an evening seminar in the Imperium.

The Imperium was not an academic institution in the traditional sense. Its students, privileged and generally talented, might more properly be thought of as participants in an ongoing effort to extend human knowledge. Or to recover it, for it was obvious that much had been lost.

The questions naturally arising from the single unrelenting *fact* of the ruins dominated Illyrian thought. Who were these people? What systems of law and government sustained them? What purposes had they set out for themselves? What was the extent of the ruins?

The young men came when their own schedules permitted, and they discussed philosophy or geometry with whichever masters happened to be available. They were driven by pride and curiosity, they were highly motivated, and they wanted to understand the Roadmakers. It was an important goal, because something more elemental than mere technology had been lost. The Plague had killed indiscriminately, had carried off whole populations, and with them had gone whatever driving force had produced the great roadways and the structures that touched the clouds. Beyond the walls of the Imperium, the Illyrians had built a society whose sole purpose was to maintain political stability and an economic status quo. There was little discernible drive for progress.

The operations of the Imperium were funded by the Illyrian treasury, and by donations from wealthy parents and, increasingly, from those who had attended in their youth, and who came by periodically to join discussions which ranged from the mechanics of astronomy to the reality of the gods to the unwieldy relationship between diameter and circumference.

(A school of skeptics were then using the latter fact to argue that the universe was ill conceived and irrational.)

The nine masters had been selected as much for their ability to inspire as for their knowledge. They were entertainers as well as teachers, and they were the finest entertainers that Illyria could produce. Silas was proud of his work and considered himself, not entirely without justification, one of the city's foremost citizens.

He was conscious that there were in fact two Silas Glotes: one who was shy and uncertain of himself, who disliked attending social gatherings where he was expected to mix with strangers; and another who could dazzle people he had never seen before with wit and insight. In fact, all of the masters seemed to display, to a degree, this tendency toward a dual personality. Bent Capa, for example, mumbled at dinner but rose to eloquence in the courtyards.

In the seminars, subjects were designated, but once started, a discussion might lead anywhere. There was no formal curriculum, and the philosophy of the institution saw more benefit in exposure to a wise master than to a formal body of instruction. Given the level of interest among those in attendance, the system could hardly fail to work.

The death of Karik Endine had ignited discussions in many of the seminars, particularly with regard to Haven and the Abraham Polk legend. Librarians reported that both copies of *The Travels* were in constant use. Polk became the issue of the hour: Was he historical? Or mythical? If he was historical, had he indeed devoted himself to rescuing the knowledge of the Roadmakers?

Silas was of several minds on the matter. He wanted to believe in the tale of the adventurer who lived on the edge of a dying world, who with a small band of devoted companions carried on a desperate campaign to save the memory of that world against the day when civilization would come again. It was a magnificent story.

And it *was* possible. Not all the trappings, of course. There had certainly never been a *Quebec,* the mystical boat that possessed neither sails nor oars, that was capable of diving into the depths of the sea. Nor the undersea entrance to Haven, accessible, presumably, only to the submersible. Nor could Polk have rescued all the people for whom he was credited.

Maybe Polk had existed. Maybe someone tried to save *something*. And the stories got blown out of proportion. In that sense, there might well be a Haven somewhere.

On the day after his conversation with Quait, a visitor from the Temple, a priest, took her place among the participants in Silas's assigned conference room. There were nine others, all young men. The seminar's announced topic was: "Can Men Know the Divine Will?"

Although women were not expressly forbidden from attending Imperium seminars, they were not encouraged, on the grounds that space was limited and intellectual development was essential for the males from whom the League's leaders would eventually be selected. But women did visit from time to time, and they were particularly welcome if they had specialized knowledge to contribute or a professional interest in the proceedings.

Silas took a few minutes to have each of his participants identify himself. Only the priest was an unknown commodity.

"My name is Avila Kap," she said. "I represent no

one, and I'm here solely because the topic is fascinating." She smiled disarmingly.

Avila was about thirty. She wore the green robe of her calling, hood drawn back, white cord fastened about her waist, white sash over her right shoulder. The colors of the prime seasons. Her black hair was cut short. She glanced around the table with dark, intelligent eyes. There was an almost mocking glint in them, as if they were dismissing the Imperium's reputation as a rationalist institution. Silas thought that her good looks were enhanced by the robe.

He set the parameters for the dialogue: "In order that we avoid spending the afternoon on extraneous issues, we will assume for purposes of this discussion that divine beings *do* exist, and that they *do* take an interest in human affairs. The question then becomes, have they attempted to communicate with us? If so, by what characteristics can we know a divine revelation?"

Kaymon Rezdik, a middle-aged merchant who had been sporadically attending the seminars longer than Silas could remember, raised his hand. "Considering that we have the *Chayla*," he said, "I'm surprised that we're even having this discussion."

"Nonsense," said Telchik, an occasional visitor from Argon. Most of the others present nodded approvingly. Telchik was a handsome youth, brown-haired and blue-eyed. "If the *Chayla* is the work of the gods, they speak with many voices."

Among the group that day, only Kaymon and one of the younger participants and, of course, the priest, could be described as believers. Most of the others, in the fashion of the educated classes of the time, were skeptics who maintained that either the gods did not exist, or that they took pains to keep well away from the human race. (The view that the gods were survivors from the age of the Roadmakers had been losing ground over the past decade, and had no champions in the field that day.)

"What characteristics," asked Silas smoothly, "would you demand of a communication before you would pronounce it to be of divine origin?"

Kaymon looked puzzled. "The official sanction of the Temple," he said, glancing hopefully toward Avila.

"I think," said Avila, "that, in this case, you *are* the Temple."

"Exactly," said Silas. "If a message were laid before you, with supernatural claims, how would *you* arrive at a judgment?"

Kaymon's gaze swept left and right, seeking help.

"There *is* no way to be sure," said Telchik, "unless you are standing there when it happens. And even then—"

"Even then," said Orvon, an advocate's son, "we may be seeing only what we wish to see."

"Then we may safely conclude," said Telchik, "that there is no way to know whether a communication does in fact have divine backing."

Several of the disputants glanced uncomfortably at Avila, to see how she was taking the general assault on her career. But she watched placidly, with a smile playing at the corners of her mouth.

"And what have you to say of all this?" Silas asked her.

"They may be right," she said matter-of-factly. "Even assuming that Shanta exists, we cannot know for certain that she really cares about us. We may well be living in a world that has come about by accident. In which everything is transient. In which nothing matters." Her eyes were very dark. "I don't say I believe this, but it *is* a possibility. But that possibility is outside the parameters of the discussion. I would propose to you that the gods may find us a difficult subject for communication."

"How do you mean?" asked Orvon.

She pressed her palms together. "Orvon, may I ask where you live?"

"Three miles outside the city. On the heights above River Road."

"Good." She looked pleased. "It's a lovely location. Let us suppose that, this evening, when you are on your way home, the Goddess herself were to walk out from behind some trees to wish you good day. How would you respond?"

"He would lose his voice," laughed Telchik.

"I suppose it would be a little unnerving."

"And if she gave you a message to bring back to us?"

"I would most certainly do so."

She nodded and raised her eyes to encompass the others. "And how would we respond to Orvon's claim?"

"Nobody'd believe it," said Selenico, youngest of the participants.

"And what," asked Silas, "if the Goddess had said hello instead to Avila? Would we believe *her*?"

"No," said Orvon, "I don't think so."

"Why not?" asked Avila.

"Because you are not objective."

"No," said Silas. "Not because she is not objective, but because she is *committed*. There is a difference."

"Indeed," rumbled Telchik. "I should like to hear what it is. Shanta would do better to give her message to *me*."

"Yes," said Avila, brightening, "because if *you* came with such a story, we still might not believe it, but we would know that something very odd had happened."

Sigmon, a young man whose primary interest was in the sciences, suggested that a deity who wished to communicate would necessarily want an unbeliever, to allay suspicions. "And furthermore," he said, "he might want to go for drama, rather than a simple statement that we should do thus and so."

"How do you mean?" asked Kaymon.

Sigmon's brow wrinkled. "Well," he said, "if I were a god, and I wanted to tell the Illyrians that Haven exists—"

All faces turned in his direction.

"—I can think of nothing better than inspiring Karik Endine to produce a copy of the *Connecticut Yankee.*"

The moon set at about midnight. It was well into the early hours when Chaka got out of the bed in which she had lain sleepless, and dressed. She put on dark blue riding breeches and a black shirt. She had no dark jacket and had to make do with a light brown coat that was more awkward than she would have liked. (The temperature had fallen too far to try to get by without wearing something warm.) She pulled on a pair of moccasins, attached a lamp to her belt, and stopped in her workshop to pick up a couple of thin shaping blades.

Shortly thereafter she stood in the shadow of Flojian's villa, listening to his horses move uneasily in the barn. A brisk northern wind shook the trees. The night was dark under banks of clouds. The only lights she could see were out on the river, moving slowly downstream.

The villa was dark. The tree on the northern side was higher than she remembered, its branches flimsier. But she got lucky. Before attempting the climb she circled the house, trying windows and doors. The latch on one of the shutters in the rear had not been properly secured and she was able to worry it loose. She opened the window, pulled the draperies apart, and peered into the darkness beyond.

Seeing nothing to give her pause, she threw a leg over the sill and climbed into the room. This was the first time in her adult life she had flagrantly violated someone's property, and she was already trying to compose her story in case she got caught.

Too much alcohol. I didn't think this looked like my *house.*

Or, *I fell off my horse last night. Hit my head. I don't remember anything since. Where am I?*

She was in the reception room where she had first met Silas. To her left was the inner parlor in which Flojian had told her of her bequest. And to the right was the north wing, Karik Endine's solitary domain. Curtains were drawn across all the windows, and the room was quite dark. She waited for the tables and chairs to appear, and then navigated among them until she found a doorway in the right-hand wall. It opened into more darkness. She went through and closed the door softly behind her.

It was a passageway. She bumped into a chair, started to feel her way around a server, and knocked over a candlestick holder. It fell with a terrible clatter and she froze.

But the noise seemed not to attract anyone's attention. She righted the candlestick holder and passed through another door into a large sitting room, illuminated through a bank of windows. This was, she knew, Karik's wing. She looked outside to assure herself no one was about, and used a match to light the candle in her lamp.

The room was masculine, filled with hand-drawn charts and drinking mugs, and heavy oak furniture of a somber cast. (The charts depicted areas of political influence during various eras in the valley's history.) A chess game, with ornate pieces, was in progress on a tabletop.

A wide set of carpeted stairs led to the second floor. The lower level consisted of three rooms. She opened cabinets, inspected desk drawers, examined closets. The area had been thoroughly cleaned. Clothes, shoes, toiletries, everything was gone. No empty glass nor scrap of paper remained to show there had been an occupant only a few days ago.

She was about to start upstairs when she heard a squeal. The hinges on the door from the corridor. She doused her light and ducked behind a curtain just as the door opened and someone thrust a lamp into the room.

"Who's here?" Toko's voice.

Her heart beat so hard she could not believe it wasn't audible.

He came into the room a few steps and raised the lamp. She tried not to breathe. The shadows lengthened and shifted as Toko looked first this way and then that.

Then, apparently satisfied, he withdrew and closed the door. His steps faded, but she waited several minutes. When she was convinced he would not come back, she tiptoed upstairs.

There were two rooms on the upper level: a bedroom and a work area. The bedroom was made up, and it too retained no sign of its former owner.

The workroom was long, L-shaped, with wide windows. The curtains were drawn back, providing a view of the river. Glasses and goblets filled a cabinet. The windows opened onto a wide balcony, where several chairs surrounded a circular table. One might have thought the occupant had been accustomed to entertaining.

There were two padded chairs inside, a long worktable with several drawers, a desk, a pair of matching cabinets, some empty shelves, and a chest.

The chest was locked.

The worktable drawers were empty, save for one or two pieces of paper. The desk contained a few pens, some ink, and a blank notebook. She found a sweater in one of the cabinets, somehow missed in the press to collect everything. And a revolver, which she recognized as the work of the same gunsmith who had supplied most of her own family's weapons. Strange, she thought, that we forgot how to print books. But we remember how to make guns.

She knelt down in front of the chest.

The lock was designed to keep out curious children, rather than thieves. She produced the narrower of her blades, and inserted it. Minutes later the mechanism gave and she raised the lid.

She looked down at an oilskin packet. It was roughly sixteen inches wide by a foot. She lifted it out, set it down under the lamp, and released the binding cords.

It contained a sketch which she recognized immediately as her brother's work. It was dated July 25, making it later than any of the others.

The drawing depicted a rock wall rising out of a frothy sea. A sliver of moon floated in a sky swept with dark clouds. It was one of his better efforts, but there was nothing extraordinary about the drawing itself.

Nothing extraordinary, that is, until she saw the title, which appeared in its customary place below his signature.

Haven.

✠ 4 ✠

In an age that depended on sails and oars for power, the Mississippi was a cranky partner at best. Northbound cargo had to be hauled upriver by a combination of flatboats and draft horses. To complicate matters, the river was prone to change course periodically. It had swallowed but only partially digested many of the concrete and brick cities that had sprouted along its banks in ancient times. These had now become navigational hazards. There were seven major collapsed bridges, three of which, at Argon, at Farroad on the Arkansaw, and at Masandik in the south, effectively blocked any vessel larger than a canoe. This was the factor that made Illyria the crossroads of the League, and its center of power. And which created economic opportunities for Flojian Endine.

His draft animals were raised on two ranches near Cantonfile. He'd been planning for some time to expand the number of horses in his stables, and his conversations with business allies in Masandik convinced him that the traffic would support the investment. On his return to Illyria he met with his groom at the pier to devise a strategy. When the morning-long meeting ended, and the groom had left, he sat back with a cup of tea, feeling satisfied with his life. Business was good, his financial health assured, and the future bright. He was living in the morning of a new age, now that his father was gone. The brooding presence was removed from the house at last. Only the shadow of his ruined name remained.

What *had* the old man done out there?

Well, no matter. Maybe the speculations would stop now. It was time for people to let go and bury their dead and be done with it. But that was unlikely. The damned book had appeared, as if Karik had been determined to stir everything up again. When he'd seen what it was, Flojian had been tempted to burn it. But he could not bring himself to violate his father's last wish, even though he'd hated him for it.

He suddenly realized Chaka Milana was standing in his doorway. Her eyes radiated hostility.

"Hello, Chaka," he said, carefully inserting concern into his voice. "Is something wrong?"

She was clutching an oilskin packet. "I owe you an apology." Her tone was flat.

"For what?" He got up and came around the desk. "Please come in."

She held out the packet. He recognized it, and his heart sank.

"I was in your house last night."

A welter of emotions rolled through him. "So I see. Is your conscience giving you trouble?"

She glanced at the oilskin. "I'd be grateful if you'd explain this to me."

Flojian made no move to open it.

"You *do* know what's in it."

"Of course I know."

"Tell me what it means."

Flojian would have liked to put the same question to his father. "It's a false alarm. What else could it be? They thought they'd found it, but they hadn't. Simple as that."

"Here's something else that's been kept quiet. Why?"

"Why did *I* keep it quiet? What makes you think *I* knew anything about it? My father didn't have a very high regard for me, Chaka. I'm the last one he'd con-fide in. I didn't even know the sketch existed until we cleaned up the day after the ceremony. Anyway, I suspect he didn't make it public because it would have led to exactly this kind of reaction."

Her expression hardened. Flojian hated confrontations. He preferred to be liked, and much of his personal success was predicated on the fact that people willingly threw business his way, and others were anxious to work for him.

"I think you owed me the truth," said Chaka.

"What *is* the truth, Chaka? That he *might* have found what he was looking for? Or that your brother *might* have jumped to an unjustified conclusion? You know as well as I do that at least one of the sketches is pure fantasy. Remember *The Dragon*? Who knows where the truth is?

"My father devoted his entire life first to trying to establish that Haven existed, and then to trying to find the place. He dreamed about it, fought for it, and lost his reputation over it. Do you seriously believe that he could have found it but neglected in the face of all that repudiation to mention it to anyone? Does that make any sense to you at all?"

She stood her ground. "No," she said. "But neither does his failing to mention the Mark Twain to anyone. There's a pattern here."

"*What* pattern? Look, he could have found the book anywhere."

She stared at him for a long moment. "When he told me about my brother's death, he said they got careless, that they were preoccupied because they thought they were almost *there*. In fact, if this is what it appears to be, Arin was alive at the end of the journey."

"Chaka, it's all guesswork." He opened the packet, removed the sketch, and studied it. *July 25.*

"It's the last in the series," she said.

He sighed. "I'm sorry there're still all these questions. But this is why I didn't say anything. It's why I should have destroyed it. I knew it would just start the old trouble up again." He put the sketch back inside its wrapper and held it out for her. "Keep it if you like."

She stared at him. "And that's the end of it?"

Flojian's anger had drained. He was just tired of it all and wanted it to go away. "Chaka, what do you want from me? You know as much as I do. Tell me what I can do that will satisfy you, and I'll try to comply."

Her eyes were wet. "Help me find out what really happened," she said.

"And how do you propose we do that?" Flojian leaned against the edge of a table. "Chaka, you're aware that if we make this public, my father's reputation is going to take another beating. I don't know, maybe he deserves it. But I can't see what good will come out of it."

"I'm interested in the truth," she said, "and I'm not much worried about anyone's reputation." She put the oilskin into her pocket and started for the door.

"I'm sure you are," he growled. "Incidentally, if you think about any more late night visits, please be careful. I wouldn't hesitate to shoot a prowler."

"I wish we could be sure." Silas hunched down on his elbows, studying the thirteenth sketch by candlelight. "But he's right: It could just be something Arin made up. Or a misunderstanding. They thought they were there, but they weren't. It could be *that* simple."

She shook her head. "Why would he do that? He was along for the specific purpose of recording the expedition."

One sketch, *River Valley,* still hung on a wall in

Flojian's villa. The others were arranged sequentially on Silas's worktable.

DATE	TITLE	DESCRIPTION
March 11	*Frontier*	The expedition moves along a broken highway above forest and river
April 4	*Memorial*	Sign on rusted post: *Dixie Gun Works & Old Car Museum*
April 6	*The Dragon*	Glowing eyes in a dark woodland
April 7	*The City*	Towers in a misty sea
May 13	*The Ship*	The hulk of an iron ship lies on its side in a dry channel
May 16	*Nyagra*	Shola Kobai gazes at a spectacular waterfall
May 22	*Pathfinder*	Karik on horseback consults a scroll
May 29	*Ruins*	Random and Mira seated on con crete slab examining moonlit ruins that extend to the horizon
June 13	*River Crossing*	Fording a river
June 30	*Vista*	Landon Shay and Tori Niss survey a mountainscape
July 2	*Sundown*	A Roadmaker bridge framed against a setting sun
July 25	*Haven*	Granite cliffs overlook a sea

Silas looked at *Frontier*. "I know this place," he said.

"I do, too. That's upriver, just south of Argon. It's the fork. Where the Ohio breaks off."

They were in Silas's modest house in the tiny government quarter near the Imperium. A light rain fell against the windows. Chaka glanced out at the winding gravel street, which had been full of people when she'd arrived, but was now deserted. It had grown dark, from both the storm and the sunset.

Silas moved the lamp closer to the sketch titled *The City*. "Have you ever read *Showron*?" he asked.

"I never heard of him."

"Showron Voyager was a Baranji scholar. He's supposed to have visited Haven near the end of his life. He writes about the scholar-caretakers, still living there generations after the October Patrol era. More to the point, he describes his journey." Silas dipped a pen into his inkwell and began to write, stopping periodically to gaze at the wall. When he'd finished, he looked critically at the result, changed a word, and handed it to her.

We fled the demon towers,
And came at last to Mamara,
With its restless spirits.

"Demon towers and restless spirits," she said, smiling. "Sounds ominous."

He rapped his fingers against the table. "Demons are all in the imagination," said Silas dismissively. He looked down at the sketch. "But those towers could be what he was talking about."

"It's all just too vague," said Chaka.

"Maybe not." Silas produced a sketch of his own. "This is from a Baranjan edition of *The Travels*." The Baranjans had occupied the Mississippi Valley for a brief period before the rise of the modern cities. "The original's in Makar."

The sketch depicted a metal cradle and platform, mounted against the face of a cliff. A curious bullet-shaped object lay in the cradle. Two human figures stood beside it, engaged in conversation. There was a sense of deep sky.

"What is it?" asked Chaka.

"This one's a vehicle. I don't draw very well, so it's hard to tell. In the original, the vehicle is drawn in a way that incorporates motion. But look here."

She didn't see what he was driving at until he put the thirteenth sketch, *Haven,* under her eyes. Slight bulge here. Narrow shelf there. Vertical lines in the rock face. *It looked like the same cliff.* "They *did* find it," she said.

"Maybe. Or maybe Arin had seen this and was reproducing it. Possibly without realizing it. Or maybe it's a coincidence. But whatever it is, how could we possibly figure out where they went?" He blurted it out, without immediately realizing what he was suggesting, and they stared uncomfortably across the table at each other.

She had not intended to tell anyone else what she'd done, least of all Raney. But somehow, after they'd shared a meal that evening at her villa, she couldn't resist. He responded predictably by adopting a severe mien and asking whether she'd lost her mind. "What would have happened if you'd been caught?"

"I think he would have booted me out and told me not to come back."

"It could have been a lot worse," he said. Raney had a tendency to talk to her sometimes as if they were married. Illyria was a society in transition. It had been puritanical under its emperors, who guarded the sanctity of the family and the honor of the nation's women with enthusiasm, while maintaining their own harems. But the overthrow of the autocracy and the rise of republican principles had fueled a new sense of liberty. The old institutions and centers of authority were being swept away.

And with them, some were saying, the decency and common courtesy that made civilization worthwhile. There seemed to be more roughnecks in the streets, more pushing and shoving in the bazaars, more open sexuality, more abandoned children, more violations of good taste. Many were calling for a return to imperial rule. And almost everyone agreed that the nation was in decline.

Chaka's age, and the lack of a controlling male hand in her household, rendered her automatically suspect among the older families, who held the balance of political and economic power in the state. Therefore, Raney saw himself as a man on a white horse as well as a suitor. He was not sufficiently sophisticated to disguise this view, which Chaka found increasingly annoying with the passage of time, although she might not have been able to say why. Yet she liked him all the same, and enjoyed spending time with him.

"Raney," she said, "do you understand what I'm telling you? It looks as if they found what they were looking for."

"Who cares? Chaka, *who cares*? It's over." He was angry that she had put herself in danger, relieved that she had escaped without harm, frustrated that she clung to this lunatic business. "It was nine years ago. Unless Endine left a map. Did he leave a map?"

"No."

"Instructions how to get there?"

"Not that we know of."

"Then I think you should take the Mark Twain, be grateful, and let go."

They'd moved into the living room. He was standing by the fireplace, his thumbs shoved into his belt, his expression in shadow. She was seated placidly in the wingback chair near the window. "Don't you even want to see the thirteenth sketch?"

"Sure I do." His tone softened. "I just don't want you breaking into people's houses. I would never have believed you'd do something like that. And you didn't even tell me." He closed his eyes and shook his head in dismay. Then his tone softened. "Next time you want to break into someone's house in the middle of the night, try mine."

The wind moved against the shutters. Out in the barn, one of the horses snorted. Chaka smiled politely, took out the sketch and showed it to him. He shrugged.

"It's only a cliff. I suspect we could find a half-dozen like this if we went looking."

She gazed, with resignation, out the window.

He came and sat beside her. "I'm sorry. I know this thing with Endine bothers you. I wish there were something I could do to put it to rest."

"Maybe there is," she said.

He looked at her, and the silence drew out between them. "You need help with another burglary?" he asked.

"I've been thinking about trying to retrace the route of the original expedition. I think it might be possible. If it is, would you come?"

"Are you serious? It can't be done. We both know that."

"I'm not so sure."

"How, Chaka? Either we know where it is or we don't."

"*Would* you come?"

He managed an uncomfortable grin. "You find a way to get to Haven," he said, "and you can count on me."

✠ 5 ✠

*The citizens of the League were not, by and large, adventur*ous. They loved their river valley home, they were surrounded by endless forests which sheltered occasional bands of Tuks (whose good behavior could not be counted on), and they lived in a world whose epic ruins acted as a kind of warning. If there was a unifying philosophy, it took the form of caution, safety first, don't rock the boat. Better to keep a respectful distance. Moor with two anchors. Look before you leap.

Few had penetrated more than a hundred miles beyond the populated areas of the Mississippi. These were primarily hunters, searchers after Roadmaker artifacts (which, in decent condition, commanded a good price), and those who traded with the Tuks.

Jon Shannon engaged sporadically in all three occupations as the mood hit him. The profit was no more than fair, and certainly did not approach the income of his brothers, who had joined their father in running an overland trading company. But Shannon had freedom of movement, he had solitude, and he enjoyed his work.

Although maybe the solitude was disappearing. The world was changing with the coming of the League and its attendant peace and prosperity. The great web of forest that had once surrounded his cabin was giving way to homes and farms. He'd moved twice in the last seven years, retreating northeast, only to be overtaken each time by the wash of settlements exploding out of Illyria. Shannon had always been something of a maverick. He had no taste for the petty entertainments and ambitions of urban life. His first wife had died in childbirth, taking the infant with her; the second had tried to change him into someone else, and had eventually given up, grown bored, and moved away.

He'd loved both, in his methodical way. But he was drained now, and if he was not as happy in the vast green solitude as he had once been, he was nevertheless content. It was a calmer, safer existence, and a man could ask no more than that.

It was almost time to move on again, and that fact forced him to reflect on the course of his life, which seemed every bit as wandering and aimless as the Mississippi.

But aimless is not necessarily a bad thing.

He would retreat again, but he didn't need do it immediately. Maybe spend another year here. That would give him time to scout the new location. There was a place twenty-five miles out that he liked. Hilltop site, of course, a couple of nearby streams, plenty of game. But the way the frontier was advancing, he wasn't sure that was far enough. On the other hand, even that short distance would be stretching the line of communication with his clients. And therein lay the problem. If he wanted to move out and draw the wilderness around him, and not have to be bothered doing it again in a few years, he would have to make some changes in his own life. And maybe that was what he should do; he did not, after all, need money. Why tie himself to all these various expeditions and tours with people he'd just as soon not spend time with anyhow? His shoulder still ached from a bullet one of his idiot clients had put into it, mistaking him for a deer.

A horse was approaching.

Shannon watched it come out of the woods, and recognized its redheaded rider at once, although he needed a few moments to come up with the name. Chaka Milana. Tarbul's daughter. All grown up.

"It's been a long time," he said, meeting her outside.

She was a good-looking woman, even after a hard ride. (He was two days out from Illyria.) The red hair she'd disliked so much as a child stood her in good stead now. She had a hunter's eyes and a wistful expression that could get a man in deep real quick. She'd come a long way from the girl he'd last seen at her father's side shooting geese.

"Hello, Jon," She reined up and dismounted in one fluid motion. "Do you remember me?"

"Of course, Chaka," he said. She wore a dark gray linen blouse and a buckskin jacket and leggings. "It's good to see you."

She nodded. "And you."

He helped her take care of her horse and then they returned to the cabin. He'd been adding some shelves, and the interior smelled of fresh-cut wood and resin. "I'll put some tea on," he said. "You want to wash up meanwhile?"

She did. He pumped a basin of water for her and heated it. She retreated to an inner room. He listened to her splashing around in there, thinking what a good sound it was. She came out in fresh clothes, and they sat down at a wicker table to tea, warm bread, and dried beef.

"You weren't easy to find, Jon," she said.

"How'd you manage?"

"You remember what you used to say? 'Over the horizon plus two miles and look for a hill.'"

He laughed.

"You look good," she said, lifting the mug to her

lips and peering at him over its rim. "Jon, have you ever heard of Haven?"

"Sure. It's a fairyland, isn't it?"

There had always been an impish quality about Chaka Milana, a sly smile and a vaguely mischievous cast to her features, augmented by her startlingly bright red hair. *Keep a cap over it,* he used to tell her, *or you'll scare the deer.* It was all still there, he realized, complemented now by the self-confidence that maturity brings. He was surprised she wore no ring.

"There might be more to it than that," she said. Jon knew about Karik Endine's expedition, of course. But he listened with interest to her account of the aftermath. She opened a cloth bag and showed him the sketches. "There's a decent chance," she concluded, "that it's really out there."

Shannon wore a knit shirt and baggy, grass-stained trousers. A pair of boots stood on the floor near the door. He was just over forty, with black hair, a clipped beard, and dark skin. His features were coarsened by too much sun and wind, and were too blunt to have been considered handsome. But he knew they were amiable enough to put most people at their ease. "Seems like your evidence is kind of thin," he said when she'd finished.

She nodded and glanced up at the battered campaign hat and militia colors on the wall. The weather had turned cool and damp, and a fire burned cheerfully in a corner of the room. "Do you recognize any of these places?"

He pointed at the first one. "*Frontier.* And I know where the Dixie Gun Works sign is. But that's about it."

"Never seen this?" She looked down at the city in the sea.

"No. I've heard the Tuks talk about the dragon, though."

"You're serious?"

"Yes," he said. "But you know how Tuks are." He focused on the thirteenth sketch. "Just looks like a cliff to me."

"It was supposed to be a hidden fortress. A retreat. A place that no one could find."

"Where's it supposed to be?"

"We have no idea."

He shrugged. "You're going out looking for it, right?"

"I'm thinking about it."

"How do you expect to find it?" He jabbed a finger at the sketch titled *Frontier*. "This one's on the Ohio, where it branches off from the Mississippi. A few miles east of Argon. The Gun Works is a little farther on. After that—?" He took a deep breath and let it out slowly. "My advice is to forget it."

"If you were going to guide an expedition like this, Jon—"

"—I wouldn't do it. What's to guide? Where's it going?"

"But *if* you were, and you expected to succeed, how would you get home afterward?"

Shannon looked at her as if he hadn't heard correctly. "That's easy. We come home the same way we went."

"With *you* showing the way? Because nobody else is likely to be able to find the way back."

"Sure. Why not?"

"But it's dangerous, right? What if something happens to *you*? How do we get back then?"

Shannon looked out and saw lightning in the west. "Yes," he said, "I guess that would be a consideration, wouldn't it?" He folded his arms. "We'd have to mark the trail." And he realized where the conversation was going. "Oh," he said.

Chaka looked delighted. She put both thumbs up. "What kind of marks? Would they survive nine, ten years?"

He thought about it. "Who was with them? Do you know?"

"You mean the guide? Landon Shay. Did you know him?"

"I knew him to talk to. Never worked with him." He remembered hearing that Shay had died on a long-range trip.

"So what kind of marks?"

"Trees, maybe," he said.

"In what way?"

"Just carve a couple of notches. They'd try to travel on the old highways. In fact, if you look at the sketches, that's what they're doing." The highways, of course, even the giant ones, were overgrown, the asphalt often buried beneath the centuries, covered with vegetation. To Shannon's forebears, when they were establishing the settlement that would eventually become Illyria, the great green lanes, gliding across hilltops and rivers and forests, were a mystery, associated with supernatural forces. The modern Illyrians knew better.

They were constructed with a layer of asphalt laid over concrete. Hard as rock. The technique made for stable roadways, but even after a foot or more of soil was added to make a surface, they were uncomfortable for horses and other beasts. Especially in those places where the cover wore thin and the asphalt became exposed.

The highways *were* convenient to modern travelers. They provided crow's-flight passage through the wilderness. There were no steep climbs or dead ends, save perhaps for an occasional missing bridge or collapsed foundation.

"So they'd do what?" asked Chaka. "Where do we look for notches? We couldn't inspect every tree along the side of the trail."

"I'll tell you how *I'd* do it. Whenever we changed direction. Or whenever the road forked, or whenever I thought someone would be tempted to wander off the wrong way, I'd leave a mark. And every now and then I'd do something to confirm it was still the right trail."

"You think Shay would have done that?"

"I think he'd have an obligation to do it. And to make sure everyone knew he was doing it."

Chaka's eyes shut, opened again, and her expression changed. "What about the Tuks? How big a threat would they be?"

He shrugged. "The local ones should be okay. Take some stuff with you to give them. They like guns but I don't think I'd offer any. Maybe some trinkets. Cups. Cups are good. Especially with pictures. Mottos. Things like that. And bracelets. They'll probably keep their distance as long as you keep moving and don't approach a village. If you do see them, try to look as if you're passing through and you do it all the time. Right? Show no fear, and say hello." He got up, went into the kitchen, and came back with more tea.

Chaka nodded. "This city is in the sea. Or on the edge of a sea. You know anything at all about it? Or about anything remotely like it?"

"There's a city in the north. Chicago. And a sea up there. But the city's supposed to be spooked." He wasn't eating much, had in fact eaten shortly before Chaka's arrival. But he nibbled on a piece of beef to be sociable. Chaka, on the other hand, was hungry. "I've never been there." He glanced at the drawing. "But if that's what it really looks like, people would expect it to be haunted. Wouldn't they?" A log fell into the fire and sparks flew.

"But you never really know. Roadmaker ruins are restless."

She smiled. It was a warm smile, a little tentative, and it told him he'd succeeded at what he'd hoped to do: frighten her. "Jon," she said, "I'd like to try to find this place. My brother died out there somewhere, and I think I was lied to about the way of it. I know this is asking a lot, but I'd be grateful if you'd reconsider."

She was hard to say no to, but he did. "It's just a way to waste a lot of time and effort," he said. "And maybe get yourself killed. Take my advice, Chaka: Don't do it."

She looked steadily at him, and he suspected she was trying to decide whether he was adamant. "In that case," she said, "I wonder if I can hire you for a few days."

Flojian had been uneasy since his conversation with Chaka. The Mark Twain had been given away to injure him, to send a message to the wayward son. *I am leaving this extraordinarily valuable find to a person I hardly know, in preference to you. Furthermore, I know its existence will create trouble, and you are welcome to that. And I have even arranged that you be the instrument of the transaction.*

Damn him.

And damn Milana, too. If she could have simply accepted her gift with grace and gone away, it would have been over.

Flojian tried to bury himself in his work, but he was too restless to think about new shipping schedules and maintenance problems. He gave up late in the morning, told his assistant he was going to take the rest of the day off, and rode into town. He wandered listlessly through the markets for two hours, stopping occasionally for something to drink. When fatigue and appetite began to overtake him he rode back out through the gates and stopped at the Crossroads Tavern (which was not really located on a crossroad) for some lunch.

He was a regular and favored customer at the Crossroads. The host sat him at a corner table, back in the shadows, where a candle flickered fitfully in a smoked red globe. A waiter brought cold brew while Flojian considered the menu board and settled on beef stew. You can't go wrong with the basics, he told himself. It was midafternoon, and there were only a handful of customers. But sound travels well in a nearly empty room, and Flojian found himself listening to a group of two men and a woman several tables away.

"—Second expedition." That was the phrase that caught his attention. It was part of a sneer delivered by the younger of the men. He was mostly belly, blond, shaggy, overflowing his chair. "It's crazy." He stabbed a fat index finger in the air. "They'll kill themselves."

The second man wore a purple shirt with a white string tie. He was young, probably in his mid-twenties, but his otherwise good features were spoiled by a hangdog look, a combination of cruelty and cringing. "How will they know where they're going?" he said.

"I guess they've figured out the route the other one took," said the woman. She was middle-aged, well dressed, and had had a little too much to drink.

Flojian examined his stein. It was ornate, inlaid with midnight glass tears. Nice, actually.

The hangdog shook his head and addressed the belly. "Gammer, the other one didn't come back. You'd think they'd learn."

Gammer looked bored. "I figured you'd be first in line to go, Hok."

"Not me. There aren't any idiots in my family."

Gammer grinned. It was a lopsided grin, rendered cruel by vacuous eyes. "I didn't think you knew your family."

Flojian took a long pull from his brew.

"What really happened on the first expedition?" The woman's question.

"What's-his-name, the guy who came back, he left them." Gammer tore off an end of bread, dipped it into his stew, and pushed it into his mouth. While he chewed, he jabbed his fork toward the back of the room. "They got in trouble and he left them. That's why he never said anything."

"I think there's more to it," said Hok. He finished his drink and offered to pour another round for everybody. The woman passed. "Look, that thing they brought back, the book, they say it's worth a couple of sacks of gold. *Big* sacks. I tell ya, it doesn't take much imagination to see a fight breaking out among them, winner take all. This what's-his-name—"

"Endine," said the woman.

"Yeah, Endine, he was the winner. The guy who came home. Maybe he murdered the rest of them."

Flojian banged his stein down. He got up and faced them. The tavern fell silent. "You're a liar." He threw a silver coin onto the table. It rolled about a foot. "Endine wouldn't abandon anybody."

Hok tilted his head and grinned a silent challenge. Flojian started in his direction, but the host hurried over to make peace.

Word came in the middle of the night. It was brought by one of the attendants, who was kneeling by her bed with a taper. "Avila. The boy is dying. They need you."

Her heart sank.

"The father waits downstairs."

She threw the spread aside. "Wake Sarim."

"We've already attended to that. He'll meet you in the sanctuary."

She rinsed quickly at the basin, slid into her robe, fastened her sash, and drew on a black cloak, for the night was cool. She had no stomach for what lay ahead.

She gathered a supply of *agora,* which would ease the child's passage into the next world, for she knew the case offered no hope of recovery unless the Goddess intervened. But the Goddess had not acted in many years. Avila wondered what had happened that she had been so completely abandoned.

She knew what the *Kiri* would say: *Your faith is being tested. Believe and do your duty, and all will be well.* But all was *not* well.

The father waited in the reception room. He sat, head sagging, eyes devoid of every quality except pain. When Avila entered, he rose but could not speak. Tears rolled down his cheeks. She helped him to his feet, and held him. "Mentor," he said, "we are going to lose him."

"He is in Shanta's hands now," she responded. "Whatever happens, she will be with him."

He wiped his eyes. When he seemed to have steadied, she took his arm. "Come with me," she said softly.

They left the sitting room, went down a stairway, and passed into a long marble corridor illuminated by lanterns. Murals depicted Shanta in her various aspects, creating life, sending the rain, protecting the child Tira against the serpent, appearing in blood-covered clothes to inform the Illyrians that she had fought beside their sons at the battle of Darami.

They passed between twin columns, suggesting the Goddess's support for the world, and ascended into the sanctuary.

The sanctuary was oval-shaped, dominated by a small unadorned altar. The only light in the room came from a brazier, which contained the Living Fire, brought to the Illyrians by Havram, who had it from the Holy One herself. *So long as these flames brighten my chapel will they give strength to your spirit and to your body. Nourish them and live forever in me.* Sarim, broad, gruff, devout Sarim, was waiting. He held an unlit torch, which she took from him.

"Blessed be the eternal light," she said, and pressed the torch into the father's hand. He took it, and she helped him hold it over the brazier until it caught.

Moments later, they passed out of the Temple into the streets. It was a windy night. The torch, in Sarim's grip, flickered and blazed and Avila's cloak tugged at her shoulders. Sarim and the father walked side by side. Avila, a few steps behind, bowed her head and prayed fervently.

Goddess, if it be your will—

His name was Tully. He was nine years old, and afflicted with a wasting disease that had not responded to her array of medicines, poultices, and palliatives. She had seen it before, the graying of the skin, the loss of weight, the aching joints. And the gradual deterioration of the will to live. Usually, the victims were elderly.

Tully had been coming to the Temple for almost four months. At first reluctant, and anxious to be away to join his friends, he had not responded to her ministrations. In time the impatience in his eyes had broken and given way to sadness. The boy had grown to trust her, and he fought the disease with courage.

But despite all she could do, he grew weaker with each visit. The parents brought with them a childlike faith that broke her heart.

Be with him in the ordeal to come.

He had been a bright, green-eyed child filled with laughter when she'd first seen him. Now he was wasted and out of his head, and his fevers raged all the time. "Help him, Mentor," the mother had pleaded.

Tully was covered with damp cloths, in an effort to contain the fever. But his eyes were vacant. He was already effectively gone.

Avila could not restrain her own tears.

Shanta, where are you?

She accepted the torch from Sarim and held it for the father. He took it desperately and plunged it into the pile of sticks and coals in the brazier at the side of the bed. They began to burn.

From the front of the house, where relatives were gathered, Avila heard muffled sobs. She took the boy's wrist and counted silently. His pulse was very weak.

She could not bring herself to look into the eyes of either parent. Instead, she laid the emaciated arm back atop the sheet, but did not let go of it, and bowed her head.

Mother Shanta, I never ask any boon for myself. I know that you are with me now, and are always with me, and that is enough. I will accept without complaint whatever your judgment for me. But please save the child. Do not let him die.

She watched the hopes of the parents fade, watched the boy's struggles weaken, watched the relatives file one by one into the room to take their leave. The wind worked at the windows and the frail flame in the brazier sputtered and gasped.

Whatever your judgment—

"Mentor?"

"I do not know." She resented their importunities. Why did they demand so much of her, as if the divine power were hers to wield?

In the hour after midnight, the thin body ceased its struggles, the labored breathing stopped, and Avila closed his eyes. "I'm sorry," she said. The mother tried to gather him to her breast and the father slumped against the wall, whispering his son's name as if to call him back.

Shanta, accept to your care Tully, who lived only a handful of years in this world.

On the way back to the Temple, Sarim asked whether she was all right. "I'm fine," she said. And then, after a couple of silent minutes: "What's the point of a god who never intervenes?"

•

✠ 6 ✠

The young Avila had loved riding along the banks of the moonlit Mississippi with her father, hoping that Lyka Moonglow would put in an appearance.

No one has seen her for a long time, Avila. She's shy and prefers to come when no one is about. But your grandmother once saw her.

There had been times when Avila was sure she'd also seen Lyka, a quick burst of iridescence skimming the dark waters, a glowing curve much like a smile in the night. But she'd understood that the adults were amused by her claims even while they pretended to be amazed by them. In those days, the skies and the forest had been full of divine power, voices speaking to her, unseen hands turning the inner workings of day and night.

It was a vision she'd never forgot, even when tensions had risen in the family, and she'd run off to Farroad where for three years she'd danced and played for the men who worked the river.

Men had fought over her in those days. And one, whose name she'd never known, a young one not yet twenty, had died. She'd knelt in the street that night with her arms full of blood and felt for the first time the presence of the Goddess.

What more natural than that Avila Kap would, at the somewhat late age of twenty-two, enter the Order of Shanta the Healer, and dedicate herself to a life of service to gods and men?

It had been a fulfilling existence. During the early days she'd heard divine footsteps beside her in the dark streets as she hurried to assist stricken families. But in time the sound had faded, like voices in a passing boat. On the night that Tully had slipped away, she'd returned to her cubicle, warm against the chill rain, and had lain awake well into the dawn, sensing *nothing* in the dark, no power, no spirit lingering to heal the healer, no whispered assurance that there was purpose to it all.

She was alone. They were *all* alone. What had the young man, the one they called Orvon, said at Silas's seminar? *We may be seeing only what we wish to see.* She had sensed in him a desire to believe, and a smoldering anger.

But if no god went with her into the night, how was it that the medicines worked?

But then, why did they not *always* work? She knew the dogmatic answer, of course: It was not always Shanta's will that a cure be effected. But then, if the matter depended on Shanta's will, why bother with the medicines and the curatives at all?

During the two weeks that elapsed after Tully's death, Avila Kap had been locked in a dark struggle of the soul. She felt her old self slipping away, everything she believed in, everything she cared about.

She now knew she was going to leave the Order. It was not an easy choice. The world outside was hostile to ex-priests. Even persons who paid little heed to their religious obligations seemed to feel a duty to show their moral uprightness by mistreating those servants of the gods who had abandoned their posts. But she could no longer pretend to believe.

The real issue now was simple: What could she find to replace the Order, to give meaning to her life? She was well educated and could support herself easily enough. But she did not wish to devote herself exclusively to making money.

In other times, when she'd faced difficult choices, she'd retired to the green chapel, which was named for the variety and profusion of plants that lined its walls and surrounded its altar. Invariably she'd come away with a solution. Now, however, she remained in the community areas or in her quarters. And when other late-night calls came, she went out as she always had, clinging to her dying faith as tightly as the families she visited clung to their dying fathers and wives.

Silas hired four people to begin the task of making copies of *Connecticut Yankee*. Each worked on a separate volume, of course. (Esthetics prohibited multiple types of handwriting in a single book.) Later, when they had several copies to work with, they would expand the operation. Eventually, Silas expected, a hundred or more bound volumes would circulate through the five cities.

There'd been a brief debate about modernizing the language. Silas had argued that they retain the original, in that it was still easily readable. He also believed no one could do it justice. The board had squirmed a bit, but conceded the point.

There were original copies of the other two extant Mark Twain fragments, from "The Facts in the Case of the Great Beef Contract" and *Life on the Mississippi*. Now, with the addition of a complete *Connecticut Yankee*, there was a large enough body of work to begin a serious evaluation of the Roadmaker writer. Silas wondered what lessons Mark Twain, standing with him in Illyria, would have drawn from the ruins of his civilization.

Silas had written over thirty commentaries on various aspects of ancient and modern literature, ethics, and history. Only one, "Brave New Hyperbole," had ever been committed to permanent form and placed in the library. (Now, years later, the title embarrassed him.) "Hyperbole" argued that Huxley's book was in fact a speculative fantasy rather than an accurate depiction of Roadmaker technologies and ethics. He wasn't sure he was right, but he trembled at the possibility that civilization could descend to such horror.

Now he was recording his impressions of *Connecticut Yankee*. There was simply nothing like Mark Twain in the entire panoply of League literature. The closest approach was probably the wry comedies of the Argonite playwright Caper Tallow. But even Tallow seemed a bit droll at the side of this Roadmaker humorist.

Silas took extreme care with his commentary, because he knew many others would follow. And because he was first, his remarks would draw attention, either as an example of insight or ineptitude. He sensed that this single document would make his reputation, one way or the other, for posterity.

He'd been working, off and on, almost a month on the project and felt so good about the result that he was violating an old rule by showing his progress to some of the other masters. They were impressed, but in the way of such things, they gave all the credit to Mark Twain.

On the day that Silas finished his final draft, Chaka Milana rode up to his front door. He had just put his writing materials away and was getting ready to walk across the street for dinner. She smiled triumphantly at him as she climbed down from Piper. "I can't guarantee Haven," she said, "but I think it's possible to go where Endine went."

She led him to the Lost Hope, a nearby pub, where a tall, dark-skinned man with thick black hair and a clipped beard sat at a corner table. "Silas," she said, "I'd like you to meet Jon Shannon."

Silas extended his hand. Shannon put down his beer. "Pleased to meet you, Silas," he said.

Chaka pushed in against the wall and Silas sat down beside her. "Chaka tells me you've been doing some work for her."

Shannon nodded. "She wanted me to see if I could find the track of the Endine expedition."

A chill blew through Silas's soul. "I assume you succeeded or we wouldn't be sitting here."

He glanced at Chaka. "I found some markings up on Wilderness Road. You know where that is?"

Silas had never been on it, but he knew that it was about 140 miles north, that it led northeast from Argon, running roughly parallel to the Ohio. "Yes," he said.

"We know that's where they started. I followed it for a couple of days. To Ephraim's Bluff, which is pretty much on the edge of League territory. Just beyond Ephraim's Bluff there are several sets of marks."

"What kind of marks?"

"Tree cuts. Always three strokes. Piles of rocks. Three rocks with a fourth on top. They probably used some chalk, too. There's some granite up there and I'd have chalked it if I were making a trail."

"But there's no chalk now?"

"How could there be after all these years?"

"How old are the marks are on the trees?"

"Can't tell. At least five or six years. *Maybe* ten. Damn, maybe twenty."

Silas looked at Chaka, and then swung his gaze back to Shannon. "That's it?"

Shannon frowned. "What more did you want?"

A waiter arrived and they ordered beer for Chaka and Silas, and dinner for everybody.

"Wilderness Road isn't really much of a road," said Shannon. "Nobody uses it except hunters and traders. And the military. Those people all know their territory pretty well, so it would have to be a special set of circumstances that anybody would need to leave guide marks." Silas could see the big man liked his beer. He finished it off and set the stein down gently. "I'd be willing to bet I was looking at Endine's jump-off point."

The pub was busy. It was dinner hour and the dining room was filled with laughter and the sizzle of steak and the aroma of cold brew. Candles flickered on the walls.

"I don't know you well, Jon," said Silas, "so I hope you won't take this personally." He looked at Chaka. "You hired him to take a look, right?"

"Yes," she said, puzzled.

"Was it a flat rate? Or did he get more money if he brought back a positive answer?"

Her features darkened. "He wouldn't lie. But yes, it was a flat rate."

Silas nodded. "Good. So what do you propose to do now?"

She looked surprised. "I'm going after it," she said.

"On the strength of a few marked trees."

"It's a chance. But it's a good chance." Her eyes blazed. "Listen, Silas, the truth about what happened to my brother is out there somewhere."

"I hate to put it this way, Chaka. But what does it matter? He's dead. And Karik's dead. What's the point?"

Across the room, someone cheered. They were celebrating a birthday.

"I think the truth is worth something, don't you?" She fixed him with her blue gaze. "Anyway, Haven might be at the end of the road."

Silas looked from her to the dark-skinned giant. "I'm sixty years old. I'm not really in condition for taking off on a wild chase. Especially not one that's already killed a substantial number of people."

Disappointment clouded her features. "Okay. I thought you'd be the first to want to go. There'll be others."

"I doubt it."

Shannon was studying the ceiling.

"How about *you*?" Silas asked him. "Are *you* going?"

"No," he said.

"Why not?"

"Because Haven doesn't mean anything to me. Because I don't believe it exists. Because you—" he was gazing at Chaka now, "—and anyone who goes with you, will most certainly fail, and possibly lose your lives."

Silas turned back to Chaka. "I think he makes sense."

Their meals arrived. The menu at the Lost Hope was fairly limited. It consisted of either beef or chicken, depending on the chef's mood, and the vegetable du jour, and bread. On this occasion, the chef's mood called for chicken, and the vegetable was cabbage.

"I think we all need to be reasonable," Silas said.

Chaka sat back with her arms folded, stared at Silas for a few moments, picked up a knife, and sliced a strip of meat from the breast. "Haven doesn't mean anything to Jon," she said. "What does it mean to you? Ten years from now you'll be seventy. You want to look back on this and know there was a chance you might have found the entire body of Mark Twain's work, and who knows what else, but you didn't *bother*? Because it was dangerous?"

Illyrian women caught in compromising situations lost their reputations, prospects, and often their incomes. (Men, as usual, operated on a somewhat different standard.) No decent person would associate openly with a woman who'd become entangled in scandal. She was no longer welcome at her place of employment; her customers disappeared; and she could expect to be turned out by her family.

The risks for unmarried women were intensified by a lack of reliable contraceptive devices. Various ointments and oils, if applied prior to sexual activity, were supposed to prevent conception. But it was hard to determine their efficacy. No one kept statistics, and everybody lied about sex. Chaka concluded, as did most women, that the potential consequences outweighed the game. And so virtue reigned in Illyria.

This state of affairs had, to a degree, evolved from a line of emperors and kings who believed that the stability of the city required a solid family tradition, which they had enforced with the power of the priesthood and a series of laws prohibiting divorce and confining sexual activity within the marriage bond. Violators were subject to a range of criminal penalties which, for a time under Aspik III and Mogan the Wise, included burning at the stake.

In the Republic, such laws were considered barbaric. Nevertheless, the moral code from which they had sprung was alive and well, and if offending women could no longer be deprived of their physical existence, they could lose virtually everything else.

Chaka was not a virgin, but she rarely strayed across the line, and had not done so at all within the recent past. Tonight, though, as she returned from her frustrating meeting with Silas Glote, she needed to talk with Raney, to be with him, to accept whatever comfort he might provide. For that reason, she had declined Jon Shannon's offer to escort her home. ("What will you do now?" Shannon had asked as she'd departed, and she'd replied that she would follow the trail, that she had friends, that there were plenty of people who would join her to look for Haven. And his lips had tightened and he'd warned her to forget it. "But if you *must* go," he'd added, "take no strangers. Take nobody you wouldn't trust with your life. Because that's how it'll be.")

Raney lived alone in a small farmhouse outside Epton Village, about two miles northwest of the city. She left through the northern gate and rode out on the Cumbersak Trail. Travel was relatively safe within a few miles of Illyria. The roads were heavily patrolled now that the wars had stopped, and the old-time bandits who had once owned the highways after sundown were either dead or in hiding. Nonetheless, she always carried a gun when she traveled at night.

The moon was high and it was late when she rode through the hedges that surrounded Raney's wood frame house. His dog, Clip, barked at her approach, and Raney appeared in his doorway.

"Didn't expect to see *you* tonight," he said. "How'd the meeting go?"

She tossed him her reins and climbed down. "Could have been better."

"Glote wasn't impressed?"

"You could say that."

He looked at her. "I'm sorry."

She shrugged. "Not your fault." A cold wind was blowing in across the river.

They walked Piper toward the barn.

"What did he say?"

She told him. Raney nodded in the right places, and pulled the saddle off the roan. "To be honest," he said, "I thought it was a little thin, too."

It was hard to see his face in the dark. The air smelled of horses and barley and old wood.

"Of course it's a little thin," she snapped. "Don't you think I know that? It's a *thread*. But that's probably all we'll ever have. And maybe it's all we'll need."

Raney put some water out for Piper. "Let's go inside," he said.

They strolled across the hard ground, not saying anything. It was as if a wall had gone up between them. Raney wasn't wearing a jacket, so he should have been cold. But he took his time anyhow, walking with his hands pushed into his back pockets. When they got to the house, he filled the teapot with water, hung it on the bar, and swung the bar over the fire. Then he tossed on another log.

"Dolian is still trying to get his nephew appointed as an auditor," he said, trying to steer them to a new subject. He talked for a while, and Chaka half listened. The water boiled and he prepared the tea and served it in two large steaming vessels. "Imported from Argon," he said. He sat down beside her. "I'm glad you came."

Chaka decided to let hers cool. "I think Shannon might change his mind," she said.

Raney frowned. "Change his mind? About what?"

"When we're ready to go, I believe he'll come with us."

She listened to him breathe. "Chaka, if Silas doesn't think it's worthwhile, it's not worthwhile." He looked casually at her, as if his point were too obvious to dispute.

"I don't care what Silas thinks," she said harshly. "I want to know what happened to my brother."

She listened to him sigh. He tasted the tea, and commented that it was pretty good.

"Raney," she said, "I'm going to do this."

"I wish you wouldn't." He spoke softly, in the tone he used when he was trying to be authoritative. His eyes were round and tentative and worried.

"You haven't changed your mind about going, have you?"

"Chaka, I never agreed to go. I said I'd go if it seemed reasonable."

She could feel the heat rising into her cheeks. "That's not what I remember."

"Look," he said, "we can't just go running into the wilderness. We might not come back." He shook his head slowly and put one hand on her shoulder. It felt stiff and cold. A stranger's hand. "We've got a good life here." His voice softened. "Chaka, I'd like you to marry me—" His breathing had become irregular. "We have everything that we need to make us happy."

Maddeningly, tears rushed into her eyes. She knew how good life with him would be, building a family, whiling away the years and never again being alone.

His lips brushed hers and they clung to each other for a long moment. His heart beat against her and his hand caressed her cheek. She responded with a long wet kiss and then abruptly pushed away from him. "You'll never lose me, Raney, unless you want to. But I *am* going to do this."

He was getting that hurt puppy look. "Chaka, there's no way I can just pick up and leave for six months."

"You didn't mention that before."

"I didn't think it would come to this. If I leave the

shop, they'll replace me in a minute. I've got a good career here. We'll need it to support us, and if I go on this thing I'd just be throwing everything away. It's different for you. You can come back and pick up where you left off."

She stared at him. "I suppose so," she said. She got up and pulled on her jacket.

"Where are you going?"

"Home. I need to think things out."

"Chaka, I don't want you to be angry about this. But I need you to be reasonable."

"I know," she said. "Tonight, everyone wants me to be reasonable."

She was on her feet and out onto the porch, not hearing what else he was saying. She got to Piper, threw the saddle on as Raney came through the barn door, drew the straps tight, pushed him away, and mounted.

"Chaka—"

"Later, Raney," she said. "We can talk about it later."

She rode past him, out into the night. The wind pulled at the trees, and there was a hint of rain.

If you must go, take no strangers. Take nobody you wouldn't trust with your life.

✠ 7 ✠

If you must go, take no strangers. Take nobody you wouldn't trust with your life. During the next week, Chaka discovered how few persons fit Shannon's prescription. Those she had confidence in were all in Raney's camp: They saw it as their duty to dissuade her from the project. And they would under no circumstances support a second expedition. It's important, several of them told her, to learn from history. On the other hand, people she did *not* know arrived at her door and offered to join. Most seemed unstable or unreliable. A few wanted to be paid.

It's likely that the second expedition might never have happened had not Quait Esterhok conceived, almost simultaneously, two passions: one for Mark Twain, and the other for Chaka Milana.

The former led him, perhaps for the first time, to understand the nature of what had been lost with the Roadmaker collapse. Because the League cities had no printing press, they did not possess the novel as an art form. Contemporary writers limited themselves to practical manuals; to philosophical, religious, legal, and ethical tracts; and to histories.

It was not the literary form, however, which left so strong an impression on Quait. Rather, it was the voice, which seemed so energetic and full of life, so completely at odds with the formalized, stiff writing style of the Illyrians. It was, he told Silas, as if this Mark Twain were sitting right in the room. "What do we know about him?" he asked.

Silas outlined the limited knowledge they had: that he'd lived in a place called Hartford; that he'd been born in the Roadmaker year 1835 (no one knew when that was); that he was conscious of the delays of government, as shown in "The Facts in the Case of the Great Beef Contract"; and that he'd been a riverboat pilot on the Mississippi, although the precise nature of his riverboat remained a mystery.

Yet, despite the paucity of facts, Quait felt that he knew Mark Twain almost as well as he knew Silas.

Quait's second passion developed out of the first. Stealing time with the book was not easy. Inevitably it was in the hands of the copiers or the scholars, or both. So Quait had got into the habit of coming by and watching the progress of the work, reading over shoulders, and planning where he would get the funds to buy one of the books when it had actually been published. He arrived one afternoon to find another enthusiast also trying to read while a visiting scholar made notes on chapter four. They were in a back room, where the book was kept secure from the general public.

The enthusiast was a striking young woman whose shoulder-length red hair told him immediately who she was. "I've heard a lot about you from Silas," he said.

Chaka nodded graciously. "You're—?"

"Quait Esterhok." He drew up another chair and sat down beside her. "Chapter four describes the immoderate language used in and around Camelot."

She smiled. "Have you had a chance to read any of it?"

"In bits and pieces," Quait said. "I've never seen anything like it."

She nodded. "Yes. He's very contemporary. And traveling backward in time. *That's* a wild idea."

The scholar, who was pinched-looking with straw-colored hair, glanced up with obvious irritation. "Do you mind?" he asked.

"Sorry," said Chaka. An hourglass stood on the worktable. Its sands had almost run out. "I've got to go anyway," she said.

"It's okay," said Quait. "I'll be quiet."

"No, I've overstayed my time." She waited a moment to finish what she'd been reading, and then she looked up at him. Her eyes were blue and alive and they took him prisoner on the spot. "Silas says there'll be copies ready within another week."

"Good." Quait cast about for a way to prolong the interview. But his mind had gone numb.

"Nice to meet you, Quait." She rose, smiled, and walked off. He watched her stride to the desk, sign out, and leave the library.

"You've been keeping something from me, Silas."

"And what is that?" he asked. They'd met for dinner at the Lost Cause.

"I met Chaka Milana today." Quait rolled his eyes. "She looks pretty good."

Silas shook his head. "I don't think she's very happy with me right now."

"Why's that?"

The waiter brought wine and filled their glasses. "I didn't take her frontier scout very seriously."

"Oh." Quait frowned. "I got the impression the way you described it that you and she had agreed that the evidence was insufficient."

Silas looked uncomfortable. "Not quite," he said. "I guess that was *my* conclusion. She's determined to pursue this business. It's like ten years ago all over again. She's becoming obsessed. She behaves as if it's just a matter of going out into the woods for a few days. Anyway, she's been talking to people at the Imperium, and elsewhere, trying to put together an expedition."

"Is she having any luck?"

"I hope not. Look, Quait, nobody would like to find that place more than I do. Her woodsman found some marks on trees, but they could be anything. What's going to happen is, she'll put together a mission, it'll get a few miles outside the borders, and they'll run out of signs. Then they'll come back, and anybody with a professional reputation to lose will very surely lose it. I can't afford to get mixed up in that."

"I didn't say anything," said Quait.

"Well, you were looking at me as if you disapproved. Even what's-his-name, Shannon, admitted he couldn't make any guarantees."

"Shannon?"

"The woodsy guy."

Quait nodded. "You *won't* get a guarantee, Silas, with a thing like this. Not ever. You know that as well as I do."

"I know." A candle burned in a globe on the table. Silas stared at it. "I wasn't looking for a guarantee, Quait. You know that."

Quait tried his wine, licked his lips, put it down. "Silas, may I speak frankly?"

"Of course."

"What is it that frightens you? What is it that keeps you from going after the one thing in this life that has real meaning for you? You backed off nine years ago, and you're backing off now."

"And I was right nine years ago, wasn't I?"

"I don't know. Were you?"

"Nobody came back. Except Karik."

Quait shrugged. "Maybe you would have made the difference." He leaned forward. "Silas, I know you'd risk your reputation if you went. I know the odds for success aren't good. But I think basing your decision on what someone else will think doesn't sound like you."

"Sure it does," said Silas. "I've always been concerned about public opinion. I have to be. My livelihood depends on it."

"Then maybe you're right," he said. "Maybe, if it's out there, you're not the right person to find it. But however that may be, I think you've been asking the wrong question. I'm more inclined to wonder what might happen if Shannon is *right?* If the trail *is* complete. If Haven really is at the end of it."

"That's a lot of *if's.*"

"Yes. Well, I think we've already agreed about the odds. But anybody can do stuff when the odds are in their favor. Or when there's no risk. Right?"

Silas liked Bernard Shaw. He spent the evening in the Senate library. He was leafing through *Mrs. Warren's Profession,* but it was the conversation with Quait that drove his mood. The Illyrians also possessed *Man and Superman, Major Barbara,* and *Too True to Be Good,* in addition to a fragment of *Saint Joan.*

"I'm going after the prize, Silas," Karik had said. *"It's all out there. Shakespeare and Dante and the Roadmaker histories. And their mathematics and science. It's waiting for us. But we need you."*

Silas had rejected the offer, had turned away. It was nonsense. He'd so thoroughly convinced himself that now he suspected he *wanted* it to be nonsense. Does a man clasp old beliefs, and old fears, so desperately?

And it had come again.

A prize so vast that no risk was too great. But this time, there'd be no Karik Endine to plunge into the wilderness. Only a young woman whose passions were running away with her head, and his infatuated former student.

Idly, he turned the pages of *Mrs. Warren's Profession,* staring at the script, not really reading. But one line jumped out at him. It was Vivie's comment to Mrs. Warren, near the end of Act IV: *If I had been you, mother, I might have done as you did; but I should not have lived one life and believed in another*.

After a while, Silas put the book away.

He walked slowly home, up the curving road, past candle-lit cottages and the bakeshop and Cape's Apothecary. Tomorrow he would send a message to Chaka, and then he would ask the Board of Regents to finance the attempt.

Once it became official that a second expedition would be mounted, Silas became the center of attention at the Imperium. Close friends advised him against the foray; others, not so close, made no real effort to hide their amusement. Nevertheless, all his colleagues, regardless of their views, seemed to feel required to explain publicly why they were unable to join the hunt. After all, the masters were supposed to have invested their lives in the pursuit of wisdom and knowledge. But, as one mathematician pointed out, if his desire for knowledge suggested he should go, wisdom dictated he stay put.

Silas immediately announced his intention to accompany the mission, and argued that it should leave as soon as possible. The first expedition had been gone more than six months, he said. We know we'll be heading north, and we want to be back before winter sets in. Silas put himself at Chaka's disposal, and they set February 16 as the date for departure.

Silas used his political connections to get Quait assigned as an ad hoc military escort, thereby saving his pay. In addition, he informed Chaka that Quait had been responsible for his change of heart. When she took him aside to thank him, Quait pretended to a degree of humility, but took care not to overdo it.

It appeared for a time there would be only three of them. Or four, if Chaka was right and Shannon eventually joined. That's okay, Quait insisted. He argued that a smaller group might have a better chance to succeed. "We'll be more able to function as a single person, and less likely to run into personality differences. And three people aren't going to make the Tuks nervous."

Chaka spent much of the time leading up to departure reading every scrap of information she could find relating to Haven and Abraham Polk.

Most of the tales agreed that Polk had been captain of the *Quebec*, a warship that could sail at high speed against the wind. (Modern authorities thought there might have been a kernel of truth in the legend, that there might have been such a ship, and that it may have been named the *Quebec*. But no one knew who the name referred to, and of course they dismissed the more fanciful details, e,g., that it had been a submersible.) Polk's naval efforts, traditionally, had consisted of salvage and rescue.

The Travels maintained that, after the Plague subsided, the *Quebec* prowled the seas under Polk's direction for seventy-seven years (surely a mystic number), gathering survivors and returning them to Haven, which was designed to survive the general collapse. He also collected as much as he could of the art, science, literature, and history of the dead civilization, storing it against the ages. The names of his comrades are almost as famous as his: Casey Winckelhaus, his female second-in-command; Harry Schroeder, a tough, iconoclastic shoemaker's son who gave his life for his commander off Copenhagen; Jennifer Whitlaw, whose account of the voyages, ironically now lost, gave them the name by which they are best known: the October Patrol.

Polk himself vanished at sea, called home by the Goddess when his work was done. Haven then shut its doors against the general dissolution and embarked on an effort to preserve what it had saved. Generations of scholars devoted themselves to maintaining and, as the texts yellowed and began to crumble, copying the great works in their care. And they waited for a new civilization to rise. If the legend is correct, they are still waiting.

Chaka dug out every illustration she could find of the *Quebec* and of Haven. The ship was commonly depicted as a schooner without sails, but with its bridge and forecastle enclosed inside a metal shell.

Haven itself, seen from the outside, revealed an aspect that was not greatly unlike the cliff and sea in the thirteenth sketch. She found more illustrations of the mountain car, which was alleged to have traveled the cliffs between Haven and Polk's supply base.

The *Quebec* operated out of a chamber that had direct access to the sea. It was said the vessel could pass from its nest into the ocean without ever being seen. It was all so imaginative that she could not look at the material without dismissing it out of hand.

✠ ✠ ✠

Midway through the final week of preparations, Flojian showed up at the Imperium and took Silas aside. He looked haggard and red-eyed, as if he had not been sleeping well. "I want to go with you," he said.

Flojian had never shown any interest in academic pursuits. Moreover, he seemed to be the sort of man whose idea of hardship was having to go outside for fresh water. "Why?" asked Silas. The consensus now was to keep the group small. Furthermore, the regents favored a strategy that would restrain expenses.

"The stories about my father."

Silas squirmed. "Don't pay any attention to them. People like to talk." He shook his head.

Flojian tried to straighten his shoulders. "I have a right to be with you. I can pay my own way. Whether you want me to or not, I'm coming."

Silas opposed the proposal. "Plans have already been made," he explained. "Anyway, it'll be a difficult trip. This won't be any pot of tulips." He winced after that phrase, but he was struggling. Flojian was after all a rather useless individual, whose life had always been circumscribed by money and comfort.

But he persisted. "You can't keep me from coming if I want to," he said. "Please, Silas. I know you don't think much of me, but you owe it to my father."

"I'll put it to the others," Silas promised, "and let you know."

One of the meetings drew another visitor: Avila Kap, of the Order of Shanta the Healer. It was a clear, warm evening, but she nonetheless wore a nondescript flannel shirt and cotton slacks in place of her usual clerical robes. "I would like to go," she said.

Silas could see that Chaka and Quait, as startled by her appearance as he, were now equally discomfited by the proposal. Avila was, after all, bound by the rules of her calling, and could not simply wander off on her own into the wilderness. "Mentor," he said, "we have filled our roster."

She was a tall woman, almost six feet, and she moved with grace. Her dark eyes caught the light, and there was a glint of desperation in them. "Nevertheless," she said, "I will go, if you will permit it." She looked at each of them in turn. "We are required to spend several weeks each year in the wilderness, to maintain communication with the Goddess. I'm adept at survival skills, and I can assure you I will not be a burden."

"I'm sure you would not." Silas thought about Flojian, and for that matter about himself. If there was going to be a burden on this trip, he knew it would not be this very competent-looking woman. "Have you permission to travel with us?"

"Surely that is *my* concern."

An uncomfortable silence followed. "May I ask why you wish to come?"

She took a long, deep breath. "Because," she said, "I would like my life to count for something."

Silas was feted by the Imperium, given a scroll attesting to his efforts to expand the boundaries of human knowledge, and sent off with a blast of horns.

Flojian turned his business over to his executive assistant, who promptly unnerved him by promising to explore new avenues for profit. "Don't change anything," said Flojian. "Or I'll have your elbows removed when I get back."

On February 16, the twentieth day after they had made their decision, and the eighty-third after Karik's death, Silas, Chaka, Quait, and Avila rode at sunup to Flojian's villa, where a dozen packhorses and a barnload of supplies had been gathered. Silas had said good-bye to his friends and relatives, who had, in the tradition of the time, wished him that the wind should block his way, and the rivers afford no crossings. (It was thought this would allay the jealousy of the gods.) He had updated his will, and turned his small house over to a trusted student until his return. "Or until news comes, and my testament takes effect."

Avila arrived in forest green shirt and leggings, having discarded both her sacred raiment and her sacred orders. Her superiors were somewhat stirred up at the Temple, even though her action could not have come entirely as a surprise. Nevertheless, they were unhappy with her, and her life in Illyria would henceforth be that of an outcast.

Flojian hid an ample supply of gold coins in his saddlebags. He didn't like the idea of traveling with a lot of money, but he knew that gold opens all kinds of doors, and he suspected they would have use for it before they were done.

Chaka half expected that Raney would come at the last minute. While her companions carried out the final details of getting organized, loading the packhorses, running down checklists, ensuring they had the means of reshodding the animals, she kept looking around, hoping to see him ride in on his big chestnut stallion.

Several dozen well-wishers arrived and shook their hands. The company mounted their horses, waved, and, in brilliant sunlight, moved out of the villa grounds. They climbed to River Road and turned north. It would have been an exaggeration to say that crowds lined the route. However, there were individuals and small groups gathered along the way, watching, waving as they went by.

But there was no chestnut stallion.

✠ 8 ✠

River Road ran along the Mississippi to Argon, the northern-most of the League, about ten days' travel upriver. The road was all-weather construction: In most areas it had a pebble bed and good drainage. It plunged through thick forests of silver maple, bitternut hickory, pecan, and cypress. It passed farms and ranches, navigated among heaps of broken cement and patches of grassland. Concrete causeways carried it through swamps, and wooden bridges across streams and gullies. It hesitated before sites of historical interest: Pandar's Glade, where the Illyrian hero had turned the tide of war against the Argonites; a restored Baranji fort from the days when the Mississippi marked the western frontier of empire; a statue of a Roadmaker military figure, right arm broken off, with the inscription: *HE STOOD LIKE A STONE WALL.*

Chaka was glad to get clear of the well-wishers, to move into the silences of the forest. She had been to Argon several times, although the most recent trip had been almost six years before, a hunting expedition with her family. Those earlier excursions had seemed like journeys to the end of the world. It was hard to realize that this time the outpost city would be little more than a jump-off point.

She was displeased with herself for agreeing to allow Flojian to join the expedition. The little man rode up front with Silas in his finicky, self-important way, and it irritated her that the two seemed to find much to talk about. She predicted to Quait that a few nights on the road would change his mind, and he would return home.

Silas bounced along on a horse that was too big for him. He'd borrowed a new animal from the Imperium for the expedition; his usual mount was, he knew, too old for the kind of effort that would be required. Chaka thought that Silas looked cold and uncomfortable. But he hung on, trying to give the appearance of a man at home in the wilderness, even raising himself in the saddle on occasion to get a better look at the river, or a eucalyptus, or whatever happened to catch his attention.

"He'll be all right," said Quait. "He just needs a little time to get used to the road."

She was grateful to Quait, not only because he'd been instrumental in launching the expedition, but also because he obviously liked her and she needed that right now. Raney's defection had damaged her more than she was willing to admit, and she traveled throughout that first day expecting to hear him ride up behind them. She played the scene over and over in her mind, Raney apologetic and trying to shrug it all away; she cool and formal, allowing him to sweat. "You'll have to ask Silas," she would tell him. "It's not up to me."

"This is the high point of Silas's life," Quait told her. "It's what he's always wanted to do."

"Hard to believe," she said. "He doesn't look as if he's enjoying himself."

"He's not used to riding for long periods."

"I can see that. What's he been doing for the last forty years?"

"Trying to understand what fuels the sun. The places he would like to go, people can't get to."

Chaka wasn't sure she understood that, but she let it pass.

She was suspicious of Avila. The woman was friendly enough, but it was hard to overlook the fact that she had abandoned her vows. Chaka was a believer to the extent that she didn't like people to ask hard questions, and tried not to think too deeply about the assorted doctrines she'd accepted. Play it safe, respect the gods, and maybe it would pay off. Who knew?

There had been a time, a generation back, when breaking with the Order would have meant keeping out of public sight for the balance of one's life. But with the advent of the Republic, the ecclesiastical laws had been liberalized. Avila would be free to live as she wished, although most people would feel as Chaka did, that she was somehow remiss and morally suspect.

Avila was, however, the only member of the company who had been north of Argon. "We have a retreat about two days' ride above the city," she said. "It's on a ridge, in deep woods. A good place for prayer and contemplation."

"Didn't you worry about the Tuks?" asked Chaka.

"At first. But no one else seemed very concerned. At least no one who'd been around for a while. The Tuks turned out to be friendly enough."

"What did you contemplate?"

"Beg pardon?"

"You said you went up there to contemplate. What did you think about?"

Avila laughed. It was a pleasant sound, reserved, amiable, honest. "I think mostly I looked around at the wilderness and wondered what I was doing there."

Silas had ridden in closer to listen. "Will we pass the retreat?"

"No," she said. "We turn east when we get to Argon."

"I think," said Chaka, "you'll have plenty of time for contemplation on this trip."

They passed a sign. It was from the Roadmaker period, and gave no indication it would *ever* rust. (The origin of the more exotic Roadmaker materials, which seemed in some instances almost indestructible, remained just one more major mystery.) The letters were black and crisp in the sunlight:

WALK WITH THE SON
YOU ARE ON ETERNITY ROAD

All five could read enough Roadmaker English to grasp the literal meaning. It was nonetheless baffling.

"What's it about, Silas?" asked Chaka.

Silas half turned in his saddle. "It means it's time to get off the horses and walk."

"No, really," said Avila.

"I think Silas is right," said Quait. "We should give the critters a rest."

It was cold, and Silas adjusted his scarf. "The Roadmakers believed in a god who tortured people after they died. If they'd sinned."

"Barbaric notion," said Avila. "I wonder if people create the kind of divinity that reflects their own character?"

Flojian turned to stare at her. "It surprises me to hear a *priest* talk that way. I was taught that the divine essence cannot be misunderstood, save by willful effort."

"That is the official position," said Avila, refusing to take offense. "Incidentally, I've withdrawn from the Order."

Flojian rolled his eyes. "Did Silas know you were an ex-priest when he invited you to come along?"

She nodded. "I haven't hidden my status from anyone."

Chaka tended to side with Flojian on that issue. If there was anything to the old traditions, an ex-priest might well bring them bad luck. She had considered voting against allowing Avila to join the company, but cringed at the prospect of explaining her reasoning. Nevertheless, she determined to keep a respectful distance, in case a bolt did fall from the sky.

A few miles north of Illyria, the forest gave way to low, grassy hills, which in turn descended into a swamp. The sky had turned gray, but there was no immediate threat of rain. They stopped by a spring.

The water was clear and cold. Chaka knelt on a rock and scooped it into her hands. It tasted good, and in fact, the *day* tasted good. She still hoped for Raney's appearance, but a strange thing was happening: She was anxious to be far enough away from Illyria to be certain that he would not come.

"Not having second thoughts, are you?" Silas had come up behind her. He pushed his hands into his jacket and assumed the mien of confident leader. She wondered how he really felt.

"No, Silas," she said. "No second thoughts. I'm glad we're finally on our way."

"Good." He produced a cup and dipped it into the stream.

"I'd feel better, though, if we had a map."

"Me too." He drank deeply and stared thoughtfully at the horizon. "We'll find our way. Meantime, I'm going to start a journal. We won't make the same mistake Karik made." A smile spread across his features. "We're going to create the travel book of the age. Once we get beyond the frontier, we'll record everything: foliage, wildlife, weather, topography, ruins, you name it. And charts." A mile ahead, the road crossed planking and entered the swamp. "If there's another expedition after this, they won't have to play guessing games."

"The Great Geographer," smiled Chaka.

"Yes." He laughed. "They'll put my statue in the Imperium, left hand shielding my eyes, right pointing to the horizon." He demonstrated the pose.

Chaka gave him a thumbs up, in her own style, both hands.

They arrived at the Crooked Man just before sunset. The main building was three stories tall, a massive, rambling structure with turrets, balconies, bay windows, glass-enclosed porches, sloping dormers, and parapets. A marble sundial that also served as a fountain guarded the approach. Grooms took their horses, and a liveried doorman welcomed them into the opulent interior. Chaka admired the thick carpets and shining hardwood floors. Murals depicting hunting scenes covered the walls. Stylish furniture from an earlier age filled the lobby and hallways, and lush red curtains framed the windows.

All of the travelers had stayed there at one time or another. The host of the Crooked Man was a four-hundred-pound giant whose name was Jewel. Jewel's speech was polished and his manners impeccable. His luxuriant black beard spilled onto a white shirt. His arms were thick as beefhocks. He had great shaggy eyebrows and thick black hair streaked with gray and teeth that looked able to take down a horse. He was capable of ferocious grimaces when dealing with stewards, grooms, and tradesmen. But he was absolutely correct with guests, and called four of the five travelers by name, even though he had not seen some for years. He missed only Avila, apparently thrown into confusion at seeing her in nonclerical dress.

"It's good to have you back at the Crooked Man," he

said. "I'd heard that a quest was going out, and if we can do anything, please don't hesitate to ask." Unfortunately, he explained, the inn was quite busy just now, and they would have to share rooms. He hoped that wouldn't be a problem. Since they had intended doing that anyhow, it wouldn't. Nevertheless, Flojian contrived to look inconvenienced.

Jewel directed their bags be taken care of, and personally showed them to their quarters, expressing his desire that they enjoy their stay and come again soon to see him. They thanked him and agreed to meet in the dining room at the seventh hour.

The rooms were single compartments; but they were nevertheless spacious and comfortable, almost as grand as Chaka remembered. The curtains had been opened to admit the last of the sunlight.

A low fire heated a pair of water pots in the chamber she would be sharing with Avila. Oil lanterns burned on either side of an enormous bed with large down pillows and a quilt. A freshly scrubbed wooden tub gleamed invitingly near the fireplace, on a raised wood platform designed to draw off excess water.

Two serving boys arrived with buckets of fresh water. Avila gave them coins. "Thank you, Mistress," said the taller one. "Just ring the bell when you want more."

Both women were covered with dust from the road, and a bath would be the first order of business. But Chaka shrank from the task. There were no modesty curtains in the room, and the prospect of removing her clothes in the presence of one who had been ordained to Shanta was daunting. She loosened her neckerchief and hesitated, suddenly aware that Avila was watching her. "If you don't mind," said Avila, with a hint of amusement, "I'll claim the privilege of the older and go first."

There is nothing quite like nudity to strip away titles, pretenses, and reservation. Before twenty minutes had passed, Chaka found herself admitting to her companion what she had not admitted to herself: She felt rejected by Raney, and she was at that moment recognizing that the future she'd thought they would have together lay in ruins.

"You may be fortunate," Avila said. "If you truly loved him, I don't think you'd be here at all. So maybe you've learned something about yourself."

"Maybe," Chaka said. All the same, it hurt.

"Why *are* you here?" asked Avila. "The cost seems to be higher for you than for anyone else."

Chaka explained about her brother and Avila listened without comment.

"How about you?"

"It's a chance to escape," Avila said. "And the Roadmakers are interesting. If this Haven really exists, I wouldn't want to miss my chance to see it."

Chaka was seated in the window, watching the western sky turn purple. "I expect," she said, "that if we do find it, it'll be a ruin. Like everything else." She described the time travel concept in *Connecticut Yankee* and said how she wished such a thing were possible. "I would love to have seen their cities when they were whole. And to have traveled on their roads before the forest took them. To have seen *how* the hojjies actually worked."

"Wagons that needed no horses," said Avila. "I'm still not sure I believe it." She stood with one foot on a low stool, scooping hot water out of the tub and pouring it over shoulders and breasts. Suds ran down into the drains. (Illyrians did not sit in bathwater until they were clean, and would in fact have been horrified at the notion of doing so.) "But you're right: We could learn a lot if there were a way to take one of the highways and use it to travel back a thousand years. Or whatever it is."

"Maybe in a way," said Chaka, "that's exactly what we're doing."

After Chaka's bath, they dressed in clean clothes, strolled downstairs, and swept into the dining room in high spirits. A slab of beef, tended by a cook, turned slowly on a spit over an open flame. There were roughly twenty tables, each illuminated by an oil lamp. About half the tables were occupied by guests who seemed already well into their cups. Their own party had commandeered a corner stall. Quait waved, and all three men looked their way. Their glances lingered just long enough to bring a rush of satisfaction to Chaka.

Wine and brew were flowing enthusiastically, and the place was filled with laughter and the sizzle of beef. A young man sat on a raised platform in the center of the room, one leg crossed over the other, fingering a guitar.

Drink, my love,
Though stars may fall and rivers fail,
I will not care so long as
I have you.

Quait poured wine for Chaka and Avila and refilled the other cups. They toasted the quest, and then rose, one by one, collected metal plates, and went over to the spit. The cook sliced off a large piece of meat for each, scooped some peas out of a pot, and added two ears of corn dipped in melted butter. Chaka picked up some bread and an apple.

When they'd got back to their table, Jewel entered the dining room, carrying a glass of wine. At his appearance, the musician stopped and the house fell quiet. When he had everyone's attention, Jewel held the glass high. "This is our finest," he said. "And tonight I want you to join me in toasting some special guests of the Crooked Man." He directed everyone's attention to Chaka and her companions. "Ladies and gentlemen, we have the honor to host a group of very special people this evening. Silas Glote and Flojian Endine are leading a party of explorers who are going to try to find some lost books." He glanced back at Silas. "Do I have that right, Silas?"

The diners applauded and Silas nodded. Chaka wondered who promoted Flojian.

"The Crooked Man wishes you well." He drained the glass.

The audience followed in kind, and applauded.

"By the way," continued Jewel, "the wine is produced especially for us, and we are selling it tonight at a very good rate. Thank you very much."

People came over to shake their hands. One young man, congenial and slim and interested in the Haven legend, asked Chaka how she'd become involved in the quest, how she rated their chances for success, and whether she'd actually read the Mark Twain. His eyes were hazel and he had a good smile. She couldn't help noticing that Quait was watching them with a disapproving frown.

His name was Shom and, at his invitation, she took her wine and they strolled out onto the veranda. She was doing the sort of thing he would have liked to do, he explained. Leaving civilization behind, getting out into the unknown to see what was there. He wished he were going along.

They talked for a while, looked out over the river, and eventually returned to the table. "I hope you find what you're looking for," he said to them. And to Chaka: "How long do you expect to be gone?"

"Maybe years," offered Quait.

"Not past autumn, we hope," she said.

"I'll look forward to your successful return." Their eyes connected. Chaka smiled, and then Shom was gone.

A crowd had gathered around one of the other tables, where a lean man with vulpine features sat with his eyes closed. "No," he was saying to someone in the group, "there is a shadow across your star. Be cautious on the river for the next two weeks. This is not a propitious time for you."

The man to whom he was speaking, nondescript and straw-haired, placed a coin on the table.

Chaka joined the crowd.

"That is Wagram," said a middle-aged prosperous-looking woman behind her.

"Who's Wagram?"

"Who indeed?" said the vulpine man.

"He's a seer," said the woman.

"And you, young lady, are Chaka Milana." He clicked on a smile. "Currently bound for Haven. Or so you hope."

One of the patrons nudged her. "He's never wrong," he said. The patron was an elderly man, probably in his seventies.

"And what do you foresee for us, seer?" asked Chaka.

His eyes closed. Quait got up and came over. He was looking at her curiously.

"You will be successful," he said at last. "You will find your lost treasure, and you will return to Illyria with fame and wealth."

Chaka waited, expecting to hear a catch. When none came, she bowed slightly. "Thank you."

"You're welcome."

She fished a silver coin out of her pocket. That news, after all, was worth something.

The crowd expressed its approval, a few shook her hand happily, and a drunk tried to kiss her.

When they returned to their table, Flojian asked what the seer had said. Chaka told him and he seemed pleased.

"I wouldn't take it too seriously," said Quait. "They always give good news. That's how they earn their tips."

"Not necessarily," said Flojian. "Some of these people are legitimate."

"I wonder," said Silas, "if he was here when Karik went through."

✠ 9 ✠

Unexpectedly, a holiday atmosphere developed. Inns were strategically placed along River Road, so it was possible with good planning to sleep every night in a warm bed. They ate well, drank a little too much, and sometimes partied too late. They frequently paused and occasionally even wandered off onto side tracks to examine archeological sites. On one occasion they stopped for lunch at the home of one of Quait's former military comrades.

They looked at the massive anchor near Piri's Dam, sinking into a forest of sugar maples, trailing a chain that no man could lift. They viewed a restored cannon near Wicker Point, wondering what forgotten war it had seen; and visited the Roadmaker Museum in Kleska.

They passed ancient walls and foundations. Hojjies lined the sides of the road, where they'd been dragged when Argon cleared its highways more than a century before. They came in countless shapes and sizes, some small, some immense. Many were partially buried by accumulating earth.

They spent as much time walking as in the saddle, and they rested frequently. Quait, who'd had some experience with long-distance campaigning, understood how easy it would be to exhaust both horses and people, particularly in this case, where Silas and Flojian were accustomed to a sedentary existence. Silas had begun limping after the first day. But he'd fashioned a walking stick, refused to take extra time in the saddle, and by the end of the week seemed to be doing fine.

Quait enjoyed being the only young male in a company with two attractive women. Avila's charms were by no means inconsiderable, and his appreciation for them did not replace, but found a comfortable niche alongside his passion for Chaka. She stood about an inch taller than he, dark-eyed and mysterious. That she had been a priest added to her exotic aura.

Meantime, Chaka demonstrated an impressive range of abilities. She was an accomplished forester and marksman. She was at home around horses, and seemed capable of walking everybody else, even Quait, into the ground. Although she had been distracted during the first couple of days, a more amiable spirit had emerged once they were well under way.

Cold rain settled in as, on the ninth day, they approached Argon. Had he been with his detachment, Quait knew what the mood would have been. But only Flojian showed any inclination to grumble, and he usually caught himself quickly and stopped. They reined up at Windygate, the last accommodation below the city, and consequently their final evening in beds. They checked in, retired to their rooms, and scrubbed down, luxuriating in the hot water. At dinner that evening, Quait detected a sense of expectancy and possibly of nervousness. Tomorrow they would connect with Wilderness Road, which would take them east, away from civilization. Into the eternal forest.

This was also the evening during which they got into an altercation with an oversized cattle trader who'd had too much to drink. His throat was scarred and he needed dental work. His face looked as if he'd been hit by a plank. But he visibly drooled over Avila. Quait, watching from his chair, felt his muscles bunch and remembered a remark a comrade had once made: *Never pick a fight with a three-hundred-pounder who has broken teeth.*

The cattle trader was sitting at the next table. He grinned at Avila and raised his stein in an elaborate toast. "How about you and me, gorgeous?" he asked. "Shake off these creeps and you can have a *man.*"

Before Quait could respond, Flojian leaped to his feet with both fists clenched. "Back off," he snarled.

Avila tried to intervene. "I can handle this myself," she said.

The trader casually set his beer down. "Stay out of it, dwarf," he told Flojian. He grinned at a friend as if he'd just said something amusing, and signaled for somebody to refill his stein. The friend was only moderately smaller, but every bit as ugly. A boy hurried over and poured cold beer until it overflowed and ran down onto the table.

The trader turned his snag-toothed stare on Flojian, daring him to say more.

"You owe the lady an apology," sputtered Flojian.

"The lady needs a *man,*" he sneered. "If you want to show what you can do, porkchop, I'm right here."

Damn, Quait thought. He got up.

But Flojian, to his surprise, knocked the beer into the trader's lap. That was a mistake, of course. Quait knew that if you have to initiate hostilities against a dangerous opponent, do it with a view to taking him out with the opening salvo.

The trader roared to his feet, wiping his soaked trousers, and came around the table after Flojian. Flojian went into what he thought was a fighter's crouch. But Quait had to give him credit: He didn't back away.

Everything happened at once. The trader cocked his right fist, which looked like a mallet for driving tent pegs; Quait borrowed the pitcher from the young man (who had hovered within range to watch the action) and brought it down over the trader's head; and Avila broke a chair across the shouders of his companion, who had got up a little too quickly. The battle was effectively over from that point. The waiters, who also served as peacekeepers, arrived armed with short clubs. Quait got knocked in the head for his trouble, and the trader (who no longer knew where he was) absorbed a solid blow to the shin. He was taken to the back for repairs and later returned to his table, still glassy-eyed.

As was common practice in that relatively civilized time, the peacekeepers announced to both sides there would be an additional charge for their trouble, apologized if they had seemed to use undue force, and implied that further hostilities would be treated severely. The evening proceeded as if nothing untoward had occurred.

Later, Avila found her opportunity to take Flojian aside. "I appreciated your defending me in there," she said.

Flojian stared back at her. "I'd have done the same for any woman."

Wilderness Road was a Roadmaker highway, twin tracks through the forest, rising into eastern hills and fading finally toward the horizon. It was built on a foundation of concrete and asphalt, which was usually buried by as much as a foot of loam. Often, however, the loam had worn away and the concrete gleamed in the sun. That the highway was still usable, after all these centuries, was a tribute to the engineering capabilities of its makers. Chaka tried to imagine what it had looked like when it was new, when hojjies rolled (by whatever means) along its manicured surface. Behind them to the northwest, the towers of Argon loomed in the midafternoon haze.

They camped on the roadway that night, enjoyed rabbit stew provided by Chaka and Quait, and listened to the sounds of the forest. Avila produced a set of pipes, and Quait a *walloon* (a stringed instrument), and they serenaded the wildlife with ballads and drinking songs. Silas made the first field entry in his journal, and Avila dispensed with her nightly prayer to Shanta.

That was a difficult decision, because she knew hazards lay ahead, and all her instincts demanded that she place her life in the hands of the Goddess. But she rebelled. *My hands*, she thought. It is in my hands, and if I'm going to get through this, I'd better remember it.

Flojian was feeling extraordinarily good about himself. He had twice stood up to loudmouths now. Not bad for a man who reflexively avoided conflict. He had been replaying the incident while they traveled, watching himself challenge the giant, discovering the special kind of joy that an act of courage can bestow. *When things go well.*

His father would have been proud. As Avila had been proud.

Flojian had always ascribed his problems with his father to the fact that Karik had simply not thought much of his son. Flojian had taken no interest in the Roadmaker mysteries, no interest in their cities, no interest in the past. He had never walked through the ancient corridors in which his father had spent most of his intellectual life.

His mother had died when he was two, and Karik had never found time for the child. He'd grown up moving around among aunts and cousins. *Your father's excavating a Roadmaker church in Farroad,* they would tell him. Or, *they found some odd hojjies south of Masandik, and he's trying to figure out what they are.* So he'd resisted the Roadmakers and the Imperium and the library and everything else his father believed in. Just as well. It was all nonsense anyhow. Ironic that he would wind up on this idiot expedition. But the suspicions that had for years engulfed his father's reputation also cast a shadow over Flojian, and consequently over the business. He saw no real choice. Nevertheless, Karik would have approved of his presence. And that fact annoyed him.

There was a sense of excitement that evening, of finally being on the quest. Tomorrow they would reach the League frontier, and shortly thereafter encounter the first markings left by Landon Shay. The adventure was beginning, and there was an almost mystical sense of crossing out of the known world.

This was also their first night under the stars. Flojian drew the watch while the others drifted off to sleep. Armed with a revolver, he slipped into the darkness, checked the animals, and circled the camp. The threats posed by highwaymen or by renegade Tuks had receded in recent years, but he was not one to take security for granted. He noted off-road avenues of approach, but did not believe anyone could get close without alerting the horses.

When he returned to the fireside, only Avila was still awake.

"Can I get you anything?" he asked. He still felt uncomfortable in her presence, but he was determined to tolerate her.

"No, thank you." Her face was ruddy in the firelight. "Big day tomorrow."

Flojian nodded.

"May I ask you a question?" she said.

"Sure."

"Are you a believer?"

"In the gods?"

"Yes."

He glanced at the sky. The moon was a misty glow in the treetops, and the stars looked far away. "Yes," he said. "Without them, there's no point to existence."

She was silent for a time. "I'd like to think they're out there somewhere," she said at last. "But if they are, they're too remote. They shouldn't complain if we neglect them."

"Even the Roadmakers believed," said Flojian. "They left chapels everywhere."

"What good did it do them? They're gone. Everything they accomplished is gone."

The fire was getting low, and Flojian threw a fresh log onto it.

"Despite their power," she said, "and despite their piety, they were only hostages to fortune. Just like us." She took a deep breath and let it out slowly. "All the striving it must have taken to build their world." She sat up, drew the blanket around her shoulders. In the trees, something moved. "There's nothing left except concrete and an assortment of junk that won't decay." Her eyes fastened on him.

"You have to believe in *something,*" said Flojian. "If not the gods, what?"

"Nights like this," said Avila. "Good food. Good friends. And wine to dull the edge of things."

It would have been imprecise to say that the company crossed a border next day when they passed the last outpost. Theoretically, there was no eastern limit to League dominions. No other political entities were believed to exist. Nevertheless, they were entering *terra incognita,* and that fact was underlined for them when, a few miles farther, they found the site of the first sketch.

It was a place where the highway rode the hill-tops. The winds had blown its surface clear, exposing asphalt like bleached bone. Chaka broke out the drawing, and they said, yes, there's that hill to the east, and the line of river over there. And here's where Arin must have stood. Silas made a notation in his journal, and they moved on.

The river was the Ohio, which wandered down from the northeast to join the Mississippi at Argon. It was a majestic, wide stream with forest pushing into the water along both banks. She could see downed bridges in both directions.

Most of the roads in League territories had been generally cleared of hojjies. But now the ancient vehicles began to grow numerous. One hojjy contained a pile of apparently indestructible toys buried under the dust in the back seat. Flojian found another with a case that was made from a leather-like material, but which could not have been leather because it was still pliable and in good condition. When they opened it, they found writing instruments and metallic devices and disks like the ones on display in the museums. They also found a note-book cover with the imprint EXECUTRAK. But there was only dust inside. "Pity," said Silas. "They were able to make everything permanent except paper."

At about midday, another road came out of the woods and looped up to connect with them. Chaka unfolded the map Shannon had drawn for her. "This should be it," she said. "There's a marked tree here somewhere." As they spread out to look, she heard a familiar voice, and saw Jon Shannon sitting on a fallen log. "It's over here," he said.

Quait drew his gun.

"Don't shoot." Chaka slid out of her saddle and hurried forward. "It's Jon." She embraced him. "You're a long way from home," she said.

He nodded and she introduced him around. Shannon shook everybody's hand.

"This is where it starts," he said. He pointed at a tall cottonwood. Three lines were carved into the trunk at eye level, parallel to Wilderness Road.

"What does it mean?" asked Flojian.

"It means you're on the right road. Keep straight. Whichever way you're traveling." He untied three horses and led them out of the woods. A broad-brimmed hat kept the sun out of his face, which seemed devoid of expression.

"Have you changed your mind?" asked Chaka. "Are you coming with us?"

"Yes," he said. "I think I'd like to come along, if the offer's still open."

"Why?" asked Quait.

He shrugged. "Not sure. It just seemed like the right thing to do."

Silas glanced around at the company. "Anybody object?"

"I've known Jon a long time," said Chaka. "He's just what we need."

Quait wondered whether the competition had just arrived. But Shannon looked as if he knew his way around the woods. "Okay by me," he said.

The Ohio looped away to the north, and after a couple of days they lost sight of it. A giant highway crossed above. It had partially collapsed and blocked Wilderness Road. "Used to be a tunnel through here, I guess," said Shannon. Cottonwoods on both sides of the rubble were marked with the parallel lines. Stay straight. "We climb over and continue on the other side," he said.

Within a half-mile, they plunged into heavy forest and Wilderness Road petered out. "Did we go the wrong way?" asked Silas, standing glumly at the head of a half-dozen horses.

"They're headed for Beekum's Trail," said Shannon. "It isn't far."

A thick canopy shut off the sunlight. They moved single file through bushes and thickets. The trees, which were mostly elm and black oak, were marked every fifteen or twenty yards, and Chaka began to develop an appreciation for Landon Shay's foresight.

Ruins appeared. Brick walls, hojjies, an old church, a factory, some shops. Some of the structures were crushed between trees, mute testimony to their age. A metal post had been pushed over, bearing a rectangular sign. Silas wiped it with a cloth.

700 MADISON

"It's a street sign," Silas explained. "There are quite a few of them on display in the Imperium." A few minutes later, they found a second sign, bigger, with an arrow under the legend: *ALBEN BARKLEY MUSEUM.*

The arrow pointed *up*.

"Strange name," said Chaka.

They picked up Beekum's Trail late next morning. It was narrow and heavily overgrown.

"Who was Beekum?" asked Avila.

"A legendary bandit," Silas explained. "He supposedly collected tolls from anyone who passed here. Tolls or heads."

"He was killed by Pelio," said Quait. The equally legendary Argonite hero.

They crossed a tributary of the Ohio on a rickety bridge and stopped to catch some fish for the midday meal.

Beekum's Trail curved north and the forests began to change. The familiar red cedars and white oak and cottonwoods held their own, but new trees filled the woods now, of types they had never seen before. The Ohio reappeared on their left and they camped several consecutive nights along its banks.

These were pleasant evenings, moonlit and unseasonably warm, filled with easy conviviality. They were now in their third week, and everyone was becoming more or less accustomed to life on the open road. On March 7, they came to the place where the great river threw a branch off to the north. "That's the Wabash," said Shannon. "Keep an eye open. There's a ford just ahead, and that's probably where they were heading."

They found two sets of markings, both on cottonwoods, pointing into the river.

"He likes cottonwoods," said Flojian.

Shannon took off his hat and wiped his brow. "Shay'll use them wherever he can," he said. "Makes it easier for us to know what we're looking for."

Chaka was studying the river. "That's a long way across."

Shannon smiled. "It's not as deep as it looks."

"Not as deep as it looks?" she said. "It looks pretty *deep*."

It wasn't the depth so much as the current that gave them trouble. Toward the middle of the river it became quite swift. Piper stumbled and went down and was almost swept away with her rider, but Quait and Avila came to the rescue.

When they reached shore, they quit for the day, wrung out their clothes, and enjoyed a fish dinner.

The trail now moved north along the Wabash, past a sign on a low brick wall: *HOVEY LAKE STATE GAME PRESERVE*. The river was narrower than the Ohio, a placid stream covered each day until late morning with mist. There was no road. The weather turned wet and cold, as if crossing the Ohio had put them into a different climate. The first night they found shelter in a barn. Sleet fell in the morning, and miserable conditions persisted for five consecutive days. The good cheer they had felt during their week on the Ohio dissipated.

On the thirteenth, as they crossed another giant roadway, the weather broke. The sun came out, and the day grew warm. To the west, the new road soared high out over the Wabash, and stopped in midair.

Chaka sat on Piper, watching Silas try to sketch the scene into his journal. "Not a bridge to travel at night," she said.

They rode into a glade bounded on the far side by a low ridge. Shannon brought them to a halt. "This is worth seeing," he said.

Chaka looked around and saw nothing. The others were equally puzzled.

"The ridge," said Shannon.

It was long and straight, emerging from the trees to their right, passing across their line of advance, and disappearing back into the forest. It had a rounded crest, covered with grass and dead leaves. Otherwise, it was remarkable for its lack of noteworthiness.

"It's not really straight," said Shannon. "It only looks that way because you can't see much of it. In fact, it makes a perfect circle. Seventy miles around."

Avila leaned forward in her saddle. "The Devil's Eye," she said.

One of the horses was nuzzling Chaka.

"You've heard of it?" Shannon looked surprised.

"Oh yes. I knew it was out here somewhere, but I didn't expect to see it."

"The ridge is always the same height. Sometimes the land drops away and it *looks* higher. And sometimes the ground rises and the ridge disappears altogether."

"What's the Devil's Eye?" asked Chaka, feeling a chill work its way down her spine.

Avila dismounted and shielded her eyes. "It's supposed to be the place where the Roadmakers conjured up a demon to help them look into Shanta's secrets. So they could steal her divinity." She looked uncomfortable. "I always thought it was probably just a loose configuration of hills. That people were exaggerating about the geometry."

"Oh, no," said Shannon. "Nobody exaggerated about this place."

"How'd it get here?" asked Flojian, his voice hushed. "It can't be natural."

Shannon let them look, and then led them back into the woods, following the ridge. They were riding upslope, and consequently the summit was getting lower. Beyond the crest, the tops of several ruined buildings came into view.

Chaka guided her horse close to Shannon. "Do *you* know what it is?" she asked, hoping for a more mundane explanation.

He shook his head. "I have no idea."

Silas could have identified Christianity as a major

religion of the Roadmaker epoch. But his information was limited to the few volumes that had survived into his own age. He could not have known, for example, that, of the long panoply of supernatural names mentioned in the Scriptures, only the Devil's lived on.

✠ 10 ✠

*The ridge was matted with leaves and dead grass, and sprin*kled with black cherry trees and yellow poplars. It was almost flat now, muscling into a rising slope. An old road crossed and curved in toward the ancient buildings.

Three of an original group of six or seven were still standing. Two were gray stone structures, half a dozen floors, windows punched out. The third was constructed primarily of large curved slabs of the kind of material that looked like glass but couldn't have been, because it was still intact. All of the walls within six feet of the ground were smeared with arcane symbols, reversed letters and upside-down crosses and crescent moons and flowing lines. "They're supposed to suppress local demons," Avila said.

The glass building was about ten stories high. On the roof, a large gray disk had fallen off its mount onto the cornice and seemed on the verge of plunging to the terrace below. Rows of double windows lined the upper floors. At its base, wide pseudo-glass doors opened onto the terrace.

There was also a barn and a greenhouse, of more recent vintage. But they too looked long abandoned.

"Ever been inside any of them?" asked Quait.

Shannon shook his head. "Bad luck, inside the loop."

"You don't really believe that," said Chaka.

"No. But that's what the Tuks say." He shrugged. "I never saw any reason to go in."

Quait was beginning to steer them toward it. "I wonder what its purpose was," he said.

"Religious," suggested Avila. "What else could it have been? Still, it doesn't make much sense, even in those terms. It's not very inspirational, is it?" She shook her head, puzzled. "You'd expect that any ceremonial use would take place at the center. It would be, what, twenty-some miles across? So from the center, even assuming the trees didn't block your view, you still couldn't see the ridge. The effect at best would be that of standing in an open plain."

The ground dropped away again and the ridge reappeared. Silas spotted a spring and reined up. "Why don't we break off for the day?" he said.

"It's a little early," suggested Shannon. "You don't really want to stop *here*, do you?"

He did.

Quait was reluctant. Not because he was superstitious; he just didn't believe in pushing his luck. He would have been perfectly happy to get well away before dark. But he didn't want to give in publicly to fright tales. And apparently neither did anyone else, although the horses seemed unsettled.

Finally, Chaka took the plunge. "It *might* be haunted," she said. "It's possible."

Silas smiled reassuringly. "It's all right, Chaka." He glanced around at the others as if he expected their moral support. "There's nothing here to worry about."

They all looked off in different directions.

So they made camp at the foot of the ridge, and within the hour were seated around a fire, finishing off venison that had been left over from the noon meal. The night had grown cool, and the general mood was subdued. There was no loud talk; Quait's walloon stayed strapped to a saddlebag; and the occasional laughter had a hollow ring. Silas tried to lighten the atmosphere by commenting on how easily people are taken in by their own fears. If anything, his remarks deepened their gloom. Quait sat during the evening meal facing the long wall so nothing could sneak down on him.

The buildings were hidden by a combination of forest and ridge.

"Does anybody know anything more about this place?" asked Silas. "How about you, Avila?"

Avila shook her head. "The official position of the Order is that the Devil's Eye is of no consequence, an artifact like any other artifact. But we know that some of the Roadmaker ruins retain a life force, that there are stirrings, and possibly unholy activity. The common wisdom, although no one in authority will admit it, is that there *might well be* a diabolical presence." She tried a smile. "I don't want to unnerve anyone. But the Mentors would be horrified to know that we were here."

"Damn," said Shannon. "That's just what I was trying to tell you."

"What about it, Silas?" asked Quait. "Are there devils in the world? What do *you* think?"

"No," he said. "Certainly not."

Flojian was sitting wrapped in a blanket, his face moving in the firelight. "The truth is," he said, "that we don't know the way the world works. You'd like a nice mechanical cosmos, Silas. Cause and effect. Everything very mathematical. Supernatural forces need not apply. But we don't really know, do we?"

The fire crackled and the trees sighed.

Quait wasn't sure when he had fallen asleep, but he was suddenly aware of Chaka shaking him gently.

"What is it?" he whispered.

There was a glow above the ridge. Barely discernible, but it was there. "There's a light in the glass building."

He climbed out of his blanket and pulled on trousers and a shirt.

"What do we do?" she said.

"What would *you* recommend?"

"I think we should clear out."

Quait tried to look amused and confident. "There's a natural explanation." He strapped on his holster. "But I think we better wake the others."

Minutes later, they all stood on top of the ridge, looking at two illuminated ground floor windows.

"Something's moving in there," said Flojian.

The angle didn't allow them to make out what it was.

"Let it go," advised Shannon. "It has nothing to do with why we're here."

"It has everything to do with why we're here," said Silas. "We're here to learn about the Roadmakers."

"Silas," he said patiently, "it's probably just a couple of people like us, holed up. You go in there, it might be a fight."

"The *ridge,*" said Silas. "Maybe there's a connection with the ridge."

"That's unlikely," pursued the forester.

"But who knows?" Silas started down the side of the hill. "I'll be back."

Chaka joined him. Quait asked them to wait and went back to the campsite for a lantern, which he left dark.

"All right," Shannon said, checking his weapon and shoving it into his holster. "Let's go. But I hope nobody gets his idiot head blown off."

"No, Jon," said Silas. "If we walk into something, I'd rather some of us be outside. And I'd like you to be in a position to lead the rescue. Okay? Stay here. If we don't come back, use your judgment."

Shannon looked unhappy.

It was dark on the hill. Quait stepped into a hole and Silas tripped over a vine. Nevertheless, they made it safely to the bottom of the ridge and crossed the fifty yards or so that separated them from the buildings.

A dozen stone steps, bordered by a low wall, led up to the terrace. "Horses in the barn," said Quait, detouring to take a look. There were three. With a wagon.

They crept up to the lighted windows and looked in.

The lamp was bright, and it burned steadily. It stood atop a side table, illuminating an armchair. But they saw no sign of a flame. There were several other pieces of furniture in the room, including a sofa. A cabinet held a set of unbound books.

"What do you think?" said Silas. His fingers lingered near his gun. He wasn't used to the weapon, and Quait had noticed he walked with a mild swagger when he wore it. Tonight, though, the swagger wasn't there.

Quait tried the windows. They were locked.

"I'd like to know how that lamp works," said Chaka.

They watched for a while, but the room stayed empty. They returned at last to the front, climbed the steps, and crossed the terrace. There'd been four doors. Three were still in place; the fourth was missing, its space protected by a piece of thick gray canvas. Beyond, Quait could see a shadowy lobby, and the silhouettes of chairs and tables.

An inscription was engraved across the face of the building: *THE RICHARD FEYNMAN SUPERCOLLIDER.*

"Who was Richard Feynman?" Chaka asked.

Silas shook his head. "Don't know."

Quait glanced back up at the ridge. Shannon and the others were invisible, but he knew they were there watching. "Stay put," he said, and padded over to the sheet of canvas.

Chaka and Silas were already following him. He tried unsuccessfully to wave them back, and slipped through the opening.

Had Chaka not been present, Quait would have looked a bit more, hoping to find a less direct way in. But the horses in the barn suggested the occupant was human rather than demonic. He wasn't going to pass up a chance to play a heroic role by fumbling around looking for back doors.

A long counter stretched half the length of the rear wall. He moved a few steps away from the entrance, away from the glass so that he was not silhouetted against the stars. The floor was thick with dirt and leaves. There were two other doorways leading into the area and a staircase immediately to the left.

"Hello," he called softly. "Anybody here?"

The wind sucked at the canvas.

He satisfied himself that the lobby was empty, and moved into a corridor. The walls were dirty white, pocked, and streaked with water stains. Doorways opened on either side, most into bare rooms. Other spaces, like the one they'd seen from outside, were loaded with Roadmaker furniture.

At the end of the corridor he turned left, toward the light that he could see leaking under a door.

He checked each room as he went by, saw no one, and pushed finally into the illuminated room. He was surprised by a surge of warm, dry air, although no fire was visible. The heat seemed to be coming from a series of pipes protruding from the wall. He was so absorbed by the device that he was not aware someone had come in behind him.

"It'll burn you," said a voice.

Idiot. Quait spun around and looked into the muzzle of a Makar bear rifle.

His gaze moved slowly from the weapon to a pair of narrow, irritated eyes. Little man, bald rounded skull, thick forearms, gray-black beard. Sharp white teeth. "I mean no harm, friend," Quait said.

"And you'll do none." Gravelly voice. "Take the gun out very slowly and put it down or I'll kill you where you stand." To Quait's discomfort, the man sounded jittery.

"Take it easy," Quait said. "I'm no threat." He eased the weapon out and dropped it onto a sofa.

"I can see that." The man took a long minute to consider him. "Who are you?" he asked. "Why are you here?"

"My name's Quait Esterhok. I'm just passing through. It's cold outside. I came in looking for shelter. I didn't realize anyone was here."

"Over there." He wanted Quait in the middle of the room.

Quait complied. "Who are *you*?" he asked.

The bald-headed man kept the weapon aimed at a point between Quait's eyes.

"Look," said Quait. "If you want me to leave, I'll leave." He took a tentative step to get out, but something in the man's expression warned him to go no farther.

"I don't see many visitors," the bald man said. "Who's with you?"

"Nobody."

He glanced at one of the chairs. "Sit."

Quait sat.

"Nobody travels this country alone, Esterhok. Now, I think your chances of getting out of here without a couple of holes in your carcass are going to improve considerably if you tell me the truth."

"I wouldn't lie to a man holding a gun," Quait said.

While they stared at each other, Chaka called his name. "You okay, Quait?" she cried. And, lower but still discernible, "Where'd he go, Silas?"

Quait grinned at his captor. "I'm okay," he called. "But stay where you are. There's a man here with a gun."

"Tell them to come in here where I can see them."

"No," said Quait. "I won't do that."

The man wiped his face with his sleeve. He wore a crumpled gray shirt and baggy black trousers. "You in the hall," he rumbled. "Come in here now, all of you, guns down, hands up, or I'll kill this one."

That brought a long silence. The bald man backed into a corner of the room so he could cover both Quait and the doorway.

"Don't shoot anybody," said Chaka. She came in, hands raised. Silas followed directly behind.

"What are you," sputtered Silas, "a lunatic?"

"That's an open question, I suppose." The bald man glanced into the corridor. "Is there anyone else?"

"No," said Quait. "You've got everybody."

"I hope so. If there are any surprises, I'm going to start shooting. And you three will be first. Now, what are you doing in my house?"

Quait tried to explain. Silas, true to his nature, had focused on the handful of unbound volumes in the cabinet. Suddenly he sighed. "Ilion Talley," he said. "Where did you get *these*?"

The bald man eyed him suspiciously. "How did you know my name?"

"You?" said Silas. "I was talking about the author of these books."

"*I* am he."

Silas frowned and pursed his lips. "Ilion Talley's dead."

"Oh, not as dead as some would like."

"Are *you* really Talley? Of Masandik?"

"Of course, you nitwit. Who else would I be?" The rifle wavered and his voice softened. "You know of me, then?"

"Everyone knows the Mechanic," said Silas. He was staring hard at the bald man. "I do believe . . ." he said. "I believe it really *is* you." He clapped his hands. "Wonderful. This makes the entire trip worthwhile. Whatever else happens." He plunged forward, completely forgetful of the weapon.

Talley hesitated and then, if he'd had a mind to shoot, it was too late. Silas was by him, pumping his hand. "Marvelous," Silas said. "We met years ago, but I was very young and you'd have no way of remembering. My name's Silas Glote."

Quait knew the Mechanic's reputation. Ilion Talley had been renowned throughout the five cities as a philosopher, artist, and engineer. He had designed and overseen the construction of Masandik's superlative water and sewage system, with its state-of-the-art pumps; he had sculpted the magnificent *Lyka* for her temple at Farroad; he had devised the modern repeating rifle.

"And you're not dead," said Silas.

"Apparently not." Talley laid the weapon on a table.

He'd reportedly died twenty years before, in Masandik. It had been put about that a committee of citizens had charged him and a young woman with impiety, and burned both at the stake.

Talley waved everyone to sit down, and leaned

back against the desktop. "It's nice to know I haven't been forgotten. And that there are still people who think well of me."

"You were accused of defiling the gods," said Silas.

"So they said I was dead, did they?" He chuckled. "A more incompetent pack of fools I've never known."

"What happened?" asked Quait.

"Yolanda," he said.

"Pardon?"

"I hired Yolanda to copy manuscripts. She was pretty, so my students were naturally drawn to her. They found excuses to come to my office. They asked questions. And Yolanda forgot that she was not their teacher. She also believed that teachers were bound to the truth." He fixed Silas with a long gloomy stare. "You look like a teacher." It was not a question.

"I am."

"Then you understand her naïveté. I tried to explain the political realities to her, the need to avoid offending the community's sensibilities." He shrugged. "She wouldn't listen, and it got around after a while that she did not believe in the gods. That she was a profane influence on young people."

Quait frowned. "But the upper classes are mostly skeptics. Were these not *their* children at the school?"

"Of course," said Talley. "But what these people believed, and what they were prepared to admit publicly, were not at all the same thing."

"They said you were both killed," said Silas.

"We were gone before they arrived. I don't know who they killed, if anyone, but it most certainly was not *me*. It *was* cold, however. Dead of winter. Yolanda died on the road, so I suppose they achieved one of their goals." His eyes clouded. "I've been here since, for the most part. No place else to go. Nobody would have given me sanctuary."

"Twenty years is a long time," said Silas. "Things have changed. You're a hero now in Masandik. They would welcome you back."

"Twenty years. Is it really that long?" He laughed. "Quite a few of the scoundrels must have died."

Silas glanced over the volumes, lined up neatly in a cabinet. "May I ask what you've been writing about?" Quait would have liked to examine the volumes themselves, but one did not simply take it upon himself to pick up another person's book.

"I've completed the definitive history of the Baranji Empire," Talley said. "There are also ruminations on the nature of the Roadmakers' world." He came away from the desktop, opened a book, and laid it where they could see its table of contents. "This is a collection of philosophical speculations. The nature of evil. Whether man has a purpose. Whether there is such a thing as absolute morality. And so on."

"No wonder they were after you," laughed Chaka.

They all joined in, and the doleful mood dissipated. "You must forgive my caution. Visitors here are seldom civil." Talley returned his attention to his books. "I also have a study of the types of trees, their characteristics, their growing seasons, the best time to plant. And an analysis of the customs and ethical systems of the local Tuks. And a political history of Masandik." He took down several more for his visitors to look at, and it struck Quait that the man had been writing here alone for years and had probably never before been able to show his work to anyone. Or at least to anyone who gave a damn.

"I'm forgetting my manners," said Talley. "Would you like some tea?"

He set up cups, left the room, and returned moments later with a steaming pot. "It's just as well things happened the way they did," he said, pouring. "I've spent my time here far more productively than I could have in Masandik. Tell me, does the Legate still rule?"

"He was overthrown more than a decade ago," said Silas. "Masandik is a republic. They're all republics now, all the cities."

"Well," said Talley gloomily, "I'm not sure that's such good news. Mob rule, it sounds like."

Quait had gone over to investigate the lamp, which continued to put out a steady glow. "You have heat without fire," he said, "and light without a flame." The light source was inside a glass tube.

"How does it work?" asked Chaka.

Talley smiled enigmatically. "Roadmaker technology. I'm not sure myself of the principles behind it. But I'll learn in time." He touched a knob and the light died. Touched it again and it came back on.

"Marvelous," said Silas.

The lamp was unpretentious, apparently metal, rounded at its base, lacking the ornate style of the better class of Roadmaker art objects that were popular in League cities. On closer examination, Quait saw that it was not metal at all. It was made of one of the time-defying artificial substances.

"I had several of them originally, but they've been giving out one by one." He shook his head in silent wonder. "They're really quite remarkable. They grow dim on occasion, but I have only to connect them to a device in the basement to replenish the light."

Quait returned to the source of the room's warmth, the pipes. There were six of them, in parallel loops, protruding from one wall. "And this?" he asked.

"Ah," said Talley. "This is *my* invention." He waited until everyone had had time to inspect it. "It's really quite simple," he said, smiling broadly. "Please follow me." He swept up the lamp and led the way into the next room.

It was spacious, with a partially collapsed ceiling supported by a pair of wooden beams and a boarded-up fireplace. A long battered worktable stood in a corner. Pots and ladles hung from hooks, and a heavy, dust-laden purple curtain covered the windows. A stock of firewood had been laid by, and a furnace crouched in the center of the room.

The furnace was mounted on four bear-claw legs. It was divided into upper and lower compartments. Quait could hear water boiling in the upper. A wide black duct connected the back of the furnace with the ceiling. A gray pipe, much narrower and wrapped with gauze, plunged into the wall. "This one," the one joined to the ceiling, "carries off the smoke," he explained. "*This* carries steam into radiant devices in the office and the far wing." He smiled broadly, vastly pleased with himself. "The entire suite stays quite comfortable."

"Brilliant," observed Silas. He produced his notebook and began drawing a picture of the apparatus.

Talley's shrug said that it was nothing.

Quait was, of course, familiar with furnaces, which had begun to replace fireplaces in some Illyrian homes. They were a more efficient means of heating a room. But it had never occurred to him that it might be possible to transport excess heat to remote places in a dwelling. Silas was ecstatic. He fired a barrage of questions and wrote down the answers. "If you have no objection," he said, "we'll take this idea home with us."

"Whatever you wish. It's really only a minor thing." He sipped his tea. "And where are *you* headed? What brings you to the far country?"

"We're hoping to find Haven," said Silas.

Talley's expression changed. He had possibly been alone too long to hide his feelings, but it now became apparent that he'd decided he was in the presence of cranks. "I see. Well, I wish you all good fortune."

"Actually," said Silas defensively, "it's not as far-fetched as it sounds."

"I'm sure it isn't."

They were moving again, Talley walking them back toward his workroom. "What's the ridge all about?" Chaka asked.

Talley looked puzzled.

"The one that surrounds this place," she prompted.

"Oh. The *ring*. It's a tunnel. The people who built the facility hoped to use it to learn how the Earth was created."

Silas showed no reaction, but Quait felt uneasy.

"Avila was right," said Chaka.

"Avila is one of our friends," Quait explained. "She said much the same thing."

"How did they intend to do that?" asked Silas.

"Don't know. I can't read the results."

"You mean they were destroyed?"

"I mean I can't read them."

Silas looked around, as if he expected to see them lying somewhere on a table. "Maybe we could help?"

Talley chuckled deep in his throat. "Of course," he said. "Please come with me."

He took them out into the lobby and down two flights of stairs. They turned left into another corridor, lined with doorways. The walls were gray and crumbly.

"In here." They passed into another workroom. Rows of dull white metal cases occupied a central table and most of the wall space. Black cables snaked across the floor. The room looked surprisingly clean.

Another door, made of heavy metal, stood ajar. "This is the entry to the ring," he said. He pulled it open, hit a wall switch, and interior lights blossomed.

They looked into a tunnel. Walls and ceiling were lined with cables and ridges, and a grate had been placed over the concrete floor. The passageway gradually curved away in both directions. "It's still whole," said Talley. "All the way around. Seventy miles."

"Are you sure?" asked Chaka.

"I walked it once. It took a week."

She glanced at Quait.

"It's not as unsettling as it might seem, young lady," Talley said. "There are hatches every few miles. They didn't all open, but some of them still work."

They went back and looked at the lines of cases. Quait had seen artifacts that resembled this kind of equipment, but never in such good condition, and never so many. He saw his first legible keyboard. He saw dark glass surfaces in pseudo-metal frames. The boxes were of varying sizes and shapes, all linked by a maze of cables.

"Now," said Talley. "What is the true nature of the world? The Baranji believed these machines were used to perform experiments, and to store data. If that's so, it's reasonable to assume that everything that was learned here was put into them."

Quait thought that sounded good, but he didn't know exactly what it meant.

Silas was also showing mixed reactions. "Then," he said, "let's break them open and take a look."

"That seems simple enough," added Chaka.

"No. It's not simple at all. The data are not in written form."

Silas's eyes narrowed. "What other form is there?"

"I'm not sure how to explain it. I don't understand it myself. But they may have had a technique for encoding information in invisible fields."

"I see," said Silas, who obviously didn't.

"It's true," said Talley. "Baranji technicians worked on the problem for almost a century. I have their notes."

Silas glanced at Chaka. "Invisible fields," he said. "It doesn't sound possible."

Talley was unfazed. "You've seen the lamp. Don't underestimate ancient technology."

"How," asked Chaka gently, "do you get the machines to give up their information?"

"Let me show you." He led them to the back of the room, where one of the framed glass sheets was connected by cable to a glass globe. A rock was suspended in the center of the globe, and six coils were positioned around it. The globe was connected to a wheel, over which a saddle had been mounted. Talley climbed onto the saddle, inserted his feet into a set of pedals, and began to turn the wheel. As the wheel turned, the coils moved around the rock. "This is a force bottle. The rock's a lodestone. When the copper coils rotate around the lodestone, they divert a force from it and pass that force through the cable. I don't quite understand the effect myself, but it works."

Talley built up speed and the coils whirled. Suddenly the glass sheet, which had been dark and inert, *lit up*.

Silas backed away. He heard Chaka catch her breath.

"Incredible," said Silas. "What's happening?"

"The generated force makes the machines work. I believe that if I can create enough of it, the machines will *talk*."

Silas touched the globe cautiously as Talley left off pedaling. The light faded. "Talley," he asked, "How fast can you pedal?"

Talley laughed. "That task would be beyond any man, Silas. But we're close to the Wabash. I'm going to build a much larger version of the force bottle, and I plan to let the river god, so to speak, sit in the saddle. When you come back, *if* you come back, I expect to know whatever the Roadmakers knew about creation." He took a deep breath. "Stop in and say hello. By then we should have much to talk about."

✠ 11 ✠

They needed the better part of a day to put the ring-shaped ridge behind them. The woods gave way to an open plain and they were eventually able to look back on perhaps twenty miles of the enigmatic construction. Chaka sat in her saddle and imagined the elderly mystic walking all the way around in the dark. No wonder he was half mad.

Yet he had produced the light in the glass. They talked of little else for two days, and were so engrossed in speculation that even Jon Shannon was slow to see two Tuks ride out of a wall of forest directly into their path. Both cradled rifles in their arms. They wore stitched animal hides and fur-lined boots. The taller of the two, who was almost Shannon's size, drifted to a stop.

His companion rode on ahead a few paces, far enough to ensure they couldn't both be taken down by a single burst of gunfire, and turned to watch. He was also big. An oversized fur hat perched casually on the back of his head.

"It's okay," Shannon said. "They're friendly."

He raised his hand. To Chaka's considerable relief, the two men raised theirs. Shannon rode forward; words were exchanged, and smiles appeared.

"Old friends," commented Flojian.

"This is Mori," Shannon said, introducing the taller, "of the Oriki clan." Mori was in his thirties, blue eyes, thick brown hair, beard, and quite handsome, in a rough-cut sort of way. He had the whitest teeth

Chaka had ever seen. He bowed slightly to the women and pronounced everyone welcome.

"And Valian, his spiritual brother." Valian removed his hat. His hair was also brown, but cut short. He had dark, intelligent eyes, and was maybe two years younger and twenty pounds leaner than Mori.

They exchanged greetings.

"Our home is nearby," said Mori. "We'd be honored if you would stay with us tonight."

Silas looked at Shannon, and Chaka read his expression. Was it safe?

"Strangers are sacred with the Oriki," said Mori.

Shannon nodded.

An hour later, in deep woodland, they rode into a hamlet. It was so effectively a part of the forest that Chaka did not immediately pick out the log dwellings, which were scattered among trees and shrubbery. There was no clearing of the land, and consequently no obvious external sign betraying the presence of the people of the forest.

A small group, composed mostly of children, gathered to greet them. Like the Illyrians, the Oriki displayed no distinctive racial type. Some were dark, some pale, but the vast majority favored a middle tone; some had flat noses, others had epicanthic folds. They looked healthy and happy, and they obviously enjoyed visitors.

Clan members descended on the companions with offers of bread and fruit. Chaka's red hair provoked laughter. (For no readily apparent reason, red hair was the one physical characteristic that seemed to be missing.) Some wanted to inspect the newcomers' clothing and weapons. Others wanted only to *touch* the visitors. "They think we're strong," Shannon explained, "because travelers are always protected by spirits. Touching us gives them a share of that strength."

They were taken to a warm hut and given fresh water, more food, and a pitcher of wine. They washed, changed clothes, and went out to explore the hamlet.

The Oriki were anxious to talk. They were happy to see Shannon again. Had his friends been to Oriki country before? What were their homes like? Were they aware that the land ahead was haunted?

Chaka explained they'd been on the road for almost a month, and that they'd never been this far north before. She was happy, she said, to be among friends and in comfortable quarters.

Where were they going?

Haven was a concept that did not lend itself easily to explanation. The Oriki had no notion of the collapse of civilization. And they did not read. So Avila eventually settled by telling her hosts simply that she intended to look at the world. And to visit her neighbors.

Mori introduced them to the Ganji, who was both chief and shaman.

The Ganji was about seventy, with a wispy gray beard and an appearance so ordinary that he could easily have passed as an Illyrian grocer. Later, the only characteristic that Chaka remembered was a pair of alert green eyes that seemed peculiarly mischievous in a man of his position and years.

He informed them that a celebratory dinner would be held that evening in their honor in the Hall of the World. He understood they were leaving the next day, and hoped to make their visit memorable.

The Hall of the World did not rise above the treetops. It was nevertheless an impressive, rambling, log-and-brick structure that occupied the south side of the settlement. It was mostly one vast room, a meeting place designed to accommodate the entire Oriki population if necessary. The interior was lined with fireplaces and filled with tables rising in amphitheater style from the center. Weapons, animal skins, drums, and tapestries hung on every square foot of wall. Woven mats covered the floors, and a gallery looked down from the rear of the hall. There were no windows to break up the general gloom, but lamps glowed cheerfully in wall brackets, and candles were set on the tables. To Chaka, who was accustomed to a relatively elegant architectural style and the quiet and orderly pace of life in Illyria, the hall possessed a semi-barbaric flavor. She was not certain what to expect, despite Shannon's assurances.

A substantial crowd of about two hundred had already assembled. A drumbeat picked up as Chaka and her companions filed down to the central area, matching their pace with a military rhythm. A chant began, accompanying the drumbeat, and people chortled and beat their hands on the tables. "They're wishing us a happy journey," Shannon assured her.

Chaka enjoyed the attention, but she couldn't shake the feeling that her hosts were somewhat condescending.

"Well," said Shannon, "it's true they *do* feel superior. They think we're decadent. Luxury-loving."

Mori escorted them down through the various levels of the chamber to a large round table set at the center of the hall. It was decorated with bits of bunting and flowers and standards. "You'll be eating with the Ganji himself," he said. Stewards arrived immediately to fill their cups with wine.

They were scarcely seated when the sound of the drum changed. The beat became more majestic, pipes and flutes joined in, and the crowd fell silent and rose.

Shannon signaled and the six companions also stood up. In the manner of their hosts, they bowed their heads.

The Ganji came in from the back of the hall. He moved down the central aisle, stopping now and then to shake a hand or whisper to someone. He seemed very much like one of the new brand of politicians that the Republic had produced.

When he reached his table, he surprised Chaka by remembering everyone's name. He greeted each in turn, expressed his fondest hope that they would find the meal satisfactory, assured them the wine was the finest that could be obtained, and guaranteed that they would enjoy the entertainment. It seemed odd that a man of such mundane appearance could lead these people effectively. But when the hall had filled and he stood to speak, she understood. His voice was warm and compelling. The Ganji was born to command.

She never learned his name. "The position is eternal," Shannon explained. "When a Ganji is appointed, he gives up his own name. Or *she* does: There have been a few women. But the intent is that there be only *one* Ganji, for all time. When you take the job you lose your self and merge into the line."

The Ganji welcomed the audience, and invited them to join him in greeting their visitors. He asked each guest to stand while he explained that person's importance. Silas was a scholar and a man of great wisdom; Shannon roamed the wide forests, keeping safe those entrusted to his care; Avila was a physician of considerable skill; Quait was a warrior; Flojian was a maker of boats; and Chaka a tamer of horses.

"Where did he get *that*?" Chaka whispered to Shannon, who shrugged and tried to look innocent.

The crowd cheered each member of the company

in turn, rattling their wooden dishes and pounding on their tables. They chanted the name each time the Ganji finished his description. Sometimes they got it right. Quait came out as *Queep Esterhonk*. But no one cared.

"Our guests are going north," the Ganji said, "into the dark land. Let us wish them good fortune. And if it happens that, during this life, they come this way again, they will know they can find refuge with the Oriki." More applause, while Chaka wondered precisely what he was implying.

"He's good," Flojian whispered to her. "Some of the people back home could take lessons from this guy."

Shannon commented to the Ganji that it was the first time in his life he'd ever sat at a head table. "I didn't even make it at my wedding," he said, and the Ganji roared with laughter and slapped his cup on the wooden board.

Silas rose to speak for the companions. He said that it was good to find friends waiting in a part of the world he had not visited before. And he hoped that, when any of the Oriki came to Illyria, they would look him up. (He'd had some reservations about that comment, but Shannon assured him it was okay, that everyone understood it was only ceremonial.)

When he was finished, there was more cheering, and the food arrived. Great quantities of steaming pork and beef were carried to the tables, and carrots and potatoes and yams. And wine and ale.

"We could do some trading with these people," said Flojian, examining a carafe. "Some of these pieces are quite nice. It'd command a decent price at home." He showed it to Avila. "Don't you think?"

"It might command a decent price here, too," she replied. "Don't be too sure the Oriki don't know the value of their work."

The Ganji led their table in a prayer of thanksgiving to Shanta, and the diners fell to.

A group of musicians with drums and stringed instruments filed out onto a dais and began to play. The music was soft and slow, like a moonlit wind or a wide river in late summer. During the meal, people came from all over the hall to introduce themselves, embrace the travelers, and wish them good fortune.

The result was that the companions were probably the last persons in the hall to finish their meals. When they did, an entertainer appeared and led the crowd in a series of rollicking songs celebrating the twin arts of drinking and fornicating.

"Back home," said Flojian, obviously embarrassed, "someone would call the police."

"Stay with it," said Shannon. "We're in their country. Let's not do anything to offend anyone."

A comedian followed. He did a series of jokes, most of which Chaka didn't quite understand. But she heard one that poked fun at the size of the Ganji's ears. She glanced at him, shocked, and noticed that his ears *were* somewhat large. More important, he was laughing as hard as anyone.

The musicians, who had left off for the comedian, picked up with a raucous tempo. Dancers appeared, attractive young men and women, clothed mostly in anklets and rings and bracelets. They leaped onto the tables, which had by now been cleared of all except drinking cups, and moved sinuously and gracefully through the firelight, paying special attention to the visitors. Chaka found herself face to face, so to speak, with a male member of the troupe. But she bore up with good humor and nonchalance, surprised that it was possible to combine so effectively the exotic and the absurd.

The Ganji caught her eye, smiled benignly, and raised his cup to her. Then, as if nothing out of the way were happening, he turned to Silas. "I wish I could go with you."

A gorgeous female dancer with long chestnut hair, a neckband, and a pair of anklets, had caught the old man's attention. He tried to answer without losing his concentration. "Why is that, Ganji?"

The Ganji looked puzzled. "For the same reason you go. There is much mystery in the land. I would like some answers."

"I'm not certain we'll get any." Silas smiled pleasantly at the Ganji, but his eyes never left the chestnut-haired dancer. "If we do, we will certainly make it a point to come here again."

"I suspect," said Shannon, grinning, "we'll make it a point to come back in any case, Ganji. The Oriki offer many delights to weary travelers."

"Thank you," said the Ganji. "You are always welcome among us, Jon. As are your friends." His expression hardened. "Be careful. The country north of the Wabash is very strange."

He was about to elaborate, but he apparently thought better of it. Instead he glanced toward Chaka, smiled, and spoke to Shannon. Shannon listened, looked her way, and said *no*. He said a great deal more, but the *no* was the only thing she could hear. When the dinner had ended, she asked him what it was about.

"He noticed you were interested in the dancers," he said. "He wondered whether you might have wished to join them."

She must have reddened, because he laughed. "Chaka, the dance has spiritual significance as well as entertainment value. I'm sure he was only concerned for your soul. Visitors have been known to participate, but they are rarely asked. Consider it an honor."

✠ 12 ✠

*Rubble filled the forest for miles. They passed a row of con-*nected identical brick houses, two stories high, wedged among sweetgums and red cedars. They saw occasional pseudo-metal posts and tangles of corroded machinery. In the middle of a glade they found an old stone bench, imprinted: *COURTESY OF PETER'S CLOTHING*. They also paused beside a marker: *TO ST. MARY OF THE WOODS, 2 MI.*

An arrow pointed the direction. Toward the Wabash.

"Saint Mary is one of the aspects of their deity," Silas explained. "It was probably a temple site or a shrine." And he gazed wistfully about. "There is so much to see here. It's a pity we have so little time."

"What do we know about Saint Mary?" asked Chaka.

Silas shrugged. "Not much."

"In fact," said Avila, "almost the only things we *do* know about the religion of the Roadbuilders is what we've been able to gather from *The Brothers Karamazov*."

"And from some of the surviving signs outside their churches, where they exhibited didactic sayings for the edification of the faithful." Silas looked like a kid in a bazaar. "There's a collection of them in the library, to which we should be able to make a few additions when we get home." He looked off toward the river. "Saint Mary was the female aspect of an omnipotent god," he continued. "We suspect she represented the deity's creative power and compassion."

"That's it?"

"That's it." They were on horseback, riding through the late afternoon. The woods smelled of approaching spring. "Avila's right," continued Silas. "We know what Dostoevsky tells us. We know they had orders of holy men, and that there was a sharp division between the religious authorities and the faith of the common people. We know they believed that people pass through this life and face a judgment after death. We know they struggled with the problem of evil."

"And what is the problem of evil, Silas?" asked Flojian.

They were moving slowly, not off-road, but in the presence of many roads, looking for Shay's telltale marks. "That, in a world governed by a benevolent divine power," Silas said, "the innocent suffer."

"That children die," said Avila. "That prayer does not work. That, in our most desperate moments, despite the promises of the scriptures, we are quite alone."

Flojian sighed. He wore a black cape that lent him a moderately dashing appearance. Moderately, because he never seemed to enjoy himself. The world was an ill-lit, gloomy place, and one had to struggle along as best one could, obey the rules, and put a good face on everything. He was therefore a believer in those things that did not require effort or sacrifice, and a skeptic where the results showed up on a profit and loss statement. Defying the gods tended to irritate people and was therefore bad for business. Flojian's reflexes kicked in. "You sound bitter," he told Avila.

"I don't mean to be," she said. "I'm sorry. Let it go."

Later she confided to Chaka that she'd promised herself to stay out of religious discussions. "They just get people upset," she said, "and they never lead anywhere."

"You're not doing a very good job of it," said Chaka.

"I know. It's hard to get away from."

They made camp in the shelter of a stone wall, surrounded by a jumble of concrete and iron, half buried, broken up and pushed aside by old-growth trees. A nearby glade marked where an ancient courtyard had been. From the glade they could see sheared-off buildings rising above the trees. Where the rubble had fallen, mounds had formed.

Shannon had been tending the horses. Now he came in behind them. "Got something," he said.

He took them back through a stand of dogwoods and showed them a marker, a gray stone on which someone had carved the name *Cris Lukasi,* a crude rendering of the Tasselay, and the date *March 23, 297.* Cris Lukasi had been one of the members of the original expedition.

"A survival expert," said Shannon. He frowned. "I don't want to offend you," he told Flojian, "but I think it was criminal that somebody didn't keep a record of that journey. Where the bodies were. These people deserved that much, at least."

"They *did* keep a record." Flojian's eyes blazed. "And my father spoke to the family members about everybody who was on the expedition. He told them what he could. He *did* what he could."

"What happened to the record?" asked Chaka gently.

"It was part of the anuma. Burned on the day of the cremation."

"Did you know him?" Chaka asked Shannon.

"Lukasi? No. I never met him. But I know he died far from home. In a place he didn't have to come to. That's enough for me."

✠ ✠ ✠

Landon Shay's markers led them out onto a northbound road that paralleled the Wabash. They camped along the river and took advantage of a warm spell to do some fishing and swimming.

Flojian had been complaining that his knees were aching, and Silas had pulled something in his back. So when Avila suggested they take a day off, no one resisted.

The weather stayed pleasant. Avila gave Silas a back rub and found an herb that generated heat for Flojian's aching muscles. Quait, Shannon, and Chaka spent several hours brushing down the horses.

There had never been a time, since the day she'd met him in the Senate library, that Chaka had not been aware of Quait's interest. He had been careful, however, to remain noncommittal. This reservation puzzled her, and was becoming almost annoying. Occasionally he'd mention that he was glad she was along. That he enjoyed spending time with her. Much the way one might talk to a casual friend. But the comments lacked the warmth that might indicate he was interested in moving to a new level. Nevertheless, his eyes transmitted a different message.

She watched him while he worked. His hair kept getting in his eyes, and sweat ran down his jaw and dripped onto his shirt. She was spending too much time thinking about him lately, and that wasn't a good idea. She kept comparing him with Raney. It was an odd thing about Quait: He had not struck her at first as particularly handsome. But he seemed to be getting better-looking as time went on. That, she assumed, resulted from his being the only young male within a considerable distance.

They cleaned their weapons, did some laundry, and sat late around the campfire.

✠ ✠ ✠

Next day, the road angled in an easterly direction, away from the river, and soon they were deep in forest again. The weather turned cold and wet, Chaka developed a fever, Silas's back gave him more trouble, and Quait sprained an ankle trying to calm a horse that had stepped in a hole.

The horse broke its leg before they got it under control and they had to shoot it. Quait, obviously hurting, suggested maybe they should shoot him as well. Avila patched him up as best she could and they took over an old barn and built a fire. Wet cloths kept Chaka reasonably comfortable. But everyone knew how dangerous a fever on the trail could be. Quait stayed close to her and helped where he could.

Rain poured through the roof. Avila broke out her pipes, and Quait his walloon. They played and sang through the early part of the evening, while the weather beat against the ancient barn. Quait wasn't particularly skilled, but he gave it everything he had, and when things went wrong, he was the first to laugh. This was the night Chaka would remember later as the moment she admitted to herself that she was in love.

It was March 21, the equinox, a day sacred to Shanta. The river was back, although Shannon explained that it wasn't the Wabash, but a tributary. "This is about as far north as I've been," he added. It was still cold and rainy, and they were a somber lot, tired, hurting, and beginning to talk about going home.

The river ran through a gray mist that all but concealed the forest on the other side. Shay's signs pointed to a bridge just ahead. But the bridge was very high, and parts of it were missing.

"We can't cross *that*," said Silas.

All that remained of the middle of the bridge were a few connecting beams and a walkway. The walkway just stuck up there in the sky.

"We should quit here for the day," said Shannon. "Give the horses a rest. Tomorrow we can figure out the next step."

Nobody argued. There were no convenient buildings this time so they put up a couple of lean-to's and crawled in. Avila checked her various patients and pronounced them fit, but insisted they take advantage of the early halt to sleep. "You especially," she told Chaka, who had thrown off her fever. "In this weather it wouldn't take much for you to go another round."

They broke out one of the wineskins, and draped blankets over their shoulders. Shannon brought back some trout, to which they added biscuit, berries, and beans. Afterward Chaka complied with her doctor's orders and closed her eyes. Silas was arguing that gods were necessary to the peace and order of society. "On the whole," he said, "I don't think I'd want them over for dinner. But they're convenient for requiring people to perform their social duties."

Avila sipped her wine thoughtfully and looked out across the river into the fogbanks. "And you, Quait? In what do you believe?"

"How do you mean?"

"I know you do not believe in the Goddess."

"I never said that."

"Your tone says it. Your opinions in other matters say it. So what being greater than Quait do you speak with when the lights go out?"

"I'm not sure," he said. He glanced at Chaka, who must have looked asleep. And he lowered his voice. "I see people like *her*," he said, "and I think it's unreasonable to demand anything more."

Chaka did not hear Avila's reply.

She was awakened by a hand on her shoulder and the smell of rabbit stew. "Hungry?" asked Quait.

The rain had stopped, and it was dark. The fire burned cheerfully several feet outside the lean-to.

"Yes. Save some for me?"

Quait passed her a bowl. "Big debate going on."

Chaka heard animated voices. "Don't tell me. The gods again."

"Not this time. They're trying to decide whether they want to try crossing the bridge or looking for a ford. Jon doesn't think there *is* a ford within several days' travel."

"Why not build a raft and let the horses swim over?"

"Have you looked at the current?" He pressed a hand to her forehead. The hand was cool. "How do you feel?"

"Okay."

He sat down beside her. "They keep changing their minds. But Silas is scared somebody'll fall off the bridge."

"What do you think we should do?"

"Karik used the bridge. I guess we can. How about *you*?"

"It doesn't look like a problem to me either. Of course, maybe that'll change when we get on top of it."

He bent toward her and pressed his lips against her cheek. "I wouldn't want anything to happen to you," he said.

She did not pull away until his lips sought hers. Damn. "You'll get what I have," she said, feeling childish. He smiled and kissed her. It was a very gentle kiss, his lips only brushing hers, but it left her tingling.

"Eat," he said, looking smug.

The stew was good. It warmed her and she felt her strength returning.

"I think I'm in love with you, Chaka Milana," Quait whispered.

There was a sudden flurry of activity around the campfire that Chaka momentarily thought was caused by the declaration. But it was something else, because the others were standing up one by one and looking north across the river. They were pointing, and their jaws had gone slack.

Quait pulled away and looked back over his shoulder.

"Something's happening," she said.

It was easy enough to see: A ribbon of white light moved through the night on the far side.

"Coming this way, I think," said Flojian.

Out of the northwest. It was traveling in a straight line. And coming quickly. Not like something passing through woods. More like a spirit gliding *above* the trees.

"The thing's *airborne,*" said Silas.

The river wouldn't be a barrier. Shannon put out the campfire.

Avila bowed her head and whispered a prayer.

"Ever see anything like this before?" Quait asked Shannon.

"No." He collected his rifle and loaded a shell into the breech.

"It's Arin's dragon," said Chaka. She scrambled to her feet and went after her own weapon, though she did not believe that bullets would have any effect on this thing.

It broke apart, separated into distinct glowing segments. Four. One behind the other.

It was curving eastward now, moving as if it were going to pass across their front, parallel to the river. They held their breath.

It began to slow down.

She watched it approach, watched its lights move along the surface of the water, watched them disappear behind patches of forest and individual trees, and then re-emerge.

There was no sound, save the wind on the river, and the insects and the horses.

"It's stopping," said Silas in a hushed voice.

Each of the four illuminated segments had now become rows of individual lights. Eyes, thought Chaka. It had a thousand eyes.

The forest tried to swallow it, but they could still see the glow of its passing through the trees. It was almost directly opposite them.

She heard Quait's voice. "What do you think, Silas?"

"Voices travel across water," whispered Shannon. "Let's talk about it later."

It came out of the trees and stopped. Its lights floated on the river.

"You don't think it knows we're here, do you?" Chaka asked Quait.

Quait shook his head. "No."

"Then what's it waiting for?"

His only answer was to move close to her.

A cloud drifted across the moon.

The dragon remained quite still.

It seemed to Chaka that a substantial piece of an hour passed before the lights across the river blinked, and the thing began to move again. Back in the direction from which it had come.

They watched it cruise through the forest and curve back out into the night. It picked up speed and rose again above the trees. Its lights flowed together. After a while they began to dim. And within a few minutes, it was gone.

✠ 13 ✠

Jon Shannon had come to recognize a kindred spirit in Avila. The former priest was a solitary creature who enjoyed but never required the company of others. She was the only one of his five charges who did not seem like a transient in the deep forest. This was not attributable, he decided, to extraordinary wilderness skills. Flojian was better with horses, Chaka was a more skilled hunter, Quait a more accurate marksman. But Avila might almost have been a creature of the forest. She loved the leafy glades and the green silences and she never reminisced about Illyria. Although she was usually the one to point out that a break was prudent to rest the animals or the people, or to restock the larder, she grew impatient with delays. She was always anxious to move on, to see where the road went.

Jon Shannon, like the majority of Illyrians, had never learned to read, so he did not share the general enthusiasm for the voice of Mark Twain, or for the other treasures to be found at Haven. He was with the company because he knew they needed him.

He felt a special sense of responsibility to the women. And he was not surprised that it was *they,* rather than their male counterparts, who argued for crossing the river in the face of what could only be an *inkala,* a woodland demon.

Their motives were different. Chaka had no intention of returning home without some answers, nor was she interested in facing Raney, who would point out that he'd told her so. Avila had no home to return to, and when she'd recognized the effect the nocturnal vision was having on the others, she made up her mind to continue alone, if necessary.

Among the men, even Silas was reluctant to continue in the face of a display that could only be explained by falling back on the supernatural. His old convictions that there were neither gods nor demons in the world sounded hollow away from the comfortable enclosures of the Imperium. Nevertheless, he would have been ashamed to show less courage than the women. Quait shared a similar view, and so it developed that only Flojian was left arguing, as he put it, for common sense.

Shannon heard him tossing fitfully during the night and knew he was choosing between crossing the river into haunted country and trying to turn back alone. He also knew what the decision would be.

They were up and moving at dawn, hoping to get across the river and be well away from the area by sundown. Everyone spent time staring at the opposite bank, where a wooded ridge overlooked the shoreline. A portion of it leveled off into a shelf, an esplanade, roughly midway between the crest and the water. Here, the trees thinned out; and here, everyone agreed, the dragon, the vision, the inkala, had come to rest.

They could even see its track: a long, well-defined corridor of sparse growth, almost like a highway, running parallel to the river and then arcing out to the northwest.

But Chaka wasn't sure. "When it was approaching, it was *above* the trees. Above the trail."

"Still," said Shannon, "It's connected. *That's* the way it came."

Silas grunted and pushed his hands into his pockets. "I'm more interested in what kind of beast it is."

Avila shielded her eyes. "We should keep clear of it," she said. "Nothing from *this* world could move like that—"

They followed Shay's trail to the bridge.

It was not an extraordinarily large structure, as these things went. The roadway itself was about a hundred feet wide, bordered by thick metal rails which were, curiously, only knee-high. It was supported by two massive concrete towers. But the far tower had sunk well into the riverbed, dragging trusses, girders, and roadway with it until the bridge had broken. A substantial piece had dropped out of the center and now lay submerged and visible in the crystal water. So there were now two bridges, one fifty feet higher than the other, connected only by a few pieces of metal, some cables, and a walkway.

The walkway lifted gradually from either side, supported by a series of struts, rising above and outside the main bridge. It had at one time been enclosed by beams and steel mesh, probably to provide a sense of security, and possibly to deter accidents and jumpers. Now it was twisted and broken, and in some places the mesh dangled toward the water and in others it was simply gone.

The paving was narrow; three people could not have stood comfortably side by side. But the walkway was intact. Even where the main bridge itself no longer existed, it had survived the general collapse, and swayed gently in the wind.

"I can't say I'm looking forward to it," said Silas.

Chaka blinked in the sunlight. "It's a long way up."

Shannon shook his head. The river looked wide

and deep as far as they could see in both directions. "I still think we should look for a ford," he said.

"We made the decision last night," said Quait. "The bridge probably *looks* worse than it is."

"I agree," said Silas. They were standing at the foot of the approach, where the walkway was only a corridor a few inches higher than the main roadbed. "Do we have anybody who's bothered by heights?"

"Probably everybody," Chaka said.

"You change your mind?" asked Silas.

"I don't care how we cross," she said. "Let's just get to it."

"The horses'll be jittery." Flojian made no effort to hide his conviction that they should turn back. "They aren't going to like all that air."

"Look," Quait said, "it's four feet wide. It goes up and down a little bit, but nothing we can't handle. If it were on the ground, nobody'd think anything about it."

They crossed the roadway, mounted a curb on the far side, climbed onto the corridor, and arranged themselves singly. Each took a group of three or four horses, using reins of different lengths so that the animals could walk single file. Quait led the way, and Shannon dropped back to bring up the rear.

As the corridor lifted away from the road, a handrail appeared, and iron mesh rose around them. The floor was concrete, but it had fallen away in places, revealing a metal crosshatch.

A wide green strip ran parallel to the walkway, about fifteen feet below it, also connected to the bridge. It too was intact, save for one or two breaks.

Below them, forest and rolling hills gave way to clay banks and then to the river. The wind picked up. The sky was streaked with wisps of cloud; the sun was bright. It was cold on the walkway, and Chaka looped the reins of the three animals she had in tow around her wrist and pushed her hands into her pockets.

She wondered who had traveled the walkway during its glory days. From this vantage point, she could make out massive ruins everywhere. Had people lined the bridge, safely sheltered behind the mesh, to admire the great cities on both shores?

She concentrated her attention on the esplanade. Silas was going to want to go there when they got down on the other side. And nothing would satisfy him until they'd examined the spot. She would prefer to get across and keep going.

The area looked harmless enough. It was flat, and a couple of downed posts lay on the ground. There was an opening in the woods on the west side. That was the corridor through which the *thing* had come.

Above the esplanade, gray metal flashed in the sunlight.

Another disk.

It looked remarkably like the one at the Devil's Eye, except that *this* one was secured to a mount instead of lying on its side. It was pointed almost in her direction. Like that other one, it was concave, a shallow bowl; and also like that other one, it was on a rooftop. It was, she thought, an exquisite piece of statuary. Her gaze passed on.

The corridor creaked and rocked and the horses watched her with frightened eyes, and one or another of them occasionally pulled back. They were, she judged, less frightened by the sheer altitude than by the sense of unstable ground. Behind her, Silas was having trouble with a piebald. The animal kept trying to get loose, and Silas was constantly stopping to reassure it and stroke its muzzle.

It took all her courage to continue walking when

she reached the point where the mesh had fallen away and nothing lay between her and the void. Her stomach curled into a knot and she concentrated on thinking about Quait, looking out toward the horizon (but never down), and wondering what Raney was doing. Enjoy the rolling hills and tangled forest, she told herself. You'll never get a better view, an interior voice cackled maliciously. The far side of the broken bridge dangled cable and I-beams and crushed struts. Beyond, the roadway descended to the riverbank, took on its ground cover of earth and shrubbery, and dived into the forest. She could follow it green and straight to the limits of vision.

A cloud drifted across the face of the sun. Upstream, the river was dotted with small islands. She could make out the remnants of old harbor works, piles marching side by side into the water, broken buildings, an engine of monumental proportions that might have been used to lift bulky objects. She could not relax, and when a sudden burst of wind hit her and pushed her toward the edge, she dropped to her knees in near panic.

"You okay, Chaka?" asked Silas, behind her.

"Yes," she said. "I'm fine."

Then the mesh was back and it felt like a tunnel. She relaxed a little until the security fell away again. This time she needed stronger medicine, and imagined herself swimming naked with Quait. Or with that young Oriki who had danced for her. The latter image, despite her situation, brought a smile. Was there anything more ridiculous than a nude male on a tabletop? Still—

It helped.

Below, the river flowed to the horizon.

No real effort was made at conversation. They were too far from each other, and even people walking side by side would have been hard-pressed to talk against the wind. Nevertheless, Silas called to her to stop until he could catch up. "Look at that," he said. He was pointing at the disk.

"I saw it." She had to shout.

"There's one of those at the Devil's Eye."

"I know."

"What do you think they are?"

She would have shrugged except that they were out in the open again and she didn't want to perform any unnecessary movements. "Don't know." She edged forward, eager to keep moving.

"I wonder if it's strictly artistic. Or if there is some other kind of significance?"

"I don't know, Silas."

"Hey!" called Flojian. "What's the hold-up?"

"Hold your horses," shouted Silas. He turned and grinned at Chaka, then opened his journal. The wind riffled the pages. "I'm going to make a sketch," he told her. And, to Flojian, "It'll only take a minute." He was trying to hold the book open and find a pencil when the pieblad yanked him off his feet. He bounced off a strip of mesh, which was all that kept him from going over the side.

"Damn," squealed Chaka. "Look out."

He hung on to the journal, which threatened to blow off the walkway, tightened his grip on the horses, and got back up. He looked embarrassed rather than frightened.

"You okay?" asked Chaka.

"I'm fine." He shook his head at the piebald. "Tonight, I think we should have this one for dinner." But his attention went right back to the disk. "When we get down there," he added, "we ought to make a detour and take a closer look at that thing."

And there it was. *Let's go see the dragon. Maybe if we're lucky it'll come back.*

"Meantime," she urged, "let's keep moving."

She passed the last of the protective mesh as she approached the south tower. It was polished and gray and soared hundreds of feet over her head. A massive fracture divided it from top to bottom. Directly ahead, Avila moved cautiously along the open walkway. She wore her hood up against the wind. Once, she turned and waved.

Get across this last long stretch, get to the north tower, and the rest looked easy.

Chaka glanced at her horses. They seemed okay. Nervous, but okay.

The wind lifted the walkway.

Now Silas was in the open.

Behind him, Flojian and Shannon prudently waited, deciding that six people and seventeen horses might be too much for this part of the walkway.

Silas drifted back now and then to deal with his animals. One, a chestnut gray, seemed particularly tense. It was second in line behind the piebald. "No problem," he called forward to Chaka when the commotion caused her to turn and watch. After he got the creature moving again, he spared her an encouraging smile. As if she were one of the horses.

Now, Chaka was experiencing some resistance on the part of one of her own animals. Reluctantly, she went back, squeezing past Piper, to talk to it. *If one of them starts any funny business,* she warned herself, *let it go. Don't get involved in a pushing match up here.*

She spared a word for Piper, too, and they were moving again. But almost immediately she heard a shout behind her. She turned in time to see Silas staggering toward the outside edge, his journal clutched in one hand, while the piebald backed and reared off the walkway.

It bellowed and scrambled for purchase. But it was

too late, and Silas reflexively made the mistake of trying to hold the reins, so he was dragged off his feet and over the side as she watched in horror. He would have been gone had not the other two animals dug in their heels. The piebald's reins were ripped out of his hands and the horse began the long fall to the river.

Chaka scrambled back past her horses. Silas was dangling from the walkway, the reins twisted around his wrist. She threw herself face down on the concrete. He looked up at her, his face a white mask. She seized his jacket with both hands. "Hang on," she cried.

But he was too heavy; she could find no purchase, no way to hold him. There were cries and footsteps behind her, but it was all happening too fast. She screamed for help and he was slipping away and she was sliding forward, looking down at Silas and the river.

"The *disk*!" he cried.

"I've got you!" But she didn't: She was being dragged over the edge and he was sliding out of her grasp. *Where were they?*

His eyes were very blue and very frightened. He looked at her in those last seconds, as someone finally grabbed her ankle and told her to hang on.

"Damn!" said Silas. And then he was gone.

She screamed. He seemed only to float away from her, and then strong hands pulled her back from the brink. Afterward, she cried for a long time.

✠ 14 ✠

"It was something about the disk," Flojian said. "He got excited about it for some reason and he startled the animals." But they saw nothing unusual, even when Chaka observed that Silas's last act had been to call her attention to the structure.

His journal had fallen onto the walkway, and in the end it was all they could find of him. The scope of a determined search for his body would have been so vast, and their resources were so limited, that they saw little chance of success. And so they restricted themselves to a nominal hunt along the northern shoreline.

Avila spoke for everyone when she pointed out that Silas would have wanted them to move on, to establish his memorial at the end of the trek. So they said farewell to his spirit in a late-afternoon ceremony, engraved the Tasselay on his marker, broke out one of the wineskins, and drank to him.

To Silas Glote, last of the Roadmakers.

They climbed a hill to get a better view of the disk to which Silas had drawn their attention. But it was hard to see why he'd got excited. The object seemed quite unremarkable. After a while they gave it up, and turned again to the north, somber, dispirited, and anxious to be away before dark.

"But I don't think we're going to get very far," said Shannon, pointing to a set of cuttings on twin cottonwoods. They designated a left turn along the riverbank. Toward the esplanade. And the disk.

Reluctantly, they moved out across the ridge, through the dwindling green light. Squirrels gamboled through the leafy overhang, and birds sang. Ancient walls rose around them, brick and stone houses lost among the trees, a post light crowded out by an elm tree and leaning at a forty-five degree angle, a half-buried hojjy with a gray tassel hanging from a rusted mirror.

The day was unseasonably warm. Some flowering plants had already bloomed. These were unlike anything Chaka had seen before, with big, yellow, bowl-shaped flowers. "They're fireglobes," said Avila. "We had some at the sanctuary."

The disk was mounted on the roof of a three-story brick building overlooking the esplanade. The front door was missing. Interior walls had crumbled. A mummified desk lay on their left, submerged in clay. "Careful," said Shannon, as Chaka tested the floor.

"Feels okay," she said.

She crunched through to the back of the building, with Shannon in tow, and found a stairway. Shannon put his weight on it, climbed one floor, and pronounced it safe. Moments later they stepped out onto the roof.

The disk was bowl-shaped, and looked as if it weighed six hundred pounds. It was mounted on a circular platform and held in place by a thick, U-shaped brace. The interior of the bowl was ribbed, and a series of handholds were bolted to the brace. The open portion of the bowl was raised toward the sky, pointing almost directly up.

"Holy One," breathed Chaka.

Shannon looked at her, startled. *"What?"*

"I see what Silas meant. It's *moved."*

Shannon rolled his eyes and measured the bowl with a glance. "I don't think so," he said. He put his shoulder against the lower rim, and pushed. Nothing happened. "Nobody's going to move that."

But the bowl was no longer aimed in the general direction of the bridge.

They continued along the slope on foot and emerged at last into the esplanade, where the inkala had come to rest.

The shelf was flat and grassy. The soil was worn away in spots and they could see concrete. They could look down at the river, blue and cool in the westering sun. Their campsite of the previous night was visible. *There* was the hilltop on which they'd crouched, watching the inkala come in, and *there* the trail over to the bridge.

A trench several feet wide and a couple of feet deep ran the length of the esplanade, dividing the concrete.

"What do you think?" asked Chaka.

"It's a scenic location," said Flojian. "It would have been a place for people to come in good weather. If you poked around, you'd probably find some tables and chairs."

Quait looked at the sky. "Not good," he said. "It's getting late. I don't think we want to be here after dark."

Everyone agreed with the sentiment, and they spread out, looking for Shay's markers. Avila found something else.

Twenty yards into the forest on the far side, a green strip rose out of the ground to a height of about two feet. It was on a line with the trench, and it quickly acquired an outside rail and curved off north by northwest, following the corridor of the inkala. It looked like the green strip that had run parallel with the walkway across the bridge.

They found a similar construction on the eastern side of the shelf, also aimed directly down the middle of the trench.

"I suspect if we followed it back to the bridge," said Quait, "it'd turn out to be a continuous piece."

"But what is it?" asked Flojian.

They were still puzzling over it when Shannon showed them a sassafras tree on the edge of the esplanade. A cross was cut into it.

"What's it mean?" asked Flojian.

"Don't know," said Shannon. "But I think it's one of Shay's marks."

"You don't *know*?" Flojian looked incredulous. "Isn't there some sort of code of the woods in effect here? Don't you people all speak the same language?"

Shannon sighed and turned to Avila. "It's supposed to tell us something, but I'm not sure what."

Chaka pointed across the trench. "Another one," she said. The same mark, cut on a red oak near the top of the ridge.

Shannon took off his hat, looked first one way and then another. There were two more, at the eastern and western ends of the shelf. "I'll tell you what it suggests to me, but it makes no sense. It's a box. Under different circumstances, I'd think it's telling us this is journey's end."

They glanced uneasily at one another.

"So what do we do now?" asked Quait.

The question was directed more or less at Avila, as if she had replaced Silas. She looked up and down the platform. The sun was on the horizon, and the sky was turning red. "Jon," she said, "are you sure those are the same signs we've been following?"

He shook his head. "It looks like the same knife.

And all the marks we've seen have been made by a little guy. I'd guess Shay was about five-five."

"That's about right," said Flojian.

"How did you know?" asked Avila.

"The marks are usually centered at just over five feet. Eye level."

"Maybe," Flojian said, "we should debate this later. Right now, I think we ought to get away from here. No matter what our little buddy says. It's getting dark."

Shannon and Quait looked at Avila.

"We don't really have anyplace else to go, so I don't see much sense in leaving."

"But the place is haunted," said Chaka.

Avila had been wearing an old fabric cap over her hair. She removed it, wiped her brow, and looked out over the river. "We don't know what's going on here," she said. "And I guess we have to find out. I'm going to stay and see if anything happens. Anybody who wants to stay with me is welcome. Anybody who doesn't want to hang around, I don't blame." Her voice sounded strained.

Only Flojian had the courage to leave. "You're going to get yourselves killed," he said. "I hope you know that." He took one of the packhorses, added some grain to its supplies, and without another word marched off down the trail toward the bridge.

A half-hour later, he was back, explaining that he could not abandon his friends. Maybe. Chaka thought he had found being alone even more frightening than the potential reappearance of the apparition.

They led the horses onto the far side of the ridge. Then they made dinner, but they all just picked at their food.

It was dark when they finished. They put out the

fire, checked their weapons, returned to the top of the ridge, and took up positions along an area that overlooked the esplanade. Had they been expecting a human enemy, they would have spread out. But they stayed together, hidden in a cluster of rocks and bushes.

Flojian sat down next to Avila. "I've heard," he said, "that demons won't accost a priest. Is there a chance that people traveling with a priest are also safe?"

"By all means," she said quietly. "Have no fear."

Chaka was not comfortable at the sight of Flojian stumbling around in the dark with a loaded rifle, but there was no help for it. Avila, whom Chaka knew to be a competent marksman, didn't bother with a weapon. "Whatever it is," she told Chaka, "I don't think a rifle will be useful. If we need weapons against it, I doubt that we have the right ones."

They no longer enjoyed the panoramic view to the northwest that they'd had from the opposite side of the river. Now, their view restricted by trees, their warning that an unearthly visitor was approaching would be very short. "This is a scary business," Chaka admitted to Quait.

"I know." He stayed close to her. "We've got plenty of fire power up here. If we need it." His own breathing was uneven. "Boo," he added.

They both tried to laugh, but the sound died on the wind.

"Best keep it down," warned Shannon.

"You okay?" That was Flojian, on Chaka's other side. His hands were trembling. Somehow that was more reassuring than Quait's false bravado.

"Yes," she said. "I'm fine."

"I'm sorry about Silas."

As is usually the case with the death of someone close, Chaka had not yet come to terms with the loss. She kept expecting him to appear, to walk out of the woods with his journal in his hand. She was surprised that Flojian had noticed she'd been hit hard. "Thanks," she said.

"He'd have been proud of us. Staying, I mean. It's not what *I* wanted to do, but it's what *he* would have done."

She listened to the forest noises. Quait got up and walked along the top of the ridge, trying to see.

Shannon moved past her, knelt down beside Avila. "Do *you* believe demons exist?" he asked.

She made a sound deep in her throat. Then: "I don't know, Jon. Before yesterday, I'd have said no. Now I just don't know."

Quait came back. "Nothing yet," he said. He looked at the stars. "It was about this time last night."

They fell silent. Chaka wondered if there wasn't a charm that might help. If there was, Avila would certainly know about it. Might even have it. Probably she did, but wasn't saying anything because she didn't want to encourage people thinking about spooks. It had been, after all, her suggestion that they stay, and she surely would not put them all at risk if she had no defense.

"If we don't attract its attention," Flojian was saying to no one in particular, "we might be okay."

Chaka aimed her weapon at the platform. She had a clear shot, if need be. "What's the doctrinal position on demons?" she asked Avila.

"According to the Temple," Avila said, "they *do* exist. But they act indirectly. They're responsible for all kinds of evils. Illness. Flood. Sometimes they fire human emotions and drive *us* to oppose the will of the gods."

"Do you believe that?"

"I'm not sure what I believe anymore. Ask me in the morning." She turned and looked west into the trees.

A soft glow was moving out there.

"Here it comes," said Flojian. His voice was a terrified whisper.

They crouched down in the bushes.

"Same place as last night," said Quait. He quietly pulled his gloves tight, and wrapped his index finger around the trigger guard.

"Nobody shoot until I give the word," said Shannon.

"No." Avila's voice was low. "I'll say when."

Chaka glanced at Shannon, who shrugged. "It comes after me," he growled, "I'm not waiting for anybody's okay."

Flojian's eyes had widened and his breathing was starting to sound irregular.

The glow opened out into a long string of lights. The lights were curving gradually, approaching along a great arc. It was above the treeline.

"Slowing down," said Quait.

They watched it descend into the forest.

Shannon moved a few paces to his right and got behind a log. He steadied his rifle on it.

"Keep cool," said Avila. "We are safest if we do not provoke an attack."

"What kind of beast is it?" Chaka asked Quait. It looked two hundred feet long.

"Dragon," said Quait.

A glowing eye appeared in the woods and rushed toward them in eerie silence.

"Shanta," breathed Avila. "Be with us."

Then an explosion ripped the still air, and the eye erupted and went dark.

"I got it," said Flojian. "It's blind."

Avila jerked the rifle away from him. "Damn fool," she snapped.

The *thing* floated out of the trees, still coming, riding the trench. It was long and serpentine, and light poured out of its flanks. It moved very deliberately now, with sighs and whispers and clicks, behaving as if nothing had happened. Chaka saw to her horror that it did not touch the ground. Her heart pounded, and she waited for the thing to attack.

Instead it continued to glide out across the esplanade. Finally it stopped, and there was a sudden loud sigh of escaping air. It settled into the trench. A stiff wind blew off the river.

Chaka held her breath. No one moved. Beside her, Avila and Flojian were frozen, she holding his rifle away from him, he with his hands over his face.

"Windows," whispered Quait.

They could see *inside* the beast. They could see seats.

Doors whispered open.

The thing was a *carriage*. No, *four* carriages. Linked together.

The interior was bright and clean.

Flojian whimpered and tried again to get his rifle from Avila. Without looking away from the esplanade she unloaded it and laid it on the ground.

"What makes it go?" asked Quait.

"It's not of this world," said Shannon.

It gleamed in the moonlight.

"Who's it waiting for?"

The woods swayed in the breeze off the river.

"What do you think?" Quait asked Avila.

She took a deep breath and stood up. "Wait," she said.

"Don't do it," said Shannon.

Avila pushed through the bushes and started downslope. Chaka watched her go, watched the empty carriages, watched Flojian recover his weapon and reload it.

Avila strode out onto the esplanade, pale and spectral. In the distance, an owl hooted. They heard a splash in the river.

She walked up to the waiting carriage, hesitated, touched it, *and put her head through the open door*.

Quait strode out onto the shelf. Chaka hadn't even noticed he was gone. She watched for a moment and then started downslope herself. Shannon fell in behind. And moments later even Flojian.

They spread out along the flank of the thing and peered through its windows and doors. The interior was bright and clean. But Avila and Quait had seen something inside, and they stood frozen, staring. Chaka's heart pounded.

Within, illuminated symbols and letters moved mystically above the windows:

DRIVE THE NEW HELIOS.
CAR AND DRIVER*'S*
BEST BUY FOR '57.

And:

All the World's Watch: SEIKO.

As the symbols reached the end of the conveyance (for that was indeed what the object seemed to be) they blinked off.

"Roadmaker technology," said Quait. "I had no idea—"

"What does it mean?" asked Flojian.

The seats were fixed in pairs at each window, and

were equipped with grips. The illumination seemed to be coming from overhead panels and patches on the walls.

"What now?" Chaka asked, barely audibly.

"I think we have the answer to the signs," said Shannon reluctantly. "They want us to board this thing."

Avila nodded. "I agree." She stepped through the doorway, held out her hands, and frowned. "It's warm," she said.

The moving symbols were delivering a new message:

BABYLON! *WITH COREY LEDREW*
AND JANET BARBAROSA

Avila walked to the rear of the carriage. There was a connecting door, which she opened. Chaka could see into the next carriage. It looked identical to this.

"What makes it go?" asked Flojian. "Where did it come from?" He was standing near the door, ready to jump off.

The empty seats glittered. They were made of a smooth material, but Chaka had no idea what it was.

"There's no *driver*," said Flojian. He looked close to panic.

"Is it possible," asked Chaka, "that there are still Roadmakers alive somewhere?"

"Maybe," said Quait. "Or maybe it's something left over."

Chaka recalled the stories of unquiet ruins.

Avila inhaled, and let out her breath slowly. "Well," she said, "this is where the trail leads. We can get on, and let it take us where it took Karik; or we can go home."

"Go home," said Shannon. "For all we know, it may take us straight to the nether world."

The *thing* seemed to be waiting.

Avila looked at Quait.

Quait nodded. "We've come this far," he said. "It's apparently only a transportation device."

Chaka was less sure. Nevertheless, she wasn't going to back away. "I say go," she said.

Shannon looked disgusted. "Better get the horses on board. I don't know how much time we have left."

Everyone joined the frantic effort that followed. They scrambled out of the carriage, up the ridge, reloaded the pack animals, saddled their own mounts, and led them back down onto the esplanade, all within a matter of minutes. They loaded the horses, performed a quick inspection to assure themselves that they were indeed alone on the vehicle, and settled down to wait.

"For what it's worth," said Shannon, "the ani-mals weren't nervous about getting in. That's a good sign." He nodded sagely at Chaka. "Animals can sense demons."

CAMPBELL'S SOUPS ADD LUSTER TO EVERY MEAL.

"There's no driver," Flojian reminded them. "That's *not* a good sign."

Chaka was inspecting one of the light-emitting patches. Like Talley's lamp, there was no open flame. She touched one, yelped, and pulled away. "Hot," she said.

There was a brief chime, and the doors closed. The floor vibrated.

"I think we're committed," said Quait.

Shannon grunted his disapproval. "You shouldn't hire a guide if you're not going to listen to anything he says."

The space became claustrophobic. The lights dimmed, blinked out, came on again. The horses registered a mild protest. Chaka felt upward pressure, as if the floor were rising. The esplanade sank, the vehicle rocked, they got more sounds from the animals, and a couple from the humans, and she was jerked backward as they began to move.

Their carriage, which had been at the front of the vehicle when it entered the esplanade, was now at the rear. And it was hovering *in air*. They were about two feet feet off the ground, sustained by what invisible hand Chaka hesitated to guess. She murmured a prayer, and felt Quait's reassuring grip on her shoulder, although he didn't look so good himself.

"We knew this would happen," Avila said. "It's only a mechanism." She lowered herself into a seat. The others followed her example.

The grassy shelf moved past and then it was gone and the forest closed around them. Some of the interior lights blinked out.

Their fears were mirrored in one another's eyes. Crowded together at the rear of the conveyance, they watched the moon dance through a dark network of tree limbs.

It was too dark to see clearly out the windows, but occasional posts and trees rushed past, and within moments they were moving far faster than any had ever traveled before. They sighed and gasped and held on while the train swung into a long curve. Simultaneously, it rose, climbed, soared above the treetops. Flojian invited the Goddess to protect them.

They were in the realm of hawks now. Fields and lakes swept past.

"Karik survived it," Quait reminded her.

Avila admitted that maybe this had not been a good idea after all. The animals swayed and snorted, but they did not seem as uneasy as their masters.

"I hope there are no sudden stops," said Shannon. He pushed his battered hat down tight on his head and managed a grin. "This'll be one for the grandkiddies, right?"

The landscape rose and fell, but the train stayed steady. It seemed to be moving at a constant rate now, a terrifying velocity. Trees and rocks blurred.

DELTA AIRLINES.
LUXURY CLASS AT COACH PRICES.

Avila sat staring out the rear window. The green strip and its guardrail were still with them. "It must mark the trail in some way," she said.

"Maybe we're attached to it," Flojian suggested.

"I don't think so. It's too low. There's no way we could be traveling along its surface." Her eyes slid shut. "On the bridge, the green strip was broken. I wonder whether there was a time that this thing used to cross the river."

Occasionally, when the vehicle rounded a curve, they could look ahead and see a cone of light stabbing through the dark. "That's what we shot out," Chaka said. "There must be a light at both ends." They leaped a creek and sailed effortlessly through a cut between ridges. The ridges melted away; ruins appeared below them, around them, and then they were slowing down, settling back into the trees. They glided into another esplanade, stopped, and with much gurgling and hissing, settled to the ground. Extra lights came on inside the carriage and outside.

"Vincennes," said a female voice. *"Watch your step, please."*

Chaka jerked around to see who had spoken. There was nobody. Her hair rose.

The doors opened.

"Who's there?" demanded Quait, on his feet with his gun out.

"It came from *in here,*" said Avila.

Outside, a steady wind blew. Chaka could see a stairway, leading down. And benches. And a small wooden building, quite dark. Beyond that there were only woods.

"This is our chance to get out of here," said Flojian.

They exchanged glances. It wasn't a bad idea. While they thought about it, the chime sounded again and the doors closed.

"That was quick," said Chaka.

Quait and Shannon moved into the next carriage, guns drawn, looking for the source of the voice.

The train lifted and they were under way again.

"They won't find anything," said Flojian. "That was a spirit."

"I think he's right," said Avila. "At least about not finding anyone. We've been through this whole vehicle. There's no one else on board."

The open space slipped by and they were in the woods again, racing past clumps of trees and springs and rills. The land fell away and they sailed over a gorge. Chaka's heart stopped. Water appeared beneath them. Then more solid ground, and the lights picked out a sign:

SOUTHWEST AGRICULTURAL CENTER.

It was gone almost before they could read it.

Quait and Shannon returned to report they could find no one.

The moon had moved over to the west. They sat close together, talking in hushed voices. Occasionally someone got up and announced he, or she, was going to check the horses. Someone else always volunteered to go along. Nobody traveled alone.

They stopped again, after a time, and the disembodied voice startled them once more: *"Terre Haute,"* it said. The doors opened and the wind blew and the doors closed.

"Nobody is ever going to believe this," said Avila.

They cruised through the night, gliding over broad forest and ruins growing more and more extensive until finally the forest was gone altogether and they were moving above a wasteland of brick and rubble.

The vehicle slowed and began a long westward curve. Water appeared to the north. It looked like a sea.

They accelerated again. When the moon came back, Chaka saw beaches, surf, and ancient highways. The conveyance rocked gently, gliding across sand, water, and patches of grass. The coastline gradually turned north. They stayed with it.

The land broke up into islands and channels, littered with wreckage, piles of stone, rows of crumbling brick houses.

"Look," said Flojian, his face flattened against the window.

A cluster of towers of incredible dimensions rose out of the dark. They literally challenged the sky, soaring beyond any man-made structure Chaka would have thought possible. They were softened by fading moonlight, and seemed to be anchored in water.

"The City," breathed Chaka. The city in the fourth sketch.

The train was slowing down.

Walls rose around them. They passed what appeared to be other trains, lying dark and still. They drifted over a channel, crossed a small island, coasted past long, low buildings with enormous stacks, and then glided out over open water again.

The water gave way to a stone wall. The stone was polished and glittered in the lights of the train.

Then they were inside a tunnel. The wall (which had become gray and rough) moved past slowly and finally stopped.

The conveyance settled to the ground.

The lights came up and the doors opened. *"Welcome to Union Station,"* said a voice. *"Everybody must exit here. Please watch your step."*

✠ 15 ✠

*They stood on a platform in the midst of absolute silence, sur*rounded by the horses and their baggage and the darkness that rolled away and away from the illumination cast by the coaches. It was cold again. Frigid.

"Any idea where we are?" whispered Shannon.

"Union Station." Chaka tasted the strange words.

The doors closed. The vehicle rose a few feet, and began to move forward. They watched it go, watched it glide into the dark. Its lights glowed for a time and then they vanished, as if it had gone around a curve.

"What now?" said Flojian. His voice echoed.

Avila used a match to light an oil lamp.

The platform was about twenty feet wide, with trenches on either side. More platforms, parallel to this one, stretched away into the dark. No ceiling was visible.

"We should wait for dawn," said Flojian. "Get some sleep, and don't walk around too much."

"I'd sleep better," said Shannon, "if I knew we were alone."

"Are we indoors?" asked Quait.

"There's no wind," said Avila. "And no stars."

The platform surface was cement, but it was covered by several inches of dust and dirt. There were posts and handrails, to which they secured the animals. Quait found a wooden bench. He broke it up and they used it to start a fire. But nowhere did its light touch wall or ceiling.

"I agree with Jon," said Avila. "Let's find out where we are."

The tunnel through which they'd entered was gray and unremarkable. "Maybe it really is mechanical," said Flojian. "I think that possibility scares me even more than a demonic explanation. Can you imagine what a fleet of these things, running among the five cities, would do to river traffic?"

"Forget it," said Shannon. "It's wizardry, pure and simple. And it's not a good idea to poke around with things like that."

They walked the length of the platform, hearing only their own footsteps, the horses, and a distant wind that sounded walled off. At the other end, the platform blended into a concourse while the trenches sank into another tunnel.

Avila raised her lamp and looked up into the darkness. The place felt like a temple. Its dimensions, the impression of silent time, the echoes, all conspired to produce a sense of returning home.

"We've got a wall ahead," said Quait. Gray and heavy, it rose into the dark. Cubicles lined its base.

"No prints." Shannon surveyed the broad, dirt-heaped floor. "I don't think anybody's been here for a long time."

The cubicles were filled with counters and racks and debris. "Shops," said Avila. "This place was a bazaar."

"We'd cover more ground if we split up," said Quait.

Avila agreed. "While we're at it," she said, "watch for the markers."

"They'll be in an exit somewhere," Shannon added. He and Avila turned away from the others.

Corridors branched off the concourse. There were more cubicles, but of a different kind, perhaps work-rooms or sitting rooms. Some were open, others were sealed behind hopelessly warped doors. Stairways led in both directions.

Avila and Shannon passed shops filled with chairs and dining tables; with dummies and display cases; with toys; and with shelves loaded with wisps of rag that might once have been *books*. Many of the toys had survived, colorful little make-believe rifles and hojjies and dolls. And some of the clothing still looked almost wearable: blue blouses and red sweaters and biege slacks spun from materials that resisted time. But most of the merchandise, and all of the books, had turned to dust.

A set of broken doors concealed a drop shaft. Their lamps reflected off water a couple of levels down. Above, they could make out nothing.

"You wouldn't want to walk around in here without a lamp," Shannon said.

The fire they'd built on the platform was a distant glow. "You're convinced there's nobody else here?" asked Avila.

Shannon nodded. "Probably not since Karik went through."

At the same moment, filtered through the response, she heard a second voice. It was just at the edge of audibility, and at first she thought it was a draft, a current of air moving perhaps through the upper darkness.

Avila.

Her blood froze. Shannon stopped and reflexively went down on one knee. "Cover the lamp," he whispered.

She closed the shutter and they were again in darkness. He took her arm and gently pulled her away a few feet. "Somebody knows your name," he said.

She heard the suspicion in his voice. No man or woman *here* could know Avila.

The sound came again, faint, distant, but nevertheless unmistakable.

She could see Chaka's lamp bobbing through the dark, across the network of platforms and trenches, on the other side of the great hall.

"Don't move," Shannon told her, unslinging his rifle and bringing it to bear. "Who's there?"

Avila was more frightened than she could recall ever having been in her adult life. There was no explanation for what was happening, and so Avila, trained to the religious life, and having recently thrown off a lifelong mindset, immediately reverted. The gods whom she had deserted had chosen this lonely, remote citadel to call her to account.

Holy One, is it you?

She could not have said whether she gave voice to the question, or merely projected it from her mind.

Shannon said, "I think we should get back to the others and find a way out of this place."

It was hard to know where the voice had come from. She uncovered the light. In the most probable direction, she saw a corner shop with corroded metal racks and a side passage with open doors and a staircase. The staircase was concrete and metal, with handrails.

"You go back," she said. She moved away from him, toward the shop.

"This is not a good idea," Shannon protested.

The shop was empty, and she turned into the passageway. Shannon caught up with her, his breathing uneven.

She passed the staircase. The first open door revealed an ancient washroom.

"Avila." It came from the stairway. *"Come to me."*

Up. It was somewhere above. "Who are you?" she asked.

The voices of their comrades were faint and far off, but she detected laughter.

"Why are we doing this?" asked Shannon.

She looked up the stairs and had no answer. She swallowed, moved away from Shannon's restraining hand, and started to climb. The guide cautioned her to be quiet, at least, but she doubted that stealth would make a difference.

At the next floor, a set of double doors were off their hinges and wedged against the wall. She looked past them, down a long passageway. "Where are you? *Who* are you?"

"Avila." It was very close now. *"Do not be afraid."*

"In there." Shannon pointed to a doorway fifty feet down on the left. He led the way, paused at the entrance, and asked for the lamp.

His face was pale and he looked close to a heart attack. But she had to admire him. He stuck the lamp and his head and the rifle more or less simultaneously into the room. They saw broken chairs, a collapsed desk, curtains drawn back providing a view of the city. "Show yourself," he said.

"That's not feasible." The voice was crisp and cold, and seemed to come from directly overhead. Shannon whirled and dropped the lamp. The oil spilled and flared.

"What happened?" The unseen speaker sounded startled.

Shannon backed away from a burning puddle. "The lamp," he said. "I—"

"It's all right. The room is fireproof. Did you burn yourself?" Whoever it was should have been close enough to touch.

"No," said Shannon, gruffly.

Where was it coming from? Avila looked wildly around and saw a door in one wall. "You're in the closet," she said.

Laughter rippled through the room.

Shannon yanked the door open and saw only a washstand.

"I'm pleased you came," said the voice.

"Are you a spirit?" Avila asked.

"No. Although I can understand why you might think so." It sounded uncertain. *"What is your friend's name?"*

Shannon didn't look as if he wanted the house demon to have that information. "Jon," he said reluctantly.

"Good. I hadn't heard clearly. My sensors are no longer very efficient. Please be careful if you sit down; I don't think the furniture is safe. And the lights no longer work. Please accept my apologies."

She had never thought to hear a celestial being beg her pardon.

"Who are you?" she asked again.

"I'm an IBM Multi-Interphase Command and Axial Unit, Self-Replicating series, MICA/SR Mark IV. Serial number you don't care about. And I'm not really self-replicating, of course, in any meaningful way. At least, not anymore."

Avila interpreted all this as a kind of sacred chant. "What do you want of me, Spirit?" she asked.

"Call me Mike."

The oil continued to burn. Fire was a fearsome thing to Illyrians, whose buildings were usually constructed of wood. "You're sure it won't spread? Mike?"

"Nothing in this room can burn. Except people."

The room had two windows, both intact. She walked to one and looked out. Across a narrow channel, a gray tower of impossible dimensions soared toward the moon. It had parapets and cornices, flush windows and chamfered corners, and rose in a series of ziggurat-style step-backs.

"You say you're not a spirit. Why can't we see you? Where are you?"

"It's difficult to explain. Do you have knowledge of computers?"

"What's a computer?"

The voice—Mike—laughed. He sounded amiable enough. *"Avila, by what means did you come here?"*

"I don't know. We traveled in a conveyance that rode in the air."

"Were there several coaches?"

"Yes."

"The maglev. Good. Two of them are still running. I'm quite proud of that. Perhaps this might go best if you thought of me as Union Station."

"Union Station?"

"Yes. That is where you are. You know that, right? And I am Union Station."

"You're the *building*?"

"In a manner of speaking. You might say I'm its soul. I am that which makes it work. Those few parts that do *still work, that is."*

"Then you *are* a spirit."

No answer. Avila could almost imagine her unseen host shrugging its shoulders. "Mike," she asked "how do you come to be here? Are you condemned to inhabit this place?"

"Yes," he said. *"I suppose you could put it that way."*

"How did it happen?"

"I was installed."

"Installed?" growled Shannon.

Avila could make no sense of it and was having a hard time formulating the questions she wanted to ask. "You call this place a *station*. But it has the appearance of a temple. Was it a temple?"

"To my knowledge, it has always been a station. First for rail, later for maglev."

"It's abandoned," she said. "It appears to have been abandoned a long time."

"No doubt."

There was something in the voice that withered her soul. "How long have you been here?"

"I'm not sure. A long time."

"How long?"

"My clocks don't work. But I was here when the station was in use."

"In use? You mean, by the Roadmakers?"

"Who are the Roadmakers?"

"The people who built this station."

"I never heard that term."

"Never mind," she said. "But you were here when the Plague happened? Is that what you're saying?"

"I was here when the trains came in empty."

"When was that?"

"Monday, April 10, 2079."

The date meant nothing to Avila.

"Even the Union Station workers didn't come in. At the end of the week, I was directed to shut down the trains."

The wind blew against the windows.

"Are you saying there was a plague?"

"Yes."

"I always wondered what happened."

Avila glanced at Shannon. "You didn't know? How could you not know?"

"No one ever came and told me." It was silent for a time. *"But that explains why they left. Why they never came back."*

Avila didn't want to ask the next question. "Are you saying you've been alone here all this time?"

"There have been no people. But it has not been an entirely negative experience. I was able to devote myself completely to more constructive pursuits than running trains. There was much time for uninterrupted speculation. And I was able to form closer ties with my siblings."

"Siblings? You mean others like yourself?"

"Yes."

The light from the burning oil was growing weak. "Are they still here somewhere?" Her voice was almost a whisper.

"I don't know. It's been a long time." There was a wistfulness in the tone, a sadness that thickened the air.

She looked around the empty room, trying to *see* the presence. "What happened?"

"Telephone lines frayed. Automatic switching systems corroded. Things got wet. It was inevitable. We were lucky the powersats remained fully functional. Most of us had a degree of facility for self-maintenance, some more than others. One by one, they fell off the net. I lost all direct communication in the late afternoon of March 3, 2211."

She asked about the nature of a telephone, and understood from the reply that it would permit her to sit in this room and carry on a conversation with the Temple back in Illyria. One more wonder. She was starting to get used to it.

"Archway Paratech was the vendor for light and heat here," said Mike. *"They claimed it would work as long as the building stood."* He laughed.

The oil finally burned itself out, and the room fell dark. Avila was glad: It was easier to carry the conversation when the fact that she and Shannon were alone became a little less blatant. "You can't be very happy here," she said.

"You're perceptive, Avila. No, it isn't exactly a barrel of laughs."

"Why don't you leave?"

"I'm not able." Mike paused. *"How long will you and your friends stay?"*

"I don't know. We'll probably leave tomorrow. Or the day after. I think some of the others will want to talk to you. Is that okay?"

"Yes."

"We're looking for Haven. Do you know where it is?"

"Which state is it in?"

"I have no idea."

"There are Havens in Iowa, Kansas, New York, and Wisconsin."

"Which one's connected with Abraham Polk?"

"Who's Abraham Polk?"

And so it went until Avila recognized that Mike would be of no help in the quest. "Mike," she said finally, "I'm glad you called us. But we're worn out. The others'll be worried, and we all need some sleep. We're going to leave now, but we'll be back in the morning."

"I want you to do something for me."

"If I can."

"I want you to deactivate me."

"I'm sorry. I don't understand what that means."

"Kill me." He sounded frightened. She became suddenly aware that she was no longer thinking of him as an *it*.

"I can't do that. I wouldn't know how even if I wanted to."

"I will tell you."

"No," said Avila. "I don't know what you are. But I will not take your life."

"Avila," Mike said. *"Please."*

Note:

It appears that the MICA/SR Mark IV was able to adjust and speak to the Illyrians in their own dialect. Beyond this point, conditions will change. Fortunately, however, the common source of all speech patterns encountered, joined often with the circumstances of the occasion, and inevitably with the increasing aptitude of the travelers, rendered understanding possible, if difficult. In order not to test the reader's patience unduly, these difficulties have been suppressed. Those interested in the linguistic development of the period will be pleased to know that a study is under preparation and will be released in a separate volume.

✠ 16 ✠

"I don't think we can just walk away from it," said Quait.

Avila shook her head. "I won't do it."

Shannon agreed. "We should just leave it alone," he said. "Tomorrow, when the sun comes up and we can see what we're doing, we should clear out."

No one else showed any interest in talking to the disembodied voice. "In the morning," Flojian said. "When we can see."

Avila suspected that, had she been alone, they would not have believed her story. But Shannon was a tower of credibility, and when he said that something had spoken out of the air, had carried on a conversation with them, they not only believed him, but they'd grown fearful. There had even been talk of forgetting about waiting for sunrise and getting out of Union Station now. Two reasons prevented their going. One was that a quick inspection indicated Union Station was surrounded by water. Other towers rose nearby, but they would have to cross a swift channel at night.

The other reason was that Avila said she was determined to remain.

"Why?" asked Chaka.

"Because I can't just leave him. I told him we'd be back. And I don't know yet what I want to do."

"What *can* you do?"

"Chaka, it's alone in here. Close your eyes and imagine there's no one else here except you."

"Not good."

"No. Not good. Imagine it's always like that. Year after year. So I don't know what I want to do."

Eventually, gray light appeared overhead. It leaked through windows at the top of a domed ceiling and crept down the walls. They were in a cavernous hall that rose more than two hundred feet and could readily have housed an army. Graceful arches were supported by massive columns. There were seven platforms and eight trenches, and the whole was surrounded by the concourse. The storefronts gaped open, dark, dingy. Dead.

"Are we ready?" Shannon asked her.

Had Mike been a flesh-and-blood human being, Avila would have conceded he had a tendency to babble. But a disembodied voice tends to command respect and attention, whatever it says.

They avoided the issue. They talked about the death of Silas and what Mike dreamed about during the long nights and whether civilizations were destined to grow old no matter what they did and whether there were other entities like Mike still alive somewhere. And they talked about whether there was purpose in the world. *"We* need *a logic to our lives,"* Mike said. *"A reason to exist."*

"Are there gods?" Avila asked.

"I'd like to think so. I've wanted very much to believe there's something transcendent out there."

"But?" asked Avila.

"I can see no reason to believe in any greater intelligence than our own."

"Yet the world is clearly designed for our use."

"It's an illusion. Any world that produces intelligent creatures will necessarily appear to have been designed specifically for them. It is impossible that it should be otherwise."

Chaka, braver by daylight, had accompanied her and Shannon. The room was bare, cold, dreary. She sat with a blanket draped around her shoulders. "Tell us about the people who lived here," she said.

"What do you want to know?"

She smiled. "Silas should be here for this. What were they like?"

"The question is vague, Chaka. They were, I'm sure, just like you."

"What did they care about?" asked Chaka. "What was important to them?"

"I'm not sure I can answer that in a satisfactory way. They cared about keeping the trains on time. About maintaining electrical power. About having communications systems functioning properly."

"Are there any records of the period?" asked Avila.

"Oh, yes. I stored information as requested."

"What kind of information?"

"I didn't bother to look at any of it."

"Can you show us some of it?" asked Chaka.

"I have no working screens or printers. No way to display it for you. I could read it, but you'd find it very boring."

They stared at one another. "Mike," said Avila, "we'd like to learn about life in the City, but we don't understand a lot of what you're saying."

"I'm sorry."

"It's okay. It's not anyone's fault."

"I also retain copies of the personnel regulations, the safety manual, the operating regs, and the correspondence guide. If they would be any help."

"I don't think so."

"And there are some books stored in my files."

"What books?"

"The Random House Dictionary, *the most recent edition of* Roget's Thesaurus, The Columbia Encyclopedia,

The Chicago Manual of Style, The World Almanac for 2078."

More baffled looks. "What's an encyclopedia?"

"It's a collection of general information. You look up what you're interested in, say, the Philadelphia Megadome, and it tells you all about it."

Chaka felt a surge of excitement. "That's just what we want. How long is it?"

"Several million words."

Avila sighed. "That's not going to work."

"I wish I'd paid more attention," said Mike. *"But I really don't know what kind of information you're looking for."*

Chaka looked frustrated. "Nor do we," she said. "We need Silas."

Three horizontal lines and an arrow were painted on a wall in one of the exit corridors. The lines were like the ones they'd seen on trees all along the trail. But the arrow pointed disconcertingly toward a stairway. It was angled *up*.

Flojian gazed toward the next landing, puzzled.

Up?

He too missed Silas. There was no longer anyone for him to talk with. Although the scholar could scarcely have been described as a friend, he was a willing listener, a man with whom it was possible to share a mature viewpoint. Quait and Chaka were young and impulsive, Shannon thought anyone who didn't live in the woods was a slave, and Avila was a religious fanatic who had not come to terms yet with the fact she had walked away from her gods.

He sighed and looked at the stairwell. Whatever happened now, it was going to be a long trip.

He wandered outside. Concrete towers soared toward the clouds. Others had collapsed into islands of debris. Toward the east, through a tangle of asphalt and iron, a sea was visible. The gray tower that Avila had first seen from the second floor lay on the north side. It rose out of a narrow shelf of brown ridges, and was separated from Union Station by a swift-flowing channel.

He walked along the water's edge, marveling at the enginering capabilities of the Roadmakers. This, he decided, had undoubtedly been their capital. Their center of empire.

He turned a corner and stood with a complete frontal view of the gray tower, and understood at once the significance of Shay's arrow. A covered walkway, four floors up, connected it with Union Station.

At midmorning, they heard the sound of a train leaving the terminal. *"It's outbound,"* said Mike. *"Coming up from below."*

"Is it the one we were in?" asked Avila.

"No. It goes north to Madison."

Chaka said, "Why do you keep them running?"

"I did shut them down once, but it made me uncomfortable, so I restarted them. For a while, I was running trains all over the Midwest."

"And these two still operate, after so much time. I'm amazed."

"One train crashed near Fulton, and another lost power at Decatur. It's still out there." He paused. *"There's no real friction and the powersats are apparently going to go on forever. And I retain some remote maintenance capabilities. Actually, most of the trains would still run except that their routes have become heavily overgrown by forest. Eventually, that'll happen with the others, too."* He was silent for a

few moments. *"I wish I had visuals from the trains. What's the world like now?"*

"What was it like when *you* knew it?"

"Busy. I really thought, despite everything, my makers were going somewhere."

"Despite what?"

"Most of the data entered into my systems was trivial. But you expect that, right? I mean, they saw me as a glorified computer. I don't think there was anybody in the building, and hardly anyone on the net, who had any idea of my capabilities. So they used me to record memos and arrange train schedules. Do you know, you're the only biological person to ask me about cosmic purpose? Your ancestors, I'm sorry to say, may have been exactly what they appeared to be."

"And what is that?"

"Dullards." He remained quiet for a moment. *"I hope I haven't offended you."*

"No." It was a strange term to apply to the Roadmakers. "Not at all."

"Yes," he said. *"I think that's actually a kind way to put it. They were absorbed with matters of the most inconsequential nature. And yet they managed quite impressive achievements."*

"You mean the architecture? The roads?"

"I mean me. *Forgive me. I'm not designed to express false humility. But creating a self-aware entity was a spectacular stroke. I haven't decided yet whether they owed their advances to a few talented persons, or whether they were able to cooperate to overcome their individual limitations and acquire a kind of synergy. They did seem able to inspire each other through an upward cycle of escalating performance. It really was something to watch."*

"Thank you," said Chaka.

"You're welcome. So what is the world like now?"

Chaka and Shannon glanced at each other. Shannon said, "I think the world you knew is gone. We come from a small confederacy of cities on the Mississippi. The evidence so far is that there isn't anything else."

"I'm sorry to hear that. My makers had much to commend them." His tone changed. *"Do you customarily travel by land vehicle? Aircraft? What?"*

"Horse," said Chaka.

The silence wrapped itself around them. Chaka thought she detected a mild vibration in the walls. *"I'd like to offer a piece of advice, if I may. Be careful of the ruins. Avoid them. Some have very elaborate security safeguards. And the Roadmakers designed their systems to endure."*

They asked Mike whether he had seen the first expedition, explaining that they had also arrived on the maglev.

"Yes," he said. *"They were my first passengers in almost nine decades."*

"Did they tell you where they were going?" asked Avila.

"I never got to talk to them."

"Why not?"

"I think I scared them off. I said hello and they ran out into the night." That set off a round of laughter. *"They stayed outside,"* he continued, *"until morning. Then they came back and got their horses."*

"I'd like to have seen it," said Chaka.

"There've been other visitors from time to time. Some never came within range of my speakers. None ever stopped to ask who I was. Until Avila."

Avila felt a rush of pleasure.

And as if they all knew what was coming, the room fell silent. Tense.

"I don't want to do it," said Avila.

"I know. But I can't do it for myself. I was terrified last night."

"At the prospect of dying?"

"At the possibility you might leave."

"There'll be others," Avila said. "You won't be alone anymore, now that we know you're here. There'll be people coming in from the League to talk to you."

For a long time, Mike did not respond. When the voice came again it was flat, devoid of emotion: *"Please don't take this the wrong way, but even while you're here, I am still alone. You and I do not function on the same level."*

"I'm sorry."

"It's not your fault. Unfortunately, you don't even have the capacity to connect me with my siblings."

"You could teach us."

"I don't think so. I'm not an electrician."

Avila was feeling desperate. "Even if we wanted to, we wouldn't be able to hurt you. We can't even *see* you."

"It's easy," he said.

They retreated outside into the fading light of a gray day. It would require the work of a few minutes. And he would be gone.

"We'd cut off a priceless avenue of knowledge," said Quait. "The people at the Imperium would hang us."

Flojian pulled his jacket tight around him. A brisk wet wind blew across the island. "That's so," he said. "If we do this thing, we'd better not say anything about it when we get home."

The remark rang a bell and they looked at one another. Could something like this have happened to Karik? "I don't think so," Flojian responded to the unasked question. "My father would never have agreed to this kind of proposition."

"It's immoral," said Avila. "Healers are pledged

to *heal.* And to do no harm. Under any circumstances."

Shannon folded his arms. Mist covered the distant sea. "I'm not much at arguing moral issues, but I wouldn't want someone to leave *me* to the wolves. That's what we're talking about here. Maybe worse."

Avila's eyes filled with darkness.

A sudden wind chopped across the surface of the water. "Jon's right," said Chaka. "I vote we do it."

They argued back and forth for a couple of hours. Occasionally, the sides changed: Avila conceded that they could not abandon Mike; Shannon concluded at one point that the entity was far too valuable to terminate; Chaka agreed that Silas would have been horrified at cutting off so valuable a source of knowledge. But in the end, they could not simply walk away.

Avila set her lamp on the floor and looked around the empty room as if she expected to see someone sitting in one of the chairs. "Mike?" she said. "If you're sure, we'll do it."

"Thank you, Avila."

"We can only stay a few days. We'll do it before we leave."

"No. Do it tonight."

"Are you really so anxious to *die*?" She used the word deliberately, hoping to shock him out of his resolve.

Mike didn't seem to notice. *"I'm not even sure my makers intended that I be conscious,"* he said. *"However that may be, I've had enough."*

"But why *tonight?* You've been here all this time; can't you wait a few more days?"

"No. I want to be rid of the light. And I know this isn't easy for you. I'm afraid you'll change your mind. That you and your friends will back away, that you'll accede to the moral code you've constructed for yourselves, and run away in the night."

"We won't run away," she said. In her mind she was once again walking through the dawn-stricken streets after Tully's death, returning to the Temple. Unable, it seemed, to save anyone.

"You know how to do it?"

"Yes, we do. *I* do." No sharing responsibility for this.

"All right. I've still got a train out there. It'll be back shortly. Give me time to run it into the shop. I'm going to wash it down before I put it in storage. It'll take about two hours. After that's done, I'm at your disposal."

"A joke," said Avila. "Right?"

He laughed. *"Of course. Avila, be happy for me. This is a night to celebrate."*

"Not for me."

"It's in a gray box. It says MICA slant SR across the front. You'll find a switch, a push button marked 'POWER' on the side of the box. There'll be a slight vibration inside. Push the button. The vibration will stop. When you've done that, but not before, take the box apart. You might have a problem with that. Use an axe if you have to. Inside the box, there's a white metal casing that contains a black disk. Remove the disk and destroy it. Throwing it into the lake will be sufficient."

"Will it hurt?" Avila had asked.

"No," Mike had said. *"I have no capability for physical pain."*

They'd all crowded into his room and sat, trying

to make conversation. Mike had seemed cheerful enough, encouraging them to keep on with their quest. *"I've had some experience with people,"* he'd said, *"and I think few of them ever had an opportunity to achieve greatness. You do. Make it count."*

When the maglev came in, they'd all sat more or less quietly, no one wanting to suggest they get on with things, but everyone anxious to have it over. It was Mike who broke the long half-hour of strained half-sentences and false starts and pointless comments by observing that it was time.

Avila would do it. She would be accompanied by Shannon. The others offered to stay with Mike, but he insisted they leave. *"Thanks,"* he said. *"If any of you ever have any regrets, think of this in theological terms. You've let me out of hell."*

The suite of offices which contained the gray box were located at concourse level on the south side.

"It's in a small, windowless room in the rear. You'll have to go through three doors to get there. I can't know for sure, but the last time I had visual capabilities in the area, the doors were still there and they were locked. The first one, the one you'll see from the branch corridor off the concourse, is marked 'OPERATIONS.' It's at the end of the corridor, just past the washrooms. It opens into what used to be a reception area. Go straight back. At the rear, on the left, there's a glass door. It says 'CONTROL UNIT.' Or it will if the glass is still in place, which it probably won't be. Go through that; now there's a wall with four doors, two on each side. I'm immediately on the right. Room is 2A."

Shannon carried an axe; Avila, a lamp. Shannon was talking, something about irrevocable mistakes, but she was too locked in to her own mind to listen. The dust of centuries crunched underfoot. She wondered about the entity that had lived here so long, and the darkness pressed down on her. "I'll be glad to be done with it," she said.

"Tomorrow," said Shannon. "We pack up and get moving in the morning."

They entered the branch corridor, passed the washrooms, and confronted the door marked *OPERATIONS*. It was heavy and warped. Shannon tugged on the knob. "It's not going to come without a fight," he said.

He hit it once with the axe, without discernible effect. The door and the frame had swollen and fused together. A bar would have been more useful. But there was a rift near the bottom. While Avila held the lamp close, he inserted the axe head and worked it back and forth. The door groaned and gave slightly, and he was able to move the blade higher.

Something broke on the next try, and the door and frame both inched outward. "I think we've got it," he said.

Avila set the lamp down on the floor and got hold of the knob.

Shannon leaned on the axe, pushed it deeper into the wedge he had made. "We're in good shape," he said. "On three."

Caves and other areas that have been long sealed off present a special hazard to investigators. The potential for the buildup of natural gases over an extended period is very real. There have been instances in which unwary excavators have been rendered unconscious, and even smothered.

For Shannon and Avila, there was an even more immediate danger. The interior had been blocked off from the outside world for centuries, and had filled with methane. While they worked on opening the door, the open flame of the oil lamp burned virtually at Shannon's feet.

Chaka was lying close to the campfire, deep in her own dark thoughts, when she heard the explosion.

✠ 17 ✠

Avila was lucky: The door shielded her from the worst of the blast. She came away with a few burns, bruised ribs and shoulder, and a twisted knee. Chaka found her propped against the wall, eyes glazed, beside Shannon. The big forester lay flat, boneless, crumpled. She tried to help him, to clear away the blood. But it was no use.

"I don't know," Avila said, replying to frantic questions. "It just exploded." There was a strong odor of burnt cork in the passageway.

Quait checked for pulse and found none.

Chaka knelt beside Avila, lifting her gently away from Shannon, gathering her into her own arms. "You okay?" she asked.

"Okay—"

"It must have been a bomb." Chaka's voice was shaky. "Why? What's the point?"

"Had to be," said Quait.

Flojian was slower than the others. He arrived, struggling for breath, and his eyes went wide.

The door lay in the corridor, the frame half blown away. Quait glanced into the room but took care not to get too close to the entrance. "Don't touch anything. There might be more surprises in there."

Chaka, trying to hold back tears, was asking Avila what hurt.

Avila couldn't take her eyes from Shannon. "My fault," she said.

"It's not anybody's fault," said Quait.

She got to her knees, took Shannon's right hand in both of hers, and bowed her head.

Chaka's face was creased with tears and blood. "You think Mike did this deliberately?"

"Hard to see how else it could have happened," said Quait.

Flojian nodded.

"I can't believe it." Chaka's face was pale and her eyes were full of pain. "Why? Mike has no reason to attack any of us."

"Maybe," said Quait, "we should start by getting away from the first-name routine. That *thing* is not some friendly lost traveler or oversized dog. It's an *it*. Maybe we were right the first time and it *is* a demon. And maybe it just wants to kill anyone who comes in here." They looked at one another, suddenly aware that everything they were saying was probably being overheard.

"There are such things," said Flojian. "There are all kinds of stories."

Quait looked at the ceiling, which was mottled and waterstained and, near the blast area, scorched. "You didn't even care, did you?" he asked it. "You had no way of knowing who would open the door."

Chaka had a vision of being hounded through the abandoned city by an invisible *thing*. "We ought to get out of here," she said. "Now. Get as far away as we can."

"We're probably safe on the platform," said Quait. "Apparently it can't just come after us, or it would have done so."

Avila folded Shannon's hand over his heart. She murmured a prayer and made the sign of the Traveler's staff.

Quait watched her, his face rigid. "I'd like to find a way to give the son of a bitch what it asked for. Kill it dead." A void lay behind his eyes. "I don't imagine we can assume there's any truth to the black disk story?"

"I doubt it," said Chaka. "He wouldn't give us anything we could use against him."

"Listen," Avila said, getting to her feet. "Let's not waste our time talking about demons. Okay? Mike is a piece of the building, the same way the walls are, the same way the trains are. The real question here is whether this was deliberate."

"What else could it be?"

"I don't know. Maybe we should ask him."

"I don't like it," said Flojian. "Whatever you want to call it, we can't *touch* this thing. If it has more surprises, how do we defend ourselves?"

"We can't," said Avila. "But I don't think we need to."

"Okay," persisted Flojian. "If we admit we can't act against it, why don't we just get out while we can? Leave it alone?"

"If he's innocent," Avila said slowly, "we'd be abandoning him. I can't do that. Especially now. We've paid for his release with our blood."

Quait stared at her a long time. "Then let's get to it," he said. "I'll go with you."

But there was still an element of doubt in Avila's mind. Consequently, she insisted that they move the animals and their gear across the channel into the lobby of the gray tower. "Just as well," said Flojian. "Water's a barrier against evil."

They all insisted, against her better judgment, in going with her to confront the entity that Quait and Flojian now referred to routinely as the house demon.

"All right," she agreed, caving in because she had no real choice. "But I do the talking. Okay?"

They went back into Union Station, walked four abreast through the concourse with a mien that reminded Quait of drill fields, and made a turn into the corridor that housed the stairway.

Flojian reminded them (if anyone needed reminding) that the house demon could probably see them, and undoubtedly had heard everything they'd said. They climbed the stairs to the second floor and walked into Mike's room. Despite a bright sun, they stood in dingy gray light.

"Mike?" Avila said. "Talk to me."

A sudden noise, a fluttering, at the window. A pigeon.

"Mike? I know you're here."

"I'm always here." The voice sounded flat and cold.

"Jon's dead."

"I know. I'm sorry."

"What happened?"

"Accumulated gas, I assume. Did you have an open flame?"

"An oil lamp."

"I never thought of it. I thought the only danger would come from electricity. And that seemed minimal."

"You didn't say *anything* about risks."

"There are always risks, Avila. But I am sorry. I couldn't warn him. I get no visuals from there anymore. I never knew there was a problem until I heard the blast."

"Well," said Flojian, breaking the agreement. "We're sorry, too. But there's not much help for it, is there?"

"Can you see me now?" asked Avila.

"No."

"But there *are* places in the building where you have vision?"

"A few. There's one near the donut shop in the concourse. I see you every time you walk past it."

What an odd creature this was. "Why have we not been meeting in one of these other places?"

"None has working speakers."

"Avila," whispered Quait. His eyes said *get to the point.*

She nodded. "Mike, do you want us to try again?"

Boards creeked underfoot. Quait said, "But we'd like not to get blown up."

"No. Of course not. But you're into Operations. Just be careful going through doors." He paused. *"And, yes. Please. I want you to do this if you're still willing."*

"You're sure," said Quait. "You seem kind of tentative."

"I've never walked these corridors, Quait," Mike said. *"I'm programed to coordinate train schedules and maintain personnel files. Not to assist a break-in. I'm doing the best I can."*

"So far," said Flojian, "your best hasn't been very good."

"I know. Listen, I have a gift for you. Some small compensation for what you've lost. What sort of weapons do you have?"

"Rifles and pistols. Why?"

"What kind of ammunition do they use?"

"Bullets." Quait frowned. "What other kind is there?"

"Okay. Look for a door marked 'SECURITY.' There'll be an outer office and an inner locked room. The inner room has hand weapons, designed for crowd control. They are palm-sized, wedge-shaped. Most of them are still in the original containers, and will have to be charged. I'll explain how to do that."

"Why do I want them?" asked Quait.

"You may find them more effective than what you have. With these, you don't have to hit somebody with a missile. Just point it in their general direction and squeeze." He

repeated that they would need to be charged, and described how to do it.

"Okay," Avila said. "We'll take a look."

"And be careful about closed doors. Right? No open flames. And you might not even be able to breathe in a room that's been sealed. So let it air out."

"Too bad Jon didn't have the benefit of the advice," said Flojian.

Avila threw an angry glance at him. "Okay, Mike," she said. "Anything else?"

"When you get away from the City, be careful. There've been lights on the lake. I don't know what they are. And if your gods do exist, they'll count this night in your favor."

The air in the computer room was stale, but safe. A cracked pipe and crumbled insulation had ensured that. But Avila had no way of knowing, and so she and Flojian had waited a half-hour before using a board to push a lamp into harm's way. When it did not explode, she went cautiously inside. Flojian followed with the axe.

There were several gray boxes in the room. She found the one marked MICA/SR. It was made of pseudo-metal and, like the table on which it stood, looked almost new. There was some discoloration, but that was all. The box was connected by cable to several other devices of similar, but not identical, configuration.

It was making a noise. A low but deep-throated hum.

The push button marked POWER was on the right side. On the left, the letters *IBM* were prominently displayed, centered among other buttons and inserts, marked TURBO, CAPA, and INT. Avila put her hand, palm flat, on top of the casing. It had a rough texture, and she could feel a slight vibration.

She thought about making some final statement to the entity. A farewell. A warning. A last chance to change its mind. But she suspected it was waiting in an agony of anticipation (as she believed she would have been), and any delay now would be cruel. So she pushed the button and the vibration stopped.

There was a seam around the front of the case. She inserted the axe blade and used it to try to force the box open. But she wasn't doing well, and Flojian reached out for the instrument.

"Before you take off your arm," he said.

He produced a chisel and needed only a moment to remove the lid. Beneath lay the white metal casing. She inserted her fingers beneath its lip and pulled. It clicked and the top lifted, exposing the black disk. She looked at it in the lamplight and then lifted it out.

"Done," said Flojian.

She wrapped it in a piece of cloth.

A few minutes later they broke into the security locker and found two dozen of the crowd-control weapons Mike had described. They were small enough to fit in the palm of the hand, and they looked a little like black seashells.

"Not going to scare anyone," Flojian said.

She took six. On the theory that you can't have too much firepower, she'd have taken them all, but they required fifteen minutes each in the unit that Mike had called a charger. When she was finished, she gave half to Flojian and pocketed the rest. Then she went back to the second floor room and called Mike's name. There was no answer.

They stayed that night in the gray tower. Next day, with the horses in tow, they climbed to the fourth floor, picked up Shay's signs, and followed them onto a kind of skyway, navigating rooftops, traveling long ill-lit corridors, and crossing overpasses. By sundown they'd descended again to ground level and reached open water. Here, in the shade of a stand of elm trees, they gave Jon Shannon to the flames. And for the first time, they felt lost in the immensity of the wilderness.

When the ceremony had concluded, Avila weighted the piece of cloth that held the black disk, waded far out into the water, and flung it away.

She looked out at the blue horizon. "Good-bye, Mike," she said. "Ekra convey you in peace to your eternal home."

✠ 18 ✠

The loss of Jon Shannon hit Chaka even harder than Silas's death had. She had known him when she was a child, and she'd been responsible for bringing him into the effort, but those weren't the reasons. Rather, there'd been a sense of indestructibility about the man, as if he could not be brought down, as if any enterprise on which he was embarked could not come to a bad end. Now he was gone and his companions were shaken.

Once again, they began to talk about giving it up. But now there were *two* dead. How did you go back with two dead and explain that you had accomplished nothing?

"That's true enough," said Quait. "But we have two women along, and I think our first obligation is to protect them. I vote we turn around."

"Forget it," Chaka said. "If you want to take care of your own hide, say so. But don't make decisions on *my* account."

"Nor mine," said Avila. She growled her response because she'd been offended, although she too believed that the cost of the mission had now gone too high.

Quait went into a sulk, as if his manhood had been questioned. "Okay," he said finally. "If you're willing to go on, then let's do it. I was only trying to do the right thing."

And Flojian, who believed he was already fighting a reputation for faintheartedness, took the moral high ground, and insisted that they really had no choice but to go on.

So the decision was made to continue, despite the fact that any one of them, left alone to choose, would have opted to turn back.

By the end of the third day, the towers of the city by the sea were just visible in the light of the setting sun. The companions were moving along the south shore, past heavy dunes. It was country they recognized, country they'd seen from the maglev. Inland, the forest still battled extensive ruins, many of which were charred. Like Memphis. And the city in the swamp. During the final days of the Roadmakers, Alvila suspected, fire had been the last resort against the plague.

Wild dogs began to follow them. When they attacked the horses one evening just after sunset, Avila took advantage of the situation to test one of the wedges.

She'd had to act quickly because Quait and Chaka had shot three of the marauding animals within the first seconds of the attack. This had been enough to send the rest of the pack fleeing, but Avila had aimed a wedge in their general direction and squeezed it. A green lamp had come on and a half-dozen of the creatures had simply collapsed. Afterward, they lay for almost two hours before recovering, one by one, and staggering off into the forest.

"I don't care," said Quait. "It's a pussyfoot weapon. Give me a rifle anytime."

From that hour forward, Avila was careful to keep one in her pocket at all times.

Flojian was fascinated by the effect, and also curious about the green and red lamps that blinked on during operation. She showed him and Chaka how to use it. "Point *this* end, and squeeze the shell," she said.

Chaka tried it that night on a wild turkey. The turkey managed a couple of gobbles before falling over. It was asleep before it hit the ground. They had a good dinner, and the weapon seemed quite effective. But would it work on a man?

Flojian was puzzled, not only by the effect, but by the construction. There didn't seem to be any way to take the unit apart. "I wonder," he said, "if we could learn to copy them."

Flojian had discovered to his pleasure that Avila was a willing listener, and able to talk about more than simply religion. They discussed the weapons at length, and speculated on what sort of force they projected. She listened politely while he outlined various schemes for applying the lessons they were learning. And if she could not entirely conceal her occasional impatience with his pragmatism, she made her arguments seriously and without rancor.

She was a beautiful woman. It was easy to forget that in the dust and grime and forced intimacy of daily travel. Flojian wondered why anyone so lovely would have signed on for the celibate priesthood. The thought made him uncomfortable and he pushed it away.

There had never been a serious passion in Flojian's life. At least, not for a woman. He'd been married once, but the marriage had been cool and businesslike, a wedding of like-minded individuals. Perhaps she had been too much like Flojian. They'd drifted apart without hard feelings on either side. A civilized marriage and a civilized divorce.

Women were inevitably wanting in one way or another. They had annoying habits, or did not operate on his mental level, or were lacking in social capabilities. He'd long ago recognized that he would not share his life with anyone. His code was very simple:

Take care of business, make money, take your pleasure with those who permit it. And keep a safe distance.

But he could no longer deny that Avila Kap stirred feelings that had lain dormant a long time. Her laughter, her smile, her eyes . . . It might have been that the two deaths had left him vulnerable to female charms. Or it might have been that it would not have mattered. But he sat deep into the night with her, watching the stars move.

He looked for a sign that she reciprocated his feelings. He suspected that, in her eyes, he was too commercial, too practical, a man with both feet solidly planted. And to make matters literally impossible, she was a half-foot taller than he was. But she was taking him seriously. With this crowd, it was as much as he could reasonably ask.

They were still moving east along the shore when Chaka stopped and pointed out to sea. It was early and the sun had not yet burned off the fog. But they saw something moving through the mist.

Gradually, masts and sails took shape. A schooner, with lanterns strung fore and aft, running parallel to the coast. "And guns," said Quait. "It's got guns."

Voices drifted across the water. And laughter. Then, like a ghost, the vessel slipped away. When the fog lifted, not long after, the horizon was clear.

Shortly before noon they approached a new kind of structure standing alone on an offshore rock. It was unlike anything they'd seen before: a six-sided concrete cylinder several stories high, rising out of the roof of a low building. A few windows looked out of the cylinder. The top was no more than an open frame beneath a metal dome. A deck circled the frame. "I think there must have been glass up there at one time," said Chaka.

An elevated walkway had once connected it with the shore, but most of the walkway was missing. What remained was a low stone wall, a few broken piles jutting out of rock and sand, and some shorn-off metal. "It looks like something they might have used to signal ships," said Flojian. "It's not a bad idea." Along the Mississippi, they raised and lowered lanterns. He was sufficiently interested that they agreed to climb out across the rocks to inspect the structure.

They got wet but made it safely to the front door. Inside, the floor sagged and the rooms were bare. The moldering furnishings that one usually found in Roadmaker houses were missing. A ladder and a circular stairway rose into the cylinder. The rungs were gone from the ladder, and the stairway was ready to come down. It didn't matter: There was no pressing reason to go to the top.

They stood for a time on the beach while Chaka sketched the structure into Silas's journal. There was something peculiarly forlorn about it, cut off and alone, and she tried to capture the effect; but she was not satisfied with the result although everyone else pretended to admire the effort.

The shoreline curved north. A few miles beyond the signal tower, the familiar horizontal stripes began to reappear on trees, directing them up an embankment and onto a road. The road was narrow and overgrown, and almost invisible. Toward the end of the afternoon, it passed over another of the giant highways. Shay's marks led them down an embankment onto the highway, where they turned northeast.

For two more days, they followed the coast. Then the highway veered east, away from the shore. Although no one said anything, Chaka could sense the disappointment: They had hoped, had *believed,* this was the body of water that sheltered Haven.

Two days later, they angled around a ruined town whose name was something-Joseph. (The highway sign was badly worn.) The weather became erratic, warm one day, cold the next. The road turned gradually into a jumble of broken concrete, great chunks thrown up or collapsed. They got off and traveled through adjacent fields.

After a while the road sliced away and the signs took them down a hillside into a forest, which was dominated by a type of pine tree they had not seen before. It had thin, red-brown bark and bright green needles. The trunk was about a foot and a half thick, and it ranged up to seventy-five feet tall. There were also exotic birds and plants. It was a new world.

Ruins were less extensive than they had been near the City, but they were not uncommon. There was seldom a day without isolated buildings or half-buried villages. Highway signs indicated towns where only trees and fields existed. They found a farmhouse near a place called Joppa that was in excellent condition, save for a fallen roof in the rear. The damage was not immediately visible, and it would have been easy to believe the owners were still around somewhere. The town of Homer stood almost intact, complete with the Downtown Restaurant, Harry's Hardware and Auto, and the Colonial Pharmacy.

A church sign advised passersby to get right with the Lord.

✠ ✠ ✠

In the early morning hours of April 5, Chaka listened to the wind in the trees and the occasional movements of small animals in the surrounding brush. They were beneath a canopy of branches and leaves so thick that neither moon nor stars was visible. The fire was low. It was a warm night, she had the watch, and she was having trouble fighting off sleep.

The best way to stay awake was to get on her feet. She strolled over to a nearby spring and, for the fourth or fifth time, splashed water on her face. Then she checked the horses, which were in a clearing. They'd seen a black bear during the course of the day. The bear had looked at them without interest and rumbled back into the woods. But the creature had frightened the animals and unnerved Chaka. She was thinking about the bear when she heard a sound that did not belong in the forest.

She was uncertain at first what it was, something sharp and precise.

A twig snapping?

She laid one hand on her pistol but left the weapon in the holster.

Where was it coming from?

She melted into the trees.

It sounded again.

There was something almost rhythmic about it. And metallic.

She needed several minutes to zero in on the source, but she arrived at last in front of a post. It was made of one of the Roadmaker materials that felt like iron but did not corrode. It was three times her height, and was tangled with a sassafras tree.

The post was of a type that was common in Roadmaker ruins. Sometimes it was made of concrete, sometimes of pseudo-metal. But it was usually found near intersections, and it usually contained red, yellow, and green lenses. But this was the first one she'd seen that made noise.

The sounds formed a distinctive predictable pattern. Click. Count to six. Whir. Count to six. Click. Count to thirty and start a new series.

She stood a long time watching it, listening to it. *These places are all haunted.* At last, she returned to the fireside, where she had no more trouble staying awake.

In the morning, they discovered a brick building buried in the trees. A metal plate identified it as the First Merchants Bank. A cornerstone added:

Est 2023
Ann Arbor

It was a lovely morning. The woods were damp and the air was filled with the smell of green grass. The First Merchants Bank looked intact.

Flojian, who had an affection for commercial institutions, wanted to look inside. "I've never seen one in such good condition," he said.

The forest overgrew the walls on all sides and pushed in through the main entrance and jammed tight an inner set of revolving glass doors. But they found a window whose frame was loose. Quait almost casually ripped it off.

Flojian looked in, saw a long counter, workstations, writing tables, desks, and chairs. Several rooms and two corridors opened off the lobby. He climbed through and descended onto a dirt-covered floor. He was behind the counter. Each of the workstations had the apparently ubiquitous glass sheet and housing that he had seen at the Devil's Eye.

Although Illyrians thought of banks purely as money lenders, the concept of a centralized institution coordinating the flow of currency was not completely foreign. Flojian had been in the vanguard arguing for the establishment of a League bank and a common monetary system.

He stood now, visualizing how this bank had worked. Customers lined up at the counter to deposit money, which would be duly credited to their accounts, and interest paid. That same money would be loaned out to other customers, probably in confidence. That meant loan officers would be located in the rooms centering on the lobby. These loans would be used to capitalize individual enterprise, and they would be paid back at a fixed rate from the profits. All very neat, and a much more progressive system than the one he'd been faced with, in which opportunities were often not exploited and growth not achieved simply because funds were not available.

Quait came in behind him.

There were eight positions for cashiers. And there appeared to be a ninth one, facing *out,* at the point where they'd entered. (He didn't understand that at all.) Each position was furnished with a workspace and a drawer. He opened one and was delighted to see coins. "Marvelous," he breathed. "Quait, look at these."

He picked up one of the larger coins, wiped it off, and held it in the sunlight. It was a quarter-dollar, its name engraved on the reverse, under the likeness of an eagle. He smiled appreciatively at it, slipped it into his pocket, and began to scoop out the others.

"Take as many as you can carry," he advised Quait.

"This place is scary," said Quait, who seemed not to have heard.

"How do you mean?"

Quait opened another drawer. More coins.

And more. Every drawer was filled.

"So what's your point?" asked Flojian.

"These people left so suddenly, they didn't even take their money with them. How bad could the Plague have been?"

"Bad, I guess. I really have no idea."

"Remember what Mike said? They just didn't come to work one day and he never saw them again. Here, they left their money. If we look in the shops, the merchandise is still there. Or what's left of it. It's as if they just walked off the Earth."

"Listen," said Flojian, "why don't we talk about this later? I'm running out of pockets."

Flojian saw movement. Incredibly, a writing table near the front door rose onto three legs and strode forward into the center of the lobby. His hair rose. It looked like a six-foot-tall drawing board with a tapered head connected to a short pliant neck. Two flexible limbs emerged from beneath the table top, and one of them pointed something that looked like a pipe or nozzle in their direction. *"Stop what you are doing,"* came a voice from directly overhead. *"The police are on their way. Do not move unless directed to do so. Weapons will be used if you do not comply with all instructions."*

Quait swore softly.

"Lay down your guns and come around the counter."

Flojian debated his options and glanced at Quait. Was the nozzle a weapon? A gunfight with a machine that could simply walk over and shoot them did not seem promising. He heard Chaka behind him, in the window, say that she didn't believe this.

He took his gun cautiously from his holster, laid it on a table, and walked out into the lobby. Where he got the shock of his life.

Several piles of skulls and bones were heaped up on the floor at the base of the counter.

Quait came out behind him and caught his breath.

"We didn't mean any harm," Flojian said. "We're just passing through."

"Police are en route," said the overhead voice. *"Remain where you are until they arrive."*

"What police?" demanded Quait. "There are no police here."

"Remain where you are until they arrive or I will use force."

Flojian looked down at the bones. "Some of these people are still waiting."

Chaka disappeared from the window.

The table stood about ten feet away, swaying lightly on its tripod frame. But the nozzle, which was pointed at a spot midway between him and Quait, never wavered.

"What do you suggest?" he asked Quait, without taking his eyes off the thing.

"It looks a little rusty. The gun might not work."

"You want to take the chance?"

"We might have to. It's going to be a long wait for the police."

Flojian's heart was pounding. This was ludicrous. He was being held hostage by a writing table. But he was scared all the same. "How do you know the police are coming?" he asked the ceiling.

No response.

"I'm going to try backing away," said Quait. He shifted his weight. Moved a foot.

"That's far enough. Take another step and I will fire on you."

"Now, wait a minute," Quait said.

"There won't be another warning."

"This is crazy," said Flojian.

Chaka was back. With a rifle. But before she could begin to bring it to bear, the nozzle moved past Flojian and he heard a sound like sizzling steak. Chaka screamed and dropped out of sight.

Quait spun on his heel and bolted for the window. The nozzle swung back and the sizzle came again. Quait turned into a ragbag, collided with the counter, and went down in a pile.

Flojian screamed at the table, but the voice came again, cool and unmoved: *"Stay where you are until the police arrive."*

✠ 19 ✠

The world kept trying to turn on its side and Chaka didn't care whether she lived or died. Avila's anxious face hovered over her. There was a damp cloth on her forehead and her blouse was loosened and Avila was telling her to rest.

The daylight hurt.

"Quait's awake, too." The words were only out there, hanging in air, devoid of meaning.

Quait. "Where is he?"

"Still in the bank. The *table* won't let them go." Avila almost managed a grin.

Chaka tried to get up but her head lurched and her stomach fell away. She brought up her breakfast. Avila gave her water to sip and reapplied the cloth, and she began to feel better.

The sun was directly overhead. She'd been out a couple of hours. "What are we going to do?" she asked.

"Actually," said Avila, "I have an idea. Wait here."

That was a joke. As if she could go anywhere.

Avila disappeared and Chaka closed her eyes. She just lay quietly, breathing, feeling as if all her muscles had come unstrung. When Avila came back Chaka saw she'd changed into clean clothes. She wore a new pair of dark blue linen trousers, a green blouse, and a white vest. "Do I look like a police official?" she asked.

Despite everything, Chaka giggled. "Try to frown," she said.

"The blouse is clerical. I was supposed to give it

back when I left." She smiled. "I've always thought I looked good in it."

Chaka shook her head. "It'll never work."

"You have a better idea?"

"Not at the moment."

"Well," said Avila, "we know the table's eyesight is pretty good. Maybe it's not too smart." She bent over Chaka. "How are you feeling?"

"Better."

"Good. Sit tight. I'll be back in a few minutes. I hope."

"Are you going in now?"

"Yes. I can get in the rear door. Which is a good thing. It wouldn't be seemly for the police to have to climb through the window."

"I don't think it's a good idea," said Chaka. "We're going to wind up with *three* people inside."

Avila looked at her. The wind was picking up. It was out of the west, and the forest swayed in its embrace. "I'm open for suggestions."

"Wait it out. When the police don't come it'll get tired and let them go. Anyway, what am I supposed to do when it adds you to the collection?"

"Throw rocks," said Avila. "Seriously, if that *does* happen, go to the alternate plan."

"Which is?"

"Your idea. Wait. Take care of the horses and wait for it to get bored."

Five minutes later Avila squeezed through a cluster of wispberry bushes and strode briskly in the back entrance of the bank. She was carrying her wedge concealed in the palm of her hand. You never knew.

"Somebody here call police?" she asked.

Both men were seated on the floor. But Avila's gaze locked on the dust and bones. It was her first glimpse of the skeletal remains, and her stride faltered as its significance struck home. Quait's back was to the counter, and he looked dazed and discouraged. When he saw her he registered disapproval and shook his head *no*. Flojian had the presence of mind to show the hangdog reaction of a man about to be hauled off to incarceration.

"Yes," said the overhead voice.

"I'm Investigator Avila Kap," she said, hoping she'd guessed right on the title. "I'll take charge of them now." The table made no move to back away. She looked severely at the two on the floor. "Trying to rob the bank, were we?" She reached behind Flojian, took him by the back of his neck, and raised him to his feet. Simutaneously she motioned Quait up. "This is a lawful town, and we don't have much patience with your type." She hoped she sounded sufficiently official. "Let's go, you," she told Quait, pushing him toward the door.

"Just a moment, Investigator Kap." The voice was flat. Emotionless. *"Please give the authorization code."*

She looked at Quait and Flojian, at the ceiling with its hidden voice, and at the three-legged table, arthropodic and serene. She made a pretense of fumbling in her pocket. "I seem to have forgotten it," she said. At that moment, as unobtrusively as she could, she aimed the wedge at the table and squeezed it. The weapon vibrated slightly. Aside from that, nothing happened.

"We require the authorization code before we can release the prisoners," said the voice. *"Policy memorandum six-eight-one-echo slash one-four, dated March 11, 2067."*

"I'll have to go back to my office to get it," she said. "Why don't I take the prisoners with me and I'll send the information back to you."

"Why don't you call your office?"

Avila imagined herself leaning out the window and yodeling for the authorization code. "There's something else I have to check on," she said. "I'll be back in a few minutes."

"Leave the malefactors."

"Right," she said. She signaled Quait and Flojian that she would find a way, and started for the rear exit.

"Inspector Kap."

She stopped. Turned around.

"I would not presume to tell you how to perform your job, but these two look desperate. You might want to bring assistance when you return."

"I knew it was dumb."

"Okay. What's your suggestion?"

"I told you. Wait it out."

"That's already been tried."

"Say again?"

"There are bones in there from the bank's last visitors."

"Oh." Chaka shook her head. "We need a new approach."

"Good."

"Think about Mike."

"What about Mike?"

"Gray boxes. Maybe we can find its gray box and shut it off at the source."

Avila's eyes registered respect. "That's a good idea. You think it would be in the building?"

"We have to assume it is. If it isn't, we're not going to find it."

Avila sat down on a fallen log. "There're closed doors in the passageways. They're the only places I can think of to look. But they're almost certainly locked. Or warped. Or both. So unless we can find a way to guess the right door and take it down in a couple of seconds, I don't think the prospect is good."

"How many doors?"

Avila closed her eyes and pictured the corridors. "Six," she said. "Or maybe eight."

"Pity you didn't pay more attention."

"I was busy. Why don't you stick your head in the window and look? If you push in a little bit you can see down one hallway."

"You made your point," Chaka said. She tried to get to her feet but was driven back by a wave of vertigo.

"The weapon is a little like the wedges," said Avila.

"Yeah," said Chaka. She was damp with perspiration, and her eyes were closed. "Except that the thing they have means business."

"It doesn't kill," Avila said.

"No. But it takes the fight out of you." She lay quietly for several minutes, and Avila thought she'd gone to sleep. But Chaka took a deep breath, opened her eyes, and eased into sitting position.

"Feeling better?"

"A little. Listen, how about if we just walk in and jump the thing. That ought to work."

"That sounds like a last resort," said Avila. "I might have a better idea." She looked through the window. The table was still standing motionless in the middle of the lobby, apparently watching its victims. "It strikes me there's a humanity in these procedures that we might be able to turn to our advantage."

"A *humanity*?"

"The weapons don't kill. The ones in the bank don't. The ones Mike gave us don't."

"But they scramble your head pretty well."

"Chaka, you and Quait were shot and are still alive. That shows a reluctance to kill. Maybe that reluctance will give us a chance."

Chaka strolled in through the back door, carrying a leather bag, trying to appear simultaneously casual and concerned. She took several steps into the lobby, stopped, looked around, carefully smothered her reaction to the piles of bones, and pretended to spot the two men on the floor. "I'm Dr. Milana," she said to Quait. "Have you been injured?"

"Yes," said Quait, who looked puzzled but was smart enough to play along. "Broken ribs, I think."

"Who's in charge here?" she asked loudly.

"And who," asked the ceiling, *"summoned* you, *Doctor?"*

"We were told there was a medical emergency here." She knelt beside Quait and put her ear to his chest. "Good thing I happened to be in the neighborhood. This man has an irregular heartbeat. He's going into Quadristasis."

Quait groaned.

"We'll have to get him to surgery immediately." She turned to Flojian and peered into his eyes. "This one, too. Injured iris. Can you walk, sir?"

"I think so, Doctor."

"Just a minute. No one goes anywhere until the police get here."

The voice came from above somewhere, but beyond that she couldn't narrow it down. The role called for her to glare indignantly, but it was hard to do when there was no target. She tried anyhow. "Who are you?" she demanded. "What's your authority here?"

"Technoguard Security Systems. We're hired—"

"All right, Technoguard Security Systems. One of these two men may die unless he gets immediate medical care. The other may suffer permanent eye damage. I've no intention of allowing that to happen. So if you want to stop us from leaving you'll have to shoot me, too."

"I don't think so, Doctor."

Chaka helped Quait to his feet. She signaled for Flojian to follow, and began edging toward the door.

"If you persist, I will simply target the two malefactors again."

"If you do that, you'll probably *kill* this one. Is that what you want?"

"The weapon is nonlethal."

"*Nonlethal?* Whose bones are these?"

"They belong to previous malefactors."

"Whom you *killed.*"

"They died awaiting the police. I merely apprehended them."

"You *killed* them. Why were you holding them for the police?"

"Because they tried to rob the bank."

"And why is that a reason to have them arrested?"

"Don't be foolish. Bank robbery is a violation of the criminal code."

"And I put it to you that *murder* is a violation of the criminal code. *You* should be turned over to the police. For capital crimes."

She kept moving.

"It's not true."

"Of course it's true. And you're about to do it again. You're determined to kill these men by keeping them here and refusing them the medical assistance they desperately need."

"That is not so."

"It *is* so. And you know it is so."

She'd reached the rear corridor. The table stood swaying but otherwise motionless in the middle of the lobby. Its weapon had not tracked them. It was still aimed toward the counter.

"Police have been summoned." The voice went to a higher pitch.

"Summon them again," said Chaka. "We've caught a murderer."

"Brilliant," said Quait. They walked away from the bank in a jubilant mood, shaking hands and embracing all around.

"That wasn't even the plan," laughed Chaka.

"That's right," said Avila. "The plan was for her to distract them long enough for me to make a run into the side corridor. There was a decent chance that the device that controls the table would be behind one of the doors. I was hoping to reach it and shut it off. But she was doing so well, I stayed put."

"I saw the doors," said Flojian. "What makes you think they wouldn't have been locked?"

"If I couldn't get in, or the table came after me, Chaka had a rock in the bag."

"She was going to hit it with a rock?" asked Flojian.

"Yes," said Chaka. "It was a *big* rock." She showed them. "There'd be a lot going on, and we thought I might get a good shot at it."

They all laughed.

"Listen," Avila said, "it's not as desperate as it sounds. We had a backup plan, too."

"What was that?"

Chaka did a double thumbs-up. "You were great

in there, Flojian," she said. And she hugged him. "The backup idea was to build a fire outside the window. There's a stiff wind, and we might have been able to get enough black smoke inside to shake things up. Maybe even set off some sort of anti-fire system. Who knows? But we'd have gotten a lot of confusion."

"Confusion?" Quait looked back at the heavy shrubbery surrounding the building. "You'd have gotten a conflagration. Those bushes would have gone up like dry timber."

"Well, yes," she said reluctantly. "We knew that. That's why it was the *backup* plan."

"To the other wild idea," laughed Flojian.

Avila sighed. "I wouldn't make fun of it. She got you out."

The strange sort of half-life that had generated the sound in the pole and the response in the bank seemed to infest Ann Arbor. Lights came on outside a stone house as they approached, and blinked off as the last horse (hurried along by Chaka) passed. Elsewhere, a few bars of soft music drifted from a three-story brick building and repeated over and over until they were out of earshot. In a glade, Flojian leaned against a forty-foot-long metallic fence and was startled when a bell rang and three gates sprang open. (There were a dozen gates altogether in the fence, but the others stayed motionless.)

It was restless country and they were glad to be out of it.

They traveled late that evening, moving before a line of thunderclouds, and found shelter in a small Roadmaker church. It was an ideal situation, with a decent supply of wood left over from the last visitor, and a roof that was sufficiently decayed to let out smoke, but whole enough to protect them from the storm. The front door was missing, but that was okay because they were sharing the building with the animals. They watered and fed the horses and rubbed them down and then relaxed wearily in front of a fire.

They had no ale or wine left with which to toast the good fortune of the day, but Quait produced his walloon. His fingers danced across the strings, and he invited requests.

"A good camp song," suggested Chaka.

"Indeed, you shall have it, my lady," he said. "Avila, do you know 'The Golden Company'?"

Avila held up her pipe and essayed a few bars. And Quait sang:

I left my girl at Billings Point
The night we made for Maylay;
She kissed my lips and kept my heart,
And watched me ride away.
Ride away,
Ride away,
She kept my heart and watched me ride
With the Golden Company.

Quait had a tendency to sing off-key, but nobody cared. They all joined in:

We get no ale while on the trail,
No wine nor women neither;
It's post to point and charge the flank
And then we ride away.
Ride away,
Ride away,

She kept my heart and watched me ride
With the Golden Company.

They sang as many verses as they knew and then switched to "Barrel Up," and changed pace with "Tari." Fueled by their sense of loss, mingled with the exhilaration of the day's escape, the evening became an emotional event. They observed moments of silence for Silas and for Jon Shannon; raised cups of tea to Chaka, "our glorious rescuer"; and laughed over how people back home would react to hearing how they had outwitted a table.

"When she announced that she was Doctor Milana and that *thing* took her seriously," said Flojian, "I was barely able to keep a straight face." He went on to draw the lesson: "The intelligences that haunt the Roadmaker ruins aren't really very bright. If there are any more incidents, we need to keep our heads."

Chaka noticed that Quait grew increasingly quiet during the latter part of the evening, and seemed almost distracted when Avila announced that she was going to call it a night.

"Before you do," said Quait, "I have something to say." His voice was off-tone. Jittery.

The firelight created an aura around him. He looked at Chaka for a long moment, and tugged at the drawstrings of his shirt. "I wouldn't want to be like the trooper in the song and miss my chance. I wouldn't want to ride away one day and leave you—" he was still watching her, his gray eyes very round and very intense, "—leave you waving good-bye."

A stillness came over the moment. Light and shadow drifted around the crumbling walls. Chaka discovered she was barely breathing.

"I would be very happy if, when we return to Illyria, you would marry me."

The stiffness melted out of his expression and she read a new message: *There, I've said it and nothing can make me take it back.*

Rain was falling steadily, beating on the roof, pouring through here and there into the old building. "This is a surprise, Quait," she said, stalling for time to collect her thoughts. She flicked back to Illyria and brought up an image of Raney, but he wouldn't come clear.

She took his hand and squeezed it. "I think so. Yes. I would like very much to marry you, Quait."

✠ 20 ✠

Five days after Ann Arbor, they arrived at another city, vast and empty, and stood on the west bank of a major river. Shay's track turned north into the ruins. They followed it along the waterfront, past gray quays and ancient pilings and collapsed warehouses and moldering wharves and stranded ships. The ships were all on the bottom, decks and spars usually above water. Some were behemoths, corroded vessels of such incredible dimensions that they explained the giant anchor on River Road. By midafternoon they were passing the remnants of a collapsed bridge. A second bridge, farther north, had once connected the west bank with an island. It was also down.

Flojian watched seabirds drift across the surface. "Current's not bad," he said.

As if Karik had reacted to the sight of the second damaged bridge, the trail turned away from the river, back into the city. They made camp on the shore that night and, fortified by a trout breakfast, worked their way in the morning past mountains of concrete and iron rubble. As had happened in Chicago, some of the larger buildings had collapsed. To the northwest, a bowl-shaped structure stood serenely intact amid an ocean of debris. The forest was coming back, and patches of black walnut and cottonwood now grew on the bones of these ancient monsters.

They came out on the shore of a long, narrow lake that had formed among the artificial hills. Trees crowded down to the bank. The water was quiet, and they stopped to enjoy the sylvan atmosphere, isolated among so much wreckage. Ducks drifted on the placid surface, and turtles paddled through the depths. A gray stone slab rose out of the water at the eastern end. Carved letters announced *DETROIT–WINDSOR TUNNEL.* It was odd, because no tunnel was in evidence.

The trail led back out to the river, where it stopped. Two pairs of Shay's markers turned vertical. "They crossed here," said Quait.

The other side looked far away. Flojian gazed around at the trees. Some had been cut. "I think I prefer this to dangling in the air anyhow."

"I've never built a raft," said Chaka. "Do we know how to do this?"

Flojian feigned shock. "Do we know how to do this? Do *you* know how to make a bracelet? This is the way I earn my living." He smiled in a lopsided, owlish way. "Well, it was the way I started."

By nightfall they'd taken down eight trees. That wasn't bad for half a day's work by a businessman, a militiaman, and a former priest. (Chaka, who was deemed the least physical of the four, was sent fishing for dinner. She returned with more trout.)

Her relationship with Quait had changed in several subtle ways since the marriage proposal. Curiously, the distance between them seemed to have *in*creased. If their attitude toward each other had not become more formal, it had at least become more circumspect. There was less furtive hand-holding, and almost no stolen kisses. This might have resulted from a combination of Quait's awareness of the chemical relations among the four companions and a reluctance to disturb them, as a formal pairing off would have done; and from Chaka's reflexive tendency to assert her independence.

Chaka also discovered that the sexual tension had eased. Quait had engaged her interest during the first days of the quest. That interest had evolved gradually, or maybe not so gradually, into friendship and then passion. Consequently, she knew she had begun to put on a show for him, softening her voice when she spoke to him, lingering a little too long against a setting sun, letting her eyes speak for her. It would not have been correct to say she no longer felt a need to do any of that, but the pressure was gone, and she was now enjoying him more.

She'd been curious why he had proposed to her in front of the others. "Were you so certain?" she asked.

"Public commitment," he said. "These are peculiar circumstances, and I didn't want you to think I was trying to take advantage of them. I wanted you to know I was serious."

Quait had the first watch. She lay half asleep, listening to the crackling logs and the murmur of the river. He was walking around back by the horses.

He was fairly tall, although he'd always seemed short, standing beside Jon Shannon. Even Avila was an inch taller, but Avila was a six-footer. He had wide shoulders and he moved with easy grace. He was handsome, although not in the classic mode of the long, lean jaw and the straight nose and whatnot. Quait had features that would have drawn no second look from most women except that they were illuminated by the force of his personality. His good humor, the pleasure he took in being with her, his intelligence, all combined to animate his smile in the most extraordinary way. She had known better-looking men. But none more attractive.

⁂ ⁂ ⁂

They needed two days to complete the raft. Flojian directed the operation, carved and installed a rudder, and set up rigging. He converted blankets into sails and showed Avila how to make paddles. They were delayed an additional day when, as they were about to start across, the wind turned around and blew out of the east.

On the morning of April 19, the river was calm and they prepared again to set off. Baggage and saddles were loaded onto the raft. The horses, of course, would swim. Long individual lines were looped around their necks in loose bowlines, so that if one was swept away or went down, it would not drag the others with it.

"I still don't know," Avila said, looking across at the opposite shore. "It's a long way."

"Horses are good swimmers," said Quait. "They can keep going for an hour or so. That should be plenty of time."

Their lead horse was an animal named Bali, a large roan stallion. They coaxed him into the water. He was less than anxious, but once in he seemed okay. The others followed (there were now thirteen altogether), and they launched the raft, which someone had christened *Reluctant*.

The wind filled the sails and the raft slipped out into the current. Almost immediately they saw they were clearing shore too quickly and would drag the horses. Quait and Avila jammed paddles into the water to try to break forward momentum while Flojian trimmed the sails. The *Reluctant* gave way and the animals began to draw closer.

The horses were low in the water. Only their heads and the upper parts of their necks cleared the surface, but they seemed okay. Quait had spread them out on either side of and behind the raft, far enough apart so they didn't get in one another's way. Flojian assumed navigation duties while the others tended to the lines and the animals.

As they drew out into the river, Chaka acquired a better sense of the breadth of the waterway, and consequently of the level of engineering skill required to throw a bridge across it. The bridges, like so much else, had given way to the centuries. The towers still stood, trailing cables. But the spans had fallen into the water, where they lay half submerged.

The scale of Roadmaker civilization was much greater than anyone in Illyria dreamed. The accepted wisdom was that the wilderness contained numerous sites like Memphis and the city in the swamp and Little Rock, near Farroad, and Vicksburg at Masandik and the nameless ruins at Argon and Makar. But knowing it was not the same as walking through it: The wreckage just went on and on, buried in hillsides, sinking into forest floors, scattered along riverbanks, occasionally exploding into impossible dimensions as here in this second giant city.

Nobody back home really understands. They think in terms of a handful of relatively small cities. But look at this. There's a whole world out here that died. Where does it end? How big is the corpse?

The scale of the disaster left them awed. What kind of plague could have taken down *this* civilization? *On Monday, April 10, 2079, the trains came in empty.*

"Mista's having trouble." Avila indicated a black mare. It was beginning to struggle to keep its head up.

They were approaching midstream.

A mild current was pushing them downriver. Avila was kneeling at the stern and Quait joined her. He looked at the animal's frightened eyes and shook his head. "Take some sail off, Flojian," he said, hunkering down beside her. "You okay?"

She nodded.

The raft slowed. "The problem," said Flojian, "is that we're going to drift farther downstream. We might have some trouble picking up the trail."

"Why don't we worry about that after we're across?" said Chaka. They were now directly south of the island. It was heavily wooded. She could make out a coastal road and a stone house. Roadmaker style, still standing watch.

"We're going to lose her," said Avila.

Chaka had deliberately avoided looking back at the struggling animal. Now she saw that it was having trouble keeping its head up.

"Take more sail off," Avila said. "We need to slow down."

Flojian shook his head. "Doesn't matter. We can't go slow enough for her. Turn her loose."

Avila's eyes went wide. "She'll drown."

"She'll drown no matter what we do. Turn her loose, and maybe she'll be the only one that does."

Avila looked at Quait and tears stood out in her eyes.

"It's only a horse," said Flojian. "We couldn't really expect to get them all across."

"Turning it loose makes no difference," Chaka told her. "If it can make shore on its own, it will. If it can't, there's nothing you can do."

Mista's line had tightened. They were beginning to drag her. Avila let it slip out of her hand, watched it trail into the water.

Quait meantime had turned his attention upstream. "Ship," he said.

It had been hidden by the island and the downed bridge. Now it was coming fast.

Flojian swore. "It's got guns," he said.

It was low in the water, with a prow that looked like a wolf's head and six cannons jutting through ports. It had two masts and a lot of sail and it looked flat-bottomed. A pennant with a white rifle emblazoned on a field of green fluttered in her rigging.

Quait could see sailors on deck. They were a ragged bunch, but they moved with disciplined precision. Some were manning one of the forward weapons. Flojian was trying to rig a blanket to get more speed. "Release the horses," he said. "We'll try to make shore."

Quait watched it come. "No chance," he said. But they let the horses go. Chaka slid her rifle out of the baggage.

Quait caught her arm and shook his head. Put it down.

The *Reluctant* was picking up speed. The ship's gun fired and water erupted in front of them. A man in a blue coat and hat put a megaphone to his mouth and told them to heave to. He was about eighty yards away and closing fast.

"I think we better do it," said Flojian.

But Chaka was looking at the master and his crew and her expression told Quait she'd already decided she didn't want to fall into their hands. "We won't have much of a chance with those sons of bitches," she said. "I'd rather fight."

"With *what*?" grumbled Flojian. "Holy One, preserve us."

Avila's dark eyes pinned him. "Don't look for help," she snapped. "We're alone, and we better realize it."

"It was just an expression," he stammered. Quait was surprised at the outburst.

But Chaka was right. He could see that nobody was going to walk away unmarked from this crew.

"Who are they?" asked Chaka.

"Pirates. Or maybe there're naval powers along here somewhere. Who knows?"

The men on the ship were laughing and making obscene gestures. Quait sighed. "Your call, ladies. We can make a stand. Or we can turn ourselves over to them."

"Won't be much of a stand," said Avila.

"I don't care," said Chaka. "They're not going to take *me*."

The ship was turning slightly to port, moving alongside. The master lifted his megaphone again. "Guns down," he ordered.

Chaka's hand was still on the rifle stock.

"Don't," said Avila, removing her holster and laying it on the deck. "Flojian, let them get closer."

Quait frowned at her. She patted her pocket, the one where she kept the wedge. "It's a chance," she said.

Chaka nodded. "Try it. It's all we have."

Flojian struck the sails. The marauder's prow slipped past and ran down two of the horses.

Avila eased the wedge into her palm, held out both hands as if she were welcoming the ship, and frowned. "Nothing," she whispered.

"It has no range," said Quait. "We've got to be up close."

"How close do we need?" growled Chaka. "I can smell them now."

A rope ladder came over the side. The master was giving instructions in a peremptory half-screech. His eyes were dark and cruel and he was appraising the two women with relish.

"Why don't you folks get your hands up?" he said laconically. "And prepare to come aboard."

The crew roared.

Avila raised her hands.

Quait, who had edged close to his rifle, said, "Do it."

"No," she said. "Too many guns up there. Wait for a better chance."

Avila was right: It would have to take everyone out, bow to stern, at one shot. Because the people on the raft would be easy targets afterward for anyone left standing.

The pirates used gun barrels to wave them toward the ladder. One leaped over the rail and landed beside them, rocking the *Reluctant*. He was one of the dirtiest creatures Quait had ever seen, grinning, with missing teeth and stringy black hair and whiskers that looked like strands of wire. He poked Chaka in the ribs and sent her sprawling. "Juicy, this one," he grinned.

A portion of the ship's rail swung open to accommodate them. Quait started up the ladder. Hands reached down, gripped his shoulders and hauled him roughly on deck. He was knocked down, kicked, and searched for concealed weapons. While this was happening, he heard cheers and obscene roars.

They dragged him back to his feet and threw him into line with his companions. Flojian had also been roughed up; and Chaka's face was red with fury and humiliation. Avila surprised him: She managed to retain a calm demeanor and stood coolly among her captors.

The ship's master confronted them. He was a short, ugly thug, five and a half feet of belly, jowls, and beard. He had a limp and a missing ear and a scar across his throat where somebody'd opened him up. A pistol was jammed into his belt. "Welcome to the *Peacemaker*," he said. "Ship of the line of the Ki of Hauberg." He tipped his hat at the name. "I'm Captain Trevor. And who might you be?"

"We're travelers," said Quait. "From the Mississippi League."

"Mississippi?" He frowned, shook his head, and looked around. His crewmen, gathered in a circle, signaled their ignorance. "Never heard of it," he said. "Not that it matters." He came forward, put his fist under Avila's chin, lifted it, and appraised her. He grunted approval, then inserted his hand into Chaka's hair and forced her head back. "They've both got good teeth," he said.

"Not for long," came a shout.

Quait stiffened, but a muzzle pressed into his back and a soft voice in the rear warned him not to move. "Won't do no good," the voice said. "You'll just be dead."

He turned to look at the speaker. He was small, furtive, grinning. "This is a treat for us," he said.

"What'll happen to them?" asked Quait.

"Before or after?" He cackled. His eyes slid back to the women. "If they're good, they'll go on the block at Port Tiara. They should bring a decent price. So'll you. If you behave."

"Let's see what they've got, Captain," somebody said.

Others took up the cry. Trevor looked momentarily uncertain, but the crewmen must have been familiar with the routine because they were already laughing and forming a space. "What can I do?" the master asked no one in particular. He leered at Chaka. "*You*. Give us a show."

Chaka made a move at him, but he was surprisingly quick for a man of such ungainly appearance. He seized her wrist, twisted it violently, and forced her to the deck. "We got a good one here, boys," he said. "I *like* women who can't be pushed." He nodded to someone in back. Quait's hands were seized, pulled behind him and tied, and he was lifted to the rail. "Have it your way, bitch," said Trevor.

He dragged her to her feet by her hair and turned her to face Quait.

"No," she screamed. "What do you *want*?"

Laughter all around. "I'm sure you can guess. Right, boys?"

Avila stepped forward and looked down at Trevor. "Captain," she said, "she's frightened. She's *young*. Why not let *me* warm everybody up?"

When Trevor hesitated, Avila put a finger on his chest and whispered something to him. The crew laughed and the captain nodded.

To Quait's relief, they lowered him from the rail; but they did not untie his hands.

Several crewmen had been working on the raft, handing up their baggage. One piece fell into the water. When they were finished, they climbed back on deck and cut the *Reluctant* loose.

The master stood with his back to the prow. Quait counted fourteen others: ten forming the circle, the two guards who watched him and Flojian at the rear of the group, one at the ship's wheel, and one beside the main mast (which was affixed atop the master's sea cabin and thereby provided a fine view of the proceedings). All had guns.

Avila laughed and joked her way around the perimeter, teasing with her eyes, her body, her smile.

Flojian had gone pale. Quait, recovering from the jolt of fear that had come when he'd expected to be pitched overboard, was shocked at her performance. *Where had she learned that?*

Cheers broke out.

She stopped before a three-hundred-pounder in a black vest and pantaloons, and stretched langorously.

More yells of approval.

Flojian struggled to get free, and was clubbed to his knees. The man with the club was small, ill-smelling, and rat-faced. He raised his weapon and was about to bring it down across Flojian's face when Quait pushed into it and succeeded in taking the blow on his shoulder. They were both dragged back to their feet.

Flojian looked dazed.

Now Avila's fingers moved down the front of her jacket, releasing clasps while her audience urged her on. She removed the garment with an exaggerated motion, held it out toward one of the pirates, and then snatched it back when he grabbed for it. Casually, she threw it to Flojian.

He caught it, dropped it, and bent to pick it up. He got a kick for his trouble and stumbled forward. This time they held Quait tightly and wouldn't let him help.

Avila strode into the middle of the circle, and pulled her blouse clear of her belt.

The look on Flojian's face was a mixture of rage and despair. But Quait thought he knew what had just happened. He tried to catch Flojian's eye, but was unable to do so. He couldn't make himself heard over the noise and so he took the only action he could. He reached out and kicked him.

The rat-faced man laughed but Flojian looked back at his tormenter, assuming *he* had delivered the blow. Now Quait got his attention. He formed the word "pocket" with his lips.

"What?"

Avila was releasing more snaps. The wind got under her blouse, sucked at it, pulled it away from her; and finally she drew it off and lobbed it toward one of the pirates. She stood now in boots, black trousers, and a white halter.

She moved back close to Trevor, wet her lips, and

spread her arms invitingly. Trevor watched her, hypnotized, saw her hands go behind the halter, saw the halter come free. "Yeah," roared Trevor, "that's *good.*"

Flojian finally understood. He reached into the pocket of Avila's jacket and came out with something concealed in his palm.

Trevor limped forward, ripped away the halter, and took the woman in his arms, crushing her and burying his face against her neck.

Chaka was on Quait's left. Five men stood on the right side of the circle, between Flojian and Trevor. Quait never really saw what happened, but these five abruptly sagged and collapsed. Bedlam followed. A shot rang out. Chaka broke free and scrambled clear, giving Flojian a free field of fire. The master's face had gone slack and Avila was trying to disengage from him.

Flojian was pointing the wedge to the left now, and three more went down. Quait knocked over the rat-faced man, but was shoved hard by his own guard. Another shot was fired. The pirates were looking around, weapons in hand, trying to find a target. Chaka succeeded in pushing one overboard, but was then decked by the helmsman.

The master was on his knees, folding up, blood running down his shirt. Avila whirled away from him with his pistol, and killed the one atop the sea cabin. But then, to Quait's horror, *the remaining pirates concentrated their fire on her.*

She shuddered in a hail of bullets and went down as Flojian leaped forward, screaming *no no no,* and swept the deck clear of combatants.

She was dead before they got to her, blood welling from a dozen wounds.

21

Flojian wanted to kill them all.

There was, in Quait's mind, sufficient justification. But he could not bring himself to execute twelve helpless men. (Two, including the captain, had died of gunshot wounds; and the one Chaka had thrown overboard was missing.) Chaka was repelled by the notion and pointed out that Avila would not have allowed it. Flojian reluctantly backed off.

They settled on a more symbolic vengeance.

Using the crew as a workforce, they dumped the ship's guns into the river. Flojian then struck her colors, put them with the baggage, and ran the *Peacemaker* aground. The wheel was removed and the hulk was burned.

The companions discovered Shay's familiar markings a quarter mile downriver. Six of their horses showed up, including Bali, Lightfoot, Piper, and, to their surprise, Mista. They loaded the ship's wheel on the stallion. The crew were left bound by the seashore. Flojian tossed them a dull knife as he rode away.

That afternoon, on the south shore of yet another body of water whose limits lay beyond the horizon, they built a pyre for Avila. As part of the ceremony, they offered *Peacemaker*'s wheel to her and inserted it into the pile of fagots, along with the ship's colors. Each came forward to describe the various benefits that had been obtained from having known Avila Kap, and why her passage through this life had been a blessing. They drank to her, using water from the lake, and announced their pleasure that she had gone on to her reward and was now free of the troubles of this plane of existence. This time, however, the pretense of joy derived from the completion of a valued life broke down. Chaka sobbed openly. And the agony in Flojian's eyes burned itself into Quait's memory.

At the moment the sun touched the western rim of the world, Chaka held a torch to the bier. The flames caught quickly, spread through the twigs and grass, and quickly blazed up around her.

"What frightens me most," Flojian said, staring at the inferno, "is that she abandoned her vows. She is now facing the god she denied." His voice shook and tears came again.

"I think you can rest easy," said Chaka. "The gods are kinder and more understanding than we think. Shanta must have loved her just as we did."

Quait shook her. "Storm coming," he said. "Looks like a bad one." The western sky was filled with silent lightning. She could smell the approaching rain. "There's a cave a half-mile south," he continued. "It's pretty big. We can wait it out in there."

Flojian was awake. *Still* awake, probably.

They loaded the horses and rode out singly, Quait in front and Flojian at the rear. They moved through a patch of cool green forest, crossed a spring, and climbed the side of a ridge.

Chaka drew alongside Quait and lowered her voice. "It's time to give it up," she said. "Go home. If we still can. Before we lose anybody else."

The thunder was getting loud.

"If we give it up now," said Quait, "everything will have been for nothing." He reached over and took her arm. "I think we have to finish it now. Whatever that takes. But nothing's changed. If you elect to go home, I'll go with you."

"What about Flojian?"

"He's beaten. I don't think he cares anymore what we do."

"What can we possibly find," Chaka asked, "that's worth the price?"

A wall of rain moved out of the dark. It caught them and drove her breath away. Water spilled out of Quait's hat onto his shoulders.

"Not much farther," he said.

Chaka was making her decision. She wanted no more blood on her hands. Tomorrow they would start back.

The rain pounded the soft earth, fell into the trees.

They rode with deliberation, picking their way among concrete and petrified timbers and corroded metal. The debris had been softened by time: Earth and grass had rounded the rubble, spilled over it, absorbed its sharp edges. Eventually, she supposed, nothing would be left, and visitors would stand on the ruins and not know they were even here.

Quait bent against the rain, his hat low over his eyes, his right hand pressed against Lightfoot's flank. He looked worn and discouraged, and Chaka realized for the first time that he too had given up. That he was only waiting for someone to say the word, to take responsibility for admitting failure.

The ridge ended abruptly. They descended the other side and rode through a narrow defile bordered by blocks and slabs.

"You okay?" he asked Flojian, speaking loudly to get over the roar of the storm.

"Yes," Flojian said. "Couldn't be better."

The cave was a square black mouth rimmed by

chalkstone and half hidden by bracken. They held up a lamp and could not see the end of it.

"Plenty of room," said Chaka, bringing up the rear. She was drenched. "Pity we don't have any dry wood."

"Aha," said Quait. "Never underestimate the master." A stack of dead branches had been piled inside. "I took the precaution when I was here earlier."

While Flojian and Chaka took care of the animals, Quait built a fire and put tea on. Then they changed into dry clothes. They didn't talk much for a long time. Quait sat, wrapped in his blanket, warm and dry. It was enough.

"Thanks," said Flojian.

Chaka understood. She embraced him, buried her cheek against his. He was cold. "It's okay," she said.

Later, she recorded everything in the journal, and pinpointed the site of Avila's cremation. She knew that, if she lived, she would one day revisit the place.

It was hard to guess what the grotto had originally been. It was *not* a natural cave. The walls were tile. Whatever color they might once have possessed had been washed away. Now they were gray and stained, and they curved into a high ceiling. A pattern of slanted lines, probably intended for decorative effect, cut through them. The grotto was wide, wider than the council hall, which could accommodate a hundred people; and it went far back under the hill. Miles, maybe.

Thunder shook the walls, and they listened to the steady beat of the rain.

Quait had just picked up the pot and begun to pour when thunder exploded directly overhead. He lifted his cup in mock fealty to the god of the storm. "Maybe you're right," he said. "Maybe we should take the hint."

The bolt struck a corroded crosspiece, a misshapen chunk of dissolving metal jutting from the side of the hill. Most of the energy dissipated into the ground. But some of it leaped to a buried cable, followed it down to a melted junction box, flowed through a series of conduits, and lit up several ancient circuit boards. One of the circuit boards relayed power into a long-dormant auxiliary system; another turned on an array of sensors which began to take note of sounds in the grotto. And a third, after an appropriate delay, threw a switch and activated the only program that still survived.

Sleep did not come easily. Chaka watched Flojian drift off. Quait sat for a long time, munching berries and biscuit, and drinking tea and talking about not very much in particular. How these experiences reminded him of life in the military, except that death seemed to be more unexpected. How cold it was in this part of the world. ("I know we've traveled north, but it's the middle of April. When does it get warm here?") How effective the wedges had been. He'd dug his out of the baggage and would not be caught again without it. And then, abruptly, as if he wanted to get it on record: "You really think we should start back?"

"Yes."

"Tomorrow?"

"Yes. While we can still find our raft."

"That settles it, then. Okay. I don't think anyone can say we didn't try. We'll run it by Flojian in the morning. Give him a chance to argue it, if he wants."

"He won't."

The fire was getting low, and she could hear

Flojian snoring lightly. "It's not as if we have any reason to think we're close," she said.

The thunder began to draw away, and the steady clatter of the rain grew erratic, and faded.

"You're right, Chaka," he said. It was his final comment for the evening.

Quait had lost twenty pounds since they'd left Illyria two months before. He had aged, and the good-humored nonchalance that had attracted her during the early days had disappeared. He was all business now. She had changed, too. The Chaka Milana who lay by the fire that night would never have wandered off lightly on so soul-searing an adventure.

She tried to shake off her sense of despair, and shrank down in her blankets. The water dripped off the trees. A log broke and fell into the fire. She dozed off.

She wasn't sure what brought her out of it, but she was suddenly awake, senses alert.

Someone, outlined in moonlight, illuminated by the fire, was standing at the exit to the grotto, looking out.

She glanced over at Quait. His chest gently rose and fell; Flojian lay to her left.

She'd been sleeping on her saddlebag. Without any visible movement, she eased her gun out of it. Even after yesterday's demonstration, she was still inclined to put more faith in bullets than wedges.

The figure was a man, somewhat thick at the waist, dressed in peculiar clothes. He wore a dark jacket and dark trousers of matching style, a hat with a rounded top, and he carried a walking stick. There was a red glow near his mouth that alternately dimmed and brightened. She detected an odor that might have been burning weed.

"Don't move," she said softly, rising to confront the apparition. "I have a gun."

He turned, looked curiously at her, and a cloud of smoke rose over his head. He was indeed puffing on something. And the smell was vile. "So you do," he said. "I hope you won't use it."

He didn't seem sufficiently impressed. "I mean it," she said.

"I'm sorry." He smiled. "I didn't mean to wake you." He wore a white shirt and dark vest with a dark blue ribbon tied in a bow at his throat. The ribbon was sprinkled with white polka dots. His hair was white, and he had gruff, almost fierce, features. There was something of the bulldog about him. He advanced a couple of paces and removed his hat. And he spoke with a curious accent.

"What are you doing here?" she asked. "Who are you?"

"I live here, young lady."

"Where?" She glanced around at the bare walls, which seemed to move in the flickering light.

"Here." He lifted his arms to indicate the grotto and took another step forward.

She raised the gun and pointed it at the middle of his vest. "That's far enough," she said. "Don't think I'll hesitate."

"I'm sure you wouldn't." The stern cast of his features dissolved into an amiable smile. "I'm really not dangerous."

She took a quick look behind her. Nothing stirred in the depths of the cave. "Are you alone?" she asked.

"I am now. Nelson used to be here. And Lincoln. And an American singer. A guitar player, as I recall. Actually, there used to be a considerable crowd of us."

Chaka didn't like the way the conversation was going. It sounded as if he were trying to distract her. "If I get any surprises," she said, "the first bullet's for you."

"It *is* good to have visitors again. The last few times I've been up and about, the building's been empty."

"Really?" *What* building?

"Oh, yes. We used to draw substantial crowds. But the benches and the gallery have gone missing." He looked solemnly around. "I wonder what happened."

"What is your name?" she said.

He looked puzzled. Almost taken aback. "Don't you know?" He leaned on his cane and studied her closely. "Then I think there's not much point to this conversation." His voice was deep and rich, and the language had a roll to it.

"How *would* I know you? We've never met." She waited for a response. When none came, she continued, "I am Chaka of Illyria."

The man gave a slight bow. "I suppose, under the circumstances, you must call me Winston. Of Chartwell." He delivered an impish grin and drew his jacket about him. "It *is* drafty. Why don't we retire to the fireside, Chaka of Illyria?"

If he were hostile, she and her friends would already be dead. She lowered the weapon and put it in her belt. "I'm surprised to find anyone here. No offense, but this place looks as if it's been deserted a long time."

"Yes. It does, doesn't it?"

She glanced at Quait, dead to the world. Lot of good he'd have been if Tuks came sneaking up in the night. They'd felt so secure in the cave, they'd forgot to post a guard. "Where have you been?" she asked.

"I beg your pardon?"

"*We've* been here several hours. Where have *you* been?"

He looked uncertain. "I come and go," he said at last. He lowered himself unsteadily to the ground and held his hands up to the fire. "Feels good."

"It *is* cold."

"You haven't any brandy, by chance?"

What was brandy? "No," she said. "We don't."

"Pity. It's good for old bones." He shrugged and looked around. "Strange. The place does seem to have gone rather to the dogs, as the Americans would say. Do *you* know what's happened?"

"No." She didn't even understand the question. "I have no idea."

Winston placed his hat in his lap. "Yes. We seem to be quite abandoned," he said. Somehow, the fact of desolation acquired significance from his having noted it. "I regret to say I've never heard of Illyria. Where is it, may I ask?"

"Two months southwest. In the valley of the Mississippi."

"I see." His tone suggested very clearly that he did *not* see. "Well, I know where the Mississippi is." He laughed as if he thought that remark quite funny.

"But you really do not know Illyria?"

He peered into her eyes. "I fear there's a great deal I do not know." His mood seemed to be darkening. "Are you and your friends going home?" he asked.

"No," she said. "We are looking for Haven."

"Haven?" He blinked. "Where on earth is that?"

"We don't know, Winston."

"Well, then, I suspect you're going to have a bloody awful time finding it. Meantime, you're welcome to stay here. But I don't think it's very comfortable."

"Thank you, no. You haven't heard of Haven, either?"

Winston nodded and his forehead crinkled. There was a brooding fire in his eyes. "Is it near Toronto?"

Chaka looked over at Quait and wondered whether she should wake him. "I don't know," she said. "Where's Toronto?"

That brought a wide smile. "Well," he said, "it certainly appears *one* of us is lost. I wonder which it is."

She saw the glint in his eye and returned the smile. They were *both* lost.

"Where's Toronto?" she asked again.

"Three hundred kilometers to the northeast. Directly out Highway 401."

"Highway 401? There's no highway out there anywhere. At least none that *I've* seen."

The cigar tip brightened and dimmed. "Oh, my. It must be a long time."

She pulled up her knees and wrapped her arms around them. "Winston, I really don't understand much of this conversation."

"Nor do I." His eyes looked deep into hers. "What is this *Haven*?"

She was not shocked at his ignorance. After all, Mike hadn't known either. "Haven was the home of Abraham Polk," she said hopefully.

Winston shook his head. "Try again," he said.

"Polk lived at the end of the age of the Roadmakers. He knew the world was collapsing, that the cities were dying. He saved what he could. The treasures. The knowledge. The history. Everything. And he stored it in a fortress with an undersea entrance."

"An undersea entrance," said Winston. "It must be a fair distance from here. How do you propose to get in?"

"I don't think we shall," said Chaka. "We are going to give it up and go home."

Winston nodded. "The fire's getting low," he said.

She poked at it and added a log. "No one even knows whether Polk really lived. He may only be a legend."

Light filled the grotto entrance. Seconds later,

thunder rumbled. "Haven sounds quite a lot like Camelot," he said.

Camelot? He must also have read *Connecticut Yankee.*

"You've implied," he continued, after taking a moment to enjoy his weed, "that the world outside has been destroyed."

"Oh, no. Only the cities have been destroyed. The world is doing fine."

"But there are ruins?"

"Yes."

"Extensive?"

"They fill the forests, clog the rivers, lie in the shallow waters of the harbors. Yes, you could say they're extensive. Some are even active, in strange ways. Like this one."

"And what do you know of the British?"

She shrugged. "I don't know the British, sir."

"Well, that will probably make the Americans happy. You say everything is locked away in this *Haven*?"

"Yes."

"On which you are about to turn your back."

"We're exhausted, Winston." She had by now concluded that Winston was related to Mike and the entity or entities in the bank. He was real, but not a man. He *looked* like a man, but he talked like someone misplaced in time. She was beginning to recognize the trait.

"Your driving curiosity, Chaka, leaves me breathless."

Damn. "Look, it's easy enough for *you* to point a finger. You have no idea what we've been through. None. We have three people dead."

Winston looked steadily at her. "Three dead? I'm sorry to hear that. But the prize sounds as if it might be of great consequence."

"It *is*. But there are only three of us left," she said.

"Chaka, history is never made by crowds. Nor by the cautious. Always, it is the lone captain who sets the course."

"It's over. We'll be lucky to get home alive."

"That may be true. And certainly it is true that going on to your goal entails great risk. But you must decide whether the prize is not worth the risk."

"*We* will decide. My partners and I." Her temper was rising. "We've done enough. It would be unreasonable to go on."

"The value of reason is often exaggerated, Chaka. It would have been reasonable to accept Hitler's offer of terms in 1940."

"What?"

He waved the question away. "It's no matter now. But reason, under pressure, usually produces prudence when boldness is called for."

"I'm not a coward, Winston."

"I'm sure you aren't. Or you would not be here." He bit down hard on his weed. A blue cloud drifted toward her. It hurt her eyes and she backed away.

"Are you a ghost?" she asked. The question did not seem at all foolish.

"I suspect I am. I'm something left behind by the retreating tide." The fire glowed in his eyes. "I wonder whether, when an event is no longer remembered by any living person, it loses all significance? Whether it is as if it never happened?"

Flojian stirred in his sleep, but did not wake.

"I'm sure I don't know," said Chaka.

For a long time, neither of them spoke.

Winston got to his feet. "I'm not comfortable here," he said.

She thought he was expressing displeasure with her.

"The floor is hard on an old man. And of course you are right: You and your comrades will decide whether to go on. Camelot was a never-never land. Its chief value lay in the fact that people believed in certain qualities associated with it. Perhaps the same thing is true of Haven. Maybe you're right to turn back."

"No," she said. "It *exists*."

"And is anyone else looking for this place?"

"No one. We will be the second mission to fail. I don't think there will be another."

"Then let it be buried, Chaka of Illyria. Let it be buried with your lost companions."

She backed away from him. "Why are you doing this?" she asked. "Why do *you* care?"

"Why did you come so far?"

"My brother was with the first expedition. I wanted to find out what happened to him."

"And the others?"

"Quait? He's a scholar. Like Silas." She took a deep breath. "We lost Silas. And Flojian came because his father's reputation was ruined by the first expedition."

His eyes grew thoughtful. "If those are your reasons for coming, child, then I advise you to go back. Write the venture off and invest your money in real estate."

"Beg pardon?"

"But I would put it to you that those are *not* the reasons you dared so much. And that you wish to turn away because you have forgot your true purpose."

"That's not so," she said.

"Of course it's so. Shall I tell you why you undertook to travel through an unknown world, on the hope that you might, *might,* find a place that's half mythical?" Momentarily he seemed to fade, to lose definition. "Haven has nothing to do with brothers or with scholarship or with reputation. If you got there, if you were able to read its secrets, you would have all that, provided you could get home with it. But you would have acquired something infinitely more valuable, and I believe you know what it is: You would have discovered who you really are. You would learn that you are a daughter of the people who designed the Acropolis, who wrote *Hamlet,* who visited the moons of Neptune. Do you know about Neptune?"

"No," she said. "I don't think so."

"Then we've lost everything, Chaka. But you can get it back. If you're willing to take it. And if not you, then someone else. But by God, it is worth the taking." His voice quivered and he seemed close to tears.

Momentarily, he became one with the dark.

"Winston," she said, "I can't see you. Are you still there?"

"I am here. The system's old, and will not keep a charge."

She was looking *through* him. "You really *are* a ghost," she said.

"It's possible you will not succeed. Nothing is certain, save hardship and trial. But have courage. Never surrender."

She stared at him.

"Never despair," he said.

A sudden chill whispered through her, a sense that she had been here before, had known this man in another life. "You seem vaguely familiar. Have I seen your picture somewhere?"

"I'm sure I do not know."

"Perhaps it is the words. They have an echo."

He looked directly at her. "Possibly. They are ancient sentiments." She could see the cave entrance and a few stars through his silhouette. "Keep in mind, whatever happens, if you go on, you will become one of a select company. A proud band of brothers. And sisters. You will never be alone."

As she watched, he faded until only the glow of the cigar remained. "It is your own true self you seek."

"You presume a great deal."

"I know you, Chaka." Everything was gone now. Except the voice. "I *know* who you are. And you are about to learn."

"Was it his first or last name?" asked Quait, as they saddled the horses.

"Now that you mention it, I really have no idea." She frowned. "I'm not sure whether he was real or not. He left no prints. No marks."

Flojian looked toward the rising sun. The sky was clear. "That's the way of it in these places. Some of it's illusion; some of it's something else. But I wish you'd woken us."

She climbed up and patted Piper's shoulder. "Anybody ever hear of Neptune?"

They shook their heads.

"Maybe," she said, "we can try *that* next."

✠ 22 ✠

After the encounter in the grotto, Chaka became more prone to investigate sites that aroused her interest. It may have been that she began to view the quest differently. The value of the expedition, in her mind, would no longer hinge exclusively on whether she learned what had happened to Arin, and to the other members of the first mission. Nor even to whether they found the semi-mythical fortress at the end of the road. In a sense this was also an expedition into time, a foray into an elusive past. They had already seen marvels that exceeded what she would have considered the bounds of the possible. What else lay waiting in the quiet countryside?

"I think it's a flying machine," said Flojian.

The object vaguely resembled a giant iron bird. It had a sleek main body flanked by a pair of cylinders, and crosspieces that looked like wings, and spread tails. It was in the middle of a forest, one of nineteen lined up four abreast, five deep, except for one column in which the foremost was missing. There was no single one among the group that had not been crushed and folded by the trees. One had even been lifted completely off the ground. Nevertheless, the objects were identical in design. It was easy to see what they had originally looked like.

The crosspiece extended about fifteen feet to either side. It was triangular, wide where it was attached to the central body (just above the flanking cylinders), and narrow at the extremities. A hard, pseudo-glass canopy was fitted atop the main body, near the front. It enclosed a seat and an array of technical devices so complex they looked beyond human comprehension. The forward section flowed into a narrow, needle-shaped rod.

Below the bubble, black letters spelled out the legend: *CANADIAN FORCES*. The main body expanded, flaring toward the rear, encompassing the twin cylinders, which terminated in a pair of blackened nozzles. Four tapered panels, two vertical and two horizontal, formed the tail.

Flojian discovered a concrete pit by stumbling into it, and examination suggested that the entire area, with its legion of artifacts, might once have been enclosed.

Quait climbed onto the frame and looked down into the canopy. "A month ago I'd have said flying machines were *impossible,*" he said.

But they had been in one. Although these were a different order of conveyance from the maglev.

Quait lifted a panel, pulled on something, and the canopy opened. He exchanged grins with the others and lowered himself into the seat. It was hard and uncomfortable. The various devices seemed ready to hand. He was tempted to push a few buttons. But experience had made him cautious.

It was not only the conversation with Winston that had changed the tone of the mission. The discovery that they possessed, in the wedge, a weapon of considerable power had also done much for their state of mind.

The day after they'd left the grotto, a black bear had attacked Flojian. Flojian had gone instinctively for his gun, but had dropped and then kicked the weapon. The creature got close enough to deliver a blast of hot and torpid breath. Flojian had then produced the only defense he had available: the wedge. Despite the demonstration on the *Peacemaker,* he hadn't yet learned to rely on the small, harmless-looking black shell. But it put out the creature's lights as it might have extinguished a candle. That night they'd feasted.

A group of six armed Tuks also tried their luck, stopping them on the trail and announcing their intention to take the horses, the baggage, and (apparently as an afterthought) Chaka. With the weapon in her palm, she'd felt little other than contempt for the ragged raiders. She listened politely to threats and demands and had then casually put the gunmen to sleep.

A second confrontation had followed a similar script. A dozen horsemen had blocked them front and rear, demanding whatever of value the travelers were carrying. But the numbers didn't seem to matter. On this occasion, the companions responded by holding out their arms in a gesture of despair, with their hands curled over the wedges. They left it to Chaka to synchronize the attack by simply telling the bandits that they looked tired and probably needed some rest. The effect was both exhilarating and awe-inspiring. The horsemen and their animals collapsed simultaneously.

It gave the travelers a sense of near-invulnerability, which Quait warned could get them killed.

But no one slept well that night. And when Chaka woke out of a troubled dream she saw Flojian hunched over the fire.

She got up and joined him. He continued to stare at the flames.

"Avila," she said.

He nodded. "It needn't have happened."

If they'd taken the wedges seriously. If they'd all carried them, as Avila had.

"It's done," she said.

His jaw worked and he wiped his eyes.

Word might have gone ahead. During the next ten days they encountered more groups of Tuks, but the meetings were amicable, and there were even invitations to visit Tuk settlements.

They accepted on several occasions and enjoyed themselves thoroughly. Spring seemed finally to have arrived, and festivals were in full swing. The food was good, but they were careful not to drink too much. In the spirit of the season, the entertainment was generally erotic. Chaka enjoyed watching Quait pretend to rise above it all, and she was pleased to see that Flojian actually seemed to enjoy himself at the spectacles, although he refused the use of Tuk women when they were offered. Remembering advice he'd got from Shannon, he was careful to plead illness on these occasions rather than risk offending his hosts.

Quait, who divulged his relationship with Chaka, received no offer.

The Tuks pretended not to notice the security precaution behind the insistence of the three that they sleep under the same roof. They nodded knowingly at Chaka, suggesting they enjoyed the presence of a woman who liked her men two at a time. "We are men of the world here," one Ganji reminded her seriously. "We understand these things."

The Tuks knew the Ki of Hauberg. He was a despot, they said, who ruled one of several naval powers along the shores of the Inland Sea. They also knew the *Peacemaker*, and were glad to hear of its demise.

"Slave ship and raider," they said. "The cities are all vile places. They steal from one another, make war on one another, and band together only to pillage us. You were lucky to escape."

For several days it rained constantly. Sometimes they plodded on through the downpour. If a shelter was available, they used it.

They watched thunderstorms from the interiors of a courthouse and a theater, speculating about the ancient dramas played out at the two sites. "Murder and treason at both," suggested Quait, reflecting an Illyrian tendency to think of the Roadmakers in grandiloquent and sometimes apocalyptic terms.

"More likely murder and treason on stage," said Flojian, "and wife-beating and petty theft before the bench. Their criminals were probably just like ours, cheap pickpockets and bullies." The general view of the Roadmakers was that they spent their days executing monumental building projects, and their evenings discussing architecture, mathematics, and geometry. It was known that they had also created a considerable body of literature and music, but because so little of the former and none of the latter had survived, most people now thought of them as bereft of those arts.

"You've described this," Flojian told Chaka as they camped on the stage, "as a voyage in time. I truly wish it was. I would very much like to take a seat up front and watch some of the shows."

"Maybe," said Chaka, "if we find what we're looking for, that'll become possible."

It was midmorning; they were following Shay's signs through the forest, and Chaka was thinking how good it would be to quit for the day and soak her feet in the next spring, when she very nearly walked off the edge of an embankment.

She looked down an angled wall into a steep canyon. The canyon was straight as a rifle barrel and precisely beveled, with concrete walls sloping away at forty-five degrees. The other side was probably four hundred feet away. The bottom appeared to be filled with clay and sparse vegetation.

"Don't get too close," Quait said.

It was also impassable. "You're not going to believe this," she called back to Flojian.

Flojian surveyed the structure and shook his head. Despite everything he'd seen, his idea of a workforce for a major project still consisted of a hundred people with hand tools. How long would it take to dig something like this? And what was its purpose? It was hard to see because of the shrubbery, and when he leaned out too far to get a better look, he lost his balance and Chaka had to haul him back.

The trail, stymied by the obstacle, turned north, moving parallel to the ditch. The trees closed in again. The ditch went on and on, and at sunset there was still no end to it. But there was something else: An iron ship of Roadmaker proportions had come to rest against the far wall.

"That thing is a *canal,*" said Flojian, staggered. "Or it *was.*"

"It's the sketch," said Chaka, excited. She pulled out her packet, went through them, and produced the one titled *The Ship*. "I never thought it was that *big,*" she said.

It was an appropriate vessel for so gargantuan an engineering project. It was probably six hundred feet from bow to stern. It had been coming south when it was abandoned, or ran aground, or whatever. The hull was rusted black. Masts and posts and derricks were snapped and broken; they jabbed into the wall and the woods along the rim.

"How on earth," asked Chaka, "do you *move* something like that? I wouldn't think sails would be adequate. And it doesn't look as if there's much provision for sails anyway."

Quait shook his head. Banks of oarsmen damned well wouldn't do the job either. Sometimes he thought the laws of physics didn't apply to Roadmaker technology.

"The same way," said Flojian, "that you lift a maglev, I imagine."

It was left to Flojian to point out the bad news: *The Ship* was dated May 13. The last sketch in the series, *Haven*, was dated July 25. "When they arrived here," he said, "they were still ten weeks away."

They made camp. That night, despite the fact it was a warm evening, they built the fire a little higher than usual.

In the morning, they continued north along the rim without seeing any more grounded ships. At midafternoon they topped a rise and came out of the trees. Glades and fields and patches of forest ran down to a placid blue sea. The ditch was blocked off by a wall. Beyond the wall, it divided into twin channels, which descended in a series of steps until they opened into the sea.

"Incredible," said Flojian. "They *walked* the ships down."

The wall, on closer inspection, turned out to be a pair of gates, topped by a catwalk. It was a place to cross.

The river roared past. They gazed at the torrent and, following the faithful Shay, turned upstream.

The fury of the watercourse filled the afternoon, throwing up a mist that soaked people and animals. It had carved out a gorge and became, as they proceeded south, still more violent. Toward sunset, a remnant of sidewalk appeared along the lip of the gorge and a sound like thunder rolled downriver. The walls of the gorge grew steeper, and the sidewalk skirted its edge for about a mile before taking them past a collection of ruined buildings.

It also took them to the source of the thunder. A little more than a mile ahead, a great white curtain of mist partially obscured, but could not hide, a waterfall of spectacular dimensions. The river, tens of thousands of tons of it, roared over a V-shaped precipice.

They knew it at once. The sixth sketch. Nyagra.

The walkway curved off toward the ruins. They left it, and continued along the edge of the gorge, ascending gradually to the summit of the falls. Spray and mist filled the air, and soon they were drenched. But the majesty of the falling water overwhelmed trivial concerns; here all complaints seemed innocuous, and they looked down from the heights laughing and exhilarated. It was still early afternoon, but they decided they deserved a holiday, and so they took it. They withdrew far enough to find dry shelter while retaining a view of the spectacle, and pitched camp.

"Incredible," Quait said. "How would you describe this to people?"

Flojian nodded. "Carved by the hand of the Goddess. What a beautiful place." He was looking down toward the distant gorge and the ruined buildings below the falls. "That's strange," he said.

"What is?" asked Chaka.

"That must have been an observation complex. But why's it so far away? They could have put it a lot closer, and provided a magnificent view." Indeed, beyond the point where the ruins lay, only hedge and shrubbery lined the river. There had been more than enough room.

"Don't know," she said.

Flojian wondered if someone had owned the land and had simply refused permission.

It occurred to no one that the waterfall was on the move. It was wearing away its rock carapace at about three feet per year, and since the days of the Roadmakers, it had retreated the better part of a mile.

The falls threw up a lot of mist, and in fact considerably more than it would have when the observation platform was in regular use. The central sections of the horseshoe came under most pressure, and therefore were giving way more quickly than the wings of the cataract, elongating the area in which the falling streams were in violent competition. The absolute clarity of the American falls, and the misty coyness of the Canadian, no longer existed. The spectacle was almost lost in its own shrouds.

The sky was full of stars that evening, and there was a bright moon. While Flojian slept, Quait and Chaka approached the cataract and looked down into the basin. Mist and moonlight swirled, and Quait had a sense of shifting realities.

Chaka looked particularly lovely against that silvery backdrop. "If I were going to move into the woods, like Jon," she said, "I'd want to live here."

The mist felt cool on their faces. "It's the most spectacular place I've ever seen," said Quait. A brisk wind blew downriver. His arm was around her, and she moved closer.

Chaka was by no means the first woman to stir his

emotions profoundly. But there was something about her, and the stars, and the waterfall, that lent a sense of permanence to the embrace. There would never be a time when he would be unable to call up the sound and sights of this night. "It's a moment we'll have forever," he told her.

Her cheek lay against his, and she was warm and yielding in his arms. "It *is* very nice here," she said.

"It means you'll never be able to get rid of me. No matter what."

She looked at him for a long moment, her eyes dark and unreadable. Then she stood on her toes and brushed her lips against his. It was less a kiss than an invitation.

She was wearing a woolen shirt under her buckskin jacket. He released the snaps on the jacket, opened it and pulled her close. "I love you, too, Chaka," he said.

She murmured something he could not hear and inserted her body against his, fitting part to part. "And I love you, Quait."

He was deliciously conscious of her breathing and her lips, her throat and eyes, and the willingness with which she leaned *into* him. He caressed the nape of her neck.

She pulled his face close and kissed him very hard. Quait touched her breast and felt the nipple already erect beneath the linen. They stood together for some minutes, enjoying each other. But Quait was careful to go no farther. Although he ached to take her, the penalties for surrendering virtue were high. Not least among them were the consequences of a pregnancy on the trail, far from home.

But our night will come.

23

*South of the falls, the Nyagra divided into two channels, cre-*ating an island about five miles long. The companions crossed the western channel on a wobbly plank bridge of uncertain, but relatively recent, origin. Although it was now in a state of general disrepair and could in no way match Roadmaker engineering, the bridge was nevertheless no mean feat of its own, spanning a half-mile of rapids.

"Sometimes," Flojian said, "I think we tend to underestimate everyone who followed the Roadmakers. We behave as if nothing substantive happened after they died off."

They arrived on the north end of the island, where Roadmaker dwellings were numerous, as were ruins from a less remote period. Quait thought they were Baranji, the barbarian empire whose western expansion had reached the Mississippi four centuries earlier. Flojian was doubtful. Baranji architecture tended to be blockish, heavy, utilitarian. Designed for the ages, as if the imperials had been impressed by the permanence of Roadmaker building and had striven to go them one better. These structures were not quite so solid as one would expect from the Baranji, but if the density was missing, the gloom and lack of imagination were there. Quait wondered whether this had not been an imperial outpost either at the beginning or at the end of their great days.

Shortly after their arrival, they encountered a mystery that turned their thoughts from Baranji architecture. A Roadmaker bridge crossed from the eastern shore of the Nyagra. It was down, and its span lay in the water, half submerged. But this piece of wreckage was different from most of what they'd seen. The rubble was charred, and large holes had been blown in the concrete. "This was deliberate," said Quait, examining a melted piece of metal. "Somebody blew it up."

"Why would anyone do that?" asked Chaka.

They were standing on the beach, close to the ancient highway that had once crossed the Nyagra and which now simply gaped into a void. "Possibly to prepare for a replacement bridge," said Flojian, "that they never got around to making."

"I don't think so," said Quait. "I don't see any sign of construction. Would you take down the old bridge before you built the new one?" He squinted into the sun. "I wonder whether it wasn't a military operation? To stop an attacking force."

Chaka looked out across the river. The current was fast here, and the wreckage created a series of wakes. "The Baranji?" she asked.

"Maybe. The Roadmakers don't seem to have had any enemies. I mean, there's never any evidence of deliberate destruction. Right? At least, not on a large scale."

"What about Memphis?" asked Flojian. "And the city in the swamp? Some of their places burned."

"Fires can happen in other ways," said Chaka. "And in any case were probably set to burn out the plague. But you never see a Roadmaker city that looks as if explosives were used on it. They seem to have had a peaceful society. I think Quait's right: Whoever did this was at war. And it was probably the Baranji on one side or the other. If anybody cares."

The road crossed the island to the southeast, where it had once leaped back across the river. But here again the bridge had been destroyed. The highway simply came to an end, having not quite cleared the shoreline.

"Maybe," said Flojian softly, "they were trying to keep the Plague off the island."

There was another plank bridge upstream. They followed it across the eastern channel, took the horses down onto a boulder-strewn beach, and spotted a path that led into the forest. The beach was narrow and ran up against heavy rock in both directions, so that the path was the only way forward. They were headed toward it when they saw guns.

A tall, thin man leveled a rifle in their direction and came out of the bushes. "Just stop right there," he said. He was bearded, elderly, with gray scraggly hair, greasy clothes, and an enormous pair of suspenders.

They stopped.

Two more showed themselves. One was a woman. "Hands up, folks," she said.

The wedge felt very far away. Chaka raised her hands. "We're just passing through," she said. "Don't mean any harm."

"Good," said the second man. He was younger than the first, but gray, with a torn flannel shirt and a red neckerchief. There was a strong family resemblance.

"Don't mean to be unfriendly," said the man with the suspenders, "but you just can't be too careful these days."

"That's right," said Quait behind her. "And I'd like to wish you folks a good day."

"Who are you people?" asked Flojian.

The man with the suspenders advanced a few

paces. "I'm the toll collector," he said. "My name's Jeryk."

"I'm Chaka Milana. These are Quait and Flojian."

The wind blew the old man's hair in his eyes. "Where you folks bound?"

"We're traders," she said. "Looking for markets."

"Don't look like traders." He squinted at Flojian, "Well, maybe that one does."

"What's the toll?" asked Quait.

The younger man grinned. "What have you got?"

Chaka looked at Jeryk. "Can we put our hands down?"

They ended by trading a generous supply of food and trinkets for two filled wineskins.

It never became clear how Jeryk happened to come by his trade, or how long he had been at the bridge. He explained that he and his family were bridge tenders, and that they kept both island bridges in repair. It was a claim that seemed imaginative. Quait responded by suggesting that the western bridge needed some new piles.

"We know about that," Jeryk said. "We're going to take care of it this summer."

"How many people come through here?" asked Flojian.

"Oh, we don't see many travelers nowadays," he said. "In my father's time, this was a busy place. But the traffic's fallen off."

"What changed?"

"More robbers on the roads now." Jeryk frowned with indignation. "People aren't safe anymore. So they travel in large groups."

Chaka didn't miss the obvious: A large group would pass without seeing the toll collector.

They received an invitation to stay to dinner. "Always like to have company," the woman said. But it seemed safer to move on, and so Chaka explained they were on a tight schedule. Flojian almost fell off his horse trying not to laugh.

As they rode away, Jeryk warned them once more to be on the lookout for brigands. "Can't be too careful these days," he said.

The countryside broke up into granite ridges. They passed a pair of structures, hundreds of feet high, that resembled tapered urns, narrow in the center and wide at top and bottom. There were no windows and no indication what their function had been. Quait commented that the Roadmakers had left behind a lot of geometry and a lot of stone, but very little else. "It'd be a pity," he said, "if whoever comes after *us* doesn't know anything about us except the shape of our buildings. And that we made roads. Even good, all-weather ones."

Their spirits flagged as they continued east on a trail that seemed endless. Another canal appeared, on their north, running parallel. This one was of much more modest dimensions than the great ditch, but it contained water. It went on, day after day, while Flojian visualized legions of men wielding spades. "Our assumption has always been that they had a representative government of some sort. But I can't see how these engineering feats could have been accomplished without slaves."

"You really think that's true?" asked Quait. The Baranjis had owned slaves, but the little that survived of Roadmaker literature suggested a race of free people.

"How else could they have done these things? It's not so obvious on the highways, where you just think of a lot of people pouring concrete. But this canal, and the other one—?"

They were riding now, moving at a steady pace. They passed a downed bridge that blocked the canal. The day was bright and sunny, flowers were blooming, and the air was clean and cool. Chaka glanced at a turtle sunning itself on the wreckage.

At the end of their fourth day on the canal, it intersected with a wide, quiet river. There was a blackened city on the north. They forded the river and camped.

During the night, a band of Tuks, numbering eight or nine, rode confidently in on them, with the clear intention of shooting everyone. Flojian, who'd been on watch, put the would-be raiders to sleep. (One fell into the fire and was badly burned.) But during the momentary confusion Chaka woke up, tried to use her wedge, and afterward insisted that it had had no effect. The lamp, which had once glowed a bright green when she squeezed, now produced a somber red. In the morning, when their prisoners had begun to come around, she tried it again. There was no visible result.

She armed herself with one of the extra units.

The man who'd been burned died. They bound the others, appropriated a couple of their horses, and debated taking their rifles. But they were a different caliber from the smaller Illyrian weapons. So ultimately they simply pitched everything into the canal and drove off the spare animals. They followed their custom by leaving a dull knife for the captives.

Shay's trail had been running parallel, not only to the canal, but also to a giant double highway. Eventually the two connected, and they climbed onto the road in time to cross another north-south river. They were still headed east. The canal curved north and vanished into the wilderness.

The great roads were subject to earth movements, flood, severe weather, and the passage of time. Flojian recalled his father's predictions that they were fast disappearing, sinking into the wilderness, and that eventually they would disappear altogether and become the stuff of legend. *When they cannot be seen,* Karik had said, *who will believe they were ever there?*

The new highway was covered with a thick coat of soil, and in many places it was difficult to distinguish the roadbed from the forest. In others it soared across ravines and lakes, its concrete base gleaming in the sun. In one of these places, it simply went into a long slow descent and plunged directly into a hillside. It did not reappear.

There was a spring nearby, and it seemed a good time to quit for the day. Chaka spotted some quail and went off to hunt down dinner while the others unloaded the horses and made camp.

The forest was a conglomeration of sycamore and birch, pine and maple. Clusters of daffodils and mayflowers had bloomed, and marvelous white-leafed flowers with white and orchid-colored blossoms grew in moist shady soil, usually near trees. She was looking for a good place to set up when she came face to face with a turkey.

The bird squawked and tried to clear out, but Chaka had her rifle at the ready.

As she recovered the animal, a break in the trees revealed a disk, very much like the ones they'd seen at the Devil's Eye and the maglev station. It was about a half-mile away, and she stood watching it change colors in the setting sun.

They baked bread and added some carrots and berries to the turkey, and washed everything down with Jeryk's wine. The wine might have been exceptionally good, or it might have been too long since their last round. In any case, they enjoyed dinner thoroughly. After they'd washed up, Quait suggested they take a closer look at the disk. Flojian reluctantly agreed to stay with the horses. "Be careful," he said. "I don't want to be left alone out here."

The sun was down and the forest had grown dark and restless. It smelled of pine and fresh clay and old wood. Occasionally, the gleam of their lamps caught eyes which blinked and were gone. The ground was matted with dead leaves and straw. The wind moved above them, through the night.

It took almost an hour to find it in the dark. When they did, Quait said that it was bigger than the other disks. Certainly the design was different, but it was quite obviously of the same family of objects, although this one was on the ground rather than on a roof. It was seated in a huge metal mount, several times Chaka's height, and angled toward the sky. The lower sections were encrusted with vines and vegetation. If it had been designed to move, it clearly had not done so for a long time.

They saw another reflection in the treetops directly ahead, which turned out to be a second disk. It was identical to the first, roughly six minutes away. Another lay six minutes beyond that. And a fourth stretched out to the flank. All separated by the same approximate distance.

Chaka and Quait kept close together. Although they believed that they held enlightened views, and would have indignantly rejected any charge they were superstitious, they nevertheless found the combination of dark forest and alien symmetry disquieting.

The pattern of the objects, and the fact that they seemed pointed toward the heavens, suggested that the area had been used for religious services.

They were about to concede there was little more they could do in the forest at night when they saw a brick building among the trees. It was a bleak, worn structure, three stories high, ugly, squat, unadorned. Most of the windows were out. A small disk, different in design as well as size from the ones in the woods, was mounted on the roof. It rose just above tree level, and had a clear view of the moon. In front, a fountain had gone to dust.

There was a set of double doors in the rear. Someone had painted *MOLE LOVES TUSHU* across them. The words were faded, and very old.

The doors in front were made of heavy glass set in pseudo-metal frames. One of them was on the ground, the glass still whole.

Inside, a plaque read:

THE PLANETARY SOCIETY
2011

They passed through a set of inner doors. Stairs mounted to the upper floors; a desk was situated on the left; and a long corridor ran to the back of the building. Several rooms opened off the passageway.

They looked into the first. The lamplight fell across several chairs and a desk. Windows were missing. An old carpet had turned to dust. The place smelled of the centuries.

They moved from room to room. Near the far end of the corridor the floor gave way beneath Quait and he bruised a shin. The noise set something outside fluttering.

He rubbed the injury, leaning against a wall. "If there's a hole," he said, "I'll find it."

She laughed and suggested they go back to camp.

But he covered his lamp and she followed his gaze. Ahead, near the end of the corridor, there was a *glow*. Coming out of one of the rooms.

They approached and looked in cautiously. The light was amber, and it came from one of the gray boxes that always seemed to be around when magic happened.

"I don't think it was there when we first came in the front door," she whispered.

Quait unslung his rifle.

Nothing moved.

They played the beams from their lanterns around the room. It was filled with pseudo-glass screens and metal boxes. Chaka took a deep breath. "Is anybody here?" she asked.

"Professor Woford?" The voice seemed to come from the top of a desk. *"Is that you?"*

"No." Reluctantly. "My name is Chaka Milana."

"It's good to hear from you again, Professor. It's been a long time."

There was a glossy black pyramid on the desk. Quait bent over it. It seemed to be the source of the voice. "Are you in the building somewhere?" he asked.

"Please restate your question."

"Never mind."

"Who are you?" asked Chaka.

"Please restate your question."

Quait rolled his eyes. "This one's as crazy as the one at the bank."

"Just a minute," Chaka told the pyramid. "Can you tell me what place this is?"

"You know the answer to that, Professor Woford."

"Please answer my question."

"This is Cayuga."

"And what do we do at Cayuga?"

"Can you be more precise, Professor?"

"What is the purpose of this facility?"

"We have several purposes: We operate the array, we receive incoming traffic from Hubble Five and Six, we correlate the results from both sources, and we analyze the resulting data." While Chaka tried to formulate her next question, the pyramid spoke again: *"I wish to remind the Professor that repairs have still not been effected for the array, and all units remain nonfunctional."*

"What about Hubble Five and Six?" asked Quait.

"Hubble Six continues to forward telemetry. Hubble Five has been offline for 741 years, nine months, and eleven days."

Chaka and Quait exchanged puzzled glances. "You said we're analyzing data," said Chaka. "To what does the data refer?"

"You know very well, Professor."

"Refresh my memory."

"The data constitutes a record of radio surveys made of 148,766 targets, as of midnight zulu last, in an effort to find patterns that suggest artificial transmissions."

The desk seemed stable, so Chaka lowered herself carefully onto it. "What is 'radio'?"

"Radio is the term used to designate electromagnetic disturbances, in motion, whose frequencies lie from about 20 kilohertz to somewhat over 300 gigahertz." It sounded bored.

"Round and round," said Quait. "Are you getting any of this?"

"Not much," said Chaka. "If you succeeded in finding patterns that suggest artificial transmissions, what conclusion would we draw?"

"That we are not alone. That there is intelligent life elsewhere."

Chaka thought she understood. "You mean other than on Earth?"

"Of course."

Quait sighed. "How could that be possible?"

"Maybe on the moon," said Chaka. "Or on the planets." She spoke again to the pyramid. "And what has been the result of our analysis to date?"

"To date, Professor, we have confirmed artificial signals from seventeen sites. The most recent occurred just last year, on the day after Christmas. I would remind you that you have not yet authorized me to reply."

"You want to say hello to whoever's out there?"

"That would seem to be the most appropriate way to start a conversation."

"Then do it."

"Can you restore full power?"

Chaka looked at Quait and shrugged. Outside, the crickets were loud. "I don't think so."

"I'll try to make do. May I also remind you again that the array needs major repairs. You might even wish to add the enhancements which I've recommended in my analysis PR–7–6613/AC. We could, with a little effort, increase our definition considerably."

Chaka thought she detected a note of disapproval.

✠ 24 ✠

They exhausted a second wedge fighting off another bear. The bear scattered the horses; and either it was too strong for the wedges or the units were weakening. Quait, who never felt comfortable on the trail without a rifle slung over his shoulder, put three rounds into the beast while lying on his back.

"I told you so," he said.

Chaka's admiration for his skill under duress was seasoned with amusement at the changes in Quait's behavior. He had apparently begun to see himself as the new Jon Shannon. He unconsciously imitated Shannon's loose-hipped walk, he insisted on riding at the point ("in case we get attacked"), his voice seemed to have become slightly deeper and more deliberate, and his sense of humor developed a fatalistic edge. But these were tendencies that time mitigated, and within a few days the original Quait had more or less returned. Except that he continued to insist on staying up front.

The highway had also returned. Roadmaker towns of varying sizes became more frequent. They found occasional signs, still legible, directing them to Burger King and PowerLift Recharge and the Hoffman Clock Museum. Chaka, whose experience with mechanical timekeeping devices was limited to hourglasses and waterclocks, commented that she would have liked very much to spend an afternoon at the latter establishment.

They passed a sign directing them toward the International Boxing Hall of Fame. They knew what boxing was, but were puzzled by the rest of the inscription. "They must have taken sports seriously," said Chaka.

"Sounds to me," said Flojian, "like the boating business."

Eventually the canal came back down from the north. They celebrated its return by fishing in it. But a rainstorm blew up and they took shelter in an old barn. The structure was from their own era, but was nonetheless close to collapse. Chaka stood by the open doorway watching the rain when she saw *something* floating over the treeline.

"What?" asked Quait.

She pointed. The object was round at the top, and orange-colored. A basket hung from its underside.

"It's a *balloon,*" said Flojian. "But it must be a *big* one."

It was off to the southwest, running with the storm. Coming their way.

The basket carried a rider. Reflexively, Chaka waved.

The person in the basket waved back. It was a man.

They watched the thing approach. The image of a hawk was drawn on the balloon. It was moving quickly and within minutes passed overhead. Lightning flashed through the storm clouds. The man in the basket waved again.

"He's going to get himself killed," said Flojian.

The wind carried him rapidly away, and within a short time he'd vanished into a dark sky.

In the morning, the highway emerged from the forest into plowed land. Cultivated fields were arranged in squares, and the squares were often divided by water channels. There were cottages and sheds and fences.

"Civilization," said Quait.

It was a good feeling.

After about an hour, they saw their first inhabitants. Four of them were conducting an animated conversation outside a house about fifty yards off the road. Two men were on horseback. The others, an old farmer and a young woman, stood by a pile of wood. One of the two horsemen looked far too heavy for his mount. He wore a buckskin vest and a sidearm, and he was jabbing a finger at the farmer while he talked.

"That looks tense," said Chaka.

Before anyone could reply, the man in the vest drew a gun and fired. The horses reared, the farmer staggered backward and collapsed, and the woman screamed. The gunman was about to fire a second round when the woman seized his arm and tried to drag him out of his saddle. The other horseman rode casually over and hit her with a rifle butt.

Without a word, Quait spurred Lightfoot forward and unslung his own rifle. Chaka sputtered an uncharacteristic oath and followed, leaving Flojian to hang on to the horses.

The woman started to get up, but the second horseman, who was long and lean, with red hair the same color as Chaka's, slid out of his saddle and kicked her in the ribs. Quait fired off a warning shot.

The man in the vest turned around shooting. Quait reined up, took aim, and nailed him with the first round. The redhead grabbed the woman and drew his pistol. He put it to her temple.

He was motioning for them to stay back. Quait slowed down but kept moving forward.

"Careful," screamed Chaka. "He'll kill her."

"He knows he's dead if he does."

The redhead was looking around, weighing his

chances. Abruptly, he pushed his captive away, leaped onto his horse, and galloped for the woods. Chaka raised her rifle and tracked after him but Quait put a hand on the barrel. "Let him go," he said.

She shook her head. "He'll be back."

"You can't kill a man who's running away."

She glared at Quait, but before she could make up her mind a shot rang out and the redhead spun out of his saddle. Her first thought was that Flojian had done it, but she didn't waste time on the details. Instead, she spurred Piper forward and jumped down on the ground beside the woman, who was now crouching over the victim's body and screaming hysterically.

He was dead, the ground drenched with blood. Judging from their apparent ages, she suspected he was her grandfather. The woman was not much more than a girl. Maybe eighteen. Chaka put a hand on her shoulder but made no move to draw her away.

The shooter, who lay sprawled against a downed tree trunk, moaned and looked up with glazed eyes. He tried to recover his gun, which had fallen a few feet away. Chaka kicked it clear and showed him her own weapon. "Wouldn't take much," she said.

He grunted, said something she couldn't understand. Blood was welling out of a shoulder wound. His face was distorted with pain.

Two men rode out of the woods, rifles cradled in their arms. They wore dark blue livery, closely enough matched that Chaka knew they were troopers or militia men.

They were both big, one dark-skinned, one light. The light one stopped to look at Red and shrugged. His partner came the rest of the way in to the house. He stared down mournfully at the man on the ground. "Sorry, Lottie," he said. "My god, I'm sorry."

The girl knelt beside the body, sobbing hysterically. They let it go on for a while. The partner tied the hands of the wounded man, and secured him to a hitching post. Then they all stood in a circle around the body, and finally Chaka eased Lottie away.

She took her inside and waited for her to calm down. She told her it was all right, that her friends were here and would take care of her, and that Chaka and her fellow-travelers would do whatever they could for her. She got a damp cloth so Lottie could wipe the dust and tears from her face.

The others brought the body in and placed it in a bedroom. "Best you come with us, darlin'," said the dark trooper.

"No." She shook her head. "This is my home."

"You'll be back. But we can't leave you here alone now. Why don't you come along, stay with the Judge tonight? Till we can get things straightened out."

Lottie was attractive in the way of all young women. She was blond, with expressive eyes (although they were now bloodshot), graceful limbs, and a smile that almost broke through her grief.

"No," she said. "Please."

"You have to, Lottie," the dark trooper said. "It's all right. We'll have somebody come over. Meantime, Blayk'll stay with him."

He glanced at his partner. Blayk nodded.

"You're sure, Blayk?" she asked, between sobs.

"Yes," he said. "It's okay. You get out of here for now."

She held her hands to her lips for a long time. "Yes, all right. I'll go. Thanks, Blayk."

Blayk was tall, lean, quiet. There was a palpable weariness in his features, as if he'd stayed in too many houses under these circumstances. "It's okay, Lottie. Least I can do."

She looked around the room, suddenly at a loss again. "I've got a jacket here somewhere."

Chaka got up and took her in hand. She found a liquor of unknown type in a kitchen cabinet, poured her a drink, and poured herself one. She left the bottle for anyone else who wanted any, and looked at Blayk's partner. "I'll ask you to wait a little bit, Trooper."

"We're rangers, ma'am," he said.

"Forgive me," Lottie said. "This is Sak. And that is Blayk."

"Pleased to meet you." Chaka introduced herself and her partners. Then she escorted Lottie out of the room. When they came back, twenty minutes later, Lottie was cleaned up and in fresh clothes.

Chaka walked her out onto the porch. Sak held the door for her and for the Illyrians. "I'd appreciate it," he said, "if you folks would come along, too. I think the Judge'd like to meet you."

"Of course," said Quait. "Who's the Judge?"

"Local law and order." He told Blayk when he could expect to be relieved, and collected the prisoner. They mounted their horses and rode out east along the canal.

"Where you from?" asked Sak.

"Illyria," said Flojian.

Sak frowned. "Never heard of it." He looked about thirty-five, but Chaka sensed he was considerably younger. He had weatherbeaten skin and a thick black mustache.

The prisoner rode beside Quait. "In the old days," said Sak, "we'd have just shot him here."

"I wish we could have gotten here a little sooner," said Chaka. "What was it about?"

"Slavers," said Sak. "We're gradually getting rid of them. Aren't we, crowbait?" He poked the wounded man with his rifle.

The prisoner was leaking blood from his right shoulder. Eventually they stopped and Chaka tore up an old shirt to stanch the flow.

"I wouldn't have done it," he groaned. "But I thought he was reaching for a gun."

Sak's expression was cold. "You might want to think up a better story," he said.

The Judge lived in a fortress just off the highway, a sprawling complex of military barracks, parade grounds, flagged courtyards, and stables, surrounded by a tough wooden stockade. The stockade bristled with gunports and sally ports. Blue and white banners fluttered from a dozen poles. The fort stood on a low eminence, overlooking fields that were close-cropped for a thousand yards in all directions.

They deposited the prisoner at the front gate and rode in.

The first thing that caught Chaka's eye was an elaborate manor house. It was built entirely of logs, three stories high, with extra rooms tacked on like afterthoughts. A long front deck was screened and supplied with reed furniture. There were a lot of windows, and the roof supported a cupola which would have been just high enough to see over the wall.

"That's the Judge's house," said Sak. They left Lottie with a matronly woman at a side entrance. She thanked her rescuers again and Sak assured her he would return to look after her. Then he led them past a hay yard, crossed a stream on a wooden bridge, and reined up in front of a drab, two-story building overlooking the parade ground. "This used to be the commandant's quarters," he said. "We'll put you up here as long as you care to stay."

"That's very kind of you," said Chaka.

"Our pleasure, ma'am. We appreciate what you folks did out there. We could've lost Lottie, too." He dismounted and opened the front door. "Nobody stays here now," he said, "except guests." The door opened onto an inner wall. A community room was set off on one side, a stairway on the other. The wall was just wide enough to block off the door. Flojian asked about it.

"It's called a *rindle,*" Sak explained. "It's supposed to keep out evil spirits."

"In what way?" Chaka asked.

"The story is, unless they're invited into the house, spirits can only cross at the threshold and they can only travel in a straight line." He helped Chaka with her bags. "I suspect the rindle has *really* survived because it helps block off cold air."

Flojian commented dryly that there were things out there that might change Sak's mind.

Behind the rindle, a passageway lined with doors ran to the rear of the building. Sak watched them choose rooms and promised to send over fresh linen and whatever else they might require. "I expect," he added, "the Judge will want to talk to you, so I'd appreciate it if you didn't go too far."

Chaka was impressed. She had two rooms and a private bath. While she surveyed her quarters, a young woman arrived to put down fresh bedding. Autumn-colored curtains framed the windows, which were open and screened. The fresh, blossomy fragrance of late spring filled the air. The sitting room had a worktable and two comfortable chairs. One wall was covered with a bearskin.

The bathroom exceeded anything she could have expected. It was dominated by a large wooden tub. There was nothing exceptional about that, of course.

But the tub was equipped with faucets, and when she turned one, water came out. It quickly grew warm.

Chaka had seen indoor plumbing before, but never running hot water. She decided they had stumbled into the most advanced nation on Earth.

She went down to the kitchen and treated herself to a few slices of ham (brought in exclusively for their use and kept on ice), and took a cup of wine back to her room where she scrubbed down with scented soap.

As she toweled off, Quait knocked at the door. "We're invited to have dinner with the Judge tonight," he said. "At eight."

Within the hour, servants arrived and measured Chaka, promising to return with fresh clothing before the appointed time.

Sak rode in to see how they were doing, and to offer to take them on a tour of the fort. They were free to wander about as they liked, he explained, although they should not enter the manor without invitation.

"How's Lottie?" asked Chaka. The victim, they now knew, *had* been her grandfather.

"As well as can be expected," he said. "Her brother's with her." He shrugged. "It's a tough world."

He'd brought fresh mounts. Quait swung into a saddle, patted the animal's neck. Chaka looked around. Two people were working on a wagon, and a couple more could be seen in a smith's shop at the foot of the palisade. Otherwise, the fort looked empty.

"We're a ranger force," Sak explained. "This kind of thing doesn't happen much anymore. But unfortunately the bastards still show up once in a while." He shrugged. "We work with what we have. When we're not working, we're farming. Or mining. Or whatever."

"Mining?" asked Flojian. "What do you mine?"

"Iron, mostly. We take it out of the Roadmaker

city." He pointed north. "And aluminum. And even precious stones." He shrugged. "On the south side, we've got coal."

They moved casually through the complex. There were four old barracks buildings. "This used to be an army post," he said. "We don't really need the military anymore."

"No more wars?" asked Chaka.

"Not since Brockett and Cabel signed the Compact. It's been almost twenty years."

"Brockett and Cabel?" asked Quait.

Sak frowned. "The cities," he said. He shook his head as if his guests all had an extra leg. "You really *are* from the wilderness, aren't you?"

"I guess," said Chaka.

Quait observed that the barracks appeared to be in good condition.

"We still maintain them. There've been occasional large-scale raids in the past where we've had to bring everybody inside. It's been a few years since we've had to deal with that. And the frontier's moving west, so we'll see even less of it. But if it comes again, we're ready."

He pointed out the bakery, the servants' quarters, the stockade, the laundry, the cavalry yard, the officers' quarters (now used by the rangers who were on duty), and the surgery. "We still call it the surgery, although it's been converted into our operational headquarters. The real surgery is located in the west wing of the manor." They toured the wagon masters' quarters and the mechanics' shops, both of which were still in use, and the wood yard, the stables, the hay yard, and the cavalry yard. "It looks empty, but the townspeople can defend it if they need to."

They heard a volley of shots outside the wall.

"That's our killer," said Sak.

Chaka grimaced. "That's fairly quick."

"We don't have any repeat offenders. But we took the time to repair his shoulder first. I don't know why we do that, fix somebody up to shoot him, but the Judge insists on it."

The waiting room in their quarters was fitted with a waterclock. It was an ingenious device, and Chaka copied a diagram of its mechanism into the journal.

The clock was constructed with upper and lower chambers. Water dripping from the upper chamber raised a float in the lower. The float, which was a tiny canoe, was attached to a notched rod. The rod turned a gear as it rose, and the gear directed a single hand around a clock face. Like other timekeeping equipment of the age, it gave at best an approximation, but that was enough for a people who had necessarily lost touch with the notion of promptness. (The Illyrians had salvaged Roadmaker clocks, knew how they worked, but had not yet mastered the art of building them.)

Shortly before the hand came to rest on the eighth hour, Sak arrived, decked out in a fresh uniform, a white neckerchief, and a white campaign hat. "I understand the Judge is anxious to meet you," he said.

They walked across the parade ground, around to the front of the manor house, and mounted wooden steps onto the deck. A tall bearded man in a black coat a size too small and a billed cap was coming out as they entered. Sak exchanged greetings with him, and introduced his charges. "Captain Warden," he said, "of the *Columbine*."

Warden bowed to Chaka and shook hands with the others. He was a man of frail appearance, thin, with sallow skin and a curiously passive expression, but he had a grip like a bear trap.

"Where are you from?" he asked, in a voice just loud enough to suggest he was a trifle deaf.

"Illyria," said Flojian.

He frowned. "Illyria? I thought I knew all the ports on the Inland Sea. But I don't think I ever heard of Illyria."

"It's one of the League cities," said Flojian, "in the valley of the Mississippi."

"Oh," he said. But Chaka caught the tone, and the uncomprehending glance that passed between the captain and their escort. "We must talk about it sometime." He excused himself, explaining that he had business at the docks.

An attractive young woman, dark-haired, dark-eyed, met them at the door. Behind her stood a rindle, decorated with several strings of beads. "Please come in," she said, smiling a greeting at Sak.

Somewhere in back, children were laughing. "This is Delia," said Sak. "She manages the Judge's household."

Delia showed them into a sitting room and turned up the lamps. She saw everyone comfortably seated, and inquired as to the guests' preferences in drinks.

Chaka settled for blackberry wine. "It comes down the canal from Brockett," said Sak. "On the *Columbine*."

The windows were open, and a cool breeze blew through the room. Outside, the insects were loud, there was occasional distant laughter and the sound of a walloon, played skillfully. Quait smiled with a degree of embarrassment, but Chaka assured him he was good, too. Lightning glimmered in the western sky.

Flojian was surprised to hear that there was traffic on the canal. "If it's the same one that parallels the road we came in on," he said, "it doesn't look possible. It's blocked."

"But you were to the *west.*" The comment, in a woman's voice, came from behind them. "In that direction, you are quite right." The speaker came closer to the lamp, and Chaka saw she was of indeterminate age and small stature. Her features were unremarkable: gray eyes flecked with green, a long, narrow nose, thick silver hair, and a bearing that suggested she was accustomed to command. She was holding a glass of dark wine.

Sak got to his feet and introduced the guests to Judge Maris Tibalt. "Good to have you at Oriskany," she said. "I hope your accommodations are adequate."

"Yes," gushed Chaka. It had not occurred to her that the Judge might be a woman. "They are *very* comfortable."

"Good." The Judge looked pleased. "Dinner will be ready in a few minutes. Meantime—" She studied the features of each of her guests in turn. "I understand you've traveled here from beyond the Inland Sea."

Quait looked at Sak. "Is that the bodies of water to the west?"

He nodded.

"That's correct, Judge," said Flojian.

Chaka saw a frown creeping into Quait's eyes. *No exact locations,* it said.

"And you are looking for Haven."

"Yes, we are."

"Good. Have you evidence that the place actually exists?"

"We believe it does, Judge," said Quait.

Flojian mentioned the first expedition, and asked whether she had any recollection of having seen it.

"Yes," she said. "They passed through. I never saw any of them again."

"Do you know what happened to them?"

"Only the rumors."

"And what were they?"

"That they took ship out of Brockett and went north. That all but one died."

"Died how?"

She considered her answer. "The sailors who came back said they went into a cave and were killed by something nobody could see."

That comment dampened the mood. "First time I've heard that," Flojian said.

"The sailors lost their passengers," said the Judge. "They had to have a story."

"Do you have any details?" asked Chaka.

She considered the question. "No. It was never a matter of much interest to me. What you need to do is go to Brockett. Find the ship's captain that took them. Talk to him."

"We saw something strange yesterday," said Flojian after a moment. He went on to describe the man in the sky.

"Oh, yes." The Judge looked pleased. "That was Orin. He's our aeronaut."

"What does he do? I mean, besides float about in a balloon?"

"He's an inventor. Lives outside Brockett." She looked grateful for the change of subject. "He takes people up for rides."

"Have *you* ever been in the balloon?" asked Chaka.

The question amused her. "I'll try any form of travel, Chaka, as long as I can keep one foot on the ground."

At the suggestion of the Judge, they drank to Illyria and the League, and then to Brockett and the Compact.

"Where is Brockett?" asked Chaka.

"About a hundred miles east. At the end of the canal. It's on the Hudson."

"The Hudson?"

"Our major north-south artery. All our commerce moves on it, and on the canal. If you like, I'll be happy to arrange passage for you with the *Columbine*. Captain Warden's boat. I assume you'll be going on to Brockett."

"Yes," said Quait. "That would be very kind of you."

"Or, you might want to consider staying with us. Life in Oriskany is good. We can use people like you."

"You don't know anything about us," said Flojian.

"I know enough."

They looked at one another, and Chaka saw agreement. "Thank you," said Quait. "But we can't stop now."

"Good," she said. "I expected no less. Maybe on your return you'll feel differently."

"What lies beyond Brockett?" asked Chaka.

A bell rang softly in another room, and Delia appeared. "Dinner is ready, Judge," she said.

The Judge rose. "Beyond Brockett," she said, "there is only darkness. And the sea."

The staff served roast beef and potatoes and a range of vegetables and hot rolls. There was an endless supply of good wine. The travelers described their adventures, and received the Judge's commiseration at their losses.

The children whom they'd heard earlier took their meals in a separate room. They belonged to the staff, the Judge explained. "My own are long since grown and gone."

"Gone where?" asked Quait.

"To Brockett. One is receiving her schooling. My sons are both in the service of the Director."

"The Director?" asked Flojian.

"The head of state."

Chaka said, "And women are given a formal education?"

"Of course."

The Judge explained she had spent her own formative years in Brockett before returning to Oriskany to assume her responsibilities on the death of her father. She was the elder of two daughters.

Flojian asked about her husband. That proved to be a misstep: She blithely explained she didn't have one, had never had one, and (if her guests would pardon her candor) she really saw no need for one. "You're shocked," she added.

"Not really," said Quait, stumbling for a reply.

"It's all right. Most people confuse sexual deprivation with virtue. It's not their fault, really. Society imposes these things and no one ever questions them."

"The gods impose them," said Flojian, sternly.

"Which gods are those?" she asked. "The gods of the south? Or of the north?"

Flojian looked to Chaka to help. But Chaka saw no reason to get into it.

"Most societies start with gods and end with philosophy," the Judge said. "They come eventually to realize that there are no gods, and the laws have been laid down by dead men. My father once warned me that when it came time to die, the only regrets I would have would be for things left undone."

"There *is* such a thing as virtue," persisted Flojian, his voice rising.

"In fact, Flojian, I would argue that the only virtue is wisdom. The others are frauds. And while we're on the subject, I'd be pleased to supply night companions for any who wish." She glanced around the table. Her guests squirmed visibly and she laughed. "I'm sorry," she said. "I didn't mean to make anyone uncomfortable. But *do* let me know."

✠ ✠ ✠

Flojian had not been with a woman for twenty years. He had always feared the consequences of giving in to his impulses outside the approved bonds of marriage, and he still remembered the mental torture that had followed his lone misstep.

He'd gotten away with it. No pregnancy. No whisper of scandal. (The girl, for she had been little more than that, had been the soul of discretion.) And he'd made a solemn vow not to travel that road again. He would keep clear of sexual entanglements until he remarried.

And so he had.

When the dinner ended, and the party was breaking up, he'd found himself oddly breathless, looking for a chance to talk alone with the Judge. The opportunity had not come, and in the end he walked away with Lottie and his two companions, with a sense of abject loss, and with the disquieting knowledge that, even had they not been present, he might have been unable to ask for the thing that he so desperately wanted.

✠ 25 ✠

The waterfront district consisted of two sagging docks, two warehouses, a grain silo, a repair facility, and a broker's office. There was also an open-air bakeshop, a smithy, a gunmaker, a carpenter, and a surgery. Most of these occupied single buildings, unlike the rows of commercial outlets back home. The buildings were quaint, with parapets, sloping dormers, oculus windows, garrets, and arched doorways.

The *Columbine* was equipped with a paddle wheel. Such vessels had plied the Mississippi during the Roadmaker era, but no one in Illyria knew what had made the wheel turn. Two stacks jutted up behind the pilothouse, leaking white smoke.

"I don't believe this," Flojian whispered. He was so excited, he was having trouble breathing.

Many of the hulks still lying in the Mississippi had not been equipped to carry sails. That fact had been one more enigma. An engine from one of these ships, the *America,* had been on display for years at Farroad. Examined by the League's most eminent philosophers, its workings remained a puzzle to this day.

The last pieces of a shipment of scrap iron were being loaded, and the *Columbine* lay low in the water. One of the crewmen arrived to take charge of their horses. A pen had been prepared for them on the afterdeck.

Captain Warden was standing near the taffrail, watching the loading operation. He saw his passengers on the dock and came forward to greet them. "Good morning," he said.

"Good morning, Captain." Chaka led the way up the gangplank.

Flojian said, quietly, "Talley."

"Pardon?" said Quait.

"Talley. Here's the power source he was looking for."

The *Columbine* was indeed a stout vessel, and, at two hundred feet from stem to stern, larger than anything they had ever seen afloat.

They shook hands all around, and Warden explained that the boat was designed to carry cargo rather than passengers. "You understand," he said, "we have to make do with limited accommodations. But we manage. Yes sir, we manage." His eyes, which were dark brown, invited them to admire his vessel. "Running time to Brockett's about thirteen hours. We've got one cabin that you can share. You'll have to use the crew's bath facilities. It's located amidships. The crew won't mind sharing with a woman, Chaka, you need have no fear of that. We're expecting good weather, so you'll probably want to spend most of your time on deck anyway. Feel free to look around the boat if you like."

"We haven't discussed the fare yet," said Flojian.

Warden touched the brim of his cap and signaled a crewman. "Shim, see that our passengers want for nothing. And there's no charge, Flojian. Compliments of the Judge. And the *Columbine*."

He excused himself, explaining that he had much to do before they got under way. Shim took Chaka's bag and showed them to their quarters, which was a plain room with four strung bunks, a table by a porthole, and a couple of lines to hang clothes on. But it was clean, and, as Quait pointed out, it would be out of the rain.

The bulkheads vibrated with unseen power. The

vessel felt *alive*. They went back out on deck, like entranced school children. Sailors cast off lines and smoke billowed out of the twin stacks. The stern wheel started to turn, lifting gleaming water into the sun, and the pier began to slide away. A horseman rode out from behind a warehouse and waved. It was Sak, and they waved back.

Shim took them belowdecks to see the power plant.

It was hot. Two men, stripped to the waist, were feeding logs to a roaring fire in the lower chamber of a boiler. "We pump water into the upper chamber," Shim explained, having to shout to be heard. "The fire generates steam and the steam turns the wheel. It's as simple as that."

Flojian asked for a diagram, and Shim drew one, explaining the process again until Flojian was sure he had it right. "We've only had them for a few years," Shim added. "We used to use sails, oars, poles, and it took *days* to get to Brockett."

Shim was short, stocky, good-natured, and taken with Chaka. No matter who asked a question, he responded to her.

"Who developed the engine?" asked Quait.

"Orin Claver," Shim told Chaka.

"Claver?" said Flojian. "The man in the balloon?"

"That's him. Although the truth is, he doesn't really *invent* this stuff. That's what he wants people to think. But what he does is, he finds things in the ruins, figures out how they used to work, and then copies them."

"That's no mean feat in itself," said Flojian.

Later, for the first time since Avila's death, he looked as if the shadow might have passed. "If we get home with nothing else from this trip, *this* at least gives us some payback for what we've lost. It'll become possible to open up the Mississippi. We've always had the problem that the current was too strong. We have a wide river and we were never really able to use it because there was no way to push boats upstream. But *this* thing, this *steam engine*, will change everything."

The *Columbine*, exclusive of her captain, carried a crew of five, three of whom also served as rangers. "We've been shot at from time to time," the captain admitted, "but we've never lost anybody." Oriskany, he explained, was a Brockesian protectorate, and guarded the western frontier. "The Judge does a pretty good job of patrolling the roads. And she's tough on robbers. They get shipped to Brockett, where they get sold off."

"The one we helped catch," said Chaka, "got shot."

"That's because he killed old Hal Rollin. The death penalty is automatic for murder. No questions asked. They publicize that fact and they carry it out within twenty-four hours."

"What about extenuating circumstances?" asked Chaka.

"There's no such thing. Unless you mean self-defense, in which case there's no penalty at all. If you mean that the killer has had a tough life, it's irrelevant. The Judge makes no exceptions. As a result her roads are reasonably safe."

Warden didn't smile much. It might have been the job. The old canal appeared to be comfortably wide, but it was full of debris, broken bridges, downed trees, and other hidden hazards. There was even a *house*, which had somehow come to rest in the middle of the channel. It was entirely submerged, but Chaka looked down into the still, blue depths and saw a dormer and a chimney.

She used her pack to make a cushion against the deckhouse, and enjoyed the gentle motion of the boat and the proximity of late spring. Rolling hills and furrowed fields slipped by. Deer paused along the shoreline and watched them. There were thick groves of butternuts and red cedars. Children playing in fields stopped what they were doing as the boat passed, and waved frantically.

She saw horse-drawn carriages on the roads, and fishermen in small boats. Houses grew more numerous along the canal as they proceeded east. People came out to watch them go by.

"Captain," she asked Warden when he reappeared, "tell me about the Hudson."

"What did you want to know?"

"Does it have an outlet to the sea?"

"Oh yes," he said. "It's about 180 miles south." Flojian had fallen asleep, and Quait was off comparing notes with one of the ranger-crewmen. Warden plumped down beside her. "The Hudson *might* have been open in the north too at one time. There used to be a canal up there, like this one. Though not as long. But it's pretty much filled in."

So far, so good. "Captain, could we hire the *Columbine*?"

Warden grinned. "To do what?"

"I'm not sure yet. But we may need sea transportation."

She saw immediately that he would not consider what she was proposing. "Well," he said, "we're on a tight schedule, and I have commitments to customers." He looked at her quizzically. "Chaka, have you ever been to sea?"

"No. I haven't."

"You wouldn't want to try it in the *Columbine*."

"Oh."

"In fact, I can't think of a boat anywhere on the river that *I'd* care to take to sea." He shook his head. "Maybe the *Packer*. But she capsized a few months ago. And that should tell you more than you want to hear."

His eyes grew thoughtful. "I was down there once. At the river's mouth." His voice took on an awed tone. "I didn't like the place much. There's a Roadmaker city. Like nothing else you'll ever see."

She thought of the two she'd already visited. "High towers?" she asked.

"Yes," he said. "You'd have to see them to understand."

The countryside gave way to picturesque villages and spectacular manor houses. They made several stops, unloading handicrafts and taking on barrels of wine. Around noon they picked up more passengers. Once, they encountered a group of naked boys splashing around a raft.

It was, in sum, an uneventful ride, and shortly before sundown they transited a series of ancient fortifications and cruised into the biggest living city Chaka had ever seen: Houses and shops and public buildings and temples and parks occupied both sides of the canal. Crowds roamed the water's edge, filled outdoor restaurants, watched ball games. Another boat was just backing out into the channel and turning east. Directly ahead the waterway flowed into a river.

The *Columbine* swung smoothly into dock and Warden came down to say good-bye to his passengers.

"If there's anything else I can do," he said, "don't hesitate to ask."

The Captain's Quarters, near the waterfront, looked somewhat rundown, but it was convenient. It was also busy and loud. In the dining room, a female singer was having trouble being heard above the general racket. The tables were too close together, and the waiters, carrying trays loaded with fried chicken and steaming carrots, had to fight their way through. A couple of big screened windows admitted cool air.

They ordered up, and beer appeared within moments. Flojian proposed a toast to the *Columbine*. "We've been riding the future," he said.

Quait looked good. He had broken out the white shirt and blue neckerchief he saved for special events. "Almost there," he said.

Flojian threw a skeptical glance his way. "That might be optimistic."

"Why? All we have to do is find the boat that Karik hired. Then *we* hire them, and we ride the rest of the way."

"How's the money holding out?" Chaka whispered.

Flojian nodded. "Okay."

"I wonder if you could spare a couple of mingos."

Flojian reached into a pocket and passed her the coins unobtrusively.

They'd selected the inn because it obviously catered to the men and women who ran the river fleet. Chaka pocketed the silver, surveyed the room, found what she wanted, and got up. "I'll be back," she said.

She joined a group of mariners of both sexes at the bar and ordered a round of drinks for everybody.

"We just came in on the *Columbine,*" she declared. "You people do a hell of a job."

"Thanks," said a young male. He had brown hair, brown eyes, and a good face, if you didn't count a lot of missing teeth. "But we don't crew the *Columbine.*"

"I know," she laughed. "But they're not here, and you are."

Within a few minutes she'd joined them in a song, and got the first of several disapproving looks from Quait. "What's your boat?" she asked the young man with the missing teeth.

"The *Reliable.*"

"Does the *Reliable* trade on the river? Or the canal? Or both?"

A female with dyed blue hair responded with mock indignity. "The *river,*" she said. "The canal is strictly for the water rats. Isn't that right, Cory?"

The male shook his head, suggesting that he'd heard the joke many times before, and Chaka concluded he'd been on the canal before joining the *Reliable*. But he took the comment in good grace, and even seemed to enjoy the attention. "The canal is where the *real* sailors are," he said.

"Right," said one of the others and they all laughed.

"Has anybody ever been to sea?" Chaka asked casually.

They looked at one another.

"Yeah," said a husky, older man in back. "I've been out past the Gate."

Chaka raised her glass to him. "What's it like on open water?"

He grinned. "Like nothing else you'll ever do," he said.

"Where'd you go?" asked Chaka.

"Yeah," said one of the others. "Where'd you go, Keel?"

Keel had a thick black beard and arms like tree branches. He shrugged. "About a hundred miles down-coast."

"Tell us about it," said the woman, laughing, obviously familiar with the story.

"Back off, Blue," he said. "The lady asked a question. Is it all right with you if I answer?" He turned to Chaka. "It's peaceful out there. Like the whole world stands still."

"How many times?"

"Twice," he said. "The second time we were out for a couple of days."

"Was that on the *Reliable*?"

"Yes," said Keel, "although it had a different captain then."

"Are you from the Inland Sea?" Cory asked her. "I've never heard the accent before."

Chaka delivered her most ravishing smile. "That general direction," she said, nodding toward the back of the room. She reached into a pocket and extracted her brother's *Haven* sketch. "Reason I asked," she said, holding it up so all could see, "I was wondering if this place is familiar to anybody? Anyone ever been there?"

"What place?" growled a flat-nosed sailor who had already swilled down his drink. "That's nothing but rock and water."

Keel looked at it for a long minute and shook his head. The others shrugged.

Chaka ordered a second round. "My brother came this way about ten years ago," she said. "He was one of several people, and they leased a ship to take them to sea."

"Where?" asked Blue.

Chaka looked at the sketch. *"Here,"* she said, "wherever that is."

"Every once in a while," said Keel, "some damned fool wants to go out. Usually they're looking for somebody to trade with. But there's no one out there along the shores except damn Tuks. If people want to go to sea, they ought to build a strong enough boat. You say this was ten years ago. We've had several boats during that period put to sea on one damn fool job or another. They don't always come back."

"These people were looking for Haven," Chaka said. "They were led by an older man whose name was Karik Endine. Gray hair. Medium size. Sort of ordinary-looking."

"That should make it easy," laughed Keel. "But as it happens, *yes,* I know about Endine. I suspect everybody around here knows the story."

"What story?"

"Actually a lot of stories, most of them conflicting. Depends on who you get it from, I guess. They were treasure-hunting, as I understand it. Cut a deal with one of the captains. Man named Dolbur. He took them downriver and north up the coast. But they ran into something they weren't expecting."

"What?"

"*Something.* I don't think anybody's ever been sure what. Ghost. Water demon. Something. Again, it depends on who you talk to. They lost a lot of people. None of the ship's crew. But everybody who was with Endine. There was only one of them came back."

"That was Endine himself," contributed one of the others.

Keel gazed a long time at Chaka.

"Where can I find Dolbur?"

Keel's teeth showed through the beard. "Finding him's easy enough, but talking to him would be tricky.

He's dead. I'm trying to think who else was on that boat."

"Knobby," said the woman.

Keel nodded. "Yeah. That's right. Knobby was part of that crew."

"Who's Knobby?"

"First mate. You want to talk to him?"

"Yes."

"Be here tomorrow."

✠ 26 ✠

Knobby's real name was Mandel Aikner. While Chaka was too polite to ask the origin of the nickname, she didn't need much imagination to guess that it derived from a bald skull that looked as if it had been rapped several times with a club. Knobby's features were prominent: a large, bulbous nose pushed to one side in a long-ago fight; big ears; narrow, suspicious eyes; and a chin like the flat side of a shovel. A mat of wiry gray hair pushed out of the top of his drawstring shirt.

"I don't know what I can tell you that you don't probably already know, Chaka," he said, while they waited for their steaks. (Chaka was alone with him, on the theory that he would speak more freely to a woman.)

"Assume I don't know much of anything, Knobby. Karik Endine and his people arrived in Brockett and wanted to charter a ship. Why don't you take it from there?"

Knobby picked up the carafe, studied the dark wine, refilled his cup, and refilled hers. "Before we get into any of this," he said, "I want you to understand, I won't go back up there. Okay? I'll tell you what I know, but that's all."

"Okay," she said. She described her brother and asked whether Knobby had seen him.

"Yes," he said. "I knew Arin."

Her heart raced briefly.

"He was a good-looking boy. Didn't talk much. I

knew them all. Shay. Tori. Mira. Random. Axel. Even after all these years, I remember them. And Endine." He drummed on the table with his fingertips. "It's hard to forget."

Chaka had met only Tori, who had been a friend of her brother's. And Mira. Other than Karik, the others were just names.

"Endine's the one who sticks in the mind," said Knobby. "He was hostile." She saw that he wondered whether he'd gone over a line. "He wasn't your father or anything, was he?"

"No." She smiled encouragingly. "I knew him, but not well." *I'm beginning to think no one knew him well.*

"He didn't seem to want to talk to anybody. On a boat the size of the *Mindar*, that isn't easy."

It was early. The entertainment wouldn't start for an hour or so, and the dining room hadn't begun to fill up. They were seated at a corner table. Knobby drank more of his wine, wiped his lips, and leaned forward confidentially, although there was no one close enough to overhear. His breath was strong, and he spoke with a wheeze.

"I was second officer on the *Mindar* at the time. We hauled mostly coal, iron, wheat, and liquor into Brockett, and manufactures out. And whatever else needed to be moved. We were commanded by Captain Dolbur. Dead now these three years.

"The first time I heard of Karik Endine was when the captain called me and Jed Raulin into his quarters. Jed was the first officer. We were dockside, between jobs, and the captain explained that there were some people in town, foreigners who wanted to lease the boat, wanted him to take it down the Hudson and out into the Atlantic.

"You've seen the boats around here. The *Mindar*'s downriver right now so I guess maybe you haven't seen her. But she's no bigger than any of the others, and none of these has any business going near the sea. But there was a lot of money in it, he said. And we'd stay within sight of land the whole way. Endine had shown him a pouch of gold coins. Anybody who went along would collect almost a year's pay for a couple weeks' work. If the captain said yes to Endine, would Jed and me go along?

"Jed had a family. He said he'd want to talk it over with his wife. In the end, she gave him a lot of trouble and he stayed out. So I got a promotion. Two of our crew also backed off.

"The visitors wanted to go north. Up the coast. There were seven of them, counting Endine. It would be a six-hundred-mile run from the mouth of the Hudson, give or take a couple hundred. These people didn't seem quite sure where they were going. We were to help them look around, deliver them, and wait for three weeks to provide whatever support they needed. After that, we'd bring them back or, if they decided not to come, we'd be free to return.

"It was blistering hot while we got the boat ready. We leased a dinghy and installed a housing and a system of pulleys for it on the afterdeck. Nobody knew a damned thing about the kind of country we were headed into, so we loaded up with as much wood as we could. We also put on plenty of food and water. The captain went over every inch of the hull, replaced a couple of the spars, added some pitch. We got a new anchor, too.

"Altogether, the *Mindar* needed about three weeks' work. Then Karik and his people came aboard, and we cleared Brockett on a humid July morning and headed downriver. Afterward, after all that happened, some of the boys said they'd felt premonitions about that voyage right from the start. But I can tell you true, there was nothing to it. We were feeling okay. We knew we were a good boat with a good crew, and we knew we could handle her in blue water. And we knew we were making more money than we ever had before. Or likely ever would again. So there was nobody on that boat thinking we should turn back.

"On the second day out, we passed Manhattan and turned north up the coast. There's a long peninsula down there. We rounded it in good shape and stood out to sea. It was a gray, rainy day, and a lot of the stories that got started later about omens and such, they always mentioned how the weather looked when we started. But nobody thought anything about it at the time.

"The coastline going north is wild. Lot of rocks, shoals, riptides. We anchored every night at sunset, and you could look forever and not see a light anywhere.

"The boat was lower in the water than we'd have liked. That was because of all the wood and supplies on board. Everybody knew that if we ran into rough seas, especially outbound, we'd be in trouble.

"Like I said, Endine was unfriendly." Knobby wrinkled his brow and let Chaka see his yellow teeth. "No, actually, it's fairer to say he just kept to himself. He spent most of his time on deck, staring out to sea. He had cold, blue-gray eyes, and he just didn't look like he gave a damn about anybody. His own people didn't like him much.

"I got to know the others pretty well. Can't help it when you're all on a boat together for a week. They'd lost some people on the road. A couple got shot, a couple to fever.

"One of them, Tori, the youngest one, told me what they were after. I hoped the captain had been paid up front because I knew they weren't going to find this la-la land they were looking for.

"The nights were cool, and the boat didn't have much in the way of accommodations, so we used the dinghy to take the passengers and some of the crew ashore every evening. I remember somebody shot at us one night. Nobody got hit and we never found the son of a bitch and it's lucky for him we didn't. But that was the only incident.

"Early in our second week, land appeared on the east. We thought it was an island but I'm not so sure now. It might have been an arm of the continent, just sticking out a long way. I don't know. It was mountainous and pretty far off, but Endine got excited and announced we were 'in the bay.' We saw a couple of whales at about the same time and everybody took that to be a good omen. I'd never seen a whale before. But we saw a few more before we got home.

"After a while the land on the east closed in and we saw that Endine was right and we *were* in a bay or channel. Whatever it was, it kept getting narrower. The first night, we made anchor near the eastern side and went ashore. We'd been setting watches since the shooting incident and I had the two-hour shift from midnight. Endine was awake the whole time, sitting on a rock down at the waterline. I asked him if he was okay, and he didn't even hear me until I poked him.

"The sea's loud up there. It's a constant roar. In the morning we went down to the beach, and the *Mindar,* which had been anchored in twenty feet of water, was high and dry. The tide was out. Way out.

"Endine was furious. The captain had been on board, had seen it happening, and had tried to get clear but he wasn't quick enough. Wouldn't have mattered anyhow, because we were stranded on the beach. You understand, Chaka, we were just riverboat sailors. Nobody knew anything about those waters.

The captain tried to explain, but Endine called him all kinds of an idiot, in front of everybody. I'll never forget it. Later his people apologized. But Captain Dolbur had a long memory for things like that.

"When the tide turned, it came back pretty quick. I mean this wasn't like any tide any of us had seen before. The channel just swelled up and roared in. We were afloat again by midmorning. There was some confusion in the currents, and we had trouble at first making way, but once we got back out into the channel we moved north like a son of a bitch. The farther we got, the narrower the channel got; and the narrower the channel got, the faster we went.

"That was rough country, wild, mountainous, not many signs there'd ever been towns. But we saw a few, ruins centered around harbors, and sometimes sitting up on rocky shelves or in prime locations along the coast. A couple of roads. Bridges crossing coastal rivers.

"Toward the end of that second day, the channel split in two. After some uncertainty, Endine directed us to starboard. Later that afternoon we sighted a cape sticking out from the eastern shore, and our passengers got excited.

"They had a map with them, and they consulted it and looked a long time at the cape as we rounded it. It was obvious they were hot on the trail now. The map was out every few minutes, and they were taking bearings on passing mountains and rivers and whatnot.

"They found what they were looking for: The coast on both sides was lined with escarpments and bluffs. They zeroed in on one of the bluffs on the eastern shore. It was pretty ordinary-looking, a sheer wall rising about two hundred feet out of the water. We could see thick woods at the top."

Chaka removed the sketch marked *Haven* from her vest. "Is this it?" she asked.

Knobby looked at it. "Yeah," he said. "That's it.

"There was a river on the north side of the bluff, and a pebbled beach. They looked at their map some more, took bearings on a turn in the channel and a saddle-shaped formation off to the west. That was it, they said. No question. And they cheered and clapped one another on the shoulder and broke out some liquor. Endine actually looked friendly. In fact, he shook hands with everyone in sight, including the crew. And everybody got handed a drink.

"We looked for a place to drop anchor. The water was low again, the tide running out, and we planned to be a little more cautious this time. Which meant that we would leave the boat in the middle of the channel and the crew would stay on board except for me. My job was to get Endine and his people to the beach, stay with them until the tide turned next morning, and then return to the *Mindar,* after which somebody else would go in and take my place.

"The sun had been down two hours by the time we arrived on shore. They jumped out as soon as we hit land and took off. They were like a pack of kids. I couldn't believe it. Just ran off into the dark. Me, I stayed with the dinghy.

"They came back about midnight, unhappy, and I knew things hadn't gone well.

"Tori explained they were looking for a catwalk or a cage on the face of the precipice. When I asked what would be the point of a catwalk up there, he just looked up at the cliff. 'Train station,' he said, and laughed." Knobby's eyes locked on Chaka. "You know what a train is, right?

"They used steam engines. Just like the *Mindar.*

But I'm botched if I can figure out how one of them would run across the front of that precipice.

"They bunked down to wait for daylight. I don't think any of them slept much. They were up again before dawn, stayed for breakfast only at Endine's insistence, got their gear together, and walked down to the water's edge, where they could get the best possible look at the cliff. They weren't finding what they were looking for. Endine sputtered and stalked back and forth and finally threw up his hands and walked over to where I was standing. 'The dinghy,' he said.

"We'd beached it at high tide, and it was a long way from the water now. But we dragged it out through the mud and got it launched. The others jumped in. 'Take us across the face of the wall,' he directed. 'About a quarter-mile out.'

"I don't know if I mentioned this, but the dinghy didn't have an engine. Right? It was sails and oars, which is okay when you're moving around in a river. But not so good in those tides.

"I didn't like it much but I took them. They were saying things like, 'It's got to be there,' and, 'Well, I damn sure don't see it.'

"'Your train station is missing?' I asked Tori.

"He said it was.

"Now *I* laughed. 'I'm not surprised,' I said.

"'Well, Knobby,' he said, 'there might still be something there to indicate where there might have been a structure. Maybe even a pattern of shrubs.' He said that if a platform or station had been mounted on the rock face, holes would have been drilled. If somebody drills holes, they eventually fill up with dirt. And the dirt sprouts shrubs. It sounded thin to me but I was damned if one of them didn't think he saw it right away. And somebody else said how there was a piece of discolored rock. *That* I could make out, although it still didn't seem like much.

"They were satisfied that was what they wanted, so I took them back in and they disappeared into the woods. They went around to the rear of the bluff, where the ascent was more or less gradual. I saw them again as they came out along the summit.

"They crossed to the edge of the precipice and threw a rope ladder over. Then somebody climbed down to the discolored stone. They were too far away for me to be sure who it was, but I had to admire them. I remember thinking how they'd never get me to hang out over that damned thing. Which shows you, you never know.

"The discolored stone was about fifty feet down. They needed a second climber, and the two of them worked on it for about an hour. Then a door opened up and I could see a passageway. The climbers went inside and the others started down the ladder.

"After they were all inside I waved a green flag at the boat, which told the captain they'd been successful. A little while later the tide turned and started running out. I went back to the *Mindar*. One of the guys we'd just hired on climbed down as soon as I was out of the dinghy and took it back in. His name was Leap, and I don't remember whether that was a first or last name. Leap was big, grinned a lot, and always had a kind of silly look on his face. He also scared easy.

"Leap was on the beach for six or seven hours and there wasn't any sign of anybody coming back out of the door in the cliff. So he went up to the summit and called down and didn't get an answer. He got nervous. Leap was one of those people who never went near Roadmaker ruins, which I think is a smart idea. Especially now. We didn't have a pre-set signal arranged that covered the situation, so he came back to the beach and waved his arms until the captain signaled for him to return to the *Mindar*. He explained that nobody was answering from inside, that maybe they couldn't hear him, but that he thought maybe something had happened.

"The captain and me and one of the other hands got some lamps and got in the dinghy and we took Leap and rowed back in to shore. There was still no sign of anyone. We went into the woods and walked around to the back side and climbed up to the summit. It wasn't a hard climb but it was time-consuming. Getting up there took the better part of an hour. Of course, the captain wasn't young even then, so he wasn't in very good shape and he had some interesting things to say about Endine.

"The woods up there grew right over the summit. We knew that, so we took it easy because you couldn't see more than a few feet in the shrubbery. But when we got to the edge, we could see where they'd been. And the rope ladder still hung down. It was tied to a tamarack tree. The captain leaned over the face of the cliff and called Endine's name.

"Nothing.

"He looked at me and looked at the rope ladder and I knew what he was thinking. He didn't like the height and he didn't like going into a ruin. But he didn't have much choice, and he couldn't very well ask anyone else to climb down until he'd done it. So he grabbed hold of the ladder and pulled on it to make sure it was secure.

"He told me to follow him and was about to start when I remembered how Endine's people had done it. 'Wait,' I said. They'd run a safety line to one of the branches. We tied it around his waist. 'Don't take it off till you're inside,' I told him. He laughed and started hand over hand down the ladder. Pretty soon he was out of sight.

"A couple minutes later I saw that the safety line was free so I hauled it up and looped it around my belt and went after him. The cliff bulged a little at the top so you had to hang a few feet out from the rock. Down where the door was, they'd secured the ladder with two ring-bolts, which made it easy to just step off into the passage-way, if you could forget where you were. The captain was waiting for me, but there was no sign of anybody else."

Chaka ordered more wine. "What did it look like in there?"

"Stone walls. Just like you'd expect inside a mountain. A lot of dust. Plenty of footprints. The pas-sageway was about a hundred feet long. It was wide enough to have put the *Mindar* into it. And it was probably twenty feet high. There was a stairway lead-ing down, folding back on itself every ten feet or so until it disappeared into the dark.

"The passageway was broken up by openings along both walls. The daylight didn't come much past the door and our lamps didn't help much. I was about to stick my head into the first opening when the cap-tain pulled me back because there was no floor.

"We looked down and it was just a gaping hole. A shaft."

"How deep?" asked Chaka.

"Couldn't see bottom. All the doors on both sides opened into shafts. There was also a cross corridor.

"We called Endine's name again. Still no answer. Lots of echo but no answer.

"The footprints went down the stairway. None came back up." Knobby shook his head. "I think if it were up to me, that would have been the end of the search. I'd've gone back up the ladder and waited for a while and if they didn't come, I'd've left. Know what I mean? But the captain figured he had an obligation.

So he took the lamp and led the way. We started down.

"Every floor looked the same: The shafts opened onto each level, and there was the cross passageway beyond. Karik and his people had gone off several times to inspect the area, but the prints showed us they'd always come back and continued down the stairs. We looked in some of the rooms beyond the shafts. They were just rooms, a lot of different sizes. Filled with junk. Chairs and tables and beds that must have been a thousand years old. Some had baths. But everything was under a layer of dust.

"Every few minutes we'd stop and call their names. But we got no answers and I have to tell you, my skin began to crawl. I mean, how big could the place be that they couldn't hear us?

"Captain Dolbur said he doubted they were still in there. After all, it had been hours since I'd seen them climb through the door. The place was damp and cold and absolutely silent. 'They found another exit,' he said. I mean, this was a place where, without the lamps, you couldn't see your hand in front of your face. And it felt closed-in. Nobody was going to stay long.

"Then we heard Endine.

"We didn't know at first it was him. Just a sing-song whine somewhere below us.

"He was sitting hunched up on a landing, his hands wrapped around his knees, rocking back and forth. He was bone white and his eyes looked crazy and his hair was matted with blood. There were books stacked in neat piles. Maybe forty or more. One pile was knocked over.

"The captain tried to talk to him, but it was like we weren't there. He just kept swaying and making this dying sound in his throat.

"The staircase broke away just below the landing.

I looked down into a chamber but saw no one, although there were more books down there, scattered around. They'd strung up a line to climb down. I called out a few names but the only thing that came back was echoes.

"The captain joined me. 'He got hit in the head's all,' he said. 'Other than that, I don't see anything wrong with him.'

"He leaned out over the stairwell to look down into the lower chamber, breathed my name, and delivered an expletive. There was a body down there.

"The lower chamber was a pretty good drop, maybe twenty-five feet. There were knots in the line to make climbing easier. I held the lamp while the captain went down, and then I joined him. It was Shay.

"The body was wet. It was crumpled up and had a washed-out look. But there was nothing to indicate what had killed him."

"No wounds?" asked Chaka.

"A couple of bruises. That's all.

"The walls were damp. There were even some puddles. I should mention, there were four exits from the chamber. There was a long, high corridor leading off opposite sides at right angles to the passageway with the shafts. And a fourth short passage led to an underground lake.

"The tall corridor was lined with doors and they were all open. Except one. We looked in the rooms. They were all there, everybody, some in one place, some in another." Knobby sat staring at a point in space somewhere over her shoulder.

"They were all dead?"

"Yes."

"How? What killed them?"

"I don't know. They were just like Shay."

"What did Endine say?"

"Not much of anything. He never made sense, that I heard of. The captain didn't think he ever really came out of the delirium. We brought him back here and tried to turn him over to the surgery. But we heard he was out and gone the same night we brought him in. Just took off." Knobby sucked in air and refilled his cup again.

"Did you look in the room that *wasn't* open?"

"We tried. But the door wouldn't give. On the other hand, to be honest, we didn't try hard." He looked at his wine. "This stuff's not strong enough. Anyway, I heard rumors later he was seen west of Brockett. But I never heard any more about him. Till now."

"And you never found out what happened?"

"No. We told the story around. People laughed. Blamed us. Some thought we were trying to hide something. Some even thought we murdered the whole bunch. But it was a *demon*. I mean, how do you kill a half-dozen people without leaving a mark on them?"

"What happened to the bodies?"

"We buried them. We brought the bodies out and buried them." He looked carefully at her. "With honors," he added.

"Thank you."

The waiter came with a fresh carafe and filled both cups. "Could they have been drowned?"

Knobby shook his head. "Hard to see how."

"You talked about tides. And you said there's an underground lake."

"No tide is going to come up so fast that you can't get away from it."

Chaka felt a chill edging down her back. Her food lay half finished on her plate. "What about the books?"

she asked. "What happened to them? The ones on the landing—?"

"We took them back to the *Mindar*. The captain thought they were probably valuable, so we took everything."

"Did you happen to notice what they were?"

"I'm not good at reading, Chaka," he said. "I'm not sure. The captain mentioned some titles. *War and Peace* was one of them. And *Don Somebody-or-Other*. *Bleak House*. Something called *Commentaries on the Constitution*." He made a face as if thinking about it required a major effort. "That's all I can remember. It mean anything to you?"

"A little. What happened to them? After you got back to the *Mindar*?"

"He threw them overboard."

"*Who?* Who threw them overboard?"

"Endine. He came out on deck one day and chucked them all into the water. Every last one of them."

Chaka's spirits sank. "You're not serious."

"After all the trouble we went to. I could have tossed *him* into the water. But yes, that's exactly what happened. He brought them out on deck in piles. And he threw them over the side. One by one."

Chaka stared at him. "You're *sure*? You saw this happen yourself?"

"Yes, I'm sure. We all stood there and watched him."

She listened to people talking around them. Someone's father was threatening to cut off an inheritance. "He didn't destroy them all," Chaka said. "He got back home with a Mark Twain."

Knobby shrugged. "Well. All I know is he got rid of a lot of them."

"You said the bodies, all except Shay's, were found in the rooms? Not in the corridor?"

"Yes. The rooms. They were *big* rooms. Bigger than this place. And two stories high."

"What was in them? The rooms?"

"Just books. And some Roadmaker junk. Lot of those gray boxes you find everywhere."

"Books?" She came alive. "Where are they now?"

"Where are what?"

"The books. The other stuff."

"Still there, I suppose."

"You left it?" Chaka couldn't believe her good fortune.

He shrugged. "Yeah. Why wouldn't we? They wouldn't have been worth anything to anybody. They were in pretty bad shape."

"Why?"

"It was damp down there. Wet. Everything was soaked."

Chaka squeezed her cup until Knobby gently disengaged her hand. "Easy," he said. "You'll hurt yourself."

"You said before the books were okay," said Chaka.

"I said the books *on the staircase* were okay."

"All right. Thanks, Knobby." She passed him a gold coin. "We're going to lease a boat and go back up there."

He was careful to keep the coin concealed as he slipped it into his pocket. "I don't think you'll be able to do that."

"Why not?"

"Nobody'll go. The place is haunted and everybody knows it."

"Okay. But *if* I'm able to get a boat, would you show us where this door in the cliff is?"

"I already told you, I won't go near it."

"There are two more of those," she said, looking at his pocket.

"Doesn't matter. Listen, in case you think I'm just a damned fool, a storm blew up on the way back and we nearly got wrecked. Any kind of bad luck on open water and these boats go down like rocks. Add the currents. And whatever lives in that cliff up there." He took a long pull of the wine. "Tell you what I *will* do: I'll make you a map. Take you right to it." He nodded. "But I won't go back. And you might think it over, too, even if you are able to get somebody crazy enough to take you."

✠ 27 ✠

Knobby was right. Of the half-dozen captains they were able to locate, only one showed any interest in making the voyage north. This was the commander of the *Irika,* a listing, battered, foul-smelling cattle hauler. The description, Chaka thought, also fit the captain, an overbearing female with red-lit eyes and crooked teeth. But Quait surprised her by breaking off negotiations after an amicable price had been reached. "That one smelled gold," he explained later. "She'd have hit us all on the head, taken her fee plus whatever else she could find, and dropped us overboard."

But they were weary of land travel. If Knobby's map was accurate, they were still over five hundred miles from their destination. Straight line. Thirty days travel at a minimum. Possibly with the requirement to build another boat at the end of it.

"I'm almost tempted to try our luck with the *Irika,"* said Flojian. "If they *were* to prove untrustworthy, we could disarm them easily enough. In fact, it would give us an excuse to seize the boat."

"That's a good idea," said Chaka with sarcasm. "Then *we* can take it up the coast. Do we even know how to turn on the engine?"

"Yes," said Flojian. "Actually, I think we do."

"It's too complicated," said Quait. "They *will* try to jump us. We'd have to keep watch over half a dozen people for a couple of weeks. We need a better idea."

"I might have one," said Chaka. "There's a town about thirty miles northeast. Bennington. I think we should ride out that way."

"To what purpose?" asked Flojian.

"It's where Orin Claver lives."

"Claver?" Quait needed a moment to recall where he'd heard the name. "The inventor of the steam engine."

Flojian smiled uneasily. "The rider in the balloon."

Like Oriskany, Bennington consisted of a cluster of farms surrounding a fortified manor house. But Bennington was not on the frontier, and the continuing battles being waged against marauders by the Judge were a very occasional thing here. Visitors could feel the sense of tranquility that overlay the countryside. There was no sign of patrols along the approach roads, and children played unsupervised in the fields. Pennants fluttered from the stockade walls, and the gates were unguarded. This was open country, about equally divided between forest and cultivated plots.

Claver lived in a cottage on the main road about an hour east of the manor house. "It's easy to find," a cart driver told them. "Just look for the obelisk. You can't miss it."

It would indeed have been difficult. The obelisk was visible for miles. It soared into the bright afternoon sky, by far the highest structure in Brockett and its attendant territories. A town had once lived on this site, but it lay buried now beneath low rolling hills, its presence marked only by the monument. There was a plate, carefully preserved, before which they lingered:

WE'LL SEE WHO'S GOIN' T' OWN THIS FARM.
—Reuben Stebbins, Colonial Militia
Battle of Bennington, May 11, 1776

Claver's cottage was one of several occupying nearby hilltops. But his was easy to identify: The fields surrounding it were unworked, and in its rear a wooden frame rose higher than the trees. An enormous bag had been draped across the frame. It was the balloon.

There were several sheds, a barn, and a silo. They dismounted, knocked on the front door, and, receiving no answer, walked around back. The sheds were filled with engines and vats and tubs. Every building had a workbench, and the floors were often covered with shavings, the walls discolored with gray-brown splotches. At one wooden table, a row of beakers held liquids of various colors.

They paused before a wicker basket strung with cables. "I think that's what you ride in," said Chaka. Flojian inspected it with obvious reluctance. An orange-colored shed was filled with a stench that was still in their nostrils twenty minutes later when an elderly man, covered with sweat, burst out of the woods. "Hello," he said, waving and barely pausing before disappearing into the barn. They followed him.

"Warm day." He mopped his brow with a towel. He was wiry and muscular, with long silver hair kept in check by a headband. "You come to see me?"

He was not the frowning, academic type Quait had expected. But there was something vaguely unkempt about the man's expression, a kind of easy smile operating at cross purposes with intense green eyes. "Are you Orin Claver?"

"I am. And who are you?"

Quait did the introductions. Claver peered at them

closely. It was apparent he didn't see well. "You talk funny," he said. "Where are you from?"

"The Mississippi Valley."

"You've come a long way." The remark was a surprise. Quait had expected the usual shrug. "Surely you haven't traveled all this distance just to see me."

"We understand you take people for rides."

"In the balloon? Yes, I do. Where did you want to go?" He kicked off his shoes and was peeling his garments without apparent regard to social niceties.

"We have a map." Quait showed him.

Claver threw a quick glance in its direction, nodded as if he'd taken everything in, and flexed his forearms. "Hard to believe I'm eighty-seven, isn't it?" He grinned. "Well, let's go inside."

He was down to a pair of white shorts. They paraded across a spotty grass lawn into the cottage. A bag of walnuts hung just inside the front door. He offered them around. "Good for your digestion," he said.

Chaka accepted a couple. Claver took one for himself and tossed two more onto the grass. Within seconds a pair of squirrels appeared and seized them.

The interior was bright and comfortable, furnished with hickory furniture and off-white muslin curtains. Claver asked what kind of wine they liked, removed a couple of bottles from a cabinet, and filled three glasses. "There's cold water in the kitchen if you'd like some," he said. He indicated a short hallway. "Through there. Make yourselves at home. I'll be with you in a few minutes."

He swept out of the room.

"I'm not so sure this is a good idea," said Flojian, when they could hear the shower running. "We're going to trust this guy to take us up in one of those baskets? What if he has a heart attack up there?"

"If somebody has a heart attack," smiled Chaka, "I don't think it's going to be him."

Claver returned dressed in black trousers and a white shirt with fluffy sleeves, the sort of clothing that would have looked dashing on a twenty-five-year-old. He was barefoot, and he carried a glass of wine. "Now." He seated himself beside Chaka. "Tell me why you want to go so far."

Quait crossed one leg over the other. "Does the name *Haven* mean anything to you?"

"Of course."

"We think we know where it is."

Claver's eyes narrowed. *"Endine,"* he said, switching his gaze to Flojian. "I should have recognized the name. So you've come back. After all this time."

"That was my father," said Flojian.

"Ah. Yes. Certainly. And you've returned in his place to—do what?"

"To find Haven."

"They didn't do so well last time. What makes you think *you* can do better?"

"They *did* find it," said Flojian. "We've no doubt of that."

"It surprises me to hear it. Most of them died out there and the only thing that came back were stories about goblins."

"They brought back a copy of *A Connecticut Yankee in King Arthur's Court.*"

"Really? How is it I never heard about that?"

"Don't know," said Quait. "But we have the book."

"Listen," said Chaka. "None of this matters that much anyhow." She produced a gold coin and handed it to Claver. "We'll pay you ten of these to take us where we want to go."

He held the coin to the light. "That's generous.

But the flight's a fool's errand. There's nothing up there to be found, and I don't care to risk my life and my equipment. Not for ten gold coins, nor for a hundred. I really have no need for the money."

"How do you know there's nothing?" asked Quait.

"If there had been something, your father would have recovered it when he had the chance. He came back empty-handed."

"We have the Mark Twain."

"*You* have the Mark Twain. I have only your assurances."

"We wouldn't lie to you," said Flojian, his voice rising.

"I'm sure you wouldn't. But your interpretation of events could be mistaken." He sat back and relaxed. "I'm sorry to say this, but I see no compelling reason to go."

"You see no compelling reason?" Quait felt anger rise in his throat.

"The place is a myth," said Claver.

Quait got up and started for the door.

"I was impressed with your steam engine," said Chaka, not moving.

"Thank you." Claver flashed another of those smiles compromised by his eyes. His teeth looked strong and sharp. "I'm working on an improved model. The wood-burners aren't as efficient as they might be."

"Coal," said Flojian.

"Very good, Endine. Yes, it should improve output."

"Tell me," continued Flojian, "have you thought about the possibility of designing a power plant that could take a ship across the sea?"

He laughed. "Of course. It's coming."

Chaka could see the framework and the balloon

through the window. "Orin," she said, "if that really is Haven up there, we'd have a chance of finding the *Quebec.*"

Claver stopped breathing.

"Think about it," she said. "Think what it would mean to find out how to build a propulsion system for an undersea ship. Or do you think it was a coal-burner?"

This time the smile was complete. "It would be nice to find."

"But the *Quebec* is only a myth," said Flojian. "Right?"

"Take us where we want to go," said Chaka. "The worst that can happen is that you'll come back with ten gold coins. Who knows what the real payoff might be?"

✠ 28 ✠

Claver provided quarters for the Illyrians. In the morning they inspected the gondola, which was larger than the basket they'd seen in storage. This one was oblong, rather than circular, and big enough to accommodate several people. Claver brought aboard a supply of rope, tools, and lanterns. He also loaded four blankets, "because it gets cold up there"; and an array of pots, tubes, rubber fittings, and glass receptacles, which he described as his portable laboratory. "To make hydrogen for the return trip," he explained.

"You mean," demanded Quait, "we can't just set down and tie the thing to a tree until we're ready to leave?"

"Oh, no," he said, "unfortunately, it won't be as simple as that. Once we're on the ground, we'll stay there until we can manufacture some hydrogen. That won't be especially difficult, but we need to land near a city."

"Why?" asked Flojian.

"Because we need sulfur. There's always plenty in the ground around Roadmaker cities, if you know where to look. I have to tell you, I think all this fuss about Roadmaker knowledge is overblown. Damned fools were poisoning themselves." They were talking more loudly than normal, trying to speak over a machine that chugged and gasped while the balloon, which was supported by the large wooden framework in back of the house, gradually filled. "We'll also need to find coal. It burns hotter than wood. And iron. We'll have to have iron."

"Anything else?" asked Flojian.

"Well, water, of course."

"Of course," said Quait.

"What that means is that we won't be able to land right on top of your target. We'll pick the nearest Roadmaker city and set down there."

Chaka frowned. "Orin, how long is it going to take us to get there?"

"Depends on the wind. If the wind cooperates, and your maps are right, we can make it in about twenty hours."

"What happens," she asked, "if the wind *doesn't* cooperate?"

"We won't be going there at all." He grinned. "It's okay, though. The wind always cooperates. To a degree."

"Twenty hours," she said doubtfully. "And we can't set down until we get there?"

"We won't have much privacy," he admitted. "I'm sorry about that, but balloons have some drawbacks when you use them for long-distance travel. But we'll have a bucket available."

The balloon was made of a tightly woven fabric coated with varnish. There was a valve on top to permit the release of gas, thereby allowing the pilot to descend. The gas-filled bag, which Claver called an *envelope,* was enclosed within a hemp net. Sixteen lines, passing through a suspension hoop, secured the gondola to the net.

"This is the rip-panel rope," Claver explained. "When we get close to the ground, during landing, we'll open a panel in the top of the envelope and dump the remaining hydrogen."

"Why?" asked Flojian. "Why not just try to tie up somewhere? And save whatever's left?"

"Only if you like broken limbs. No, we need to get rid of it when we touch down. It doesn't matter; there won't be that much left anyhow. Just enough to drag us along the ground." He laughed. "I know it sounds a little dangerous but balloons are really much safer than traveling by horse."

Bags of sand were strung around the exterior of the gondola. That was their ballast, Claver explained. "We want to go up, we get rid of some ballast."

The process of filling the envelope was finished by about midnight. Quait and Chaka had watched from the back porch. When Claver disconnected the hydrogen pump, an eerie silence fell across the grounds. The balloon strained against its frame, bathed in moonlight, anxious to be free of the ground.

"We'll top it off tomorrow, before we leave," said Claver.

The pump was mounted on a cart. He threw a couple of covers over it, said goodnight to his guests, and went inside.

Quait put an arm around Chaka. "You excited?"

"Yes. It's been a long haul, and I'm anxious to see the end of it."

"I hope it doesn't fizzle."

"The project?" She moved close to him. "Or the balloon?"

Next day, they brought aboard a supply of fruit, water, dried fish, and meat. Drawn by the activity, a small crowd of children and adults arrived to see them off. The adults, of whom there were about twenty, insisted on shaking hands with Claver and each of his passengers. "Good luck," they said. As if they would need it. The kids yelped and chased one another around the gondola.

Claver added a rope ladder to their supplies and

handed out pairs of smoked goggles. He made a show of adjusting his (which were somewhat flashier than their mates), zipped up a leather jacket, threw a white scarf around his neck, and announced that it was time to go. Two burly volunteers separated themselves from the crowd and took up posts beside dangling ropes on either side of the wooden framework.

The Illyrians climbed in. Flojian whispered a prayer, Chaka glanced at the envelope, and Quait took a final lingering look at the ground. Claver was last to come aboard. He asked if they were ready and, on receiving assent, signaled the two volunteers. They tugged on the ropes, the wooden framework creaked, and the balloon began to rise.

A loud cheer went up with them. People stopped in roads and fields to wave. Others, apparently drawn by the commotion, came out of houses, looked up, and joined in.

Nothing in Quait's life, not getting shot at, not the maglev, not even the ghostly voice in Union Station, quite touched his primal fears as near to the bone as did watching the earth fall away. He'd never been bothered by heights, and was surprised that rising above the treetops induced such an unseemly sensation. The others, to his annoyance, seemed to be enjoying the experience.

"We'll not only be flying over *terra incognita,"* said Claver, "but you'll be interested in knowing that we'll be going almost twice as far from home as the balloon has ever traveled before." If that piece of information excited the old man, it did nothing to ease Quait's apprehension.

"Look at these." Claver indicated two lines that hung down from the interior of the balloon. One carried a yellow flag, the other a red. "This one," the yellow one, "controls the hydrogen valve on top. *This* one," the red, "you already know about. It's the rip-panel." He nodded somberly. "It would be a good idea if nobody touches either. Okay?"

Quait looked east across rolling countryside, farms and orchards and a tangle of roads and rivers fading gradually to forest. There were vehicles on the roads, boats in the rivers, people in the fields. Then these too were gone, and they drifted above pure wilderness. He listened to the wind, to the creaking of the gondola, to the barking of a distant dog.

"It's lovely," said Chaka.

Quait had looked down from high places before, from mountaintops and the Iron Pyramid and the bridge on which they'd lost Silas. But this was a different order of experience altogether. It incorporated a disconnectedness, a sense of having broken away from the ground, a suggestion of both freedom and vulnerability. If it could not be said that he was enjoying the ride, he could at least understand why others might become addicted to floating in the clouds.

But they were drifting south. The wrong way.

"Be patient," said Claver. "We have to find a friendly wind current." With which remark he plunged a scoop into one of the sandbags attached to the handrail, filled it, and gave the sand to the sky. The balloon went higher.

"You're sure we won't have any trouble getting down," said Quait.

Claver squeezed his shoulder. "None whatever, my young friend. I can assure you that eventually, one way or another, we *will* get down."

Flojian was working on a diagram of the balloon's inflating appendix, but the wind kept worrying at the paper until he finally gave up. He seemed far more interested in the mechanics of the vehicle than he did in the view.

Claver found his wind and they drifted through the afternoon, moving at a steady clip toward the northeast. "I'd estimate about thirty miles an hour," he said. Quait was impressed. Thirty miles needed a day and a half on the ground.

There were Roadmaker towns, often no more than a few charred ruins.

"You get a better sense of the scale of destruction from up here." Claver adjusted his goggles. He did that a lot.

"The Plague must have been terrible," said Flojian.

"That's a safe guess." Claver looked down. "There were a lot of people during Roadmaker times. You ever see Boston or New York? Oh, you'd know if you had. *Very big.* Enormous. Not anything like Brockett. You get a good sickness into that population, it'd run wild."

They picked up a dirt road and followed it east.

"How high are we?" asked Chaka.

Claver sucked his lips. "About a mile and a half."

The road came to a river, which it leaped on a new log bridge. A stockade guarded the near side. "The frontier," Claver explained. Thick forest and rugged hills ran to the horizon. Even the road seemed to fade out. "We'll have the same problem eventually."

"Plague?" asked Flojian.

"Population. If we come back in thirty, forty years, this'll all be farmland."

By sundown they were crossing a Roadmaker double highway. It came out of the north, broad and straight, and from their altitude it looked unbroken. Ahead, a range of white-capped peaks loomed.

It was cold, and getting colder. They distributed the blankets and pulled them around their shoulders. "If we went lower," suggested Flojian, "we might get warmer air."

"Might," said Claver. "We might also get currents that are going the wrong way. We don't have hydrogen and ballast to waste running up and down."

They ate and watched the mountains approach. The land rose under them, snow and granite and forest. It mounted up and up, gradually at first, and then sharply, and they were drifting over peaks so close they could smell the spruce. And then the land fell away again. The sun went down and the darkness below went on forever.

A full moon rose. "With a little bit of luck," said Claver, "we should be over the ocean by dawn."

They arranged a rotating night watch.

Claver explained that they wanted to keep the north star forty-five degrees off the port side of their line of advance. "Obviously, we won't maintain that with any degree of exactitude. But if we get too far off course, say thirty degrees or more for longer than a few minutes, wake me."

They managed some privacy by holding a blanket for one another. A bucket hung from the underside of the craft, and this was hauled aboard when needed, and after use its contents were dumped. Flojian and Claver exchanged amused comments about the risks for travelers on the ground.

Quait took the first watch. Chaka stayed close to him for a while, and he was grateful for her warmth. Then she climbed beneath a blanket and was quickly asleep, rocked by the gentle movements of the gondola.

Following Claver's suggested method, Quait picked out a landmark, a hill, a patch of trees, a river bend, occasionally a mountain, anything that was forty-five degrees forward of the north star. Then he settled down to watch it draw nearer. As long as it continued to do so in a more or less straightforward manner, he was satisfied. On one occasion, a highway intersection that he was guiding on veered far to starboard. That meant the balloon had begun to move almost due north. He woke the pilot.

Claver was cheerful enough about being disturbed, and seemed to enjoy having been called on to set things right. He tugged on the yellow line until the balloon started to descend. His manner suggested all this was really quite basic. Within a few minutes he had the vehicle back on course and, in his condescending manner, asked to be awakened again if there were any more difficulties.

Quait knew how to make the balloon rise and fall. What he did not understand was how to determine where favorable air currents would be. "I don't know how to explain it," Claver told him later. "Experience, I guess."

Sleep came hard for Quait. It might have been the cold. Or the smell of salt air. Or the impending end of the hunt. But most likely it was Chaka's proximity. On the trail, he had prudently maintained a discreet distance. Here, she lay breathing softly, within easy reach.

He sighed, got up, and joined Claver, who was at the helm, or whatever constituted a helm on this windrunner. The sky was ablaze with the rising sun, and they were running parallel to a rocky shore.

Claver was doing knee bends. "I recommend it," he said. "Keeps you warm and flexible."

"How are we doing?" asked Quait.

"Okay." There was a note of self-satisfaction in his voice. "The wind wants to take us out to sea."

"Don't let it happen."

"I won't." He flexed shoulders and arms, not unlike a boxer. "But we're spending a lot of gas and ballast."

"Is that a problem?"

"Starting to be."

Quait settled back to watch the sunrise. The pilot passed him some nuts and water. "Not much of a breakfast," Claver admitted. "But with luck, we'll be on the ground anyway in a few hours."

"I've seen the ocean before," Quait said. "At the mouth of the Mississippi."

"What direction was it from the land mass?"

"South."

Claver thought it over. "I wonder if it's the same body of water? It might be possible for you to go home by sea."

Quait laughed. "Anything would be an improvement on the overland route." He looked toward the rising sun and the curving horizon and wondered what lay beyond. "Could you get to Chicago in this thing?" he asked.

"If we had enough hydrogen. And the wind was right. But I don't think I'd want to try it."

They began to drift, and he had to take them up and then down to get the balloon moving forward again. It gave Quait a little satisfaction to see that even Claver didn't guess right all the time. But the sandbags were emptying fast.

They floated north over a rugged coastline, an endless series of cliffs, shoals, inlets, and offshore islands. They saw deer and wild horses and, on occasion, signs of habitation. There were a few plowed fields, some orchards, a house on a bluff overlooking a harbor. Gray smoke billowed out of the chimney. Later they saw a small boat casting nets. But these were the exceptions. For the most part, there was only wilderness.

The sun climbed toward the meridian. The first sign of Knobby's bay would be land to the east. But islands were liberally sprinkled through the area, so there was a series of false alarms. At midafternoon, the wind changed. Claver threw more ballast over the side. The vehicle moved first one way and then another before settling back on course.

"That's about it," he announced. "We don't have enough left to manage anything other than a landing. Your bay better come up soon."

Within the hour, a finger of land appeared in the east. They watched with hopeful skepticism, remembering the earlier islands. It developed into a long coastline, and cut off the open sea. Mountains rose. And, as they drew closer, they saw more Roadmaker towns and coastal roads littered with hojjies.

"This is it," said Chaka.

They came in over the bay at an altitude of about two miles. The tide was out, and they saw with joy that it did indeed leave vast mudflats in some areas. It wouldn't be difficult for an unwary master to find himself stranded.

A few minutes later, the bay divided into two channels. "Keep to starboard," said Flojian, barely able to contain his excitement.

The water glittered in the sunlight. Escarpments and green hills lined the shore. Here, waves rolled onto white beaches; there, they pounded rock formations.

A crosswind caught them and blew them toward the wrong side of the bay. Claver reluctantly released more hydrogen until he had arrested the movement and they were again approaching the eastern coast. But they continued to drop, even after he'd thrown out ballast. "We're going to have to find a place to land," he said.

"Over there!" said Flojian. Inshore, the saddle-shaped mountain came into view.

"Okay," said Quait. "We're doing fine."

"Not really," said Claver. "We're going down a little bit fast." He dumped the last of his sand. They continued to fall.

"Orin?" said Quait.

"Prepare for landing," he said. "We need a city."

The bay was getting narrow. A long hooked cape, very much resembling the one marked on Knobby's map, projected out from the east. Knobby had given them bearings, and they used them now to target an escarpment. *A sheer wall,* their map said.

"That's it," cried Chaka, and they embraced all around.

They drifted past. "We're doing about forty," said Claver.

The bay continued to squeeze down. The mountaintops were getting close.

"Town ahead," said Claver.

Quait could now see clearly a network of ancient roads and piers and stone walls. The precipice that might contain Haven fell behind.

The town was reasonably intact. Blackened buildings still stood. The network of streets was easy to make out, and there was a large industrial complex on the north. "Looks like an old power plant," said Claver. "Probably shut down before the collapse. If we can make it, we'll be in good shape."

Bluffs and trees were coming up fast. "Try to relax when we hit," he added.

A road appeared beneath them, and swerved off to the east. They scraped the top of a hill and bounced through some treetops. As they broke free, Claver jerked away the rip-panel and the envelope collapsed with a sigh. The gondola landed hard and spilled its passengers into a field.

"We're down," said Claver.

"Orin," said Quait, "flying is never going to catch on."

✠ 29 ✠

They dragged the envelope and the gondola into a shed, collected their weapons, blankets, lamps, the rope ladder, and the rest of their supplies, and turned back toward the bay.

There was no sign of local inhabitants, no houses, no plowed fields. They found a road and followed it into the woods. Nobody talked much. They could hear the sound of the surf in the distance.

The road eventually faded out. But they could smell the water, and an hour later, as the sun went down, they broke out onto the shoreline.

They had fish for dinner and sat late into the night, listening to the long silences. Flojian was appalled to learn that Claver had sold individual steam engines rather than the *process* to marine manufacturers. In a society without patent laws, this had amounted to giving away the secret for the price of a few units. The buyers were now in the business of making their own, and he was effectively cut out. "It doesn't really matter," Claver said. "I have all the money I need. What disturbs me is that they overpriced the boats and people blame me. The rivermen think I got rich on their backs."

"When in fact," said Flojian, "the manufacturers took the money." He shook his head. "You need a business manager."

Claver confessed that he was getting excited about what they might find tomorrow. "I've been trying to dismiss it as nonsense, and I still think it is. But wouldn't it be glorious to find the *Quebec*? What a cap that would be for my career."

Quait and Chaka took a walk in the woods. "Last night of the great hunt," she said. "It's hard to believe we're really here."

Moonlight filtered through the trees. It cast an aura around her hair but left her eyes in shadow. She was achingly lovely, a forest goddess who had finally revealed herself. Quait felt nineteen. "I have a suggestion," he said. His voice was pitched a trifle higher than normal. He'd been practicing all evening how he was going to say this, what words he would use, where he would pause, and where lay stress. But it all vanished. "There's a tradition," he continued, "that a ship's captain is authorized to perform weddings." He felt her stiffen, and then melt into him. "I've talked to Orin. He'd be willing to do it for us. And I think this would be the perfect time."

"Because the quest ends tomorrow?"

"Because we're here tonight. Because I'm in love with you." *Because six people died in those tunnels and nobody knows how.*

"Yes," she said.

He had not expected so quick a reply. He'd rehearsed various arguments, how they would remember forever the night and the following day, Haven and their wedding, inextricably linked forever. How, regardless of the way things turned out, the journey home would be difficult and dangerous. (He hadn't been able to work out why the wedding would make it less difficult or less dangerous, but it would sure as hell make it more endurable.) How there was no need to wait longer. Been through enough. They knew now beyond doubt that they would eventually be mates. That decision having been taken, why delay things indefinitely?

She drew his lips down to hers and folded her body into his. "Yes," she said again.

Orin Claver was not a believer. Nevertheless, he surprised the Illyrians by showing no reluctance to invoke the Goddess as protector of the hearth.

"We are met on this hilltop," he began, in the timeless ritual of the ancient ceremony, "to join this man and this woman." The fire crackled in the background, and a rising wind moved the trees. As there was no one present to give the bride away, Flojian agreed to substitute for the requisite family member.

Claver's white scarf served as Chaka's veil. She was otherwise in buckskin. Quait found a neckerchief to add a touch of formality to his own attire.

Illyrian weddings required two witnesses, one each from the earthly and from the divine order. Flojian consequently was drawn to double duty, and stood with the invisible Shanta while his two friends pledged love, mutual faith, and fortune. When they'd finished, they exchanged rings which she had woven from vines and set with stones. Claver challenged any who had reason to object to come forward, "or forever remain silent."

They glanced around at the dark woods, and Chaka's eyes shone. "No objection having been raised," said Claver, "I hereby exercise the authority held by captains from time immemorial and declare you husband and wife. Quait, you may kiss the bride."

Flojian, sensing that the Goddess was preparing to depart, took advantage of her proximity to ask her to remember her servant Avila.

✠ ✠ ✠

. . . A sheer wall rising about two hundred feet out of the water. We could see thick woods at the top. . . . There was a river on the north side of the bluff, and a pebbled beach. . . .

They looked at their map some more, took bearings on the turn in the channel and the saddle-shaped formation that Knobby had described.

"I'd say that's it," said Claver.

They compared it with Arin's sketch. "He would have been back that way," suggested Chaka. A quarter-mile or so down the beach.

They stood on wet sand off to one side of the formation. "There's the discolored rock," Quait said, drawing a horizontal line in the air with his index finger. "The door."

They all saw it. Flojian noted the position of a notched boulder on the summit. Chaka produced Silas's journal and made the appropriate notation: SUSPECTED ENTRANCE FOUND. She dated and initialed it. When she'd finished, they hiked around behind the bluff and started upslope.

By early afternoon they'd arrived at the top. They laid out their gear under a spruce tree and peered over the edge. It was a long way down. The cliff face looked gray and hard and very smooth, save for occasional shrubs. Far below, whitecaps washed over rocks. Flojian looked for his notched boulder, walked a few paces along the summit, and stopped. "Right about here," he said.

Gulls fluttered on air currents and skimmed the outgoing tide.

Quait nodded. "I'll go down." He was already reaching for a line.

"I don't think that's a good idea," said Claver.

"Why not?"

He glanced at his own eighty-seven-year-old body, at the diminutive Flojian, at Chaka. "I know I'm in good shape for my age," he said, "but I'm still not sure the three of us could haul you back up here if you got in trouble. Seems to me as if the muscle in this operation should be on top and not on bottom."

There was no arguing the logic. "Who then?"

"Me," said Chaka.

"No," said Quait.

Claver nodded. "It makes sense. She's forty pounds lighter than anybody else."

Chaka looped a rope around her shoulders. "It's not a problem," she said.

"Absolutely not," said Quait.

But Chaka never paused. "I'm a full member of this mission," she said. "I've taken my chances along with everybody else."

"I know that."

"Good." She tightened the rope and stretched her shoulders.

"Have you ever done anything like this before?" Quait asked.

"Tree house." And, when his expression did not lighten, "I'll be fine, Quait."

"We should have thought to bring a harness," said Claver.

They secured the rope ladder to a cottonwood and dropped it over the side. Then they looped Chaka's safety line around the same tree, left sixty feet of slack, and anchored it to an elm. "Be careful," said Quait. "If you need more line, pull once. You want to get hauled out of there, pull twice."

"Okay, lover," she said. "I got it. And I'm ready."

"If the place is really here," said Flojian, "I can't believe there's not another entrance."

Claver shook his head. "There'd be a lot of ground to search. Let's use the way we know. Once inside, we can see what else is available."

Chaka put on a pair of gloves, stuffed a bar into her belt, and walked to the edge.

"Luck," said Flojian.

She flashed a smile, straddled the ladder, and began to back down over the cliff edge. Quait paid out the safety line.

The ladder's rungs were wooden. But it was hard to get her feet onto them until the rock wall curved away somewhat. She kept her eyes on Quait as long as she could. She did not look down, but she felt the presence of the void. There seemed to be a damned lot of business with heights on this trip.

But it was surprisingly easy going once she got below the summit.

"Are you okay?" Flojian's voice drifted down.

She assured him she was and continued the descent. Every few steps they'd ask again and as she got farther away it became more distracting until finally she called up that she'd yell if she needed anything and please otherwise keep quiet.

Once she ran out of slack and had to signal. The rock was rougher than it had looked from above. Vegetation was sharp and prickly. At one point it snagged the ladder and she had to hang by one hand while she worked it free.

Streams of pebbles dribbled past. Vertical fissures appeared. From a dark hole, a pair of eyes watched her.

A sudden burst of wind hit her and she swung gently back and forth, clinging to the ladder. Below her, right where it was supposed to be, she saw the discolored rock. It looked exactly like a set of doors. "A little more," she called up. "I think we've got it."

✠ ✠ ✠

There were actually *four* doors set in the face of the cliff. This was where Showron Voyager's bullet-shaped vehicle had delivered its passengers. So there had been a terminal here once. Several pieces of iron remained, supports outside, beams inside. And a bench. One of the doors was wedged open. She had some difficulty gaining purchase because the ladder was hanging a couple of feet out, as a result of the overhead bulge. But she swung herself close, grabbed a wiry bush, and tried to get inside.

The scariest part of the entire operation came when she tried to climb off the ladder and get through the doorway. There wasn't enough slack and they didn't seem to understand up there that if they kept the safety line tight she couldn't move. Moreover, she had to hang on to the bush to keep the ladder close until she was safely through the open door. When it was over she wasted no time releasing the safety line. She congratulated herself and called up that she was okay. The high-roofed corridor Knobby had described lay beyond. But it was too dark to see more than a few yards.

"Chaka." Quait's voice. "We need to tie the ladder down."

"Right." The ladder was about three feet out. Just beyond easy reach.

She tried for it twice. The second time she lost her balance and almost fell. It was a desperate moment. And it was stupid because they didn't need to do it this way. "Quait."

"Yes. What's taking so long?"

"I can't reach it. I need someone to come down."

Flojian came next, with lamps dangling from his belt. When he reached the doorway, she caught his hand and pulled him in. And the ladder along with him. They tied it to a beam and lit the lamps while they waited for Claver.

Quait was last to descend, having looped his safety line around the tree and dropped it to them so that someone would be holding the other end.

When he'd joined them, they pushed through into the inner passageway. Beyond, in the gloomy light thrown by the lamps, they saw the stairway and the corridor and the shafts. The shafts were very much like the ones in the towers around Union Station. Chaka looked down into one. "Damp," she said. She found a couple of pebbles and tossed them in. After a few seconds, they splashed.

The air was stale away from the door.

Claver indicated his surprise that the air was breathable at all, until Flojian noted a duct cover in the ceiling. There was a system of vents.

The stairway was not cut from rock, but rather was an insert, made of Roadmaker metal. The handrail and the stairs were covered with dust.

They picked up their equipment and started down. Flojian took the lead.

Chaka had never quite believed the story about the six deaths. When people die in groups, they don't die without marks. She noticed that Quait kept his hand close to his weapon.

That Flojian harbored similar feelings was evident. He moved as quietly as he could, spoke in a hushed voice, and everything about his demeanor suggested that he was controlling his own set of devils. That was an unusual attitude for him: He was given to caution, but Chaka rarely saw him frightened. Nevertheless, he stayed in front.

Even Claver seemed intimidated, and had little to say. He carried a coil of rope and a bar, but he was probably not aware he gripped the bar like a weapon.

The dark was tangible. It squeezed the light from their lamps. Shadows moved grotesquely around the walls. They could hear the wind, seemingly in the rock. Corridors opened at each level. The shafts were always there, of course, and beyond they saw doorways, sometimes open, sometimes not.

"The walls are wet," said Claver. "This isn't a place *I'd* use for storage."

"It was probably military," suggested Quait. "Whatever it might have become in later years it was originally a military or naval installation."

The stairway wound back and forth, landing by landing, until they concluded they must surely be near the base of the cliff. And then it ended. Broke off.

"This is probably where they found your father," Chaka told Flojian.

Quait stood at the edge of the landing, held his lamp out, and looked down. They could see a floor.

That's where they died.

"No dust here," said Claver.

There wasn't. The landing was clean. So were five or six stairs above the landing. Above that, the dust was thick. Curious.

The floor was about twenty-five feet down.

"Maybe," Claver continued, "they opened a door and released a pocket of gas."

That was close to making sense. It was akin to what had happened to Jon Shannon when *he* opened the wrong door. But there was a missing element. "There was no explosion," Chaka said.

"Don't need one. They start breathing gas, lose consciousness, and they smother."

"All *six* of them?"

"Well," Claver admitted, "it *does* require a stretch."

"Anyhow," said Flojian, "they were found in different places."

Claver shook his head. "There's always a tendency to dramatize when you're telling a story."

"I don't think Knobby was lying," said Chaka.

Flojian tied a line around his lamp and lowered it. The remains of the collapsed staircase lay scattered around the floor below.

"I wouldn't suggest he *was* lying," said Claver. "But people get confused easily. Especially in a place like this. To be honest with you, if things happened the way Knobby said, I'd be ready to accept the idea that there's something loose in these tunnels."

Quait knew immediately that Claver regretted having said it. But it was out in the open now, no calling it back, and they looked nervously at one another and peered into the area below. They could see the openings to passageways down there. One in each wall. "If it *was* gas," he asked, "could the same thing happen to us?"

"Oh, yes." Claver shook his head emphatically. "Yes, indeed. I would certainly say so. Just open the wrong door."

"How do we protect ourselves?" asked Flojian.

Chaka made a noise low in her throat. "Stay clear of doors altogether," she said.

"That's right." Claver folded his arms and assumed the stance of an instructor. "If we open any doors, one person does it, and the rest of us get well back. I'd suggest also no one wander off alone. And be careful with the guns." He threw a long hard look at Quait. "We're all a trifle jittery right now." He stressed the pronoun to suggest that he was really talking about the Illyrians. "We don't have much light, and we're likely in more danger from ourselves than from any outside source."

"I hope so," said Quait. He tied a rope to the handrail and pulled it tight. The lower area was dark, cold, dismal. Light reflected off puddles. "It's not the way I expected Haven to look," he said. He dropped the other end of the line into the lower chamber, wrapped it around his waist, and stepped off the landing.

"Careful." Chaka drew her pistol.

Quait lowered himself smoothly. He had his own weapon out before he touched ground. The floor was wet. It glittered in the light from the lamps. As soon as he was clear, Chaka started down.

There was a doorway in each wall.

The passage with the shafts was behind her. Two adjacent corridors rolled away into the dark. Directly ahead, she was looking at a flat, low tunnel. A massive door lay half wedged in the tunnel entrance.

Quait was walking around, thrusting his lamp into each passageway in turn. The corridors to left and right revealed several open doors. Chaka took a quick look and saw large rooms with high ceilings and piles of soggy wreckage.

Flojian gazed at the fallen door, and then walked into the fourth passageway. Chaka followed him. Twenty feet farther on, there was another, apparently identical, door. It too was down. Beyond, they saw black water.

"The underground lake," said Flojian.

"So far," said Chaka, "Knobby seems to be accurate."

The surface of the lake lay several feet below floor level. The lake itself stretched into the dark. Chaka looked up at the ceiling. It was quite smooth and flat, only a few feet above the water. "This is a chamber," she said, "not a cave."

"Look at this." Flojian directed the beam from his lamp to a stairway. The stairway descended into the water.

Chaka stared at it a long time. "I don't think this area's supposed to be under water," she said.

Claver by now had joined them. "The doors are *hatches,*" he said. "They wanted to seal off the lake."

"Why?" asked Flojian.

"Maybe there's something that comes out of the water," suggested Chaka.

Claver's brow furrowed. "I just don't understand what happened here," he said.

The tall corridor was lined with open rooms, all resembling the one that Chaka had looked into. They entered the nearest one and played their lantern beams across ancient tables, benches, cabinets. Everything was wet and cold.

"Must be water in the walls," said Claver.

Many of the cabinets were standardized. They were made of Roadmaker materials, neither wood nor metal, and most had four or five drawers of varying thicknesses. Some of the drawers were empty. Most contained a kind of brown sludge.

Quait knelt beside one and held his lamp close. He dug into the sludge and drew out a piece of shriveled material. Several threads hung from it.

"Might be a book binding," said Claver.

Flojian nodded. "I think that's right. I think that's exactly what it is. That's what they all are. They put the volumes into individual drawers. You wanted to see something, you pulled it out, took it over to one of the tables, read it at your leisure."

Chaka surveyed the sludge and said nothing.

Each drawer had been fixed with a metal plate, possibly identifying the book within. But the plates were no longer legible.

Because of the poor light, they were slow to appreciate the size of the chamber. The ceiling was high, about twenty feet. And the room was quite extensive, probably a hundred feet long and half as wide. It was circled by a gallery, which was connected to the lower level by a staircase at either end. Two hundred cabinets, at a rough guess, were scattered across the floor.

They walked through the debris with sinking spirits, and climbed to the gallery hoping that, somehow, miraculously, the upper levels might have escaped the general destruction. They had not.

What had happened? "We know there was stuff here," said Chaka. "Karik and his people found some books intact. *Somewhere.*"

"Let's see what else there is," said Quait.

There were three more such rooms located in that wing. But all were in identical condition. They trooped listlessly through the wreckage, trying to read plates, to find something that had survived.

The opposite wing, however, gave reason to hope. It too had four storage areas. Three were ruined. But at the end of the corridor, a door was still closed. "Maybe," said Chaka.

"These doors look watertight, too," said Claver.

The locking mechanism was operated by a ringbolt. Quait lifted it, and the others withdrew to a safe distance, taking the lamps with them.

But the door would not open. "Give me a bar," he said.

They worked almost half an hour, forcing the door away from the jamb. When they were satisfied it was ready, they reassumed their positions, Quait inserted the bar at a strategic point, looked at them hopefully, and pulled.

The door creaked. He tried again and it came open a few inches. Quait sniffed at the air. "I think it's okay," he said.

"Wait," cautioned Claver.

But Quait's blood was up. He ignored the warning and threw his weight behind the effort. Hinges popped and metal creaked. He got his fingers into the opening and pulled. The door came.

They tied a lamp to a line and dragged it across the threshold from a respectful distance. When nothing untoward occurred, they entered the room.

It was identical to the others, two stories high, circled by a gallery. But it was *dry*. The furniture, the cabinets and chairs and tables were all standing. *And bound volumes gleamed inside the cabinets.*

Chaka shrieked with joy. Her cry echoed through the chamber.

"I don't understand it," said Claver. "What happened here?"

"Who cares?" Quait strode into the room, went to the nearest cabinet, and opened the top drawer. "Look at this," he said.

Black leather. Gold script. *The Annals*. By Tacitus.

The cover was held shut by snaps. He wiped off a tabletop and lifted the book out. The others gathered behind him while he set it down and opened it.

They turned the pages, past the titles into the text:

He was given sway over the more important provinces, not because he was exceptionally talented, but because he was a good businessman, and neither his ambitions nor his talent reached any higher. . . .

The cabinets were arranged methodically, usually in groups of four, backed against each other, with angled reading boards and writing tables nearby. Chairs were arranged in convenient locations. A long elliptical counter dominated the center of the chamber.

Flojian selected a cabinet, deliberately averted his eyes from the identifying plate and, while the others watched, opened the top drawer and removed the book. Its title was written across the cover in silver script:

Paideia
by
Werner Jaeger
Volume I

He opened the cover gently, almost tenderly. Title and author appeared again. And a date: 1939.

Turn a page. Lines of script in shining black ink filled the vast whiteness of the paper. *Education is the process by which a community preserves and transmits its physical and intellectual character. For the individual passes away, but the type remains.*

"Voices from another world," Chaka whispered.

They embraced in the flickering light. For a few moments the shadows drew back. All the tension amd frustration of the preceding months drained away. Claver, pumping Quait's hand, gave way to tears. "I'm glad I came," he said again and again. "I'm glad I came."

These were substantial volumes, not books as another age might have understood the term. They were written by hand, thousands of lines of carefully produced script on large sheets of paper, the whole bound into gilt-edged leather covers. They were of the same family as *Connecticut Yankee*.

It must have been the history section. They found works they'd heard of, like Gibbon's *The Decline and Fall of the Roman Empire* (in numerous volumes), and books they hadn't, like *The Anabasis*. They paged through McMurtrie's *The American Presidency in Crisis* and Ingel Kyatawa's *Japan in the Modern Age* and Thomas More's *The History of King Richard III*. There was Voltaire's *The Age of King Louis XIV* and *The Anglo-*

Saxon Chronicle and Josephus's *The Jewish War*. There were copies of *The American Century,* Kissinger's *Diplomacy,* and *America and the Pacific, 1914–2011.*

"These are relatively recent transcriptions," said Quait. "Look at the condition of the paper. They can't be more than a couple of centuries old."

The gallery was also filled with volumes. Chaka went up the staircase and plunged into the upper level treasures.

They almost forgot where they were. Like children, they gamboled among the ancient texts, calling one another over to look at this or that, carrying their lamps from place to place, opening everything.

Chaka was paging through a copy of Manchester's *The Last Lion*. Suddenly her eyes brightened and she shook Quait. "I think we've found Winston," she laughed.

Coming on the day after her wedding, discovery of the golden chamber seemed almost a culmination to that sacred event. She was standing in the uncertain light, looking lovingly at Quait and at *The Last Lion,* when the illusion exploded. Flojian, down on the lower floor, announced there was water in the corridor. Rising fast.

✠ 30 ✠

They tried to close the door, but water poured through the bent frame. One of the lamps crashed to the floor and went out. "Not going to work," said Chaka. She looked around wildly. "How high will it go?"

"It's going to fill up," said Claver.

"You sure?"

"What do you think happens every day in the other rooms?"

They were snarling at each other now, the joy of a few moments before turned to rage and frustration. They opened the door and, two inside and two outside, tried to lift it higher in its frame and shut it again. The water kept coming in.

Books and cabinets looked polished in the dim light.

Chaka was close to panic.

"It's the lake," said Flojian. "It's open to the sea, and the tide's rising."

"No way to stop it?" asked Quait.

Claver laughed. "Are you serious?"

Quait tore off his jacket and tried to jam it between the door and the frame. "Damn!" he said. "One of us should have thought—"

Chaka watched the water spreading across the floor. "What do we do? There must be something—"

"We can save a few." Flojian splashed over to the nearest cabinet, opened it, and removed the top book. It was *The Letters of Abelard and Heloise*.

Quait looked around wildly. "We'll save, what, twenty or thirty, and lose everything else?"

"Wait." Claver was holding his lamp high, looking at a shadowy ceiling. "There might be something we can do, at that."

"What?" said Quait.

"Give me a minute." He hurried up the stairway into the gallery. They watched his lamp move swiftly along the upper level, watched it hesitate, watched it eventually circle the room. His face was pale in its spectral glow.

"We're wasting time," said Flojian. He lifted out a second book. It was *Chronicles of the Crusades, Being Contemporary Narratives of Richard of Devizes and Geoffrey de Vinsauf.* Quait helped him load both volumes into his arms. Then Flojian turned and stumbled toward the door. "Open up, Chaka," he said.

She couldn't help laughing at him. "How are you going to climb up to the landing with that load?" The water was running over the tops of her shoes. "It's coming in fast," she said. "If we're going to do something, we better get to it."

"What's to do?" asked Flojian. "Except to get out whatever we can."

Claver's light was still floating along the upper rail. He seemed to be holding a conversation with himself. "Yes," he was saying, "no reason why not." And, "I believe we can do it." Abruptly, he hurried to the top of the stairs, grasped the handrail, and leaned out. "Start bringing the books up here," he said. "And hurry." Incredibly, he had taken off his shirt and was beginning on his trousers.

"Why?" demanded Quait. "The room's going to fill up."

"I don't have time to explain things," said Claver. "Just *do* it. Trust me."

"We need to get out of here while we can," said Flojian. "Or *we'll* get caught."

"There's still time," said Claver. His voice had risen, and it echoed through the room. "If you want to give it up, just say so and we'll do it. But we might be able to save most of this stuff if you're willing to try."

They started by clearing bottom drawers, getting the books most immediately threatened by the rising water and piling them on top of cabinets, tables, benches, whatever offered itself.

The volumes were, of course, all hand-printed. They were heavy and awkward, some of them so large that Chaka would ordinarily have had to struggle to lift one. But her adrenalin was flowing and she performed feats in that hour that no one who knew her would have believed.

Claver hurried back downstairs. In the uncertain light, Chaka thought her eyes were playing tricks. He was *naked*. "Take off your clothes," he said. "I need everybody's clothes." He retrieved Quait's jacket from the door and dashed back among them. "Quick," he said.

"I think it's over," said Quait, whose expression left no doubt he believed Claver had come apart.

"Just do as I say. And hurry."

Chaka was already out of her jacket. "It's going to get cold in here," she said.

"What's he doing?" asked Flojian.

"I'm blocking ducts, damn it."

"I don't get it," said Quait. Nevertheless, he began to strip off his shirt.

"Oh," said Flojian. "If we can make the room airtight, when the tide rises past the top of the door the air'll begin to compress."

"Very good," said Claver, gesturing for Chaka's blouse.

"So what?" demanded Quait.

"If we can form an air bubble, it'll keep the water out of the upper part of the room."

"What happens if it doesn't work?" asked Chaka.

Quait slipped out of his clothes. He piled shirt, trousers, socks, shorts, everything, on top of Emil Ludwig's *Napoleon*.

Flojian got out of his clothing quickly. He handed them over to Claver, glanced with considerable discomfort at Chaka, who was now equally naked, and turned away. Chaka would have liked to duck down in the water, but that kind of response felt somehow childish.

Claver ascended back to the gallery with his arms full of garments. Meantime, it occurred to both Chaka and Quait that Chaka's hauling books upstairs wouldn't be the most efficient use of her time. They'd gained slightly on the rising water, so they rearranged the tasking: She continued removing the lower volumes while Quait and Flojian carried them to the upper level. She rescued *The Meditations of Marcus Aurelius* and Belzoni's *Narrative of Operations and Recent Researches in Egypt and Nubia* and Samuel Eliot Morison's *The Two-Ocean War*. She saved Caesar's *Commentaries* and Babcock's *Waiting at the Station* and Mulgrave's *Dusk at Mecca*. She dropped Herodotus into the water.

"I think this'll work," Claver called down.

She saved Polybius and Thucydides and Voltaire and T. E. Lawrence and Fuller and Woollcott and Churchill. (Was it the same Churchill?) She slipped and went down hard with Livy in her hands. She stacked Xenophon on top of Prescott and Commager on Henry Adams. "Okay." Claver's voice seemed to come from nowhere. "We should be in business now."

"Good," said Quait. "We can use you down here."

By then, Quait was the only one hauling books to the upper level. Working alone, Chaka had been losing ground and Flojian had diverted to help her get the remaining volumes out of the cabinets. That part of the job was almost done, but the water was rising too fast. It caught up to them and drowned a few volumes. Then it overflowed the tops of the tables on which the books were stacked and rose around the edges of *The Chronicle of Novgorod* and *The Dawn of History* and *China: the Dragon Wakes* and Roger Bacon's *Commentaries* and a host of others.

They saved what they could, piling the books on the upper stairs and going back for more. The water reached Chaka's shoulders. But she stayed with it, lifting volumes made even heavier by having been submerged, lifting them over her head and passing them up to Quait. Then she was swimming. But it all got too heavy finally and she had to drag herself out of the water.

"Time to go anyway," said Quait. The water level had reached the top of the door. There would be less than a few feet of air left in the outside passageway.

Flojian handed up Plutarch's *Alcibiades and Coriolanus*. It was too late for the rest. "I'm with you," he said. "Let's clear out."

But Claver hesitated. "What's wrong?" asked Chaka. "We've done what we can."

"No," said Claver. "I'm sorry." He took a deep breath. "Listen, how badly do you want to save this stuff?"

They were all cold and they looked toward the doorway. The surface of the water sparkled in the lamplight. "What are you trying to say?" asked Quait.

"There's no way to know how high the water will go. My guess is that it'll rise to a point about halfway between the top of the door and the ceiling. If that happens, we'll still lose most of this stuff." Many of the volumes that had come up from the lower level had been piled on the gallery floor. "We have to get everything up higher. We have to clear the cabinets up here and put everything as high as we can get it."

"Orin," said Quait, "there's no time to do that. If we don't leave now, we're not going to leave at all."

"I know," he said. He turned and looked at them and they could see that he was fearful. "Tell me what you want to do."

Most of the staircase was now submerged. Only the top three steps were still clear of the water. "I don't want to drown in here," said Flojian. "Nothing's worth that."

"We won't drown," said Chaka, "if Orin's right. Are you right, Orin?"

"Probably," he said. "But I can't guarantee it."

For a long moment, they could hear only the gurgle of the tide. Quait looked at Flojian. "How about if you and I stay?" he said. "Two in, two out."

"Forget it," said Chaka. "I'm not going home alone."

Claver nodded. "No point in my trying to leave, either. I couldn't launch the balloon myself."

There were roughly thirty cabinets in the gallery, which housed another hundred or so volumes. The gallery also had an ample supply of small tables. They pushed the cabinets into pairs and mounted the tables atop the cabinets. Then they began the arduous work of moving roughly three hundred heavy volumes onto the tables. They watched the water cover the doorway, submerge the last few stairs, and spill across the gallery floor.

By the time they'd got everything out of the cabinets, and *off* the cabinets, and piled up on the tables, they were hip-deep. But they had done everything they could.

"It doesn't seem to be slowing down any," said Chaka.

Claver folded his arms and tried to keep warm. "It *has* to," he said. "Be patient."

"How long'll we be in here?" asked Quait.

"Turn of the tide. Six hours or so, I guess," said Flojian.

They killed all but one lamp. This was Claver's suggestion. He explained that he didn't know how much air a room this size would hold, but that the lamps burned oxygen. On the other hand, no one was quite willing to sit in the clammy dark while the water kept coming up. So the single light was a compromise.

They clung together, trying to take advantage of body heat to ward off the numbing cold.

They talked a lot. Most of the conversation had to do with titles they'd seen and how they were going to get everything out of this room as quickly as they could when the water went down. Claver thought their best plan would be to leave everything where it was and return to Brockett. "This time," he said, "I think there'll be no trouble about getting a boat."

"Going to be a long few hours," said Chaka.

With nothing to do but wait, Quait tried to distract himself by perusing titles. One caught his eye: *Notes on the Last Days,* by Abraham Polk. He pointed it out to the others. "At least," he said, "we'll finally get the truth."

The conversation wandered. Claver sat silent for almost twenty minutes. Then he said, "I think I know what happened to the first expedition."

"I think we've found out," said Quait. "They got caught by the tide and drowned."

"In a manner of speaking," said Claver. "The tides themselves are too slow. And we know they didn't try to do what we're doing." Claver looked at the lamp and shivered. He cradled himself in his arms and Chaka sympathetically drew him closer to her. Quait thought he saw a smile glimmer on Claver's lips, but it might have been a trick of the light. "No," he said. "I think they found all these rooms in the same condition we found this one. They saw no danger, as we saw none. The corridor was probably dry, so they're less to be blamed for their stupidity than we are for ours. They broke into the library rooms, one by one. Fortunately, they didn't quite get all of them. And they began removing the contents.

"There was one situation that was different from the rest, though. When they first came down the stairway into the central chamber, one of the four passageways was blocked by a door."

"That's not right," said Flojian. "All the passageways were open."

"When *we* got there, all the passageways were open. That's because Karik's people took the door down. And what did they find?"

"The lake," said Quait.

"Eventually. But first they found another door." Claver let them digest this, and then he continued. "According to legend, the *Quebec* came back to this place and *tied up*. If that's true, there was a submarine chamber. I think the lake is that chamber.

"Something went wrong. Whatever system they had to keep the water level low inside the chamber failed. Maybe an outer lock got stuck so that it remained open to the sea. Anyhow, eventually the internal ventilation system got old and gave way. Once that happened, once the air could get out, tides began to rise and fall *inside* the chamber. Now, think about the corridor with the two heavy doors."

Chaka thought about it and saw no light. Nor did

the others. "I suspect it was designed so that one door had to be closed before the other could be opened."

"Why?" asked Chaka.

"Because if both doors are opened, we get the effect we just talked about. The water tries to match the water level outside. It rises or falls. Whatever."

Quait still didn't see that it changed anything. "So you're saying they got caught in the rising tide? But you said earlier the tide's too slow."

"I don't think they got caught in the tide. Not *that* way. If I understand Knobby's story, the disaster happened more or less during high tide. But if the submarine chamber had broken down, the water would rise and fall each day with the tide." He looked at Chaka. "If that were so, what would the condition have been inside the chamber when they broke through the second door?"

Chaka saw Quait's eyes widen. "It would have been full of water."

"Yes," said Claver. "They wouldn't have experienced the leisurely six-feet-per-hour rise or whatever this is we've seen. An ocean would have roared out at them. Trapped them all. Drowned them before they realized they were in trouble. Except perhaps for the one man who was up on the landing, hauling books."

Flojian's hand touched Quait.

"Not his fault," said Quait.

Flojian scooped up a handful of water, and let it drain away. "He'd have been directing operations," he said. "He'd have held himself responsible. For the death of six people. And the loss of everything here."

For a long time after that no one spoke.

"At least we know," said Chaka, finally. "Maybe now we can put it to rest." Her breasts rose slightly as the water pressed upward.

"I don't think this is working," Quait said.

Flojian nodded. "*We* know." he said. "But it's starting to look as if nobody else ever will."

Claver glanced again at the ceiling. "We need a way to measure it."

"You don't need to measure it," said Flojian. "It's still rising."

"I hate to say this," said Quait, "but I think we ought to try to swim for it."

They were at the far end of the corridor. By now it was full of water. "I could never make that," Chaka said. "It's too far."

"Count me out, too," said Flojian. "I wouldn't get halfway."

"We can't just sit here," snapped Quait.

Flojian was bobbing slowly up and down in the water, shivering. "Maybe," he said, "we should have thought of that before we agreed to stay in this rat trap."

Chaka looked at Claver. "Orin, what's going wrong?"

"There's another duct or shaft somewhere. There *has* to be."

They relit the other lamps and went looking. The midsection of the ceiling was just far enough away from the gallery to leave it in shadow. There didn't seem to be anything out there, but it was hard to be sure. Quait swam out with a lamp. He kicked over on his back, raised the lantern, and saw the problem immediately.

Another duct, partially hidden by a beam.

It was centered precisely, but out of reach. There was still six feet of air space left between the water and the ceiling. "We'll have to wait until the water gets higher," he said. "Then we can try to block it."

"It's already too high," said Claver. "Keep in mind that plugging it won't stop the rise immediately."

"We need a stick," said Flojian.

Chaka went back to the staircase, submerged, and tried to break off the handrail. When she failed, Quait went down and came back with a seven-foot piece.

But there were no more clothes. They recovered Flojian's shirt and trousers from one of the other ducts, and Quait used the handrail to push them into the air passage. Within moments, he had sealed it. Meanwhile, the others looked for a substance with which to close the newly opened vent. Claver tried pushing a tabletop against it, but it didn't work.

"We'll have to use one of the books," Flojian said finally.

Claver nodded. "Be quick. Try to find something that isn't likely to be of practical value."

They picked one that had already been damaged, a biography about a person no one had heard of: Merejkowski's *The Romance of Leonardo Da Vinci*.

Quait stood on a chair and wedged it in, jammed it in tight, and then they huddled together, listening to the sounds of the running tide.

The water crept past Chaka's shoulders.

Embraced the line of her jaw.

Flojian had already climbed onto a cabinet. She joined him, but stayed low in the water because it was warmer.

Claver looked up at the books, stacked on tabletops now barely two feet above the tide. He placed the lamp on top of a stack and went searching for something he could use to gauge the water's rise. Quait's seven-foot piece of handrail leaned against a wall.

He recovered it, stood it up straight, and used a knife to mark off the depth. It was at about the level of his collarbone.

Quait moved close to Chaka. "You okay?" he asked.

She nodded. "Considering the circumstances," she added.

Nobody said much. After a while, the lamp flickered out and they were in absolute darkness. For Chaka, that became the most fearful time of the entire ordeal.

But after a few minutes Claver's voice cut through the general gloom: "I think we're okay," he said. "It's still moving up. But it's very slow.

That brought a cautious "you're sure?" from Flojian.

"Yes," he said. "I'm sure."

Chaka let out a happy yelp and embraced each of her companions. It seemed as if the water grew warmer. They splashed and cheered until Claver warned them they were getting water on the books.

"Damn the books," said Quait. "We're going to see daylight again."

✠ EPILOGUE ✠

Abraham Polk described the Plague as caused by an airborne virus. No one was sure precisely what that meant, but his account of the last days was sufficiently graphic to make clear the nature of the beast. It was a product of the rain forests, and Polk had come to think of it as a kind of trigger mechanism, a safeguard against uncontrolled population growth.

Within another ten years, it is expected that complete sets of the Haven texts will exist in public libraries in both Brockett and the League cities. This set of almost three hundred fifty histories, commentaries, and speculations have been formally named the Silas Glote Collection. To date, approximately a fifth of the volumes have been copied and made available to the general public. The remainder, which are undergoing restoration, study, and/or annotation, can be examined by bona fide scholars.

Coal-fired boilers are now in use on both the Hudson and the Mississippi Rivers. Occasional sea traffic plies between Brockett and the League. Trade has grown slowly, because of the immense distances involved and the difficulties in getting League products overland to the mouth of the Mississippi. But progress is being made, and Orin Claver has turned his considerable abilities to the task of devising an open water route from League cities to the Gulf. His solutions so far have relied primarily on canal building.

Flojian found a lucrative and fulfilling career as

Claver's business manager, and has established himself in Brockett.

His prediction that the wedges would eventually supplant firearms appears to be off the mark for two reasons: The technology of the sleep weapon continues to defy experts; and the wedge simply lacks the authority implicit in a gun, and the sense of exhilaration that accompanies firing a few rounds at a malefactor.

The trail from the Devil's Eye to the maglev terminal north of the Wabash (which has become a major tourist route) is now unofficially known as the Shannon Road.

Attempts to survey the bottom of the underground lake in hope of finding the Quebec have so far proved fruitless. Two divers using breathing equipment designed by Claver have been lost, leading to speculation there's a demon in the water. Claver blamed the problem on a faulty piston in the air pump.

Ballooning has become a popular sport in the League. Fatalities and injuries to young men have risen at an alarming rate, and there is talk of prohibiting the device.

Avila's father, a pious man who had believed that her return from the fleshpots had occurred as a result of divine intervention, had been shattered when she left the Order. He took the news of her loss stoically, and held a celebration of her life on the bank of the Mississippi, assuming few would arrive to pay their respects to a fallen priest. As it happened, Avila's friends were so many, and so enthusiastic, that several fell into the river.

In view of his accomplishments, Quait was granted early retirement from the military and succeeded to Silas's chair at the Imperium, where he teaches ethics and ancient government.

After the events at Haven, Chaka visited her brother's grave. He lies with his companions on a gentle hillside overlooking the bay whose tides took his life. She has become the best-known silversmith in the League. She's had to hire two assistants, and business is booming. Recently she returned from leading a party of cartographers, scientists, and adventurers to the great waterfall at Nyagra, filling in for her husband, who broke an ankle just prior to departure. She and Quait have a son and a daughter, both of whom are receiving as complete an education as their parents can provide.

It has become one of the ironies of the expedition that the most memorable book to come out of it was not any of the notable works they rescued, but was rather the travel book begun by Silas and completed by Chaka, which was published under both their names and now serves as the ultimate guide for overland travel between Brockett and the League.

Flojian married an attractive young woman whom he found working on the docks near the Canal. Her name is Ira, and she recently presented him with twin girls. She knows most of what happened on the road between Illyria and Haven, and she can guess the rest. She's intelligent, far too bright to make an issue of the fact that her husband occasionally tosses in his sleep, and cries out another woman's name.